Teleworld

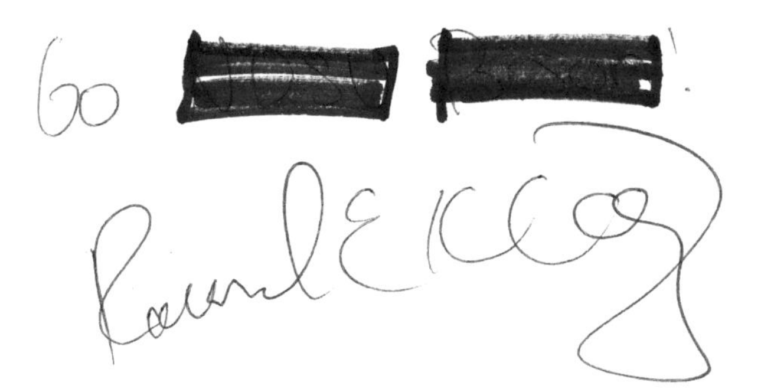

Teleworld

Book 2 of the Colorworld Series

Rachel E Kelly

Edited by Jamie Walton

Published by Rachel E Kelly, Williston, North Dakota, USA

Published by Rachel E Kelly, Williston, North Dakota, USA.
Web Site: http://www.colorworldbooks.com

ISBN-13: 978-1496156211

Cover Photograph by Richard J Heeks

Cover Design by Beth Weatherly

Acknowledgements

Humble thanks to the C.S. Lewis Company for generously allowing me the privilege of using quotes from one of the great novels of C.S. Lewis:

THE GREAT DIVORCE by C.S. Lewis copyright © C.S. Lewis Pte. Ltd. 1946. Extract reprinted by permission.

Thanks to everyone who not only works hard on my behalf in order to bring this series about, but loves what they do (which makes all the difference):

Jamie Walton, exquisitely talented editor who can always make me laugh (literally) at my piece of crap drafts. It's a gift.

Richard J. Heeks, one of the rare people who knows how to see the colorworld, and he captures it for me.

Beth Weatherly, who knows about putting love on a sandwich and that this skill ought best be employed in all endeavors of life (including my book covers).

Brad Kelly. Everyone with a dream ought to have one of you in their life.

And, of course, readers. You drive me to try harder, work longer, and produce the best work I know how.

Time is the very lens through which ye see—small and clear, as men see through the wrong end of a telescope—something that would otherwise be too big for ye to see at all... But ye can see it only through the lens of Time, in a little clear picture, through the inverted telescope. It is a picture of moments following one another and yourself in each moment making some choice that might have been otherwise.

All that are in Hell, choose it. Without that self-choice there could be no Hell. No soul that seriously and constantly desires joy will ever miss it. Those who seek find. To those who knock it is opened.

-C.S. Lewis, The Great Divorce

Part I

1

If I thought my Uncle Robert was capable of practical jokes, I would definitely think he's messing with me. This is the second time he has brought back produce that he claims is organic, but my nose tells me otherwise. Maybe he doesn't know what organic means. I'm kind of surprised the guy even knows his way around a grocery store. Phoebe, his live-in maid, usually does the shopping.

"Uh, Wen?" Ezra says from beside me, "I don't think it's necessary to scrub a peach that much. I think they're actually pretty delicate."

I ignore him as I continue to run water over the so-called organic peach. I try my best to remove the residue-attracting fuzz with an abrasive pad.

"She always does that," Gabriel says from the table. "She says it smells funny. But I feel for the poor herbs and fruits she subjects to such vigorous abstersions. You should see her with lettuce. It takes an hour just to make a salad."

"Forget this," I grumble, placing the peach back in the colander with the others. "I'll just peel the stupid things." Then I turn around carefully, placing my hands on my hips to look at Gabriel. "I would think you would be grateful that I am: A. Making dinner for you, and B. Ridding your produce of harmful pesticides. Just because *you* can't smell them doesn't mean they're not there!" I try to be serious, but I can't keep the corner of my mouth from twitching upward.

Ezra looks between Gabriel and me, rolls his eyes, and says, "Well just make sure my peaches are in one piece, 'kay?" He saunters over to where Gabriel sits at the table and flops on a chair with a Batman comic book.

Gabriel grins outright, a glint in his eye. Unable to keep my stern composure, I throw a wooden spoon at his head and turn quickly back to my work. I hear him catch the spoon and chuckle.

Even though he knows no whispered words can escape my exceptional hearing, Gabriel whispers to Ezra, "It's entirely worth it. What she can produce in the end makes up for the starvation you endure in the meantime."

Without turning, I say loudly, "If you think I'm so slow, why don't you come help speed up the process?"

I hear him rise immediately and step in my direction until he's right behind me. I stiffen. I stop peeling the peaches and deliberately watch my ungloved hands as if they might have a mind of their own. Slowly, I lift them up and grip the sides of the sink.

"What are you doing?" I ask.

Dismay sinks Gabriel's upbeat thoughts. I hate making him feel like that, but he never seems to fully grasp how easily I could kill him, just by accident, if any part of my skin touches his. He *knows* how nervous I get when my hands are exposed. If I could, just once, pick up fear from him when he's around me, I might not be so on edge.

I suppress growing exasperation. Whatever I say will not erase the difficulty of our constant search for balance in an entirely non-physical relationship.

Gabriel retreats a few steps and his voice is soft, "Sorry, Love. Sometimes I can't help my need to be near you, and I overlook how careful you are."

Sensing that he is far enough away, I turn, bringing my hands behind my back to face him. "I'm sorry," I say, distraught. "It's bad enough that you can't touch me, but it's even worse that it makes you feel like I'm rejecting you."

He braces his hands on the edge of the counter behind him, looking up at the ceiling and then down to my face. "It's my fault. It must be a ridiculous instinct of the male species to feel rejected when a woman retreats from our advances… even when the reason is justified."

For a moment, I languish in self-pity. I even allow myself to wonder who Gabriel would end up with if his super-hearing, super-sighted, super-smelling, emotion-sensing fiancé with a death-touch wasn't around to make his life difficult. It's just another day of torturing myself with my insecurities.

I smile at him though, needing him to at least know that I want him... and hoping it's enough "If I had my way," I whisper so Ezra can't hear, "I'd keep you prisoner in my bedroom, and I wouldn't have all this extra time on my hands to cook dinner."

His eyes grow wide and I hear him hold his breath for a moment as he allows himself to consider that idea. His pulse quickens for a few moments but then he shakes his head to regain composure.

"Usted mala mujer!" he whispers back. "If you're finished teasing me, is there something you actually want me to help you with?"

I snigger, satisfied with his much happier mien. I grab the bowl of peeled and sliced peaches from the sink and deposit it on the counter. "Sure, you can start some water boiling for that pasta. Then you can wash the basil for the marinara—*thoroughly*," I say, shooting him a stern look to warn against further commentary.

Gabriel can't help himself. "Shall I run it through the dishwasher then, darling?" Then he darts to the other end of my Uncle Robert's enormous kitchen to find a pot, obviously to avoid another spoon to the head.

With Gabriel helping me, I'm nervous about having my bare hands exposed. I reach under the sink and grab a pair of rubber gloves to wear and move to another part of the counter to work on the asparagus. Gloves are as essential to me as my insulin injections these days.

"Have you heard from Kaylen recently?" asks Gabriel, moving to the sink where he washes the basil.

I look up. "Not since I spoke to her that one time a month ago. Why?"

"I just want to catch up with her. I emailed her but didn't get a reply."

"Did you try calling?"

"Yes. No answer and no voicemail."

"Well… she said she was on vacation with her father for the summer," I say, recalling my last and only conversation with Kaylen. It was a couple weeks after Gabriel and I had escaped Louise. "I don't know where they went so maybe she can't get calls there… And I doubt she's staying on top of her emails."

"True," he replies. "But it would be nice to see her. Plus I'd like to speak to her father. Kaylen's been having hypno-touch for years, so her father has known Louise for longer than most. He might be able to give us some insight into Louise's mind."

"That's a good idea," I reply thoughtfully. "We should see if we can find contact information for her dad. What's her last name… Fowler?"

"It is," Gabriel replies, carefully chopping the basil. "Kevin Fowler. He's a CPA in Palm Springs. I tried his office but I only got voicemail. And I can't find a home address for him."

"I guess he's unlisted."

"Kaylen is that telekinetic you told me about?" Ezra asks, looking up from his comic book.

"Yep," I say, leaning over the counter as I wait for the water to boil so I can blanch the asparagus. I remember the day I saw Kaylen in the woods spinning giant boulders around her head. I haven't told Gabriel about that; he has no idea what she can really do. Other than my own ability, Kaylen's telekinesis was far more powerful than anything else Louise produced by hypno-touch. I wonder why? Was it because she'd been having hypno-touch so long? I'd like to ask Gabriel what he thinks, but I promised Kaylen I wouldn't tell anyone.

"What is it?" Gabriel asks.

I look over at him. I could swear Gabriel can read my thoughts sometimes. "What's what?" I ask.

"You sighed like you have something on your mind," he replies, dumping the box of pasta into the boiling water.

I furrow my brow. "I did?"

"Yes," he says, looking at me more pointedly now.

I shrug. "Well I don't have anything on my mind."

He's still looking at me expectantly and I can tell he doesn't buy it.

I ignore him, turning to arrange the asparagus in the steamer basket.

"What did I do?" he asks, genuinely worried.

I shift my attention back to his face and raise my eyebrows. "Why would you assume you'd done something?"

"Because you rolled your eyes at me."

I rolled my eyes? Gabriel's constant probing into my thoughts is not something I've gotten used to yet and he's especially interested when it's something I don't want to talk about. He makes my facial expressions a scientific study. "Gabriel," I assure him, "I was just thinking about something Kaylen told me—in *confidence.* So let it go, okay?"

"Well why didn't you say that to begin with?" he replies, turning back to the stove to dump pasta into the boiling water.

"She *did,* dude," Ezra says, breaking in with a huff. "She said she didn't have anything on her mind. That means, 'Mind your own business.' For a smart guy, you sure can be dense."

"I know exactly what it meant, Ezra," Gabriel replies, glancing at me briefly. "But Wendy knows I'm always interested in her thoughts. So if it was something she couldn't share with me out of loyalty to Kaylen, she could have put my questioning to rest right up front and spared me all the irritated glances and eye-rolling."

"What does the reason matter?" Ezra says. "If you knew she didn't want to tell you, why would you keep bugging her? Word of advice: you'll just end up pissing her off if you keep doing that."

Gabriel contemplates that honestly and then looks at me questioningly. I may think his incessant efforts to get inside my head exhausting at times, but I would never honestly tell him to stop doing it. It would make him… less *him*.

"Ezra, knock it off," I say. "We don't need relationship intervention from you. Besides, you're my brother. Our relationship is different."

"Whatever," Ezra says, leaning back in his chair. "So what about Kaylen then? Can she move *anything* telekinetically? I think if I had I choose a supernatural ability, that would be it."

"Anything but water or things with a lot of water in them," I reply, now wishing *Ezra* would drop it.

"Really?" Gabriel asks. "I never knew that… Interesting." He leaps into his intricate maneuvers of critical reasoning.

"How much can she move?" Ezra asks. "You said all the abilities there were tame. So what? A piece of paper?"

Okay, I'm perfectly willing to protect Kaylen's secret, but I do *not* like the idea of lying outright. I wait, hoping Gabriel will answer. When he doesn't, I make a show of turning to grab the steamer basket full of asparagus and taking it to the stove. "Uh huh," I reply casually.

And just like that, Gabriel's emotions shift and he's zoned in on me. I have *no* idea how he does it. It's like my tone of voice can clearly communicate my thoughts to him somehow. He definitely knows there's something up with my reply and is now wondering if he should ask about it. This is ridiculous. He's going to figure this out even without meaning to.

"That's it?" Ezra asks. "I don't get it. Why does Louise care about stuff like that if she's going to keep it so secret? And she's been doing this since Dad was alive? She sure has wasted a lot of time on shifting pencils and tweaking lightbulbs or whatever. Lame." He turns a page of his comic book.

"That is a very good question," I say. It's bugging me that I can't ask Gabriel what he thinks about Kaylen's real ability. It doesn't *seem* like something that can help me figure out my death-touch… But Kaylen has a powerful ability and so do I. It's a mystery that needs an answer and the more I think about it, the more I want an explanation. Kevin Fowler is a stone I definitely want to turn over.

Meanwhile, Gabriel's irritation has broken through my thoughts. I can tell he's thinking about this secret with Kaylen and it's bugging him. It becomes amusing after a while. He's determined not to ask me about it, but he can't stop himself from wondering and imagining possibilities. I think he has even drawn a conclusion. After pulling the asparagus from the stove and moving the peaches into a bowl with mango, I stop and watch him. Then I start laughing; the pasta is boiling over even though he is standing right next to it.

He looks up, jumps and yanks the pot from the burner.

"Are you going to be up all night now?" I ask, giggling.

"Probably," he admits, reducing the heat and moving the pot back to the burner.

"Oh. My. Gosh," Ezra says, looking up and rolling his eyes. "Really? So Gabe, if you were in an empty room with a big red button you were told not to push but they didn't tell you why, would you push it?"

"That depends," Gabriel replies "Why am I in the room? Is it an experiment? Or am I being held against my will? What kind of facility is it? What do they do there?"

Ezra stares at Gabriel with his mouth open for several seconds. Then he shakes his head. "Dude…" Then he looks at me. "Wen, is he for real?"

I laugh again and turn to my marinara sauce, tasting it to see if it's done simmering. "Yes, Ezra," I say finally. "Don't ask vague questions unless you want to be interrogated about it."

"Wendy speaks the truth," Gabriel says. "I don't deal well with ambiguity."

"Or secrets, apparently," Ezra says drily.

"Well it's not the secret so much as having a theory about what it is," Gabriel says, bringing his pasta over to the sink to drain it. "I could let it go otherwise. I just don't like not being able to speak freely about Kaylen because I'm afraid asking questions will cause Wendy to violate her promise."

"Well if it makes you feel any better, I want to tell you because I want to ask you about it," I say. "And now it's bugging *me*."

Gabriel wrinkles his nose in distaste. "Secrets. They are the bane of humanity."

I busy myself with arranging pasta bowls, portioning asparagus to each one, hoping that this once my face is impassive and none of my instantaneous dread is written there for Gabriel to pick up on. He doesn't even look my direction, too busy being aggravated about being unable to talk about Kaylen.

Secrets. I have some of those. Are you obligated to share them even if they have no bearing on the now?

I suppress a sigh. Probably. Especially when they reveal a person you hope you'll never be again, but a person you can't ever forget.

2

"Any news on Subject Number Three?" I say casually to Robert once everyone is done eating.

Robert doesn't answer right away. As usual. It makes me self-conscious. I already feel like a mooch asking Robert to foot the bill for a private investigator to find Subject Number Three, the one person we know of that has survived my death-touch, but his hesitation in answering makes me think he really doesn't want to help me like he says he does. No matter how genuine Robert's intentions seem by way of his emotions, I still feel distant from him. He comes across as one-dimensional because of how mellow and controlled his feelings are all the time.

"Not really," Robert replies after a couple pensive mouthfuls. "Langston is still working on it. The only way I know to narrow down a location for this woman is to find the others—the ones that didn't survive. Crime reports… homeless deaths… body dumps… Combing through all those records in LA County is time-consuming."

It's hard not to cringe at the reminder of what has been wrought by my lethal skin. To imagine what those poor people went through when they touched my skin is bad enough. But then to imagine how their lifeless bodies were thrown out like garbage…

I twirl angel hair pasta around my fork, twisting my outrage with Louise and shame over what I have become along with it. With my exceptional vision, I watch tiny globules of sauce squeeze out as I wind it tighter. That's exactly what my desperation looks like. Pretty soon the cords of my condition are going to squeeze too tightly. Parts of me are going to start oozing out. What will be left?

The gloominess of the future has me flirting with the idea of asking Robert a question that's been on my mind—the question I've been *wanting* to ask but have been afraid to. I still don't really know why Robert puts up with me invading his life, living in his house, eating his food…

"Uncle Rob, why can't you use your ability to locate number three?" Ezra asks.

Well that's one way to get the question out there. I look up. I'm going to have to thank Ezra later for that one. He is so much more comfortable around Robert than I am that it makes me think Robert must act differently when I'm not around. But then Ezra has always been good at skipping over convention.

Robert strokes his salt and pepper goatee. I've been trying to figure out what that means in Robert-speak. But I suck at deciphering body language. "It wouldn't work," he replies.

"Why not?" demands Ezra.

"A nameless, faceless person… Someone I've never met…" Robert says. "What's more, the goal centers around Wendy, not me. I can't get good visions on goals that don't directly relate to me. My ability is… something I've taken years to master. Some goals are feasible. Some are not. This one, unfortunately, is too vague. I'm not a missing person locator, especially of a person I've never met or seen. My ability works best when I have some*thing* in mind, not some*one.*"

I've gotten better at picking different mental states out of a group, and although Robert is on the edge of my emodar range, his regret is contorting my thoughts into a bit of a bind; he must be sorry that he can't help me. It's surprisingly strong though, especially considering his distance. It seems like more than just run-of-the-mill compassion for my situation. He's got too tight a lid on it for me to translate more.

"What about Louise then?" Gabriel says, wiping his plate with a hunk of garlic bread. "Would it be easier to find *her*? She must know where this mysterious woman is."

"You want to find Louise?" Robert asks, furrowing his brow.

"Not really," I disagree, wrinkling my nose. "Gabriel, the only reason I would want to find Louise is to make her answer for her crimes. And since I doubt anyone can *prove* she's a murderer, I'd rather steer clear."

"I agree, it would be much more pleasant to avoid her," Gabriel replies. "But she's got answers for you."

"Answers?" I say. "Like what?"

"Not just about who she tested your ability on and who survived, but most importantly she knew your father. There was a reason she wanted you to touch someone in the colorworld, and we need to get the truth out of her. Her motives are obviously more complex than we thought. And besides, I don't like not knowing what she's up to."

"Even if we *did* find her, how would we get her talking?" I say skeptically as I gather up everyone's empty plates. "You can't trust a thing she says. There were only a hundred opportunities before she kidnapped me to win me over with information. But she didn't even try. I don't think she'll give up *anything*. Chances are she'd just play mind games and waste our time."

"Oh, well, even Louise has a price," Gabriel says. "And now that she knows no amount of coercion is going to make you do what she wants, maybe she'll bargain with information instead. But either way, Louise appears to be the most direct route to your goals."

"I am with Wendy on this one," Robert says, breaking his silence. "Louise is not someone you want to *bargain* with for any price."

"Okay, fine," Gabriel sighs, propping an elbow on the table. "You don't want to *bargain* with her. Don't we at least want to know where she is and what she's doing? Don't we want to have her under some kind of surveillance? Maybe just following her will give us a lead."

"I've made attempts at keeping tabs on her in the past and my success has been spotty at best," Robert says, crossing his arms and sitting back in his chair. "I told you she knows what I can do. It's not that hard for her to avoid me. She has even shut down the compound completely. I get visions about places to accomplish my goals, but quite often that place is not somewhere I recognize. Hiding in a place I'm unfamiliar with is the perfect way to stay out of my sights."

"So how did you find *me* then?" I ask as I take out dessert plates. Robert's ability makes no sense. Gabriel is at least right that we need to figure out what Louise is up to.

I look behind me briefly to catch Robert amid another long pause. I turn back to the ice cream, scooping it with irritated vigor as I roll my eyes. One day I'm going to figure Robert out. I swear if the guy wasn't so ridiculously nice on the surface, and if I weren't living under his roof scot-free, I'd have blown up at him a long time ago.

"I found you by what I call a compounding vision," Robert says finally. "I almost always avoid using them, but you were in danger so I made an exception. When I wanted to locate you, I got the room Louise had you held in. Then I visualized a *new* goal to locate the place I saw in my vision. That's how I got that area in San Bernardino: a vision within a vision. The problem with compound visions like that is that they never go the way you expect. Remember that it was just Ezra and me that showed up there without all my men? That's what happens when I use compounding visions to accomplish something. People can be killed. Things don't go right. I'm not comfortable using my ability that way to find Louise, someone I already think you should avoid."

I've stopped what I'm doing to look at Robert, surprised. I had never considered Robert's ability might be dangerous like that…

He looks truly uncomfortable with the interrogation. I feel bad asking him at all. I sigh. I hate this weird, undefined relationship I have with my uncle. I just don't know where I stand.

"That's fascinating," Gabriel says. He sits back in his chair with his arms crossed behind his head, deep in thought.

I turn back to the counter and start distributing dessert—a sweet corn and rice pudding ice cream in churro bowls with a mango and peach compote. I'm nervous because it's my first attempt at serving Gabriel something that has Hispanic origins.

"We should attempt to locate Louise conventionally then," Gabriel says. "She'd like us to be intimidated by her, but I think we should be aggressive. She's probably not prepared for that." He looks down at the dessert in front of him. "El Ceilo, mi encantadora doncella! How do you come up with these fanciful culinary creations? With you around I may have to double my fitness regimen."

"Don't get excited yet," I say. "You haven't even tried it."

"Ommmm," Ezra says through a mouthful, having already dug into his portion. He closes his eyes, swallows, and says, "I don't know what that was, but my taste buds don't care. This totally makes up for that asparagus.

I roll my eyes and sit down. "I *like* asparagus, Ezra. It's not all about you."

"Yeah, I know," Ezra says. "But you know I don't like it. You could have at least put it on the side."

"But then you wouldn't have eaten it," I say. "And you need your green veggies."

"*Nobody* likes asparagus but you, Wen," Ezra says, putting another bite of ice cream in his mouth and closing his eyes.

"Oh please," I say. Then I turn to Gabriel. "Do *you* like asparagus?"

He wrinkles his nose and shakes his head. "The marinara was delightful, but I'm afraid I'm in line with Ezra on this one."

"Really?" I say, surprised and a little disappointed. Here I've been worried about the dessert all this time and he didn't even like the *dinner.* "Why didn't you say anything when I started putting the asparagus in?"

"That would have been rude," he replies, examining his dessert. "It's not like I hurl at the thought of asparagus. I just don't prefer it. So what do you call this?" He turns the bowl to get a different view.

"It doesn't have a name," I say, *really* nervous now. He may be excited about trying it, but what if he hates peaches or something? I never once picked up on his feelings about asparagus while I was preparing it. I adjust myself, at first offended that he didn't like it, but then settling into this new brand of honesty—one in which I may not like what I hear. I like knowing that I can count on him that way… It puts a smile on my face.

"Party in your mouth," Ezra says when Gabriel continues to admire his dessert. "That's what it's called. Will you stop analyzing it and just eat it?"

"Ezra, your sister obviously put a lot of effort into presentation. I have no doubt it tastes divine. But there's more to food than the taste." He glances at me pointedly "There are *lots* of other aspects. You'll miss out if you don't fully appreciate them all."

If he wasn't in my emodar, I wouldn't have recognized the suggestiveness of that comment. I think I blush. "It's going to melt, so can you taste it already?" I say, stealing a quick look at Ezra to make sure he didn't pick up on that. But he's busy shoveling ice cream and churro into his mouth.

"Of course," Gabriel says, his eyes finding mine and not leaving for several beats. Goosebumps travel down my back as if he has just pulled me in and his hand has caressed the length of my curvature. My heart flutters in anticipation. If Ezra wasn't busy with his food, I'm sure he'd be grossed out by the way Gabriel just looked at me.

"Ambrosial," Gabriel says after swallowing a bite. "Who would have thought to put sweet corn in ice cream? And mango is my *favorite.* Really. How *do* you come up with these combinations?"

"I just get bored with food, I guess," I reply, pleased with his reaction. "I had sweet corn ice cream in a restaurant once. I thought it would be good with cinnamon. That made me think of rice pudding… Hispanic foods… Then it just kind of came together. I'm glad you like it."

"Like it?" he scoffs. "This is rapture for the mouth."

"Freaking fantastic, Wen," Ezra says.

Robert is the only one who hasn't said anything. I don't think he has noticed the food in front of him yet; it's melting. I look at him, wondering what's making him think so hard, and he glances over at me. "I'm sorry. I was just thinking about Louise. I'm still adamantly against seeking her help with anything. Considering what happened to my brother, she just worries me."

"Uncle Rob," Ezra garbles through a mouthful. "Forget Louise. Eat. Then your whole life will make sense."

Robert looks down finally and gives a start, spotting the dessert. "Wendy, you outdo yourself every time you get in the kitchen. I'd be happy to help you fund a restaurant."

"Thanks," I say. "But I don't know if I would like cooking if I *had* to do it all the time."

About halfway through his dessert, Gabriel sits back and says, "Your exceptional culinary skills have me once again ruminating on how lucky I am to have you as my betrothed. When, pray tell, were you planning on carrying through with our nuptials?" He gives me an expectant look.

Ezra sniggers. "Does that mumbo jumbo actually work on girls?" he asks, referring to Gabriel's frequent use of antiquated language.

"I charmed my way into your sister's heart, didn't I?" Gabriel offers.

Ezra scoffs. "Yeah, I meant on *normal* girls."

"*Normal*? I wouldn't know. The normal ones bore me. Nothing but fur coats with no knickers," Gabriel replies, waving his hand dismissively with a look of distaste. I chuckle under my breath.

"Fur coat and no knickers? What, *pray tell*, does that mean?" Ezra mocks.

"Put together on the outside with no substance underneath," Gabriel answers with a disdainful look. He turns to me again. "Your brother is as good at stalling as you are, but I won't be put off. What's the issue?"

I glance around the table. Robert and Ezra both have turned their attention to me. Gabriel asked in front of everyone on purpose and he's also laying the charm on thick, which means he's intent on getting an answer. He brought it up the first time a couple weeks after our arrival at Robert's, and I told him I wanted to spend a little time focusing on finding Subject Number Three. That is nowhere even close to happening right now, so I can't tout it as a legitimate excuse anymore.

But I don't want to say my real reason in front of the rest of the table, so I hedge, "What? So I'm solely responsible for determining a date by myself and planning it all out? It's not like there is a huge list of people I want to invite: Letty maybe... definitely Kaylen. You're the one with the big family in need of fanfare. *You* make the plans. Just let me know when and where to show up."

I hide my smile and take a bite of dessert. *That ought to shut him up.*

Gabriel observes me curiously. "Well played," he says with a raised eyebrow. We know each other so well and I often forget that he can usually see through my defenses.

He delves into his dessert with gusto, and I hope he's going to let the issue drop for now.

After a few minutes though, Gabriel puts his elbow on the table and stares off into space. "In that case, you should meet my mother. She's been begging me to bring you home. Sooner or later she's going to arrive here unannounced if we don't make a trip... I think I'll put *her* in charge of the plans then if you're leaving them to me."

He turns back to his food casually. His expression doesn't hide his obvious triumphant delight from me though.

My spoon hovers in mid-air, my jaw slack. I can't figure out what to say. Is he serious? I wouldn't put any means of manipulation past him, and the visual I have of Gabriel's mother suggests that she'd turn a wedding into a neighborhood circus. I doubt even *Gabriel* would want her planning his wedding.

I shut my mouth and lean back, looking unconcerned. "Okay, when do you want to go? I'm sure any woman who raised such a wonderful son has excellent tastes in wedding décor." I look at him eagerly. "Do you think she can suggest a good place for a dress? Maybe she has her old one? I can wear that..." I trail off, trying to look like the picture of ease, gazing up at the ceiling as if I'm contemplating all the wonderful possibilities. From the corner of my eye I catch Gabriel's mouth fall slightly open before he quickly finds his composure.

"I have an interview tomorrow, but we can go this weekend. Is that okay with you?" he asks before spooning his last bite of ice cream into his mouth and looking at me adoringly.

Okay, so he's calling my bluff. He's entirely serious, but Gabriel is *excellent* at controlling his emotions. I'm already in too deep; I am not going to be the one to back down, so I smile and say, "Of course!"

Ezra and Robert watch us with confusion and amazement. Gabriel is mostly amused, but I think I catch a millisecond of worry. It comes and leaves so quickly I can't be sure whether it's mine or his. How far will he take this charade? Past the point of no return? His determination might get me into trouble. Big poofy wedding dress trouble.

Ezra bursts out laughing. "I dunno, Wen. Maybe you ought to stick with a date at the Justice of the Peace and call it a day. I still remember what you said to Mom when she picked out that homecoming dress for you, '*Mom, I am not going to the dance looking like a doily from a nursing home!*'"

Ezra hoots, loosening a chuckle from Robert.

I can't help cracking a smile at the memory, and to go along with my façade I say with as much gooeyness as possible, "If Gabriel wants me to wear his Mamá's frilly wedding dress, I'll wear lace. Whatever makes *him* happy makes *me* happy." I bat my eyelashes at him for good measure. Ezra is hysterical by now, and I have trouble maintaining my oozing tone through the infectious laughter.

Gabriel taps his spoon on the side of his bowl, imagining it, I think. Then he says, "My mother is Hispanic. And much shorter than you are, Wendy. I'm afraid her dress would hardly be form-fitted as well as barely reach your calves."

Then he raises his spoon. "But! If you tell her you want her to take control, she would be more than pleased to pick something out for you. As for me, well I think you'd look stunning in any kind of dress."

He stares into my eyes then, amused, but I feel him trying in vain to read me. He probably wonders how long I am going to keep up this performance. So am I.

"I'm in!" I gush.

"You two are nuts," says Ezra who has finally stopped laughing long enough to scrape the remnants of ice cream from his bowl.

"Sounds like it's going to be… interesting," Robert says.

The prospect of meeting Gabriel's mother sets my nerves on edge though. "Um, Gabriel, does she *know* about me? I mean my uh, *limitations*?"

"Of course," he replies, unfazed. I don't know what to make of that. Then he hops up. "Ezra, help me with the dishes." As he gathers them up, he looks at me. "When we're done, I had hoped to take you out briefly tonight. Nothing fancy, just a walk on the beach perhaps? That is if your uncle doesn't mind consenting," he adds, looking at Robert for approval.

I open my mouth to protest the assumption that I need my uncle's permission to go out, but Robert interrupts before I can get a word out, "You shouldn't put my name, Wendy, and consent in the same sentence. I'd like to keep myself intact please."

Ezra chortles, and Gabriel grins.

I snap my mouth shut and wrinkle my nose at them.

3

"The Lone Cypress?" I ask when we reach our overlook destination on the 17-mile drive, a scenic byway just outside of Monterey.

Gabriel doesn't answer, only reaches for my hand once we're out of the car. He's been on edge since we left Robert's house, and when I asked him about it earlier, he told me he wasn't ready to tell me and then complained that my emodar ruins surprises.

I take his hand nervously because I'm afraid of whatever has him so uneasy. He leads me toward a walkway that descends into a grove of trees. It opens up to reveal a serenely picturesque view of the ocean. We're high up on a cliff that runs along the shoreline. About fifty yards away on a pedestal of rock sprouting up from the seaside stands a single ordinary-looking tree. It's kind of small and insignificant, and compared to the other trees I saw on our drive that were often wind-sculpted and twisted into tilted positions, this one stands daringly upright. The backdrop of endless sea casts focus on the lonely specimen simply because it's the only thing there.

The tree is rooted to rock from what I can tell. Even though it's braced up with cables—and maybe *because* of them—it just *exudes* perseverance. And it looks comfortable there. Like being exposed to the elements of wind and sea water alone all day is no big thing. I wonder how it ended up there and why, as a sapling, it didn't just give up? Maybe it used to have companions but they washed away with erosion.

What a story it must have. I wonder what the colorworld will reveal about it…

"Hold still," I say to Gabriel as I hover my hand above his arm.

I close my eyes and focus my senses on Gabriel's life force. The silken strands become apparent surprisingly quick.

Unprepared for the onslaught of color and light that greets my eyes, I shrink back, squinting. The sun is in my immediate line of sight. Never before have I observed it directly in the colorworld like this. Its color is unrecognizable. In the visible world, sunset brings a mystical arrangement of colors to the horizon. In the colorworld, this effect is magnified a hundred fold. The sunset presents a display of radiant and varied color streams that fluctuate outward endlessly. The sun is so fantastic that I cannot tear my eyes away. It just doesn't look *real.* And if it doesn't *look* real, do the laws of physics still apply? Will the sky swallow me up and carry me away on ribbons of color if I stay here too long? I struggle for breath, overwhelmed.

The colors of the sky have always shifted as I change my perspective, and in the face of this even more dazzling panoply that fluctuates with my slightest movement, my thoughts have slowed in utter awe. I just stare, consumed fully by the visual stimulation.

The longer I look at it, the more I think the sun doesn't supply the color as it does to the sunset in *our* world. Instead, colors seem drawn *into* it. The sun's rays reach out purposely to connect with every surface. Almost like the sun is *collecting* the color around it.

"What does it look like?" Gabriel asks, and I realize I'm gripping his arm in an effort not to be carried away with the retreating phantasm. I'm drawn toward the sun, just like the colors.

I shake my head in wonder. "Mysterious… Fantastical… The sun is less like a source of light and more like a giant reflector. Sometimes it looks like it absorbs the light and sometimes it looks like it produces it. It's hard to say." I tilt my head back and forth a few times to observe the changing colors, describing it further to him, wishing in vain that I could *show* him what it looks like.

"The ocean…" I breathe as my eyes shift lower. "I don't even recognize the ocean here."

I'm so consumed with sensory bombardment that Gabriel's fit of curiosity doesn't phase me. Instead I do my best to describe the sight. "I don't know if what I'm seeing is actually water. Instead I see… currents swirling around, sloshed about with the tide. It's like liquid rainbows instead of water—translucent though. Like a churning opalescent fog maybe, but slightly reflective of the sky." My chest is so tight with wonderment that it begins to leak warmth, sprouting goosebumps all over my skin. I move my shaking hand down Gabriel's arm to grip his hand fiercely, leaning into him to hold myself upright.

"It's the most beautiful thing I have ever seen…" I whisper. I stand for quite a while like this, wondering if the earth really has fallen away. It doesn't seem possible that this is the same planet I see day in and day out. I haven't stepped through some magical portal to another dimension; this is simply... *invisible* to other people.

I finally shift my line of sight over to the old tree—the reason I came into the colorworld in the first place. All living things have an aura about them. I wonder what the old Cypress will reveal?

The tree glows pale ice-blue and it definitely looks sentient, but that's what I perceive about everything in the colorworld. More importantly is what I see *around* the tree—around everything, actually.

"The trees and plants have something coming off of them," I say. "It's like a mirage: when you look at hot asphalt in the distance and you see the waves of heat? It's like that. It's invisible if you don't pay attention to it... The air glitters so much." I turn my attention to Gabriel. "I swear I'm—" I stop, caught up by the sight of Gabriel's life force. I've never seen it so brilliant.

"You are so breathtaking," I whisper. His light is so bright that I put my hand over my eyes as if to escape the glare of the sun. My own life force is bright as well, and placing it so close to my eyes is like shielding them with a halogen light.

I blink a few times to avoid the onslaught of visual stimulation.

"What is it?" asks Gabriel eagerly.

"Too bright," I reply. "I think you might blind me."

I turn back to the Cypress. I'm used to trees being some shade of blue in the colorworld. But this tree is nearly white. The wavering, mirage-like substance that flows from the tree looks like a vapor of some sort. And it has an iridescent quality. I first saw it as flowing *from* the tree, but as I watch, the movement is more of a rolling motion congregated *near* the tree—kind of like swirling of the ocean here. It could be coming *away* from the tree as well as *toward* it. The vapor lingers around everything that is living, from the shrubs to the little bit of grass peeking between the rocks.

"The vapor is coming off of living things," I say. "Even us. But it's not just a vapor. The way it moves around stuff... purposeful, like it could be interacting with it... Like an energy vapor?"

"Does it look any different from one life form to the next?" asks Gabriel. "You know, like plant versus person?"

I bite my lip, looking from Gabriel back to the trees. "I can't tell." I shake my head.

I sigh and move my hand away from Gabriel's arm.

When the colorworld disappears I startle briefly, thinking I've been blinded. But then I see the thumbnail of sun on the horizon; it's just nearly dark.

"Wow. That's amazing," I breathe. "I guess the lack of light on this side makes everything in the colorworld brighter. Or maybe it's just an effect of sunset…"

"We'll definitely have to do that again," Gabriel says ardently. "There might be something there."

He turns to face me. "But I did have a different reason for bringing you here, although I'm pleased that the sights were so stunning. Hopefully it set the right mood."

His stress makes an appearance once more, and I raise my eyebrows. "I have *never* seen you this nervous."

"Well I ought to crack on with it then," he says, pulling his hand from his jacket pocket and revealing a black ring box.

A smile spreads over my face. He must have a ring for me. I'm dying to see what he picked out. It's sure to be beyond my expectations—actually I have no idea *what* I expect. Simple and understated? Gaudy and outspoken?

"Well?" I demand when he doesn't immediately open it. "Do I get to see it?" I reach for the box, and he lifts it up over my head and out of reach.

"What gives?" I ask.

"Before I show you I want you to answer a question…"

His strained anticipation has tied my thoughts up. I can't stand waiting like this any longer. "Spit it out before you give yourself a hernia. I could walk on your nerves like a tightrope."

Gabriel relaxes slightly and rolls his eyes. "Your manners are impeccable, as usual. The first thing I wanted to ask was…" He clings to courage more tightly and then says, "Are you ready to get married? I mean, is it completely crazy that I wanted to marry you right off the bat? I could understand if, in the moment, you might have been moved to think you wanted marriage when, after the fact, you might have seen it as a knee-jerk decision…"

I don't think I've ever heard Gabriel ramble before, but this is the first time it feels like he's nervous about saying the wrong thing.

"Seriously?" I reply. "I haven't once rethought that decision. When I told you I wanted to marry you, I don't think I had ever thought more clearly in my life."

"Really?" He slumps against the railing in obvious relief. "Sometimes I forget that you're only nineteen. But when I do, I wonder how you could know so quickly that I was who you wanted. I'm 27. I've had plenty of time to date the wrong people. But you've barely had time to taste independence."

"Independence? To do what? Date guys not nearly as amazing as you? That sounds lame." I give him a reassuring smile.

"Oh you know what I mean," he says derisively.

I cross my arms and chuckle. "No. Not really."

He groans. "Come on, Wendy. I'm talking about meeting you and then getting engaged a month later. I'm talking about all but forcing you to tell me you wanted to marry me. It was a strained situation we were in—not really the kind of place you make life-altering decisions like that."

I crease my brow, starting to get a little worried. "Where is this coming from, Gabriel? I get that the quickness of our engagement was… unorthodox, but I knew after I met you that you were who I didn't know I wanted. You like… blew my mind in so many ways. I would have entertained marrying you without all the prodding if I had ever put any thought into what getting married really means."

He hops up to sit on the railing, releasing the rest of his tension. "I knew it," he says, shaking his head.

"Of course you did," I say. "I told you all this before."

"No, I mean my family was pretty flabbergasted when I announced I was getting married," he says. "Then when I told them you were nineteen…" Gabriel shakes his head. "That did *not* go over well. They were sure I'd pressured you. I tried to explain that they didn't know you, but then when you kept putting me off on choosing a date I worried you had started having doubts. I started thinking maybe they were right…"

Dread stops up my words. I don't like where this is going.

"Why are you so hesitant to choose a date, Wendy?" he says softly, looking directly at me now, much more confident now that I've assuaged his worry.

I take a deep breath. I knew I'd have to tell him sooner or later. I guess I'd hoped it would be later… I should know better. Gabriel never settles for assumptions for long. "I just haven't given up hope, I guess, that a solution to my problem is right around the corner." I lean on the railing and look across the horizon, which is now dark. "I hate the idea that our wedding night will be spent doing something lame like watching a movie or taking a walk." I swallow back a sob and say with staggering breath, "I hate that I can't give you anything more than being in the same room together."

"How am I supposed to know these things if you don't tell me?" Gabriel hops down and takes something else out of his pocket and puts them on: gloves. Fitted like the ones I wear.

"When did you get those?" I sniffle.

"Recently. But back on topic," he says, stepping closer to me. He reaches for my face and I respond immediately, pushing off the railing to face him. His touch is hesitant and gentle as his palm comes to rest under my chin. I close my eyes. His other hand glides across my cheek as he brushes the hair away from my face. Touching a face is probably more mundane to most people, but this is the first time Gabriel has touched mine.

The heaviness of despondency dissolves instantly. Even with gloves, his hands feel deeply intimate. He touches me as if I am fragile, his fingers traveling the curves of my face, over my cheeks, under my eyes, up the bridge of my nose, tracing my eyebrow. I feel like a priceless treasure under his hands.

My heart races as he outlines the length of my jaw, his hand finally coming to rest at the back of my neck. He tucks my face into his chest with submissive relief at the contact. His smell overwhelms me, his warmth soaking through his light jacket and into my cheek.

"Oh, Wendy," he sighs, running a hand through the length of my hair. "All this time I've been worried about the wrong thing." He pulls away long enough to glance at my face. "I can understand my family's misgivings, but they just don't understand that I *had* to snatch you up or someone else would."

"Gabriel, nobody else would want me like this. *I* am the lucky one. You're exactly what I want *and* you are willing to take me in this state. Don't you realize that you are probably the only person alive ready to dive into a relationship—let alone a marriage—like this?"

"Yes, I do know that," he says softly. "And I hope you won't be upset with me for it but I can't help being grateful for your handicap. Because without it, who knows if I *ever* would have found you? How tragic to think I might have lived my whole life never having met you?"

His sincerity is so powerful it reaches places I didn't know were lacking warmth. "How can I possibly be upset at that?"

He exhales deeply. "Because I keep expecting you to decide one day that I'm too much. I've dated plenty of women. All different but all failed for basically the same reason: buyer's remorse. Too much. Too much adoration. Too demanding. Too critical. Too much commitment. Too much devotion. I like them too much. And they never like me enough."

I lift my face away from his chest. "I think they just don't get that you're for real. I guess it pays to be an empath. It means I get to know the real you, which is exactly the you that everyone else gets to see. That's why I love you so much. You never hide from me."

Gratitude tumbles out of him so fast that it's like the thrill of taking that first breath when you come up out of the water for air. "I cannot imagine how I deserve that kind of regard," he whispers, overcome. "And I think you give your ability too much credit. Knowing the real me *should* have had you running for the hills. It's *when* women find out I'm exactly who I presented myself to be in the first place that they act surprised. But you got me undiluted. And you wanted me anyway. I've never had that." He kisses my palm and holds it to his face.

"It's not fair that I can't share everything with you," I complain. "Or maybe it *is* fair. I guess you don't ever get everything you want. If we could actually touch each other…" I sigh longingly. "Why did I have to meet you at the worst possible time? Why not just a month earlier? At the grocery store or something? Is that too much to ask?"

"It was the perfect time for me," he says and then hops back up on the railing. "Wendy, do you know how many times my own mother has said, 'Gabe, why do you have to push and push and push? Why can't you let things be?' I hear it all the time, just in different ways and about different things. But you just let me be me… I never expected anyone to *accept* that part of me so easily. What we have *without* touch is entirely worth it to me."

Gabriel props his elbows on his knees, puts his chin in his hands, full of bewilderment I think he's not used to feeling. "I can't get over the happenstance of our meeting," he continues quietly. "And I don't *do* happenstance. I struggle to understand how or why I got so lucky but fail. When my logical requirements aren't met, I get insecure. And currently my self-confidence is at an *all-time* low.

He glances up at me, simpering. "You'll have to forgive me; I'm so eager to put a wedding band on your finger that I won't rest soundly until it's done. Until it is, there's still a good possibility that you'll decide you don't want me after all. Or you'll meet someone less complicated. Or I'll do something that turns you completely off, make you rethink putting up with me. Or you'll find a solution to your lethal touch and decide you want to explore your freedom." Gabriel's eyes lose their gleam for a moment, a hint of dread nestling uncomfortably in his mind. He says more quietly, "Sometimes I hope you *don't* find a cure. Because it means I'll likely never have to face losing you."

The earnestness behind his words floors me and my lips part in disbelief.

He hops down again and steps closer to me. He reaches out and touches my cheek with his gloved index finger as if reminding himself that I'm real. I'm speechless, and my chest is cavernous because the power of his words has expanded it so much.

He turns his hand over and grazes my cheek until he reaches my ear. He sweeps my hair behind my shoulder. "Can you understand what I mean by 'gild the lily' now?" he says, his voice choked with emotion. "Or have I moved into realms of crazed obsession?"

Obsession? Yeah, it sounds like it. But it doesn't *feel* like it. It *feels* like fondness so deep that I can't wrap my head around deserving it. As for 'Gild the lily,' it's our trigger phrase. For Gabriel it means he has everything he needs when it comes to our relationship. Anything further—like curing my lethal touch—would be bonus. And while I've known what it meant, I've never considered it quite like this. I guess I've never understood what it is about me that has managed to inspire such strong fidelity.

"It's not crazy," I reply finally. "And I… am glad I can feel your emotions. Otherwise it would be hard to believe you're real."

He wraps me in another embrace. Then he brings my hand up to his face and kisses my palm. "Too good," he sighs into my glove, the warmth of his breath pulsing me with a thrill. "Too good to be true."

For the smallest moment I panic. What I feel from Gabriel right now… the depth of his love? It *does* feel too good. How can it be real? But I can't deny that it's simply honest. Uncomplicated. Raw. I let panic go. I need to embrace this good thing. A death touch is plenty awful enough to balance out his amazing presence in my life.

"I'm not going anywhere, Gabriel" I assure him. "Death-touch or no. Obviously I've been worried that you'll change your mind also. I want to give you more than half a marriage. That's how much I love you."

"Silly woman," he says, cradling my face in his hands to look at him. "I want you to stop thinking that. It's *not* half a marriage. It's a whole marriage with roadblocks and obstacles like any other. And I want it more than life itself. Do you hear me?"

I nod, feeling immature that I need this kind of reassurance so often, but grateful he is willing to give it anyway—each time more beautifully than the last.

"Good. Now I have a plan—the other part of this—which is also why I'm so nervous." He puts both hands on my shoulders now, closes his eyes, and takes a deep breath. "So what do you think about getting married this weekend?"

"What, like in Vegas or something?" I ask, confused. I suppose that would be okay. No one there would ask me why the bride isn't kissing the groom.

"What are we? Border ruffians?" Gabriel says, appalled. "No wife of mine will have been married in a crass place like Vegas. I thought you knew me better than that?"

"Border ruffians?" I squint at him. Is he making up expletive phrases again?

"Yes, as in scalawags. Wastrals. You know," he says, looking at me expectantly.

I shake my head and laugh, "I don't think I've ever heard of a wastral."

Gabriel's brow furrows. "Really? It means—"

"Okay, okay," I giggle. "Where then?" Maybe he's thinking Justice of the Peace or something.

"Bakersfield, when we go there this weekend."

I look at him with confusion. Justice of the Peace in Bakersfield?

Gabriel continues, "When I saw how reluctant you were to choose a date, I took it upon myself to start thinking about making arrangements—I thought you might appreciate having the whole affair out of your hands—not to mention the need I've felt to secure your hand..."

I remain silent, waiting for further explanation. His nerves have wound back up to full tinsel strength.

"So I've arranged for a small ceremony at my parent's house," he finishes. "What do you think?"

He looks at me with worried grin, like a child expecting a reprimand. He's obviously torn about how he thinks I'll react. No wonder he was so nervous.

I am surprised, that's true, but a larger part of me is relieved.

"So let me get this straight: you want me to marry you in three days at a wedding I had no part in planning, at your parent's house, hosted by said parents whom I've never met before?"

"Yes," says Gabriel, twitching with anticipation. "Oh confound it! It is so dastardly unfair that I can't read *your* emotions. Please tell me I got this right. I really felt like you would appreciate this or in the very least be okay with it. My mother did most of the planning but she ran everything by me, and any time I wasn't sure, I asked Ezra, and he pointed me in the right direction. Wendy, please give me some kind of reaction here."

"Wait, Ezra was in on this?" I ask, floored. "That's why he was laughing his butt off? And you! You were totally testing the water that whole dinner conversation? I thought you were just bluffing to get me to set a date, and you were *serious?*"

"Well of course! You didn't think I would plan a wedding without making sure beforehand that he and Robert could attend, did you? And I was *trying* to get your honest opinion, but you were putting me off the whole time. Wendy! Please! You're torturous indifference is positively unbearable. What do you think? Did I do the wrong thing? The right thing? Tell me!" He nearly shakes my shoulders with impatience.

"And these past couple weeks? When you were asking me random questions like what my favorite color was... food... names of my friends... outdoors? Oh! And that day you tried to take me shopping and asked me all kinds of questions about what I like to wear? That was you digging for my opinion on things for a *wedding*?" I ask, incredulous that I have missed these signs until now. In fact, I remember asking Gabriel why he was so insistent about knowing such mundane details and he had replied,

‘I want to know *everything* about you. And you never know when such information will come in handy.’

“Yes, yes!” he replies impatiently. “Now please tell me if you’ll marry me this weekend. Usted se me torturando a propósito!”

In spite of the shock, I get more and more excited. I can’t think of any girl whose fiancé would ever take it upon himself to plan a wedding.

“You are hands-down the strangest man I have ever known, Gabriel Dumas. And it makes me even *more* thrilled to be marrying you this weekend.” My smile is so big my cheeks hurt. Giddiness energizes me. “This is like opening a really big present but I have no idea what it is!” I squeal. “I am *so* jazzed! Wait, what am I wearing? Please tell me you got me something to wear!”

“Wendy, Wendy,” says Gabriel, relief washing over him. He shakes his head but smiles hugely. “Your enthusiasm is gratifying, but your doubt is insulting. Actually, my mother and Ezra picked something out. I don’t know what it is, but Ezra swears you’ll like it—Hey! Was that a squeal from you? I don’t think I’ve heard you make that sound before. Mi encantadora doncella… you always surprise me. Your reaction is far better than anticipated!”

He reaches back into his pocket again. “Yes, I believe you deserve this now.”

He pulls out the black box.

Exuberance finds me once more as I jump up, grabbing for it. “Lemme see! Lemme see!”

Gabriel taunts me with a mischievous grin. “I must say, Miss Whitley, this side of you is incredibly alluring. I’m starting to believe you might actually be nineteen years old.”

“Oh shove it, old man!” I say, jumping at the box he holds out of my reach. “You had better give me that box right now or you’ll regret it,” I warn.

“Really?” says Gabriel, his grin turning more devilish. “I wonder… how would you make me do that? I’m *so* curious!”

“You asked for it,” I say. I round my fist and sink it into his stomach.

I doubt I’ve hurt him, but it takes him by surprise enough that he lowers his arm. I snatch the box away. He reaches for me, but I skip to the side and turn my back to him.

The sun is completely down and the moon has yet to rise, but my eyes are excellent as I flick open the lid. The ring is very unusual but contemporary: two parallel silver bands joined by two horizontal bars on either side. The stone, which isn't raised but flush with the band, is square-cut. It isn't a diamond, though it's cut and faceted like one.

I turn it this way and that to determine what it is. The color of the stone changes from green to pinkish depending on the angle of the light.

"Wow," I whisper.

"It's called Zultanite," says Gabriel from behind me, his gloved hand brushing through my hair and coming to rest on my shoulder. "It has different colors depending on the perspective, just like you. It's unusual, I know, but so am I. It seemed perfect."

"It *is*," I say softly, overcome. Gabriel, as usual, has exceeded my expectations. "You couldn't have picked anything better. Thank you."

I turn carefully to face him with a smile.

"Could I put it on you?" he asks.

"Of course," I say.

I start to pull the glove off of my left hand, but Gabriel says, "I had the ring sized a bit larger so you could wear it *over* your glove… if you like?"

I stop and look at him, my throat catching. He always thinks of everything… "Yes," I whisper so I don't start crying.

Gabriel takes my hand delicately, and it reminds me of when he introduced himself at the compound. He lifts the ring out of the box and slides it carefully on my finger. "I hope you can see it better than I can. I assume so since you could see the colors change."

"Perfectly," I answer, admiring the ring now gracing my hand.

"I can't believe you punched me," says Gabriel, smiling. "I did *not* see that coming. What a woman—can even throw a punch. And on Saturday she will be Mrs. Dumas."

He sighs. Our feelings are the same: slightly giddy, off in a daydream.

I throw my arms around him, careful to tuck my face away from his, my heart so overfull that it kind of hurts. "Thank you," I whisper. "It's perfect. The ring *and* the wedding idea."

Perfect, I think over and over as we stand in the dark. The moment invites a depressing, unbidden thought then. I tell myself it's my cynical nature choosing a vulnerable moment to sneak up on me, but I can't help being reminded of a truth I learned a long time ago: the more perfect, the more costly.

4

"There you are," a familiar, articulate voice says from across the pool. Footsteps accompany it but they stop abruptly where they are. "Yes, you are. You are definitely *all* there, aren't you? What is the occasion and why wasn't I invited?"

I open my eyes to find Gabriel standing at the patio door with his attention locked on me. His eyes move over the length of my form. My very *bare* form since I'm only in a swimsuit next to the pool. I freeze in alarm automatically at having him this close to my excessive skin exposure—even at ten yards away. "I wasn't expecting you back so early," I say, grabbing my towel, distracted by the weird mixture of relief and disappointment I feel at covering myself in front of Gabriel.

"Hola, mi habenero caliente. Mi oh mi. ¡Qué cuerpo! Mira lo que había debajo de toda esa ropa…" he says as he comes around the side of the pool.

"You do know I still don't understand Spanish, right?" I say, grabbing a t-shirt now. "I was just getting some sun—my skin has been withering under all my clothes." I don't know why I'm explaining myself—I guess I don't know how far is too far when it comes to teasing Gabriel with my body.

I sigh heavily, pulling the shirt over my head. There is probably *no* amount of teasing Gabriel wouldn't be up for.

"Ciertamente no eres marchitez…" he says in a husky voice as he stops about ten feet away—just outside of my emodar for him. "Y ahora te estás vistiendo… Tan injusto…"

"Again, no hablo español." I shoot him an expectant look.

"Yes, I know you don't understand Spanish," he says. Then he strides forward a few steps. "So let me translate in *your* language."

He sits in a chair that's just within range and my mind is suddenly hijacked. Gabriel's thoughts are normally concise in movement. Free and open yet purposeful—intricately choreographed toward a goal. This is the first time I've felt him think without a definitive direction. He's amid unpredictable rapids. And they're creating stuttered and disjointed movements like changing the channel on the TV every second. And *whatever* he's watching, it excites him more and more, deepening his breaths and making his heart patterns erratic.

I start to look around for the pants I came out here with just to remind my body who is in control. But I can't focus on anything I see except Gabriel. It's mid-July in Monterey, California, and it's already hot outside, but with each flip of the channel in his mind, the temperature rises in the surrounding air. It becomes so thick I can't tell if I'm breathing or not. But I'm too distracted with looking at him to wonder. My eyes roam over the outline his body: the curve of his shoulders beneath his slim-fitted button-down shirt, the glistening of sweat gathering on his forehead and neck, his hands tucked under his chin as he stares at me, his lips that I want more than anything to kiss right now.

My hand is on my neck and I have no memory of putting it there. And my other hand is clutching my leg behind my knee and I'm leaning toward Gabriel.

Where are my pants?

I don't see them, but I do catch sight of my water bottle. Perfect. My mouth is *definitely* dry. I reach down for it but end up knocking it over instead. I snatch it up before the contents can spill entirely. I take a swig, eying Gabriel hungrily, trying to get my thoughts to move directionally. But he looks *so* good. I have never wanted to put my lips on someone so badly.

My fingers are resting on my lips… When did that happen?

Gabriel closes his eyes for a moment as he sits back. The rapid pace of channel-shifting eases into slower movement as he phases out of whatever incredibly sensual daydream I *know* he was having. He opens his eyes and smiles lazily at me. "Was that clear enough for you? Or do you need further translation?"

Now that he has released me from the grip of passion, I glance around for my pants once and for all. As I do, I recognize that all that heavy yearning was not just his. My own body feels jittery with unspent sensual energy. I spot my pants and pull them on, my excited skin hypersensitive to the texture of the fabric as it glides over my legs. Gabriel has not come anywhere close to touching me, but my body is behaving as if he had.

With my pants on, I take several deep breaths while looking down to avoid being sucked into the weight of Gabriel's probing stare.

"Si je pourrais avoir juste une nuit avec votre corps…" he says softly as he starts giving up mental control again. "La mémoire me durerait un temps de la vie…"

My body tenses all of a sudden and instead of channel surfing through imagination, the vision becomes like static. Or maybe it's simply focus. Whatever it is, I grip the sides of my chair, closing my eyes to breathe through the hunger clenching my chest. Oh, his hands… I just want him to touch me… Just for a moment.

I clear my throat because my head is mush and I think I'm not getting any air. I don't think I can stand this anymore…

"How do you *do* that?" I croak. I want him to stop… but I *don't* want him to stop. I don't have the wherewithal to articulate how out of control I feel. It must be *his* feelings though, so he must *know.*

"Was bedeuten Sie? Liebe wird im Geist gemacht. Nicht wahr?" he asks just above the whisper. "Mein Körper kann deinen Körper nicht berühren, aber mein Geist kann deinen Geist sehr wohl erreichen. Lass uns daher mit jedem uns zur Verfügung stehenden Werkzeug Liebe machen."

"You have *got* to stop," I say, opening my eyes to look at him finally. His head is bowed, his eyes are closed, and I hear him take deliberate breaths.

He does not answer for a couple minutes at *least* and during that time he collects himself. Only then do I get that the static I felt was the cessation of intellect.

After an eternity of watching him calm himself back down, he looks up at me and smiles before saying, "Stop what?"

I cross my arms and scowl at him. "Oh please. You *really* need me to spell it out? Being so *hot.* Looking all… calendar model. And then speaking to me in other languages. Getting me all… *riled up* with your indecent thoughts."

He crosses his arms behind his head with a satisfied smile. "Well you started it. You were practically naked over there. Now I must insist that next time I be informed ahead of time."

"This is *my* fault? I told you I didn't expect you back so soon. I had my doctor's appointment today so I got off work early. I assumed I'd be safely alone for at least an hour. I never intended to taunt you with nakedness." I draw my knees up and wrap my arms around them.

"I'm not placing blame. Nor am I complaining." He looks at me pointedly. "I'm just explaining the cause and effect."

"Well I doubt I'll be *informing you ahead of time.* Otherwise you'll probably show up here in a swimsuit and *shirtless.* I'm not going to be able to pay attention to anything else, let alone how dangerous my skin is. And then if you start talking dirty in other languages while… while *thinking* like that. I don't think I have that kind of self-restraint."

I shift in my chair and fidget my hands just remembering it. "Geez, Gabriel, I have no idea how you have that kind of control. I don't think I have *ever* been that turned on before. And you weren't even touching me!"

"How do you know I was talking dirty?" he asks, instantly excited by the prospect. He takes several deep breaths again to maintain calm.

"I could *tell* because your thoughts said so. And your words are *never* at odds with your thoughts."

"I didn't *really* say anything dirty," he says. "Actually it was more like… pillow-talk." He tilts his head, his eyes glassy as his pulse speeds up again. "But tell me more about how you've never been so turned on?"

I shake my head. "No way. Dirty talk is *over.*"

He sticks his lip out, pouting. "You think I have so much self-control, but I've never seen that much of your skin. Talking dirty is simply a method of distracting myself from what I *really* want to do. All this time I've only *imagined* what you look like under all those clothes."

The fantasy channels start flipping again. "Ce que je veux vraiment faire, c'est examiner la courbe de vos lèvres avec les miennes… Et puis passer à d'autres courbes..." he says.

I put my hands over my eyes and groan. "Stop it already! I'm dying here!"

"Then stop doing things like groaning and telling me I turn you on!" he exclaims. "I'm not a robot you know!" He swallows a few times before saying, "I think I need to find some cold water. I'll be back in a moment." He hops up and heads back inside.

I collapse back against my lounge chair once he is out of range. Like Gabriel, talking was the only way I think I managed to stay away from him. Thank goodness he wasn't any closer. If I'd caught a good whiff of him…

I've definitely experienced guys who have moved from daydream into libido takeover mode, and it's somewhat… surprising to find that Gabriel, in all his mental control, still has the same primal urges as any other guy. And they are just as powerful if not more so. What impresses me is his courage to get up and walk away from it. I don't know if it's that I told him to stop or that he knew he *needed* to stop, but he was still 'reachable' even while so consumed.

Gabriel reappears then with a big grin on his face, taking the same chair as he did previously; he has settled down quite a bit.

"That was quite enjoyable," he says, clasping his hands behind his head.

I give him an odd look and shake my head. "Likewise. I think I'm starting to get that marrying you *without* the benefits of physical touch is going to easily rival what anyone else can accomplish in a marriage *with* touch... I don't know how you do it, but you don't just exceed my expectations; you annihilate them."

"I intend to pull out all the stops when it comes to keeping you satisfied."

"Satisfied?" I ask. "You don't know *how* to merely satisfy. You aren't happy until you are blowing my mind in every way."

"How would it be satisfying if I wasn't?"

I laugh. Of course Gabriel's idea of satisfaction is another's idea of mere fantasy.

"I think we both need a distraction, so tell me about your interview," I say. "How did it go?" I sit up, cross-legged.

"Excellent. They hardly interviewed me," he replies. "I guess they liked my resume. They offered me the job on the spot. Which is why I'm back so early. Thank goodness. I might have missed the sights."

"Of course they liked it," I say. "They'd be stupid not to hire *your* brilliance." I'm surprised Gabriel hasn't found a job before now. He claims that because it's late in the summer, even if most schools would love to have him, their positions have all been filled. Gabriel has two doctoral degrees and speaks at *least* ten languages that I know of. Before we met at the compound he was an adjunct professor at UCLA in their physics department. He's been published several times in physics journals, and he was voted teacher of the year by students. I wish I could see him in action in front of a class.

"How do the students usually react to you?" I ask. "Are you as... *flowery* in your language when you lecture?"

He chuckles. "No, actually." He crosses a leg over his knee. "My brother says when I'm in front of a crowd is the only time I'm human." He rolls his eyes. "He and Ezra would probably get along swimmingly."

I laugh and then say, "Well I guess they'll get a chance to bond at the wedding, right? Speaking of which, is that why you asked me about Kaylen yesterday? You tried to invite her?"

"Yes… I also mailed her an invitation a while back but I didn't get an RSVP. That's the one thing in all this that hasn't gone according to plan."

I furrow my brow. "I hate that she won't be there. I wish she'd at least answer an e-mail."

"I had Robert's private investigator look up her father's unlisted information this morning. I got an address in Palm Springs and a phone number that also goes to voicemail. Maybe the vacation she told you about took her out of the country."

"Probably so," I say, but it still bugs me. Teenagers don't typically disconnect from technology just because they're on vacation. Although Kaylen isn't typical by any means. She probably doesn't have a real circle of friends to stay connected *to.* I'm just bummed that she won't be at my wedding. "Can't win them all," I sigh.

"How did your appointment go?" he asks. "Is your A1c under control?"

"A tenth higher than six months ago," I reply.

"Really?" he asks, worried. "What did the doctor say?"

"Nothing," I reply. "He was too amazed by my history to worry about an A1c of 6.8."

"6.8?!" Gabriel asks, amazed. "That's incredible for someone with Type 1 Diabetes. Has it always been that low?"

I nod. "The doctor I always used in LA wanted to run tests on me all the time growing up, but my mom refused every time. She said my life was affected enough by the disease. I didn't need to spend it in a lab getting poked any more than I needed to be. He eventually stopped asking, but obviously this Monterey doctor Robert got me has never seen the likes of me. His eyes kept bugging out over my chart."

"No doubt," Gabriel says, in disbelief over my nonchalance. Then he starts asking about my average glucose reading, how often I test, and how much insulin I take—pretty much the same questions the doctor asked today. The truth is on a regular day I probably only test three times—something the doctor always wishes he could berate me for but can't because my A1c proves how well I'm managing my diabetes. "I'm good at gauging how much insulin I'll need for a meal," I finish. "I sometimes test afterward if I'm feeling weird, but not often. I have more problems with high blood sugar than low."

"That is so odd," Gabriel remarks. "It's like someone who was diagnosed as an adult rather than juvenile onset."

I shrug. "Well I figure I just got lucky. And considering my *other* problems right now, I think I deserve a simpler diabetes without all the whacky blood sugar swings."

Gabriel sits back in his chair. "I, too, am glad it's not more severe. But regardless, that's highly unusual—perhaps unheard of for someone diagnosed at such a young age—four you said?"

"Yep."

The phone rings from inside then.

"I'll get it," Gabriel says, hopping up. But I stand up anyway and follow him at a distance so I can get my gloves from upstairs.

From my room, while I'm checking my blood sugar—since I'm thinking about it—I hear Gabriel's side of the conversation after he picks up the phone, "Robert, how are you?"

A pause. "Excellent. I did get the job. Thank you."

Longer pause. "Really?! That's wonderful news!"

That has my interest.

"That should work," he says. "We'll wait for your call."

I hurry and finish putting my gloves on and bound down the stairs. "What is it?" I ask breathlessly once I reach the kitchen.

Gabriel, who has hung up the phone, beams at me. "Subject Number Three. Robert found her."

My jaw drops. "Really?"

"So he says. Robert's having her flown up from LA."

My heart skips in excitement. "Well let's go!" I say, stepping into my shoes by the back door.

He laughs. "It's going to take a couple of hours at least to get her up here, Love. No rush."

I take a deep breath, tempering my anticipation. "Right," I say. "But I can't very well sit here. I'm going to lose my mind waiting."

He comes to link his arm in mine, leading me toward the door. "We'll go by my apartment so I can change and then we'll go for a run. El Cielo, Wendy. You act as if the woman has a cure in a bottle."

I look over at him. "Maybe not in a bottle. But in the colorworld."

He stops with his hand on the front door. He looks at me, worried. "A cure in any form is a pretty hefty expectation, Love. I think it more likely that it's going to point us in a direction. I very much doubt it's going to explain everything we don't know."

I think he's discounting just how big this is. I'm supposed to marry him in two days. And after our poolside interlude how can I *not* dream and wish and hope that this is the *real* beginning of the end of this curse? "I know that," I say evenly. "I don't *really* think it's a cure. But this is a big step finally… Why can't I be thrilled about that? And right before our wedding? It just makes everything perfect!"

His worry stalks my own exuberance for a few more moments, finally settling on acceptance. He smiles at me. "I suppose a little progress *is* the perfect wedding gift. I just don't want you to get your hopes up too high and be disappointed."

"I'm about to meet the one person we know of that's immune to my touch," I argue. "Whatever we're about to find out, it's going to be really helpful. How could I possibly be disappointed with that?"

5

Lindsey McGrath is a young, petite, blonde with a shy disposition. But that's probably subjective. She *did* just get approached by an unfamiliar man in LA who questioned her about her dealings with an older woman with long, silver hair who had her touch a sleeping girl in a lab in Pasadena. I don't know how they talked her into coming here to Monterey, but I bet Robert's deep pockets had something to do with it. I'm less interested in the particulars of getting her here though, and more interested in what her life force will tell me.

Gabriel, the only person among us to have seen the video of her demonstrating her immunity to my touch, confirms excitedly that she is definitely Subject Number Three. I'd been halfway concerned that Robert might have the wrong girl.

Langston, Robert's PI who escorted her here, starts asking Lindsey questions about her interaction with Louise. I sit at the other end of the conference room at Robert's office, inconspicuously going into the colorworld to get a look at her. I use Gabriel as a channel. His nerves are palpable and my hands are shaking.

Lindsey sits on a chair in front of Langston with her hands fidgeting uncomfortably in her lap. She keeps glancing over at me, distracting me so that it takes longer than usual to access my sight.

Once there I zone in on her life force: it's purple and swirling like a cocoon around her body just like every other one I've seen. It also hasn't seen the hands of hypno-touch—I'm pretty sure. The perfect swirl centers over her chest, winding inward fluidly, unhindered, none of the disjointed flow I'm used to from the people on the compound.

It looks *exactly* the same as everyone else's who hasn't had hypno-touch. It looks just like Langston's who is right next to her. I look at Robert who sits nearby. He also has the same perfect swirl. The same shade of purple. The same luminous strands as Lindsey, Langston, and even Ezra who is standing a few feet away from me.

Exactly the same.

I work to get my heavy and immediate disappointment under control. Instead, I start looking more closely. I compare the speed of flow of her chest swirl to everyone else's. I compare the shades of purple more critically. I watch the way her life force moves around her body. *Nothing* stands out as noteworthy or even slightly different—not that each person's flows exactly the same, but they tend in the same direction.

Wanting desperately to escape the defeat tying up my insides, I close my eyes and inhale the scent of the colorworld that's always so calming. Lindsey is saying something about how she ended up meeting Louise but I let her voice fade into the background.

I pick up her scent then. I ease my chair closer to smell her life force better. She smells like flowers. Kind of like Baby's Breath with how saccharine sweet it is. It's the kind of smell that would perfectly compliment any flower arrangement. Actually, it would compliment *any* smell really well. I take deep breaths and let her incense take over my instincts. It reminds me of the openness I used to feel while talking to one of my professors in college. It was a woman who taught Calculus and she always seemed vested in her students. She was really good at getting people talking. Although I never got a chance to touch her, she always came across to me as genuinely interested in the details of the lives of others.

But yet again, this aspect of Lindsey's life force doesn't tell me anything helpful. It just reveals her personality and essence. I open my eyes and look at her again. She's talking about what happened after she left Pneumatikon. I barely hear her over the pounding in my chest that pulses frustrated tension into my arms and shoulders.

"Is there something else I should be looking for?" I whisper in desperation to Gabriel.

He glances over at me. "I don't know, Love," he whispers back. "You know the answer to that better than I do. Everything about her life force. The flow. The color. The makeup. Does a*nything* stand out as different?"

I shake my head and breathe deeply so I don't start crying. "The only thing different is her smell. But *everyone's* smell is different."

Gabriel's mind takes off agilely into contemplation while my eyes rake back and forth over Lindsey's life force. But I'm too upset to process anything. I've already looked at it anyway. There's nothing there to tell me why she's immune.

Ezra sees the look on my face and he comes over to where we are. He crouches down next to me. "Anything?"

I shake my head, gritting my teeth to hold the tears at bay.

"Maybe you should touch her and see what happens," Ezra says.

I look at him in shock. "No way! Are you crazy?"

"Gabe saw the video. We know she's immune. Why not?"

"Gabriel saw she was immune *then*," I correct. "There's no telling if she is now."

Ezra looks from me to Lindsey, and then back. "Robert said Dad's ability was different from one person to the next. Why would you think your ability is any different?"

"We don't have proof of anything, Ezra," I say, my voice rising involuntarily. "And Robert said he *thought* that was the case. And I'm looking at this girl who is supposedly immune to me and there is nothing about her to give me a clue as to why that is. There is *no* way I'm touching her to test it out."

I've caught Lindsey's attention. Her mouth is slightly open, confusion apparent on her face.

I stand up. "I need to go. This isn't helpful."

I walk out of the room, shutting the door behind me. I throw myself on the couch in the nearly empty lobby.

Gabriel follows me. Not that I expected anything else. I want to go home but Gabriel drove me and I doubt he's going to leave me alone without a line of questions. "I really don't want to talk," I say without looking at him.

He doesn't reply. He leans back on the couch and puts his feet up on the coffee table. His disappointment over discovering nothing of use is far less than my own. And in fact his thoughts are still in that insistent whir that I left them in. I have no idea what has engaged his intellect after that big fat nothing, but I guess Gabriel can find something fascinating in every situation. That he is clearly *not* upset just makes me irate.

"Take me home," I say after a few silent moments.

He stands up without a word and reaches for my hand. I take it because *not* taking it would make him ask me why I'm mad at him. I *don't* know why I'm mad at him. I'm just mad. And I want to be allowed to stay mad.

When my gloved hand touches his, the burning in my chest relents, leaving behind the soreness of sorrow. What I wouldn't give right now just to have the comfort of his palm against mine. Such simple contact can soften the edges of heavy moments.

Through a glove, the connection is just not the same. Pondering that makes me further upset though. People take for granted what they can accomplish through the barest of skin contact.

After an awkwardly silent ride home, we reach Robert's house, and Gabriel turns off the car. He turns toward me. "Wendy, tell me what I can do."

I cross my arms. "Nothing," I mumble.

I wish my emodar would just be silent right now. Instead I have to pick up pricks of frustration from Gabriel as he tries to work out what to do to put a smile on my face.

"Drop it," I say. "Just let me stew, okay?"

"Will that make you feel better?"

I grit my teeth in annoyance before saying, "There's nothing you can do right now to change my attitude so please stop wasting your brainwaves trying."

"There can't be *nothing,*" he replies. "If you're upset, there has to be something that will help."

"Well there's not," I snap. "Why can't you just accept that sometimes people want to be pissed off and there's nothing you can do about it? Geez, Gabriel. Stop pestering me and just let me be. There is *nothing* you can do to fix this."

"So you're planning on being upset forever then…"

I throw my head back against the seat. "Oh my gosh. Stop. You act like I have a choice in how I feel. I don't. I'm disappointed. I'm angry. And I'm going to stay that way until it wears off. You interrogating me about it is only going to make me angrier."

He settles resignedly into his seat. I can tell he doesn't understand. I marvel at this. Gabriel seems to think emotions are something you can just *command.* He sees them as a tool to accomplish his means. Sure, sometimes they sneak up on him—like right now. But he always manages them with little effort. He doesn't dwell on them like the rest of us do. When emotion is especially strong, he just *thinks* harder in order to tune it out. He is a *strange* man.

After about a minute of 'listening' to the current of his thoughts, I laugh. He's working to articulate his way to understanding what I've said. The contrast of that to what *I* am going through is bizarre enough to be humorous.

He looks at me, confused.

I shake my head. "Sometimes you just amaze me with how… unusual you are.

He's still confused.

"Forget it," I say. "But your weird quirks are interesting enough to make me feel marginally better. For now. But don't start asking me to be happy. I might just bite your head off."

"Thanks for the warning," he says, baffled. I reach for the handle of the door but my body tenses with Gabriel's disappointment. He doesn't want me to leave.

It's hard to be mad at him then. It softens my mood to realize that he loves me even when I act like this.

I sigh and turn to him. "Sorry. I just figured you wouldn't want to be around me when I'm in a rage. I know you don't like irrationality. And right now I feel *anything* but rational."

He reaches tentatively for my hand, expecting me to pull away I guess. When I don't, he takes it in his own and kisses my palm. "I hope you'll still want to be around *me* when I act in a way you don't understand. I guess I'm making plenty of deposits for when that day happens so you can remember how much I love you."

My being reaches out for him. I want the weight of his arms around me, but he only has a t-shirt on. And he has no gloves nearby to put on either. An embrace right now would be too dangerous. The familiar feeling of being strangled by my own body overtakes me like it always does. I fidget at the discomfort of having no physical outlet.

I guess I still have words. But I'm not so good at those, especially when I'm high-strung. Talking… it's so vague. Inaccurate. There are too many ways to mistranslate words. The wrong ones always come out. The right ones never do. But a hug never communicates the wrong thing. Just touching someone's hand can be so comforting. It's a genuine moment of connection that lets you know you aren't alone.

Gabriel is good at words though. Which is ironic. Sometimes he offends. Sometimes he praises. Ezra told me recently that he thinks Gabriel uses big words as a subtle way to insult him. *I* know that's not the case though. Gabriel just isn't afraid of mistranslation. He said to me when we met that he felt he was *made* for this challenge of being with someone he can't touch. I think he's absolutely right. I, on the other hand, was not.

"Will you stay with me tonight?" Gabriel asks then, interrupting my internal ruminations.

"Uhhh…" I reply, my eyes darting over to him, confused and apprehensive.

He rolls his eyes. "Wendy, will you *stay* with me, not will you *sleep* with me. I just don't like leaving you in this state. I'd rather I was close by. Otherwise I'll be up all night worrying about you. I do have an extra bed *and* a guest bedroom, as you know. Obviously I'm prepared to share a space with you considering we're supposed to be married this weekend."

"Oh," I reply, feeling silly. "Yeah, okay."

"Perfect!" he says delightedly.

"Yay!" I say, laughing at his enthusiasm as we both step out of the car. "The most G-rated sleepover ever!"

Gabriel shoots me a look over the top of the car. "Wendy, I believe I demonstrated earlier how *not* G-rated things can be even *without* touching. But since you place overabundant importance on sexuality, I think I need to now demonstrate intimacy *without* the sexual aspect."

"Oh great," I say as we walk up to Robert's front door and I pull out my key. "Crying together over a Disney movie with a box of tissues… Bring it!"

6

"This is not even a little bit fair," I whine, throwing my hand of cards on the floor in between us. "I can't move the cards fast enough with my gloves."

Gabriel laughs. "Well playing Speed was your idea, you know." He collects the cards to deal again. "How about I put gloves on, too?"

"*That* is a perfect idea," I agree.

He grabs his gloves out of a drawer and then we go again. Almost immediately I decide this is the last round of any fast-paced card game for us tonight. It's *impossible* to pick up cards with any quickness while wearing gloves. I steal a glance at Gabriel though, and find that I'm a *pro* compared to him. He's still trying to fill his hand from his deck but the cards are too slick to pick up.

I giggle and keep going, more confident because clearly my experience with wearing gloves for a few months now has given me an edge.

I go out much more quickly than he does and I throw my hands up in a touchdown sign.

"Hijo de un sacerdote casto! How on earth do you manage this?" Gabriel says, holding his gloved hands out to look at them with disgust.

"You think picking up cards is hard, you should try turning the pages of a book… or using a smart phone… or buttoning a shirt… typing… Pretty much everything, actually. Oh, except for opening a peanut butter jar. That's probably the only thing that's easier."

"Well you've obviously mastered it as well as it *can* be mastered," he says. "Because you stole my lunch during that round."

"I definitely did. But I am *done* holding cards. That was ridiculous."

"Agreed. I prefer talking anyway."

"What? No Disney movies?"

He gathers up the cards again and looks at me from under his eyelashes. "Are you being serious?"

I laugh and stand up, slightly nervous about what kind of talking Gabriel is thinking of. "No, not really." I sit on the couch instead.

Gabriel comes to sit on the other end and we each lean against an arm, facing each other, knees bent. "Why do you always avoid talking?" he asks.

"I don't avoid it."

"Wendy." He gives me a condescending look. "You do too. You avoid talking by using sarcasm and jokes to throw me off. What is it you are afraid of?"

I look away. Why does he have to be so perceptive?

"Are you still upset over this afternoon?" he asks.

I sigh. Silence stretches between us and I foolishly wish he would drop this. He just stares at me with stubborn resolve to get the truth from me though.

"Of course I am," I answer finally.

"And saying that was hard, why?"

I glance at him before looking away again. "You ask me how I feel about it as if it's not obvious, which seems like you're saying it's dumb to feel that way at all. It makes me not want to share things with you."

"No, it's *not* obvious what's going on inside your head. At all. You immediately gave me the cold shoulder after seeing Lindsey's life force like you were upset at *me* for some reason. That completely confused me since I couldn't pinpoint anything I had done. And then when I tried to ask you about it, you got even *more* upset. So I waited to let you cool down from whatever it was and now when I bring it up again, you refuse to talk about it. I'm really trying to understand, but you act like you don't *want* me to understand you."

I rub my face, exhausted that, as usual, Gabriel wants to micro-analyze everything I do. "I'm just irrational when I'm upset," I say. "I told you that in the car. I don't have a reasonable explanation for you that will make my behavior logical. I don't want to fight with you. I was giving you the cold shoulder so I wouldn't say something ugly that I'd regret."

"Again, that doesn't explain why you are *still* reluctant to address it now, after this supposed irrationality you claim has worn off. Why was your automatic impulse to lash out at *me*?"

"I don't know," I say, propping my arm on the back of the couch. "I really don't."

Gabriel is overcome with disbelief and confusion then as he thinks about that, but then he says, "Well you need to figure it out. I'm not going to be the whipping boy for your emotions."

I feel like I'm having a conversation with my mom, like Gabriel is my parent rather than my partner. Irritation blossoms like an acrid stench, summoning my rebellious nature. Intellectually I think Gabriel is right, but I don't like his tone. To demand that I should be rational when I've been so thoroughly disappointed is too much to ask. I don't *have* that kind of control when I'm upset.

I cross my arms over my chest and bite my tongue.

"And withdrawing even more is not going to help you do that," he says, watching me.

I hate that he is so annoyingly mature and level-headed. This would go a lot easier if we could scream at each other for a while and loosen all the pent-up tension. Maybe this whole marrying someone who is eight years older than me isn't such a good idea. I really don't want to be parented all the time.

"Well then how do *you* propose I do that?" I say icily.

He sighs, concern loosening the grip of his frustration. "By being honest with me, Love," he says softly. "Even when you're upset, just tell me whatever you're thinking, even if you think I don't want to hear it or I won't understand."

"Fine," I say, annoyed that he thinks hashing out every detail like this is *helpful* let alone some kind of bonding experience. What is the point of inviting emotions that are only going to devastate me?

I wish I could sit on the floor right now. But Gabriel knows that's my tell. I take a throw pillow from the couch instead and hug it to my chest, still not looking at him but at a piece of artwork he has on his wall. Gabriel is a fan of M.C. Escher, the guy who did mathematical drawings that had screwy perceptions like two hands drawing each other. The one in my view now is called *Relativity* and features stairways that appear to go both up and down at the same time.

"I'm discouraged," I say. "I saw nothing in that woman's life force that gave me any direction. I told you I wasn't expecting a cure. But I was expecting a lot more than nothing."

He remains silent although his wheels are turning.

"Gabriel, I feel like I'm being forced to accept that this is how things are, that I'm stuck like this. And I'm… mad at you because you're so *okay* with it…"

I gain steam then as I figure out how to articulate what I mean. "You're like... *light-years* ahead of me when it comes to accepting that you might never touch me. I'm too afraid to really *imagine* what my life will be like without physical contact... It's terrifying. I suck at dealing with this handicap. I can't handle the ambiguity of the future. Will I ever touch again? I want to know so I can *plan* for it. *Adjust* to it. But you're so damn good at handling it. So yeah, it makes me jealous of what you're able to do that I can't."

I sigh with some relief. "And sometimes your maturity makes me feel like a child. And that pisses me off."

More silence as Gabriel waits. When he decides I'm not going to continue, he says, "Is that all?"

I look at him. "For right now."

"Do you really think it's easy for me to deal with being unable to touch you?"

"Yes, I do. Isn't it?"

"No. It's the hardest thing I've ever done. Every moment around you is a struggle because I want that intimacy with you that comes so easily with touch. Every moment apart is a struggle because I spend it agonizing over what to do when I *am* around you. I am constantly second-guessing how I should behave, afraid I'm demanding too much or not communicating things the right way. How much flirting is too much? How much is not enough? How close can I get without you living the moment in fear of hurting me? How much do I touch what I can of you without you feeling like I'm dwelling on your body? I am *so* lost most of the time, just trying to blunder my way to meeting your expectations but not really knowing what those are. No. It is *not* easy."

I exhale hurriedly because I've been holding my breath, relieved but amazed that Gabriel is, in fact, human.

"Sorry," I say, looking down at my hands. "I didn't know." Ugh. I am *so* good at imagining I am the only person with issues worth thinking about.

"I could have told you. But of course I question how it will come across to you. Will you take it as me saying the situation is too much for me to handle? Will you feel inadequate? I have never second-guessed myself so much in my entire life as I have in the last month."

I look into his eyes. I don't think they've left me this entire time. "You must be coming to all the right conclusions because you make it look easy."

"Well *I'm* not happy with my conclusions."

I frown, trying to suppress my gut-reaction of assuming that he's saying he's done with us. That's stupid. He gave me a ring only last night…

"What conclusions are those?" I ask when I finally work through my foolishness.

"Only one really. The conclusion that you aren't happy with me."

"What?" I reply. "That's not true. I have *never* been happier."

"Then your definition of happiness must be different from mine. You just told me that you're upset that you can't adjust to your handicap. To you, I seem happy and content to deal with it indefinitely which you say is the exact *opposite* of what *you* are: terrified to really entertain a life without touching people. That tells me you still haven't found a place for me in your life that satisfies you. I'm not giving you what you need. If I was, you wouldn't be so afraid to face that kind of life. I'm not helping you handle things. You can't tell me that makes you happy."

Gabriel's logic can be so maddening. I think if I sat here and insisted I'm happy, he'd break out a chalkboard and start coming up with a mathematical proof why I'm not. While I follow what he's saying, I can't figure out how to point out where his error is. I don't know how to communicate in his language.

"What do you want from me?" I ask wearily, propping my head up with my hand on the back of the couch. "Just tell me what to do and I'll do it. I don't know how to float hope of finding a cure with acceptance of what may likely be my future. You think that until I reconcile the two and do them both at the same time, I'll never be truly happy."

He sighs. "And *you* think happiness is dependent on an outcome. But let's not argue about that. Were you serious when you asked me to tell you what to do?"

"Sure. You obviously know whether I'm happy better than I do so why *wouldn't* you have the secret formula for happiness? I'm all ears."

He gives me a withering look.

I roll my eyes, take several breaths, and reel in my sarcasm—though I don't think it works entirely. "Yes, Gabriel. Please tell me what to do."

"Have a conversation with me in which you don't hedge."

"Sure. What do you want to talk about?"

"Oh anything really." He smiles. "I just like to hear you talk."

"Well you're going to have to give this conversation more juice than that. You can't just say, 'Let's conversate' and expect things to start rolling."

"Fine..." He thinks for several beats. "Remember when I told you all those stories about my boyhood when Louise had us locked up?"

"Yeah."

"It occurred to me then that you know far more about my childhood than I know about yours. Let's remedy that. Tell me what you were like as a child."

I furrow my brow. "What do you want to know?"

He shrugs. "Did you like pretend? Did you like coloring books? Or were you into science and the outdoors? Or maybe you danced a lot... I don't know."

I don't like where this is going. But answering questions that have ugly answers is probably going to be easier than arguing with Gabriel's logic about my happiness.

"I was pretty much a regular kid. I liked to draw," I reply. "My mom said I made up songs a lot. I liked to run around outside but we didn't always live in places that allowed much of that."

"So you were more artistic as a child then... How did you end up choosing computer engineering for college?" he asks, intrigued.

"I needed a good job in order to provide for my brother. And when I researched the best paid four-year degrees, computer engineering was at the top of the list. So that's why I picked it." I notice, just in paying attention to his contentment as I answer, that Gabriel really *does* get a lot of pleasure out of hearing me talk...

I shift positions, drawing my legs under me to get more comfortable. But I think this conversation is about to get anything *but* comfortable. I consider moving to the floor again, but restrain the urge.

"So that's really it?" Gabriel replies. "You picked it based solely on income potential?"

I nod.

That confuses him. "But computer engineering is so specialized. I hear it takes a lot of brains and zeal to get through.

You must be pretty gutsy to have pointed your finger at it and said, 'I'm going to do *that.*'"

I shrug. "I didn't really have a choice. I promised my mom I wouldn't quit school if she would let me take care of Ezra. It was sink or swim. I needed money to provide for him. Computer engineering could deliver."

"You do just blossom under pressure, don't you?" he asks, although I think the question is rhetorical. "So is your passion more art-related then? You *are* an artist with food."

He's still looking at me with focused interest.

I look away, staring at *Relativity* on Gabriel's wall again, trying to comprehend going both upstairs and downstairs at the same time. "No," I reply. That's not really the truth. But it's not really a lie either.

"So what is it then? If your mom hadn't died, what would you have gone to school for?"

My chest is tight. Gabriel is swinging his branch of questioning very close to tender areas. I want him to back off. I trace my eyes up and down the stairs, never actually ending up anywhere. *Have a conversation without hedging,* I say in my head over and over to gain courage.

"I was accepted to an art school just before my junior year of high school," I say finally. "They offered me a full ride but I turned it down."

The possibility of learning this new store of facts about me has filled Gabriel with ready anticipation. But he has also picked up my reluctance. He's somewhat apprehensive about continuing his interrogation. But he does it anyway. "Why would you do that?"

Up the stairs. Down the stairs. Which way are the people in the drawing really going? Will they ever meet up at the same place?

"Because I decided not to go." I can't bring myself to continue. I'd rather him ask questions so that we end up at the truth.

He ponders my answer for a minute and I know he's going to delve deeper. I'm holding my breath. I don't want to talk about this—even though I know I ought to. I'm already so unsure all the time; I don't think I can handle Gabriel possibly thinking less of me. I still can't look at him.

"You were seventeen when you graduated from high school, weren't you?" Gabriel asks in a lower voice.

I nod. I think if I were the one on those stairs in the picture, I'd head wherever the sun was.

"That's awfully young to make a decision about your future like that. I don't blame you for putting off college. Isn't your birthday in October? Why did your mom put you in school so young?"

"I don't know. I guess I was pretty bright and she figured I was ready. Mom was… weird about school."

"Weird how?"

I struggle to explain it, grateful to be able to occupy myself with something other than dread. I even glance at Gabriel. "Um, it was kind of like she didn't think it was necessary. It was secondary to other things. I mean we went to school, but Mom was always more concerned about… letting us do what we wanted. She said we ought to do what made us happy. She took me to art museums all the time and I was always enrolled in some art class at the college. She didn't care if I had to miss school to do it either."

I pause and then laugh drily as I remember. "I swear it was like she only had me go to school because the law said I had to. But she'd pull me out of class just because she found some really great museum or sculpture garden or hole-in-the-wall boutique with local art for sale. She probably would have sent me to a private art school if she could have afforded it… She probably would have done the same with Ezra except he *loves* academic stuff and thrives on that."

"I take it you did well enough in school to merit that full scholarship offered to you as barely a junior though?" he asks.

I look down at my hands. We're rounding back to the question I don't want to answer. But what can I do but be truthful with him?

"I did pretty well," I reply. "But I got in because I was talented. They liked my portfolio."

Gabriel sighs and I can tell he is definitely concerned about what I'm avoiding so persistently.

"Wendy, why did you decide not to go to art school?" he asks, looking at me pointedly.

My eyes are back on *Relativity*. There's one man looking over the balcony. As I try to imagine what he sees from there, I recognize that from his angle of sight, everything appears normal. He can't see stairs going the wrong direction or people upside down. I have no idea how Escher accomplished that. Only the outside observer can see how bizarre those stairs are.

I take a slow breath. “Because I got pregnant.”

7

He inhales. Exhales. Does it again. Pushes forcefully past shock.

And then the inertia of sinking disappointment. It's so swift it's painful.

I can't bear to look at him. Instead I count out his heartbeats and focus on the sound so hard that all other noises drown away. I look down at the floor as I listen. And then I sink down to it because I need the security right now.

Gabriel stands up. Paces slowly between the kitchen and the living room, but I don't look up.

The more bewildered he becomes, the more worried I get. I reach for the pillow again and bury my face in it. I want to get away from his feelings; they are breathtakingly intense.

Disappointment again. It throbs heavily. I expected it, but it's even worse now that I'm *feeling* it from him. Aggravation and disconcerted questioning—he must have a *lot* of questions. He dwells on confusion the longest. And then finally he begins to think. He pauses in his step. Placates himself with something.

More pacing. Anxiety gathers and I tense, ready to spring. He's running away with some idea that leaves him devastated. He tries to reject it with the dependability of reason, but it doesn't seem to be working.

I grip my shins now, my eyes shut, my cheek against the pillow, enduring the force of his distress. I know I should complete the story. But I need to know: will his opinion of me change now?

He finally stops, comes to sit on the edge of the couch. I feel his eyes on me but I look down at the carpet.

"And then what?" he asks finally, anticipation and dread bottlenecking his thoughts.

"I put her up for open adoption," I say without looking up. "And two months after she was placed, she got RSV and died."

He gasps. More shock. Hard and lead-like. My arms are heavy and numb with it. Then a hint of lightening disbelief. But it doesn't stay long. He comes upon a conclusion only to question it. He does this over and over. I think he's trying to think of what to say. That indecision winds to a close and he opts to be silent and wait for me to talk.

"That was nearly three years ago," I say quietly, needing to answer some of his questions so the force of them whirling around so violently won't nauseate me. I even look at him to convey my sincerity, but he's not looking back. "I got accepted to art school while I was pregnant. I put her up for adoption because I thought it was the right thing to do. I wanted a second chance—I was supposed to go to the school for my junior and senior year but after she died I obviously faced the what-ifs over and over. I gave up art because it reminded me too much of choosing art school over my own child."

Gabriel looks at me finally. The lamp on the end table is the only source of light in the room. It's behind him so it makes his face appear darker—it goes well with his expression. It doesn't hide the depth of his compassionate grief though, and it releases a few tears from my eyes.

I discern a question trying to push through—one that he feels ashamed of wanting to ask. But the question remains and he gets aggravated at himself for dwelling on it. He remains silent.

I rub my eyes and clear my throat. I know what he's wondering about. "He was funny and thoughtful and really smart. I was young and stupid of course, thinking that a romance at barely sixteen was going to last forever. I trusted his emotions at the time. But when I got pregnant he wanted nothing to do with me." I sigh. "I know I expected too much from him. I was too stupid to see it then."

Gabriel has been watching my face carefully. He scoots next to me. He reaches down for my hand and tucks it under his chin. "I love you," he says.

"So that's it?" I ask skeptically. "You're not… mad at all?"

"No, I'm not mad. Just disappointed. But you can tell, can't you?"

"Yeah, I'm just having trouble believing it. I figured you'd at least be upset that I hadn't told you before."

He squeezes my hand as he thinks. "It would have come out eventually. Getting upset about timing isn't helpful."

"I can't say I would have told you before this weekend if you hadn't pressed me…" I test, annoyed for a reason I can't pinpoint.

"We've barely known each other two months. If I were to be concerned that I don't know all aspects of your life, then I only have myself to blame for wanting to marry you so quickly. And since I can't look back on *that* decision with any regret, then I have no right to be upset. So I'm not."

"Well maybe you're not angry, but you *do* seem distraught by it," I say. "I've let you down. I've... all but lied to you. That doesn't... worry you?"

He looks at me critically, perplexed. "Would you *rather* I be angry?"

I sigh, slumping against the couch. "No. I don't think so. I think I'm irritated at myself for *not* telling you sooner. If you were angry I wouldn't feel so stupid having waited so long."

"I really don't blame you for not telling me sooner, Wendy. It's not the kind of thing that comes up in the course of regular conversation. Nor is it something I have a right to know up front. I am *not* upset with you. Only sorrowful for what you've been through."

I look up into his light brown eyes again which exude nothing but concern. "I know what you feel *for* me. That's obvious. But you're also experiencing something else. Doubt. Some kind of shame—I can't translate it, I think because you're trying to avoid it. That's not like you to suppress yourself that way so it's kind of freaking me out."

He exhales through pursed lips. "You're right. I... hadn't realized how poorly I was hiding it. It's irrational and I was hoping it would go away if I didn't address it."

I draw my knees up and wrap my arms around them. "Sounds a double-standard. I'm supposed to bare three year-old baggage to you as a method of achieving happiness but you're allowed to hide your reactions to it?"

He sighs. "It is a double standard. No doubt."

I look up at him, waiting.

He wrinkles his nose at me before groaning quietly in defeat. "I'm jealous of your past sexual exploits with another man." He looks up uncomfortably.

I have no idea how to respond to that. I bite the inside of my cheek, running through various responses: *Don't be jealous, Gabriel. We will have* way *better sex than me and that other guy did.* Not. *But you are way hotter...* Like that matters. *He may have had my body, but you have my heart.* Big, fat, nauseating copout. *I never had conversations with him like I do you...* Yeah, that will *totally* erase Gabriel imagining me in the arms of another guy. I give up. There is *nothing* I can do or say to reassure him.

But I can tell I need to say *something.* He's ashamed of being jealous of events that happened years ago.

"I love you," I say. It worked on *me* after an unload; why not him?

He smiles at me and I smile back. He starts chuckling. "I cannot *stand* being insecure. It shoots my brain full of impracticality. I can't think clearly."

I roll my eyes. "Oh God forbid you not be able to think clearly."

"Insecurity is a disease, Wendy. I think one disparaging thought and a whole slew of them come forward, like when you give money to a beggar in downtown LA. Every one of them is vying for my attention."

"Don't I know it," I reply.

"Like now. I get the admission off my chest but I still can't stop wondering about him. How tall? How smart? How good-looking? What color hair? Eyes? Is he like me? Is he completely different? If he's different, why did you like him enough to explore that kind of intimacy with him? Did you like him better? Was intimacy with him so satisfying and that's why you feel bereft without it now? And in *all* that, I'm jealous that he could satisfy one of your needs that I can't." He groans, crosses his arms, and throws his head back on the arm of the couch. He looks at me out of the corner of his eye. "Irrational. I told you."

"I don't think any of those questions are irrational," I say. "Do you want me to answer them?"

He lifts his head and looks at me in shock. "No I don't! I am not going to entertain that line of thinking. You could answer every one of them satisfactorily and I'd *still* find more to wonder about and question. No. I'd rather ask you questions about *you,* not some lascivious miscreant whom I hope I never chance to meet."

"Okay," I sigh, gearing up for more emotional unloading. "But before you do, I do want to tell you that a relationship with you, *without* physical contact, has been far more intimately satisfying than anything I ever had with him." I reach for his hand and squeeze it. "Ask me whatever you want."

"That actually does make me feel better," Gabriel says. He muses over some new line of questions but he shakes his head and heads it off by looking at me. His expression softens. "I want to know more about what it was like carrying a child… then losing her. I feel inadequate though. I don't think I have a right to make you unearth those details for me to survey."

"It was long enough ago that I'm not going to lose it in talking about it," I reply. I scoot back up onto the couch near Gabriel's feet and cross my arms over his knees. "Being pregnant was terrifying. From the moment I found out, *everything* changed. Everything I had planned on was suddenly up in the air."

"Did you... *feel* her? Your daughter, I mean... Considering your empathic talent?"

I look away, my eyes filling with tears. I guess it's *not* long enough ago if this is how I react.

"I'm sorry," he says, sitting up and reaching carefully for my hand. "That was... too invasive. I meant—"

"No, it's not," I say, wiping my tears. "I just didn't expect it. That's all." I sniffle a few times. "Yes, I felt her... Although it wasn't nearly so obvious as touching other people. Babies have emotions. They just... aren't the same." I look at him, trying to explain it. "It's kind of like dreaming. You experience emotions when you dream, sometimes strong ones, but they have a different quality. They aren't as... all-consuming. And they come and go without much transition."

Gabriel is contemplating. When he finally looks up again I continue, "I guess, for babies, emotions are new so they don't quite get the implications of them enough to feel them as strongly. They don't have the defined edge of someone who is older. Kids are kind of the same. They don't... perpetuate what they feel like adults do—not usually. Kids are good at enduring feelings. They pass and kids don't look back. They move right on to the next thing like the last ten minutes didn't really matter." I smile as I remember the kids I felt in the children's ward. "That's why adults don't quite relate to kids and vice versa."

"That's fascinating," he breathes. "I honestly have never thought that our developed intelligence would make us *more* susceptible to emotion. But it makes sense that we have a harder time with them *because* we know their origin." He looks at me. "So was it gradual then? Feeling your daughter in-utero?"

I nod. "I never really acknowledged that I felt her at all until maybe the beginning of the second trimester. But even then I only picked up on her if I was paying attention. Which I usually wasn't. I was too busy wrestling with my *own* impending devastation. But by the third trimester I felt her enough that I couldn't ever ignore it. When she—" I stop because it feels like I'm about to rip the Band-Aid off of a giant gash in my heart.

Gabriel squeezes my hand and reaches for my free one as well. I find solace in his empathy, which is under control. I take a deep breath. "I had already decided to put her up for adoption. So when I went into labor, I took every drug they offered me so I could be numb. I just didn't want to—" I stop, shuddering through a few breaths. I look up and blink my eyes to make the tears go away. "I didn't touch her skin after she was born. I thought if she knew I was giving her up I wouldn't be able to handle feeling it. I didn't want to suffer more guilt over letting her go… I tried everything I could to separate myself."

I lower my eyes in shame, working through the grief, waiting for it to pass. I know it will. It's been three years almost, and while it bugs me that my emotions over it can still be so fresh, I'm positive that they are not going to last forever. Emotions *always* pass.

Gabriel's heaviness pushes into my attention finally. Sorrow for me unsettles him, but it's compassionate sorrow which is much easier to endure. I grab on to his softer emotions and ride them to the surface until I can bear to look at him again.

When he sees that he has my attention, he says, "Wendy, do you still believe it was selfish to put your child up for adoption?"

I look at him critically. "Yes. I picked something over her," I reply matter-of-factly. "And I paid for that choice."

He's deeply bothered by my answer, and I figured he would be. He doesn't like to blame me for anything, even things that are definitely my fault. I'm surprised though, that Gabriel knows all the touchiest questions to ask. But I've agonized over this one enough times that the admission comes with indifference. "If there's one thing I've learned," I say, answering his doubts, "I suck at keeping it together when I don't have responsibilities. Ezra taught me that. Because when I started working my butt off to take care of him, that's when I finally started being happy again. If I'd kept my baby, I would have discovered that about myself sooner and saved all those years of letting myself down—and saved *her*. I justified giving her up under the guise of giving her a better life. But I *know,* at the core of my being, that keeping her would have made me better and would have saved her. Giving her up made me an ugly person for a lot of years."

I can tell he wants to disagree. It doesn't matter what he says though. He doesn't know me well enough to make a valid argument otherwise.

"I've accepted it," I say. "I've moved past it and I don't agonize over the guilt anymore. I learned from it and became better… That's the least I can do in her memory. *Justifying* what I did only cheapens her death."

Gabriel sighs, restraining himself against protest. I'm glad he knows better than to argue. Gabriel is a little blind when it comes to me. He thinks I could never do anything truly horrible. But *I* know what I'm capable of. People make selfish decisions all the time. And the best you can hope to do to make up for mistakes is to learn from them.

"Is there something else you want to know?" I ask after a minute.

"Not at the moment," he replies. "I'm too busy devising ways to change your perception of yourself."

I roll my eyes. "What does it matter, Gabriel? What's done is done. I'm a better person now than I was then. Sometimes people make bad choices. They just do. No matter how much you love me now, how impossible it is for you to believe I could do something so blatantly self-centered, I did. I *refused* to touch my own daughter when she was born because I didn't want her emotions to convince me to keep her. I used to *hate* that I had to feel her inside of me all the time. I *resented* her for it. I wanted her to stop feeling so I could put a stop to the guilt. You can't change the person I was just because you want to see me through rose-colored glasses."

He leans toward me and grabs my hand, gripping it firmly. "I don't care what you say. Giving up your child was *not* selfish. I refuse to believe that you looked at your art school brochure and looked at your ultrasound picture, *felt* your baby's feelings so close, and picked one over the other. *You* are the one with a skewed perception, not me. And somehow I'm going to find a way to prove it… I'm just not sure how yet."

I sigh in exasperation, pull my hand from his. I stand up to go to the kitchen to get away from his insistence, which he's deliberately aiming at me. I don't look at him, hoping to properly convey that he needs to drop it. I'm not interested in hearing him lavish more praise on me for a situation that was *not* praise-worthy.

Rummaging through the cabinets for a snack, I end up in the one with plates and glasses instead. I'm about to shut it to look in another, but one of the glasses catches my eye. I open the door all the way and reach in, taking out the monogrammed glass, turning it around in my hands to examine it. How did Gabriel get *this*?

I turn to Gabriel who has been watching me. I can tell from the look on his face that he has been plotting most likely. "This is yours?" I hold the cup up.

He glances at it. "That's my brother's. I ended up with it somehow. Probably he left it at my place in LA when he came over, and I never got it back to him."

I look at the cup and then back at him. "Your brother? Where did *he* get it?"

Gabriel's brows pinch together as he looks at me. "Why?"

I set the glass on the counter space separating the living room from the kitchen, prop my arm up there, and stare at it like it's an oracle. It definitely *feels* that way.

The glass' shape isn't remarkable; it's the logo etched on it that caught my attention. Two hands, palms up. Above it, the words, *Detritus.* Beneath the logo is the year 2010.

"The same year," I whisper, disbelieving.

Gabriel gets up and comes to stand on the other side of the counter. He leans down, eye-level with me. "What?"

"Did your brother… go to this exhibition benefit?" I ask. "Is that how he got it?"

"Actually, we both did," he replies. "They gave all the patrons these free glasses. My brother liked them so much I gave him mine, too. What do you know about it?"

My mouth is hanging open. I hop up to sit on the counter. "Why? Are the two of you art enthusiasts or something?"

"Oh no. Neither of us was much into art. I like Escher, but only because of his genius in combining philosophical and scientific worlds in visual form. But my brother and I were looking for a gift for our mother. She really likes sculpture, and that year Detritus hosted their annual benefit to fundraise for a musculoskeletal disease charity. My mother had been a long-time volunteer for the charity so buying her a gift in which the proceeds would benefit something she loved so much added especial value." Gabriel props his elbow on the counter, lost in memory. "She cried her eyes out when we gave her what we'd picked out. I think that's probably her favorite gift from us ever."

I've been listening with bated breath. "*Whoa,*" I say after several silent moments, my head spinning.

He sits on a bar stool and watches me, curious.

"I was at that benefit," I reply, hardly believing that Gabriel was actually in the same building as me almost three years ago… "I had just finished up an intensive art camp with Detritus that summer. The benefit was the final event for the camp—it was supposed to teach us about curating."

His eyes widen in surprise. "Incredible," he says. Then he grins. "Well it's fortunate I didn't meet you there. Three years ago you would have been underage and that would definitely have complicated things, wouldn't it?"

My face darkens. "Honestly, I doubt you would have *wanted* to meet me then. It was early August, right before my senior year began. And only a week earlier I had gotten the phone call that my daughter had died. I hardly remember a thing from the event. And it was the last art exhibit I ever went to."

He reaches across the counter for my hand but doesn't say anything. The usual precision of his thoughts falters, sagging with the sadness weighing them down. Through the melancholy, however, we're both a bit awestruck by the coincidence, especially considering the conversation we *just* had.

I don't like feeling his fresh despair for me. It's bringing too much to the surface that I haven't had to endure in a long time. In an effort to shake out the sadness infecting me, I hop off the counter and grab an apple from a bowl near the sink and say, "Maybe I *was* underage, but at least I could still touch people then…" I look up. "I wonder what would have happened if I'd met you then?"

"I have to say I'm glad I didn't," Gabriel replies, moving to sit back on the couch. "But not for the same reason you claim. I simply wouldn't have wanted to face the moral conundrum of what to do about you. Undoubtedly, if I'd had any words with you at all, I would have fallen immediately in love. I don't want to think about the kind of self-restraint it would have taken to stay away from you all those years."

After a minute or so more of marveling silence, I sit on one of the barstools and say, "That is one heck of a coincidence."

Gabriel looks up at me. "I do not ever ascribe to coincidence."

I roll my eyes. "Okay. Well if you have an explanation for why we were both at the same event, three years ago, right after my child died, despite the fact that you are *not* art-inclined, and we discovered this *right* after I told you about that child, please enlighten me."

Gabriel grins at me. "Because we were meant for each other, Love. And now that I've discovered how the universe tried to bring us together even then, I have to say I'm even more confident that taking you off the market the day after tomorrow is the right thing to do."

I chuckle. "So I guess the universe doesn't honor underage laws then if it was trying to bring us together then."

He furrows his brow. "Yes, I would have thought the universe would have more sense."

"It's a senseless world, Gabriel," I say. "But I don't much care. In two days—" I notice the clock on the stove then. "Make that *tomorrow,* I will gladly begin the rest of my life with you trying to make sense of it anyway."

"Aww," Gabriel says. "I should have started having sleepovers with you earlier. Apparently after midnight is when your sentimental sweet side finally emerges."

I grin at him. "Oh, well I thought being sentimental and sweet was part of this whole G-rated intimacy you were talking about earlier."

"You're a quick study."

8

For some reason Gabriel insists on leaving Saturday morning—the day *of* the wedding. I don't question it; this is *his* production. When we reach his parent's house, however, my anxiety gathers in full force. The grandeur of the home is daunting. Robert's house is bigger, but I was never aware of how well-off Gabriel's family was. I feel like a pauper marrying a prince. In more ways than one. I wish we'd have come Friday so at least I'd be a little more comfortable in their space before the wedding.

"You grew up here?" I ask as we pull into the circular driveway.

Gabriel glances at me. "Mostly. They bought this house when I was in middle school. We lived in a smaller one before though. My mother said my brother and I would get into more trouble in a bigger one where she couldn't easily keep her eye on us. When they finally decided to buy a new house, she told us we had grown up enough to have sense to not swing from curtains or climb on the roof."

I smile. "Did you? Climb the roof, I mean."

His eyes gleam. "As far as my mother is concerned we never saw it up close." He hops out to come around and open my door. Taking my hand and pulling me out, he points to a chimney on the left. "But there's a spectacular place to admire the view from over there."

"Gabriel!" I say, smacking his arm, "You had better apologize to your mother for that!"

"Hey!" he says, cringing from my attack. "*She's* the one who said we were old enough to have sense not to. She was obviously mistaken on that count. Why should I apologize for something I never promised not to do?"

I shake my head. "Wow. Well, Gabriel, there's this thing that kids are supposed to do called obedience. It means you do what you're told even if it doesn't make sense to you."

"Why on earth would I concede to do something that doesn't make sense?"

I laugh. "Forget it," I say. I'm too nervous to argue with him right now. I take his arm for moral support.

Gabriel chuckles and pats my hand. He's a little apprehensive as well, making me even more anxious.

"Could you temper your feelings a little?" I say. "As if I wasn't nervous enough already… You think they won't like me?"

"I was under the impression that I *was* tempering my emotions for your benefit. I'm more nervous that you won't like *them*. My mother is um, a handful, to say the least."

"Seriously?" I giggle. "I mean, you're really worried that I don't like people who are 'a handful?'"

He looks a little confused at first but catches on quickly. "Good point. Still though, I hope you can handle two of us handfuls in the same room. I don't want to scare you off."

Just as he says that, the front door opens, and a small woman charges out, a huge smile on her face. "Mi muchacho!" she exclaims. "Mi bebé! Mi hijo!" She comes at Gabriel so fast that I let go of his arm and jump back.

He throws his arms around her, lifts her up, and then sets her back on the ground. "Es un gusto verlo, Mamá. And this is Wendy," he says, stepping to the side because I'm hiding behind him.

"Sí, sí. Qué chica bonita. How did you manage that, Gabriel? She's lovely!" she says, throwing the dish towel she came out of the house with over her shoulder. Her black and silver hair is braided and wound around her head. Her face is free of wrinkles but for the corners of her eyes. She takes my hand in both of hers, her dark eyes sparkling with enthusiasm. "Hello, Wendy, I am so pleased to meet you finally."

She's holding my hand so firmly I'm afraid she's going to take it a step further and hug me. When she doesn't, I smile tentatively at her. "Me too," I say. "I've heard a lot about you. Thanks for doing this."

"Don't thank *me.* I should be thanking *you,*" she says, shooting Gabriel stern look. It actually *feels* like a warning, too—the motherly kind like when mom drops you off at a friend's house and tells you to behave yourself or else. "I couldn't be happier that I am *finally* marrying this thorn in my side off so another woman can share the burden."

"Thank you, Mamá, for those kind words of affirmation," Gabriel says drily, lifting his chin like a rebellious child. "You say you're grateful, yet you aren't doing a very good job trying to retain your future daughter-in-law when you insult me."

She snatches the towel from off her shoulder and balls her hands into fists, placing them on her hips. She stares him down, (or *up* considering how much shorter she is), daring him to argue.

"I'm only making sure she knows what she's getting into. You're such a diabólico encanto, I have to make sure she's not under a spell. As your mother it's my job to make sure you conduct yourself as a gentleman."

"Oh, por amor de Dios," Gabriel drawls, rolling his eyes. "Here I was thinking that as my mother it was your job to uplift and nurture. How does calling me a thorn in your side in front of my fiancé accomplish any of that?"

His mother glares at him and then whips him in the chest with her towel so fast I startle at the sound it makes. Gabriel jumps back. Then he leans in and snags the towel from her. "Mamá!" he cries. "Dad needs to confiscate your dish towels from you one of these days. They're not weapons!"

Mrs. Dumas puts her fists on her hips again. "*That* was for using the Lord's name in vain. Don't act like you didn't know it was coming." Then she lifts her chin almost haughtily. "And if you had *any* regard for your maker, you'd have read His good book. Then you'd *know* that even the Apostle Paul was grateful for the thorn in his side. And so I am grateful for you, Mijo."

She turns to me now, ignoring my stunned look. "As I was saying, *you* are the one that deserves a thank you. And if you know any other good women so I can get rid of his brother too, send them my way. Now come on! We have so much to do. I expect people to start arriving at any moment. It doesn't matter when you tell relatives to show up, they come early, just for the 'before' party. Gabe, go find your brother. He's having an issue with the seating. I think he might be rearranging the whole living room. He swears to me you'll like it better. Cáspita! He's going to put me in a state!"

Gabriel looks at me. "Wendy? You'll be alright?"

I open my mouth to answer but Mrs. Dumas puffs, "What do you think I'm going to do? Scare away the one woman willing to put up with *you*? Now get! Or I'll tell your father you're defying your mother."

Gabriel shakes his head at her. "Mamá, you already *are* scaring her. Telling her how you want to get rid of me… I'm afraid as soon as I'm gone you're going to convince her to run as far away as possible."

She rushes at him, reaching for her towel that he's holding.

He hops away from her. "Okay, okay. I'm going. But if Wendy disappears, I know exactly who to blame."

Gabriel shoots me a grin and then bounds for the front steps. Mrs. Dumas turns to me. I haven't had a chance to speak much so I say, "It really is nice to meet you, Mrs. Dumas. Your home is lovely. And really, thank you so much for doing this. I really appreciate it."

"Call me Maris," she says, watching my face. She's in a bit of disbelief as she takes me in with a critical eye. "Así que dime. You were really okay with him springing this on you? I told him it wasn't a good idea, but he wouldn't let it go. And then he calls me yesterday and says he's bringing you *today*. There's *no* time to make adjustments if there's something you don't like." Her emotions reveal a current of expectant demand. I have the sudden urge to hum the Final Jeopardy tune to it.

"It was a shock for sure," I reply, nervous that I'm going to give the wrong answer. "But I couldn't be more grateful that he took the stress off of me. I'm actually excited to see what he came up with. He's never disappointed me."

She looks sideways at me, surprised and still somewhat disbelieving. "You're okay that your future husband planned your whole wedding without consulting you about any of it…? You are an odd one, aren't you?" Then she smiles genuinely. "Well, it would take an odd one to put up with my Gabriel. Eso me conviene. Come on then, Wendy. I'll show you what we've done."

Maris makes it a point of showing me every room in the house whether or not it has to do with the wedding. She says she wants me to think of it as my home, too, so I ought to know where every nook and cranny is. She obviously likes things lively; the house is bright and airy, accented with bold colors so tastefully distributed that I would never call it gaudy. She obviously drew a lot of inspiration from her Hispanic roots but still managed to make the colors understated enough to be refined. And Gabriel was right; she does like modern art—especially sculpture.

She finally takes me to the kitchen where she has me taste everything, watching my face for approval. I stop short when I reach the center island on which a massive spread of hors d'oeuvres is arranged.

I stare at it with my mouth open.

Maris comes up beside me. "Gabe said you liked anything with spinach and artichokes together and that I should go loco on the hors d'oeuvres with the combination. I even made this one up." Maris points to what looks like small stuffed and fried pockets of some kind. "Miniature Spinach and artichoke tamales fried and served with cheese dip."

She definitely followed Gabriel's instructions on the spinach and artichokes. There are little cups of some kind of finely chopped salad that includes the two vegetables; miniature spinach and artichoke quiches; little flat breads with spinach and artichoke, tomato and feta cheese; some kind of pastry wrapped around spinach, artichoke, bacon, cream cheese and… *jalapeños*. My cheeks flush a little.

And in the very center, a huge casserole dish of… *spinach and artichoke dip.*

I bite my lip to keep from laughing.

"Gabe said you were picky about things being organic so I was very careful," Maris says. "If you taste anything that's not up to your standards, you be sure to let me know."

"I can tell by smelling it that it's fine," I say. "And the spinach and artichokes…" I grin at the food widely. "Well, I'm excited to try everything you came up with."

At that moment a blond-haired man walks in, about Gabriel's height and build. I can tell immediately that this guy must be Gabriel's dad. He has the same nose and chin. I thought that Gabriel got his smile from his mother when I first saw her, but it's clear that he more closely resembles his dad in the curvature of his mouth.

"Wendy," the man says, holding out a hand.

I take it with my gloved one and smile shyly. Mr. Dumas strikes me as stately. The way he carries himself makes him come across as dignified.

"I'm Dan," he says, graciousness oozing from him. "It's a pleasure to meet you. Gabe has spoken of you so often we feel like we already know you. We are so pleased to have you as part of our family." He speaks with the slightest French accent and I can't help but smile, remembering what Gabriel told me about his dad who moved to the states years ago and married Maris. I wonder how that happened. The two cultures are so very different.

"It's nice to meet you, too," I say, releasing his hand. "Gabriel makes a bit more sense now that I've met his parents."

Dan chuckles. "Well it can't be *that* much more. Gabe still fails to make sense to Maris and me all the time. And we've known him his whole life."

"Ah, you've met the method behind the madness that is Gabe," an unfamiliar gruff voice says from behind me.

I turn to see a dark Hispanic man looking at me.

"Michael," Maris says, flitting to my side. "You've not met Wendy yet." She looks at me. "Wendy, this is Gabe's brother, Mike."

Mike doesn't step forward or offer me his hand, but nods once with a cordial, reserved smile. He's terrifically handsome. Not just regular handsome. Like, so handsome that I don't understand how so much in the way of good looks ended up in one family. Mike is a couple inches shorter than Gabriel, and darker-skinned. In fact, he looks like he picked up a *lot* more of the Latin side of his parentage. His jaw is more square, his eyes more round than Gabriel's slightly almond-shaped ones. And he's built like a tank. Solid and muscular; the guy must spend hours at the gym. *Geez. He's not married* either*?*

"Nice to meet you, Mike," I say, grateful I don't have to shake his hand. Everyone here is a little too comfortable around me. It's nice to see someone with caution. I'd like to get closer to him to familiarize myself with his emotions—to see how similar they are to his brother's—but Gabriel bounds up behind Mike just then, looking from his brother to me. He moves to stand slightly ahead of Mike, almost as if he's blocking him from me. Or me from Mike. I can't tell. But the placement of his body is definitely odd. It doesn't phase Mike who stands with his hands behind his back, watching me. He looks militant.

"Hello, Love. I see you've met all the important people," Gabriel says in a rush. "Mamá, have you had her try the dress yet? If alterations have to be done, I'm sure you'll need time to do them before the ceremony."

"Yes, yes, Gabe," Maris says impatiently. "If you were so concerned about alterations you might have shown up yesterday. But tuviste suerte. I can tell by looking at her that it's going to fit perfectly. Now, Mike, did you and Gabe figure out the seating situation?"

"Yes, Mamá," Mike replies, looking at Gabriel the whole time. "Gabe and I have come to an agreement."

I can't help but think that Mike's words are loaded. Gabriel is on the edge of my emodar and what I pick up is agitation. It feels like he's trying to calm himself. When I look at his face, his mouth is set in a line, but he doesn't respond. That's weird. It seems like there's tension between the two.

“Then the two of you can go set up chairs outside,” Maris says. “Come with me, Wendy. Let me show you where the ceremony will happen, and then we do need to get you into that dress.”

Maris leads me through a set of French doors into the living room. The sight of it makes me stop on the threshold and catch my breath. The first thing I notice is the vaulted ceiling: satin has been suspended in random and interspersed bands of variegated color. I know exactly what it’s supposed to look like.

The sky in the colorworld.

Someone expertly wove the fabric together in such a way that the colors blend into one another just right—yellow blends into darker yellow which blends into light orange. And the colors… I would have thought the range of colors I’ve described to Gabriel in the colorworld would be hard to duplicate this tastefully, but they are just muted enough to be elegant. And the intricacy… it’s incredible.

“How…?” I marvel.

Maris is looking up with me, pleased. “We hired someone to do it. It took her several days. I was nervous about how it would turn out, but she did an excellent job.”

“Seriously,” I say. I have described the colorworld many times for Gabriel, always feeling like I couldn’t possibly do an adequate job. But looking at this ceiling, it’s like he’s been seeing it with me all along.

I finally look down to the space beneath that incredible fabricated sky and see that it’s almost entirely white. With one exception: the aisle runner is deep purple and leads to an alter framed in purple organza. The symbolism of it—the joining of our two souls which are both purple—hits me. For Gabriel and me, this marriage is about something other than our bodies. That he would choose to make that the focus of our union touches my heart. Tears come to my eyes.

Maris sighs in relief at my reaction; she knows these are not tears of sadness.

“How does he always get things so perfect?” I whisper.

“He never *ever* settles for less. It is both a blessing and a curse, mi hija.”

***

Maris opens the closet door in the room that will be my ready room. A dress bag hangs there and she unzips it with a flourish, pulling a white satin gown out like an expert bridal consultant.

The dress is spectacular. I don't know if I would have had good enough taste to pick it out myself. It has a boat neck and short sleeves, with matching gloves that I guess will almost meet the sleeves. The gown itself is simple and there is no beading or lace anywhere that I can see, which is a relief. Instead, the bodice is accented with intricate folds, and the skirt flows like liquid satin.

"It's perfect," I breathe, admiring it.

"Try it on. Let's be sure it fits."

Until Gabriel mentioned alterations I had forgotten how customized dresses such as this should be. Maris might be confident, but I don't know that *I* am since my shape has to carry the dress. I wonder how they got my measurements? Maybe they estimated based on the size of the clothes in my closet? My wardrobe is hardly custom-fitted...

I take the dress from her and go into the bathroom.

"I'll help you with the zipper once you have it on," Maris says before I shut the door.

I see a pink gift bag on the bathroom counter as I start to undress. There is a small card attached. I open it and read:

Mi encantadora doncella,

All that skin on Thursday... I couldn't help myself. I had to go to the lingerie store. Did you know those places are lace-apaloozas? It took several hours to find anything I deemed worthy of gracing your body that you'd like. But hopefully I found something we can both be satisfied with. No pressure if you aren't ready to wear it. But it <u>*is*</u> *your fault... Too much skin, Love. Too much.*

-Gabriel

I pull out the contents of the bag and my heart skips. It's a satin underwear and bra set and it is *definitely* more revealing than my swimsuit from Thursday. And it's a pastel version of chartreuse, my favorite color. I didn't even know they made lingerie in that color... I weigh whether or not I should wear it.

That's probably not a good idea. Wearing it will only make me want to show it off. And I don't know if he *or* I are going to be able to handle that kind of intimacy without pushing boundaries we ought not to. I'm not ready to test those waters yet. Furthermore, today I just want to think about starting a life with Gabriel. I don't want to think about deprivation.

I turn to the dress finally and step into it. It feels like cool water, light and breezy. It's even more perfect now that I see it on me. I struggle in vain for the zipper then, not wanting to accept Maris' offer of help. Gabriel told me he had informed his mom about my condition, but I'm worried that he glossed over it. I don't want to explain that she shouldn't get near my skin. Then she'll realize how much of an anomaly her son is marrying and… hate me.

Just thinking of it makes my throat thick with tears. I hear the bathroom door open, and I turn my exposed skin away from Maris and back up to the sink and mirror.

"You'll never get that zipper up by yourself," Maris says calmly, striding toward me. She wears a pair of beige gloves. I relax, exhaling. I have no idea how she knew the exact moment to come in, but I guess she's as perceptive as Gabriel. I turn around, and she zips up the dress in one smooth motion while I hold my hair out of the way. I've already put the gloves on. Gloves are always the first thing I put on. They're like a security blanket. Sometimes I even sleep in them.

I let my hair fall to my back and look in the mirror.

The dress fits just right, which is both a relief and a surprise. How did they manage to get it so exact? I look really good, I have to admit. The gloves, for once, don't detract from my appearance. They extend high up and expose maybe three inches of my upper arm before the sleeves of the dress take over. I look very Audrey Hepburn.

"Perfect," I say in disbelief.

Just then, I hear Ezra's voice from the bedroom, "Wen, you in here?"

"Ezra!" I say excitedly. "I'm in the bathroom. You can come in."

Ezra appears in the doorway wearing the beginnings of a tux: a pair of black slacks with a dress shirt, but no tie or jacket. Even without the entire ensemble, he is definitely looking handsome. "Wow, Ezra," I say, "I can't believe you're looking that good and I had nothing to do with it."

He rolls his eyes at me. "I *can* dress myself, Wen."

"Yeah but even your hair is done," I say, smiling at him.

"Yes, hair gel presents a real problem if you haven't been trained properly. Forget about my hair. What do you think of the dress? It looks terrific on you," he says with a pleased smile, looking at my reflection in the mirror with me. But he's slightly nervous awaiting my reaction.

"It's perfect, Ezra. I can't believe you had it in you to choose something this nice!" I say, turning this way and that in the mirror. Maris nods appreciatively at my reflection.

"Well, Mrs. Dumas did the picking, I just did the narrowing down," says Ezra, leaning against the door jamb, clearly relieved.

"You picked this?" I ask, looking at Maris, "How did you get the fit so right?"

Maris grins and her eyes brighten just like Gabriel's. "Ezra and Gabe handled that part."

I fold my arms and look at Ezra suspiciously. "Care to share?"

"Relax, Wen. You were asleep. We uh, took a tailor's tape to you. It wasn't easy. You aren't a very sound sleeper. You kept tossing every time we tried to get the blanket back—Hey!" he says, throwing his hands up as I glare at him with my hands on my hips now. "We were careful! We both wore long sleeves and gloves! Geez ,Wendy, get a grip!"

He backs out of the door as I advance on him. "You risked your life to get measurements for a *dress*? Ezra, what were you thinking? No, what was *Gabriel* thinking? Where is he? I have a few words for him…"

"Wendy," says Maris sternly from behind me, "Perhaps now isn't the best time. We still have to do your hair, and Ezra needs to… He has other things to do, I'm sure. You can berate Gabriel later, but really, it sounds like he was very sensible about it. Don't get so upset."

Slightly miffed by her assertion that I'm overreacting, I can't deny her point about the timing, so I return to the bathroom to remove the dress which doesn't have to be worn for a while longer.

Maris follows me in and unzips the back for me. "I'll do your hair and makeup and then you can put it back on right before the ceremony."

Once I've taken the dress off she sits me down in a straight-backed chair and starts spritzing, parting, and clipping my hair.

"So what's the deal with Gabriel and his brother?" I ask. "They seem kind of… at odds."

Maris chuckles. "As competitive as always... Probably Gabe worries Mike is going to make a move on you. In fact, I think that's why Gabe decided to bring you today rather than yesterday." Maris tsk-tsks. "Los muchachos tontos."

"What?" I ask, incredulous. "That's ridiculous."

"Not really," Maris says, unconcerned. "Mike would do it just to get on Gabe's nerves. That's what they've always done—tried to steal each other's girlfriends, crushes, whatever. It's some kind of game to them. But Mike recognizes where the boundaries are. He certainly wouldn't try to flirt with his brother's wife on their *wedding* day. Gabe ought to give him more credit."

I think it's funny that Gabriel would be so insecure. Sure, Mike is *super* hot, but Gabriel is everything I want. I guess he wasn't kidding when he said he was worried I would choose someone else. Silly, of course, but I know how he feels. It is *very* easy for me to worry the same thing. And I have a lot less to offer than Gabriel does.

"Gabriel has this idea that there might actually be someone *else* out there who would put up with my… handicap," I say. "He's delusional of course. What do *you* think about this whole freak show?" I hold my gloved hands up to indicate my meaning. I feel kind of reckless in asking, but I need some kind of reassurance that what Gabriel and I are doing isn't totally crazy. I don't have personal experience with marriage. I wouldn't know what a real marriage is *supposed* to look like.

Maris doesn't miss a beat but keeps right on combing and parting and separating like I've only commented on the weather instead of the fact that her son is marrying someone he might never be able to touch. She's mostly calm, but everything else is indiscernible. I have trouble translating and separating more subtle emotions in people I don't know as well.

She sighs before she speaks. "I didn't like it at first. But Gabe won't be put off from what he wants, and you are who he wants. What can I do about that but accept it and accept *you* like the daughter you are soon to be? I don't know you very well, of course, but I know my Gabriel, and he never backs out of a commitment. So that gives me a lot of hope."

It's honest at least; that much is obvious. But pity is there again, and it's hard to ignore. I don't like to be pitied, but if anyone should be, it's probably me.

"I know what you mean," I say. "Part of me, the unselfish part, wishes he would move on and be happy and marry a normal girl and give you happy normal grandchildren. I even tried that. He wasn't having it though."

Maris laughs. "That sounds about right for my Gabriel."

I fidget my hands for a moment and then say, "But the selfish part of me wants him all to myself. I love him. I believe him when he says we can make this work. What can I do when he shows me in every way imaginable that this is what he wants and that he'll be happy even if I can never touch him?"

I can't believe I'm baring my soul to Gabriel's mother like she's my own. I must really like her. Or maybe I miss having a mother.

"Gabe has always been good at persevering," she replies, twisting and inserting bobby pins against my scalp. "But it's still going to be hard. You have to commit to doing your best. Every day."

She works silently for a moment, but I know she's not done and is considering her words. "Physical expressions of love are relationship building. It communicates a level of trust that is difficult to duplicate. You are in love now, but marriage is hard enough without complicating it further." She stops what she's doing and comes around to look at me. "It is *hard,* Mija." She looks directly in my eyes and it feels like when Gabriel is trying to read my mind. "*Muy dificil,*" she annunciates. "Some days you'll want to strangle him. You'll wonder what you were ever thinking. And when things are hard, you'll question whether the good outweighs the bad."

She moves back to work on my hair again. "You go through cycles of falling in and out of love. You have to find ways to rekindle what you once had, and physical expression is a perfect way of accomplishing that when words are not working."

She pauses for a moment, pensive. "Is it possible to be married without physically expressing that love?" she asks, as much to me as to herself. "I hope for you and for Gabe that it is. I want to believe that it is…" Her hands go still for a moment. "Oh Dios, ruego para que así sea. Por favor, bendice a mis hijos de tener éxito. Amen." she says softly and sincerely.

Did she just say a prayer?

She starts working again and says, "If you can do it, the rewards will be beautiful. I'll be cheering you on, Mija. But bear this in mind when it gets hard: this is what you signed up for."

I bite my lip. She expressed my doubts even more clearly than I have to myself. I have so few expectations when it comes to what I'm doing. I don't *know* anything about being married. I only know I want Gabriel always near me. I hope that's enough.

9

"You look terrific, Wen," Ezra says. Then he reaches a hand toward my head. I try not to flinch away but it's an automatic reaction now whenever someone moves too quickly in my personal space. "Relax," he says. "One of your flowers is coming loose."

I hold completely still as he eases it carefully back into place. Then he smiles at me. "I'm really happy for you."

"Thanks, Ezra," I say genuinely, shifting my weight from one foot to the other. We have about ten minutes before we go down the aisle. We're waiting for the cue-music. Ezra is giving me away and doubling as my 'man of honor.' I'm nervous. Not about marrying Gabriel but about going in front of all those people out there. I think there are only twenty-five or so, but I kind of wish Gabriel had made this an immediate-family-only affair.

"No, I mean I am *really* happy, Wen," Ezra says, reaching for my hand and tucking it under his arm. "I think being married to Gabe is going to take enough energy that you'll stop mothering me so much."

I scowl at him.

He laughs and then he softens. "I'm trying to say that it makes me really happy that you have someone in your life. I know you like doing everything for me, but it kind of stresses me out."

"Stresses you out?" I ask.

"Yeah… All that time it was just you and me, I was wishing every day that you'd meet someone. I didn't want you to end up like Mom."

"End up like Mom? What do you mean?"

Sadness surges through him as he thinks about her. I squeeze his arm. "Mom worked too hard," Ezra says without looking at me. "She never took time to herself. She never dated. Not once. You know that. Always made me feel like my every move determined her happiness, you know?"

I look down. "I know," I say softly. Mom mothered Ezra and me like we were her entire world in the extreme. She didn't have a life outside of us and it felt stifling at times.

"It was a lot of pressure to… be what she expected. I know that's why you—" Ezra stops but I can tell that whatever he wants to say is still bouncing around in his brain. It fills him with regret.

"What?" I say.

"Forget it," Ezra says. "Let's not talk about sad things on your wedding day."

I sigh, knowing exactly what Ezra is thinking about. "What I did, Ezra… Getting pregnant and then… Well, it wasn't Mom's fault. It was mine. Every bit of it. Mom loved us. She did her best. That's all that matters."

Ezra turns to me, indignant. "I know she did her best, Wen. And I'm grateful for it. I miss her. Every day. But I'm not going to pretend that the way she revolved her entire existence around us was healthy. All that time I got in trouble at school when Mom was alive? That was me doing the exact same thing you did. Rebelling because I was tired of her breathing down my neck. And when she died, you felt like you needed to do things exactly the way she did. I thought maybe, if I acted different with you than I did with Mom—stopped mouthing off, stopped skipping class—*you* would act different."

"Ezra… I'm sorry," I say, seeing Ezra's behavior in a whole new light. I assumed all that time that he was so well-behaved because I sucked at keeping things together and he knew it. But instead I was making his life harder because I focused on him too much.

"Oh stop it, Wen," he says, watching my expression. "Quit beating yourself up over every little thing. I didn't mean for this to turn into a criticism. I'm just trying to tell you that I am really glad that you're breaking the cycle—that you're finally free to do something for yourself that has nothing to do with me."

I look up at him—he's a couple inches taller than me now. "Me too," I say, feeling nothing but consuming happiness for me from Ezra. After several moments of thinking about it, I say, "I guess I never realized that your happiness is… connected to mine that way. That's what I was doing all that time—trying to make you happy." I smile genuinely as relief I didn't know I needed washes over me. "Ezra, thank you. Knowing that you don't feel abandoned or forgotten now that I'm getting married really makes this day perfect."

Ezra snorts. "I *definitely* do not feel abandoned. Kind of baffled… that you would pick someone like Gabe, but definitely not upset about you getting married. And Gabe obviously worships the ground you walk on. So *that* doesn't worry me. I'm just glad he's someone that thinks as highly of you as I do." He adjusts his tie uncomfortably and pulls his jacket down to straighten it. Then he holds out a hand to take mine again. "I know Mom would be happy, too."

I sigh, my chest twinging in sadness. I wish she were here, yet even that disappointment doesn't last long. It's hard to be too sad when Ezra's here next to me, about to give me away. Ironically, Ezra is the one person in this world who has a *right* to. Because Ezra was the first person that I ever really *gave* myself to. I gave him all my time and energy and love. Now Ezra is giving that to someone else. It's... genuine... and complete. I look up to the ceiling, trying not to cry so it won't mess up my makeup.

The wedding march starts and Ezra says, "We're up. Let's go make you Mrs. Dumas."

He reaches for the handle of the French doors. As he opens them, my eyes automatically find Gabriel's. He smiles at me from the other end of the room, looking absolutely gorgeous in a dark tux. But I don't dwell on that. As I walk down the aisle on my brother's arm toward Gabriel, I don't feel lacking at all. I don't begrudge my gloves the physical connection I may never have. I'm surprised by the deep contentment this moment brings. For the first time I feel like I'm in the exact place I *should* be. A thrill invigorates me as I get closer to Gabriel. I am definitely ready to be Mrs. Dumas.

***

"You like it?" Gabriel asks, guiding me to a table in the reception area that is set up on the back patio—the one place Maris *didn't* show me earlier.

"Like it?" I reply. "I cried when I saw where the ceremony was going to be." I shake my head in amazement as I look around at the space. Each table centerpiece is a bowl filled with multi-colored glass pieces that are illuminated by a light underneath. Other than these hints of color around the space, everything else is white. I love the effect—the way so much white highlights those simple splurges of color. "I had no idea you had this much class in you."

"I have to admit that the 'class' was not my doing," Gabriel replies. "*I* wanted a lot more color. I was planning on having it everywhere. But my mother and Ezra both told me that was too much. Ezra said, and I quote, 'Gabe, take what you like, tone it down about ninety-eight percent, and that's what Wen likes.' Best advice I got through the whole thing. I have to admit, what I envisioned for the ceiling inside was not *nearly* as lovely as what my mother was able to have done."

"It's stunning," I say, grateful Gabriel consulted someone other than his own tastes for the décor.

"Not nearly as stunning as you," he says, taking my hand and bringing it to his face to kiss my palm, my body warming with happiness at his nearness. I smile and imagine what it *might* have looked like if Gabriel had been left to his own devices... I think even if I'd walked into a room with floor-to-ceiling rainbows of color, I would have been just as thrilled. It would have had Gabriel written all over it; how could I hate that?

"So what about the vows?" I say. "The part about 'I take your body and soul under every condition?' That was perfect. You may not be the master of décor, but you are definitely the master of words."

"Oh of course," he replies. "I wasn't going to let my mother or your brother anywhere *near* our vows. It's frankly none of their business."

I sigh and prop my elbow on the table, which we have all to ourselves. I'm stuck in the surrealism of the moment, wishing that we were the only ones here. Eventually I'm going to have to go table to table and make nice with Gabriel's relatives—he said that's what he decided on over the traditional receiving line. They've all been duly informed to not get too friendly with me although I don't know what excuse was made for my aversion to skin-contact—Obsessive Compulsive Disorder maybe?

Maris announces that drinks and hors d'oeuvres are available so Gabriel hops up to get a plate for me.

My friend, Letty, bounds up to me then. Her presence was a surprise when I saw her at the ceremony. Although I remember mentioning that I wanted her at my wedding, I'm now kind of terrified she's going to take me into a hug unexpectedly. Fortunately, she just throws herself down in Gabriel's chair in a puff of heavy perfume, grinning. "Holy crap, Wen! *Married*? I don't even know where to start! I can't believe you didn't tell me! I can't believe Ezra and your *fiancé* planned your wedding without you knowing! I can't believe you married such a hottie! Was that his *brother*? Oh my Latino loveboat! Where did you meet him? Are you pregnant or something? Are you going—"

"Geez, Letty," I interrupt, smiling. "Are you going to ask me questions all day or do I get to talk at all?"

She slumps her shoulders like she's exhausted and throws her hands up. "I hope so. Because I have been *dying* to call you since Ezra told me."

Gabriel shows up then with two glasses of ice water in one hand and a plate in the other. He hands one glass to me and, seeing that Letty is here, hands her the other glass—which I am sure he intended for himself. He sets the plate down between us and then he holds out a hand to her with an irresistible grin. "Letty, I presume? *Such* a pleasure, señorita."

She melts internally as she takes his hand with her free one, staring at him open-mouthed. "Uh, yeah," she manages.

"Wendy and I are *so* pleased you could make it," he says, not yet releasing her hand and looking her in the eye. "And I must say, that color blue is simply striking on you. I've always thought bright colors on a Hispanic woman to be stunning."

I try to suppress my laughter at Letty's absolutely floored reaction. I know what it's like on the other side of all that alluring charm. Gabriel should have his picture next to the word 'charm' in the dictionary.

"Thanks," she says with wide eyes, unable to look away from him.

"I must ask you a question, Letty," he says in a low voice, releasing her hand finally and putting his chin between his thumb and forefinger, his gaze not varying from her face. "Mi esposa… ¿Cuántos novios en el pasado? ¿Cuántas más participaciones de matrimonio se deberán enviar?"

She giggles. "No idea," she replies. "Demasiados. If you want I can get you a list. Although, no hay anuncios necesarios. You don't have *any* competition worth mentioning."

"Demasiados?" Gabriel asks, annoyed. "One is too many. How many are we talking about?"

Letty giggles again and I raise my hand to get their attention. "Hello? Uni-lingual white girl over here. Can you people quit with the Spanish? It's rude. This is *my* wedding last time I checked. I declare it an English-only affair."

"Your wish is my command," Gabriel says. He turns to Letty who has started to get up from his chair. "No, you stay. I'll go get you a plate so you and Wendy can catch up."

After he leaves, Letty leans in conspiratorially. "María y José! Is he *always* that intense? Seriously, Wen. If you hadn't just married him I would be *all* over that. He's like Enrique Iglesias. But hotter. Although I don't know how that's possible. Enrique is my boy toy."

I giggle. "Yeah. He's like that all the time. But I hear his brother's single. Give it your best shot. Maybe we can be sisters-in-law."

Letty sits back and fans herself with her hand. "I'm gonna have to cool down first. Too much Latin hotness in too short a time."

I roll my eyes at her and laugh. Letty has a way of lightening the air with her presence. She doesn't take herself too seriously and it always makes things seem like less of a big deal. That's why she and I always got along. I always overthink everything. Letty balances me out and I've forgotten that until now.

I give her a quick version of the slightly-altered truth of meeting Gabriel. I exchange the word 'compound' for 'internship' which is where I told Letty I was going this past summer.

When I'm done she says, "So tell me, what's with the wedding? He only kissed your *hand*? If it was me, I *know* I would have been making out up there."

I laugh nervously, hoping it doesn't show. "Um, he's a gentleman. That's all. And yeah, I would have been making out, too. That's why we kept it G-rated."

"G-rated, huh?" Letty says, bobbing her eyebrows. "Saving up for later?"

I bite my lip uncomfortably, but thankfully Gabriel shows up again and hands her a plate. Letty shoots me a knowing look and hops up to sit with Ezra. I'm glad to let her think what she wants without having to manufacture more lies.

I blow air through pursed lips when she's gone and Gabriel looks at me. "I hope I did the right thing inviting her. I didn't want to leave anyone out who was important to you… I was already disappointed that I couldn't get a hold of Kaylen. I didn't want it to be *just* my relatives. Ezra told me Letty was your closest friend."

"No, I'm glad she's here," I reply. "And I think I managed it okay." I smile at him. "And she has the hots for you, of course. No surprise. You look like you stepped out of GQ Magazine."

Gabriel lays his hand on top of mine, intertwining his fingers there. But I'm thinking about Kaylen again since he mentioned her. “I think we need to exert a little more effort to connect with Kaylen,” I say. “I don’t like not knowing for sure where she is. I told her I’d be letting her know a date for the wedding and I’m really surprised she hasn’t been on the lookout for it. In fact, she was floored the last time I spoke to her that you hadn’t already insisted on setting a date…” I shake my head in disbelief. Kaylen’s intuitiveness is something I always take for granted. “She was obviously right in her guess about what you were up to.”

“Kaylen *is* quite perceptive,” Gabriel agrees. “And I agree. We can try out the home address she gave you… Ask the neighbors if they know where the Fowlers went… see if they have better contact info.”

“Robert did give me the week off from work…” I say. “Did you have honeymoon plans?”

“Actually no. I left that up in the air so that you could at least have a say in that. And personally I don’t care *where* we go as long as I’m with you.”

“Perfect,” I say, grinning. “So a road trip to Palm Springs tracking people down. Sounds like fun.”

I’m surprised that doesn’t bug me more. Going to Palm Springs to hit up an old friend isn’t what anyone else would consider a dream honeymoon. But I guess I’m finally adjusting. Gabriel kind of makes anything else impossible.

10

Relatives are eager to get an eyeful of me, asking me questions about this and that—nothing too invasive, but it still makes me uncomfortable to have to hide so much of myself from them. Gabriel is so good at avoiding lies. He doesn't tell a single one, and when someone strays into sensitive territory, he heads them off by asking a question of his own. I guess since he knows them all, he can easily ask the right questions. I even meet his Uncle Al and Aunt Lydia; Gabriel once told me he terrorized them with boyish antics while his parents went on vacation.

During picture-taking I manage to get Mike into my emodar, but all I pick up from him is stone-willed indifference. It seems as if he is *really* uncomfortable. As soon as a picture is taken, he scoots away from me and I can't tell if it's on purpose or not since I don't know if Gabriel told his family about my empathic abilities. I catch Letty at one point sidling up to where Mike's sitting and unabashedly flirting. With my excellent hearing, I'm surprised to find Mike's seemingly cold exterior dissolve instantly as he talks to Letty, clearly skilled at his own brand of charm full of warmth and everydayness. Once I see that, I can't help noticing his comfortable politeness as he talks to his relatives, clapping them on the back and laughing in conversation, delivering hugs. It confuses me and I can only take this to mean that Mike doesn't like me. Or maybe he doesn't like the idea of his brother marrying me. Maybe *that's* what they were arguing about…

I try not to let it get to me but it does. In an effort to distract my new melancholy, I excuse myself to test my blood sugar. As soon as the cool air from inside the house hits me, I realize how hot I am. There were ceiling fans and misters on the patio, but I was still sweating. My gloves stick to me now with uncomfortable clamminess. In the restroom downstairs I tug them off, sighing with the coolness on my bare skin. I lay the gloves over a vent in an attempt to dry them out while I take care of testing.

I put my rings back on and stand there for a moment, admiring them. My wedding band is simple silver, and I smile as I think about how Gabriel kissed the top of my hand when he put it on me during the ceremony. It reminded me of when I first met him at the compound. I love how he seizes every moment and has no shame in conveying his love to me in every corny way imaginable.

After I wash my hands, I dry them thoroughly so I can get my gloves back on more easily. I dab my face with the towel, wondering how much longer I'm going to be expected to remain outside. I'm dreading it now that I've tasted cooler air.

I sigh and pick up my gloves from the vent. I can tell immediately that it's going to be a chore to put them back on in their dampened state. I think maybe I can find another pair, one that's dry. They probably won't match but I really don't care. I know I have the ones I arrived in upstairs in my ready-room, and I have to go there anyway because I need an injection. I peek out of the bathroom first to be sure no one is around.

Heading for the stairs, I use both hands to hike my dress up, liberated by the sensation of actually having my hands exposed. It's so much easier to do things without gloves. I'm so focused on the stairs in front of me as I hop up them quickly as well as the delicious feeling of the silken fabric of my dress on my fingertips that I don't notice Ezra, who is just starting down.

"Oh, Wen, look out," says Ezra, stepping to the side to make way for me.

His voice takes me so utterly by surprise that I almost jump out of my skin. In the process, I lose my footing, turning my ankle to the side. Instinctively, I let go of my dress and reach for the railing. But I'm dead center of the very wide stairway and there is nothing to grab on to. I fall backward.

I think I'm falling until I realize that Ezra is gripping my arm and jerking me forward. The sensation is exquisite, tingling almost. The skin on skin contact has me momentarily distracted from the implications, and I stare at his hand on my arm, uncomprehending.

The daze does not last long, and I fling myself away from him and scream, "NO, EZRA!"

Ezra is shocked at my outburst at first but then realization hits him. Terror sets in. I continue to move away from him on hands and knees until he is entirely out of range and my back is to the stair railing.

"Ezra!" I gasp. I feel lightheaded as I descend into hyperventilation, more quickly than I ever have before. I look up at him and hug my arms around myself, struggling to slow my breaths. Thick, nauseating dread has penetrated my bones as I wait for my brother to collapse. I know I will fall apart entirely as I watch.

He's a few yards away from me, examining his hand like there might be some kind of physical manifestation of what just happened. "I think I'm okay," he says calmly after a moment. Then he notices the state I'm in and starts walking up the stairs toward me.

"No!" I gasp, pushing my back against the railing.

"Wen, I really think I'm okay. What's it supposed to feel like? I don't feel anything. Wait, I'll go get Gabe." Then he turns and runs down the stairs.

Even seeing Ezra's upright and retreating figure doesn't soothe the dread that has grabbed a hold of my lungs. In utter disbelief, I'm sure my mind is playing tricks. Ezra is really lying dead on the stairs in front of me. Maybe this is what memory repression is like.

I can't calm my breathing. No matter how hard I concentrate, I can't stop heaving and choking on the air. That's when I recognize that I'm sobbing. My dress is getting wet droplets on it, and I think fleetingly that water stains don't come out of satin. I bring my hand up to wipe the tears away but am startled to find the unexpected sensation of my own skin against my fingers. Then I remember why I'm in this state and the sobbing starts again in earnest.

"Wendy?" says a soft voice. I look up.

Gabriel. The sight of him sends my respirations into overdrive again. I look down at the floor once more and try to respire more deliberately.

"Wendy, he's alright. Are you listening? He's alright. Ezra is fine. Completely unaffected."

I look up again. "How?" I say between gasps for air.

"I don't know… maybe like Lindsey?" Gabriel replies. His expression is full of concern, but his wheels are turning. The sure movement of his controlled thoughts begins to calm me. I look into his face, which bears such familiar safety. Having watched it so often in the past, I easily remember what he looked like when he would put himself in a trance during hypno-touch. I use the memory of his even breathing to regulate my own until the heaving finally stops.

Ezra stands just beyond Gabriel with wide eyes and a pale face. I listen and hear the even thump of his heart and the air moving in and out of his lungs. Relief wins over the worry finally. He's alive and well. I shudder, loosening some of the tension in my neck and shoulders.

"Ezra," I say, looking him over from head to toe again, checking that he hasn't sustained any visible injury. "I am so sorry. That was so reckless and stupid. Why did you grab me? You should have let me fall."

"I don't know, Wen. My first thought was that those stairs were so long… You could kill yourself falling backwards down them like that. I didn't think any more than that. I just… grabbed you."

He inches a bit closer, but with a warning look from me, he stops. I'm not ready for anyone to be near me.

"Wendy," says Gabriel's low and even voice, drawing my attention back to him. "Are you alright? Are you injured in any way?"

"No, of course not," I say, annoyed. I almost killed Ezra, and he's asking how *I* am doing?

"Good. I think we can talk about this later. We should really get back downstairs though. I think most people are ready to move inside, so you should be more comfortable. Go get your gloves. We'll try to move things along," says Gabriel, standing and straightening his button-down shirt.

I stare at him for a moment, trying to get a handle on what he's saying. He acts like the whole thing was merely a passing accident that can be brushed off. But he's right about getting back to the party. I don't want people questioning why I am suddenly absent. *Yeah she's pretty shaken up. She almost killed her brother while walking up the stairs. No biggie, she's okay.* I look at Ezra again to make sure he's still standing. I move a bit closer to him to put him in my emodar, just to check. All I pick up is worry and bewilderment—none of the awful feelings I know he *would* be experiencing if he were on his way to death from my touch. Derek, though he took longer to die, was knocked unconscious. And he felt that Nothingness that was so paralyzing. I check on Ezra periodically anyway.

Just as Gabriel said, the group has moved inside when I return from my ready-room, although I barely notice the climate change. I grow more and more indignant at myself for having acted so impetuously. The heat should not have bothered me so much that I would be so careless. Where was my exceptional hearing when I needed it? I should have been paying attention to what was going on around me!

Ezra sits with Robert most of the time, and I figure he must have told him. I can eavesdrop easily, but I don't care to. Robert looks over at me on a regular basis, a look of stern concern on his face.

I can't figure out how she knows, but Maris is on to me as well. She keeps looking over at me intently from time to time, probably trying to read my expression. I also notice Mike watching as well. He hates me. I'm sure of it. The stony expression on his face can't mean anything else. I avoid his eyes, but I swear I can feel his attention on me anyway.

Through all this, Gabriel holds my hand and watches me and thinks. He grows more and more hopeful as the moments go by. I hate that he can move so rapidly to optimism after such a dangerous encounter. I'm afraid to open my mouth and say something out of gall. Gabriel is a good man. He is so good that it makes me want to be better. But his complete obliviousness as to why I'm upset only makes me more so.

I don't get why he's upbeat. So Ezra's immune… So what? Does he now think Ezra is the key to understanding my ability? Lindsey's life force didn't reveal anything. I saw Ezra's life force that day, too. Nothing was odd about it.

Gabriel's dismissal of the event shows that he isn't as concerned as I am about the need to be careful. I just proved my worst fear: I will become too comfortable, let my guard down, and kill someone.

I did all but the killing, but that was a blessed reprieve of nature. Maybe the forces of the universe felt sorry for me and gave me a freebie. I am not capable of being careful. Eventually I am going to make a mistake again. I'm only human. I shouldn't expect myself to constantly be on guard.

What am I supposed to do now?

11

"We've got to dance you know, being newly wed," Gabriel says quietly, squeezing my hand and breaking me out of my reverie.

Husband and wife. It sounds ugly now. What have I done to Gabriel? Bound him to a person like me because I'm too selfish to stay away? I should learn some restraint. I turn to Gabriel's hesitant smile and give him a tentative one, allowing him to pull me to my feet and into the middle of the spacious living room which has been cleared for dancing.

Some kind of love song emanates from the speakers, but I don't even listen long enough to hear what it is. Gabriel, who has been so hopeful, takes in my rigid posture and measured distance as we dance. His demeanor changes.

He leans forward slightly to whisper, knowing I can hear him clearly even over the music, "Aren't you supposed to be happier on your wedding day?"

I focus on breathing, trying to keep my tears at bay. It doesn't seem to be working, so I bite my lip, afraid to speak lest the torrent start.

Gabriel notes my expression with such deep concern. It plugs up the holes in the leaky boat of my mind. "No te preocupes mi encantadora doncella. Me casaría contigo en un día soleado y en un uno nublado. Las cosas nunca han sido fáciles para ti ni para mí, ¿verdad? Surely I can say something to make you smile…?" He thinks for several beats. "My mother told me just before the ceremony, 'I like her, Mijo. Don't do anything to drive her away or I'll make you suffer.' It made me wonder what you said to her… I guess I'll never know, considering you won't talk to me. That's unfortunate. I live to hang on your every word."

As he turns me around the floor I become aware of all the eyes on us. I paste a smile to my face.

Feeling a bit reckless, I say, "Your brother doesn't like me. What's his deal?"

Gabriel's tentativeness goes a bit rigid, but he releases it almost as quickly as he summoned it. "That's not true."

I glance at him and raise an eyebrow. "Then why does he avoid me like a plague and look at me like I stole his lunch money?"

"He's mad at me. Not you," Gabriel replies. "He just thought it would be funny to tease me about stealing you away. I didn't find it funny at all. And I told him so. I also told him to stay away from you. It put us at odds. But he'll get over it."

I restrain myself from rolling my eyes. Gabriel is deluded. I'm sure he's not lying and Mike actually *did* threaten to steal me. But I doubt that was the actual intent behind the words. Mike probably did it to goad Gabriel because he doesn't like the idea of Gabriel marrying me. I wish I'd been listening in on their fight. I bet there was a lot more to it than Gabriel is letting on.

"Your mom said you guys have always been competitive about women," I say, going along with Gabriel's claim just to see if I can get more. I don't know why, but I feel like I need to *prove* that Mike doesn't like me. Or maybe I just want to torture myself. "You're both so good-looking… I bet women had no idea what hit them with *you* fighting over them."

Gabriel sighs uncomfortably. "Yes, Mike and I have definitely had no holds barred when it comes to women. Which is why I've been overprotective of you. I have no intention of giving him *any* opportunity to charm you. Mike is… as relentless as I am."

I guess that's his story and he's sticking to it. "I doubt it," I mutter, giving up on my quest to prove that some member of Gabriel's family has it out for me. "I don't think you give yourself enough credit. Letty was *drooling* over you, as soon as you looked at her. And then you started telling her how hot she looked… I swear the only thing stopping her from asking for your number was me sitting right there. Speaking of which, what was that little Spanish conversation I was in the dark on?"

He turns slightly mischievous. "Oh, just trying to get a head-count of the men I might need to send marriage announcements to."

I roll my eyes. "Really? And how many did she say?"

"She said too many. I admit that had me a bit jealous. I don't like the idea of there having been so many hands or lips on you before me."

"Oh please," I reply. "That's a lie. Letty had a nickname for me: coquetear puta. Some of the few Spanish words I actually know."

"What? *Flirt whore?*" Gabriel says, aghast. "That's not very nice."

"Maybe not, but it was accurate."

"I doubt that. You're a beautiful and intelligent woman. Why *wouldn't* you have fawners? That does not make you a flirt whore."

"Whatever, Gabriel," I snap, enraged that no matter what I say to him, he still thinks I'm just as wonderful as ever. "I didn't have boyfriends. I had admirers. I had a reputation for pushing guys' self-control just because I could. I used my ability to read their emotions when I touched them so I could control them."

I groan inwardly, avoiding his face. I wish more than anything that I could give up this ridiculous façade and find a bathroom to fall apart in.

I've definitely taken him by surprise. He wavers on disbelief though, confused by my temper and wondering something—probably if I'm exaggerating.

Just the idea of him resisting any belief that I could ever be conniving sends me into further rage. "It was all a game to me," I say in a low voice. "I knew *exactly* what they were thinking and I would use it against them, *especially* when they were dirt-bags. But sometimes even the nicer ones got played if the mood struck me. I thought it was fun. And they always fell for it. I was a *master* at manipulating them..."

I close my eyes, self-loathing creeping in like an old friend.

"Wendy…" Gabriel says with soft tenderness.

"Eventually they either hated me or followed me around like puppy dogs," I interject, unable to stop acrimony from fueling my words. "And if they ever managed to make it to relationship status with me, it never lasted long. One lie, no matter how small, and I was out of there, on the hunt for another one. They were disposable. They would never be honest, so in my head they deserved what they got. Yeah, I was a flirt whore. And don't you try to tell me I was anything different. You weren't there. You don't know. It's more likely that you're going to find past boyfriends who hate me than anyone who still has a thing for me. They never got what they expected."

How true that statement still is—especially now. I clench my teeth. *Why did you do that, Wendy?*

I've been too ashamed of it to have told him before. I expected it to come up the other night when I told him about my pregnancy, but it didn't, to my relief. And now I'm throwing it in his face on our wedding day so he'll hate me.

Gabriel's feelings are in flux: a mixture of irritation and bewilderment. He can't decide how to react. He knows I'm deliberately pushing him away and the realization of that jolts his confidence painfully.

I hate myself.

The song ends. He comes to some decision as we stand there in the middle of the dance floor, some twenty-five pairs of eyes on us. He leans in, but not too much. "You are so lovely," he whispers. "In every way. You are such a beautiful story of perseverance. I love to watch you blossom. I am so privileged to now be able to watch you do so whenever I like. I am a lucky man."

My heart catches in my throat and lodges there uncomfortably. Why can't he be angry? For some reason, it hurts more to have him adore me. "Please," I whisper. "Just stop."

Gabriel sighs in disappointment and releases me. I think he's going to leave me to my own devices, but as soon as he moves out of the way I see his dad, Dan, standing there.

Dan holds out a hand. "I know you don't feel much like dancing. But I don't have any daughters of my own. This may be my only chance to dance with my daughter on her wedding day. May I?"

I can't refuse when he puts it that way, so I take his hand. He takes me in a slow waltz.

"I'm very pleased to have you in my family, Wendy," he says. "I can tell my son did well."

I avoid his face; I'm so high-strung that there's no telling what's going to set me off. "Thank you," I reply evenly. Then, because I don't like the silence, I say, "Obviously you guys did a lot to put this wedding together. I really appreciate it." I glance at his face to make sure he knows I'm genuinely grateful. Dan comes across as a reserved kind of guy, although there is a streamlined and deliberate current to his thoughts that makes me think he's pretty intelligent. He probably spends a great deal of time observing things. With Maris' more overt presence around, I don't doubt that this is the kind of dynamic they have.

"You are very welcome," he replies. "It made Maris's day to be able to play wedding planner. It was a pleasure to watch her revert to girlish youthfulness."

Dan thinks of Maris with affection.

"How did you meet her?" I ask, anticipating finally learning how Gabriel's parent's ended up together.

Dan smiles. "I was working as an intern at a law firm in LA. I became friends with a young man in operations named Alvaro who worked as a courier for the firm. It was an unlikely friendship at the time, but I've always had an interest in cultures. I studied anthropology as an undergrad. Hispanic American culture was entirely foreign to me, and befriending Alvaro was simply curiosity to start with. But I ended up loving how close-knit Alvaro's family was and how comfortable they were around me, a stuffy French academic who was studying to be a lawyer. They are a welcoming and loyal people."

Dan remembers it fondly. "Maris was Alvaro's cousin. She was the most down-to-earth person I'd ever met and I was almost immediately taken with her. I came to visit her family often under the guise of seeing Alvaro, but it was really to see her. And she and I would talk over a sink full of dishes after Sunday night meals. I would wash. She would dry. We talked about everything over those dishes… except I never confessed that I loved her. When I was away, I dreamed of seeing her again. But I never expected my dreams to become reality—we were from different worlds, and in those days it was somewhat… *taboo* to meld them."

"That's so sweet," I reply as I imagine the two of them standing in front of a sink, talking, Dan passing a wet plate to Maris. "What happened next?"

"When we finished the dishes one Sunday, and I gave her my usual goodbye, all of a sudden she swatted me with her dishtowel."

"No way!" I laugh, remembering how Maris swatted Gabriel.

"Oh yes. Took me *completely* by surprise—scared me actually. Then she put her hands on her hips and said, 'Dan, you are the *only* man in this casa who helps with the dishes. I don't know much about French culture, but here in America that means you'd like to take me somewhere *other* than a Sunday night dish washing. And francamente, Señor Dumas, I'd like to *go* somewhere other than this kitchen. If I have to dry one more plate with you and hear you say, *au revoir, mademoiselle* before you leave, I'm going to go loco.'"

My eyes have widened but a grin spreads over my face. "I can *so* see that."

"Yes, and she hasn't stopped swatting me or anyone else with dishtowels since."

"That's a great story," I say as Dan leads me once more around the dance floor. "Thanks for telling me."

The song winds to a close and Dan doesn't yet release my hand. He looks at me with clear concern and regard. "Wendy, I hope you know that if you need anything at all, Maris and I are here. It isn't my place to meddle, but I want you to know that you can trust my son. He knows how to love fiercely. And he loves you. It's not the kind of thing he is capable of ever letting go of. He will make it his life's work to make you as happy as he knows how. He doesn't know how to do anything less."

I bite my lip, hard. "I know," I nearly whisper as he lets go of my hand finally. He's jarred my tears loose again.

"Yes, I figured you did," Dan says. "But sometimes it's nice to have people confirm what you already know, isn't it?"

Gabriel appears next to my side then and takes my hand. "Would you like to sit down?" he asks.

I nod, but my chest is burning. I need a minute somewhere to compose myself. The sweetness of Dan's story has dissolved my momentary tantrum. But underneath is the frightening list of questions that now demand answers. I know now isn't the time, but I'm desperate to find some kind of closure to the day's events.

Gabriel leads me to a table on the outskirts of the dance floor. I stop before I sit down and close my eyes, still fighting tears. I don't think it's going to work. "Gabriel," I croak, trying to get the words out before I start crying. "I need a minute to get it together. I'll be right back."

I don't wait for his answer, but I can feel his darkening worry as I walk away from him. I can also tell he wants to follow me so I hold up a hand to stop him as I go. Gabriel's hovering is not something I need right now. I don't know what I need really. A good cry maybe?

Someone rushes up to me anyway though, and I nearly jump out of my skin trying to get away from them.

Then I see that it's Ezra.

I tense in anxiety and guilt. The memory of him reaching out to grab me surfaces and tears spring in earnest.

I almost killed my little brother. Stupid, stupid, stupid.

"Wen, wait," he says, his brow pinched in worry.

"No Ezra," I insist. "Please. Give me some space."

He doesn't follow me as I push through the French doors. Yes, there will definitely be crying. And on the other side of it…?

I don't know.

12

My blood sugar reading is 32.

I panic, and for a second I weigh either trying to go back down the stairs to the kitchen for some juice, or yelling.

Stairs are too dangerous. I might pass out halfway.

Why do I not have a bottle of juice in my bag?

Because you don't get lows.

Yell.

But I come out of the bathroom just in time to hear a knock on the door to my ready-room—which I had intended to hide out in for a good cry, but got side-tracked.

"Come in!" I gasp, expecting Gabriel and grateful he decided to come after me.

It's not him, though. It's Maris.

"Juice, Maris!" I say, sitting on the edge of the bed to retain my strength. "I'm diabetic and I'm low!"

Without a word, Maris spins on her heel and dashes out the door.

While I wait, I lay my head on the bed and work to keep my eyes open. It's like the mere thought of being so low has manifested the symptoms that have been fairly mild until now. I only decided to test because I couldn't understand why what were supposed to be tears of sadness morphed into tears of rage. And then my head started getting fuzzy...

"Mija!" Maris' voice rouses my eyelids back open and I spot the tall glass of juice in her hand.

I reach out but she sets it on the end-table quickly. Confused that she's making me get up for the juice, I sit up anyway. I don't have time to argue. I scoot over to the table, swiping the glass and nearly spilling the contents as I bring it to my mouth. I suck it down with iron will because I'm starting to feel nauseated and I pray I can keep it down.

Four gulps and the glass is empty. I collapse back on the pillow.

"Mija? Are you okay?" Maris asks.

"A minute," I manage to say, putting my arm over my forehead and finding that it's clammy. And that's when I remember that I'm ungloved. And that's why Maris didn't hand me the glass…

Really? I almost kill my brother. And then I almost kill Maris in the same day.

More rage.

I've got to stop trying to think through the irrationality of a diabetic low. So instead I count my breaths and listen to my own heart beat as it slows little by little.

Ten minutes in, the fog clears and I open my eyes.

Maris is nearby, staring at me and wringing her hands.

"I'm fine," I say to reassure her. "I don't know how that happened. I don't usually have sudden drops like that…"

And I really don't. I can only remember once in the last year. I've had a couple highs, but those aren't nearly so scary, and they never went into truly dangerous ranges. I think back, recalling that I took an injection only an hour or so ago right after the incident with Ezra… Did I overdose?

I don't think so. I remember shaking so badly from my anxiety attack that I checked the syringe at least twice to make sure.

No use agonizing over it. Diabetics have unexpected swings a lot. It was probably because of my pendulum of emotion. Although it's unusual for me, it does happen. I need to learn to keep juice nearby so I am better prepared.

I say that every time. But I never do it. But this time I need to. I nearly killed Maris by taking a glass of juice from her. I can't afford unconsciousness given my death-touch. I need to be a more organized person. Prepared.

"Could you bring me my test kit from the bathroom?" I ask Maris calmly in order to demonstrate to her that I'm okay.

She goes and gets it and lays it on the bed next to me. She also brings my gloves.

I test and find my glucose on the upswing. I sigh in relief and say to Maris' wide-eyed expression and anxious thoughts, "I'm fine. Really."

She looks me over and I guess I look well enough to her that she agrees. "Gracias a Dios," she says, crossing herself.

I heave in a breath. With *that* temporary crisis out of the way, the crisis that brought me into this room begins to surface. If only my death-touch were as easy to manage as an injection. "Sorry, Maris," I say, looking up at the ceiling as I put my gloves back on. "I kind of ruined everything."

She looks at me with softness and then sits on the other corner of the bed. "No you didn't. No tienes que fingir conmigo. It was an accident. You have a right to be upset."

"I don't *want* to be upset," I reply. "I want to be able to think straight. But… I'm afraid to."

She tilts her head at me. "Everything is worse in the moment, mi querida hija. I think you should stop expecting yourself to be immune to your own feelings. Allow yourself to experience them and endure them until they pass."

It would be nice if my glucose episode would have driven out the uncertainty of the day, but it seems to have exacerbated it instead. "I don't think I can go back out there," I tremble. "It's too much… Everyone expects me to put a smile on my face and pretend this is the best day ever—" I let out a sob when I think of what this day was *supposed* to be. "Gabriel… I've ruined this for him." I look at Maris. "He deserves better than this." I hold up my gloved hands.

"There you go, trying to think instead of feel again," she says, scooting over to me. She puts a hand on my back. "And no. No one here expects you to pretend. And don't worry. Gabe is already wrapping things up for you. No más del partido. No más sonriente…"

"I don't speak Spanish, Maris," I sigh.

"Si, I know. But I've always thought Español had more of a comforting lull to it than Inglés. And if I speak Spanish, you won't spend your energy analyzing what I say." She tugs on my arm. "Stand up, Mija. Let's get you to bed."

"Bed?" I ask, hesitating.

"Si, si. Levantarse." She pulls me to my feet and then goes over to the vanity to get the gloves she had on earlier when she did my hair. "Dar la vuelta," she orders, turning my back toward her. She unzips my dress.

"Usted va a dormir," she says as she goes over to a drawer and opens it. She takes out a pair of sweatpants and holds them up to look at them. "Estos encajar?" she asks, looking me over. Then she nods, seemingly to herself. "Si. Usted no puede ir mal con un par de pantalones de chándal."

She rummages in the drawer again, pulls out a t-shirt, and walks back over to me. "Poner en esto," she says, putting the clothing in my hands.

"Uh…" I say.

"Baño!" she insists, pointing at the bathroom.

I turn and walk to the bathroom and stop at the door. She expects me to just *go to bed*? "What about Gabriel?" I ask. "He's going to be worried."

"Ahora necesitas cuidados maternales, no un interrogatorio. Episodios que ponen en riesgo la vida y traumas emocionales… Deja que yo me preocupe por Gabriel."

I have no idea what she said, but I don't think she's going to take no for an answer. I sigh and go into the bathroom, take off the dress, and put on the sweatpants and t-shirt. It *does* feel good to be out of the dress.

I check my blood sugar again, satisfied that it's back in normal range. I *am* tired. It's dark outside, probably only nine or so, but late enough for bed. Just when I start to lament that I'm not even giving Gabriel my *presence* on our wedding night, I come out of the bathroom and see that Maris has turned the sheets down. It looks *awfully* inviting.

"Acuéstese," Maris insists, patting the pillow.

The bed wins.

I sit on the edge and draw my feet under the cool sheets, unable to resist sighing, though I do feel foolish with Maris hovering over me. Maris, on the other hand, is stern and decided, like a mother would be putting an unruly child to bed.

"Dormir. Y cuando se despierta," she says in a sing-song voice, tugging the blankets gently up, "su mente estará más clara. Dios obra en nosotros mientras dormimos."

She rubs my back through the blankets, speaking Spanish softly, while I try to get over being put to bed by Gabriel's mother on my wedding night.

"Deja de pensar," she says over and over.

I close my eyes then, because I think that's what she expects.

"Querido Dios Eterno," she says slowly, and with purpose. "Bendiga a este niño con un sueño reparador. Cura sus heridas y sus miedos. Envuelva ella en los brazos seguros de su amor y dé su paz. Amen."

Maris' emotions, as she speaks those words, are rife with sincerity and pleading. While her other Spanish was soothing, I can tell she *means* these words. I think she just prayed over me again. I don't have any convictions about God, and I don't think I've ever said a prayer in my life, but the idea that Maris has pled for me so genuinely stills my troubled soul, and I have nothing but love for this woman who has taken me so fully as her own daughter.

As I marvel over gaining such a wonderful family, my thoughts become heavy, fading into slumber.

***

The light from the windows is bright enough to tell me that it's past early morning. I sit up in bed and look around to find myself alone. I stretch out my hearing and pick up on a conversation happening below:

"She's not a child, Mamá," Gabriel says. "She's a capable woman. I need to know she's alright."

"Gabe," Maris chides, "I just told you she's alright. What you *really* want is to hound her about the incident yesterday without giving her time to process it."

"I don't want to *hound* her. I want to see if there's something I can do to *help* her process it. What is so wrong with that?"

"She does not need your help processing it!" Maris snaps. "She just needs time!" A chair scrapes the floor abruptly. "Dan! Talk to your son! He always thinks he knows *everything*!"

Someone sighs.

"Gabe," says Dan in his accented and fluid cadence, "please take your mother's advice. You and Mike go out together, come back at noon, and Wendy will have had some time to herself and be ready to talk to you."

"Dad… I married her because I want to be a part of her life," Gabriel says. "Not turn her over to my parents when things get rough. This is ridiculous. I'm her *husband.*"

"Yes, and an inexperienced one. You've started your married life off with a traumatizing event," Dan says. "I am positive that the way you see the event and the way she sees it are very different. If you try to talk to her in the way I know you will, you're going to drive a wedge from the get-go. Your job, as her husband, is not to fix things, but to give her what she asks of you. Let her be sure about where she stands and how she wants to move forward and *then* you can ask her what you can do to help her accomplish that."

"Gabe, are you going to listen to your know-it-all brain that drives everyone crazy—especially women—or are you going to listen to thirty years of marriage experience?" a more youthful male voice says. I think it belongs to Mike.

Gabriel huffs and I think he pushes his own chair back. "Fine," he says. Then more loudly, "Wendy, if you are awake and listening, I love you and I'm sorry my parents are meddling in our marriage already. I'll see you at noon."

"She can really hear that far?" Mike asks.

"Oh yes. Although she rarely employs her skill to eavesdrop. She has more class than that."

"Yes, Gabe," Mike groans in exasperation. "She's perfect. We all got the memo."

13

Maris pampers me for the rest of the morning. She brings me brunch in bed, and then runs a bath in her own bathroom where there is a massive jet tub. She puts all kinds of oils and salts in it to soothe my senses. I stay there for at least an hour, thinking.

Gabriel may be annoyed at his parents for stealing me away, but I can't say I agree with him. I *have* needed this time to come to grips with things. I'm slowly coming to solidify my belief that living together will be a mistake. I want Gabriel in my life; that hasn't changed. But he won't be safe with anything beyond what we've had in the past month since leaving the compound. I should stay at my Uncle's house where there is plenty of room to keep people from close quarters with me. Gabriel should stay in his apartment so that we don't get too comfortable around each other. To me, it is the only solution that will ensure his safety. I can't be trusted to be careful, therefore I have to avoid situations where I will be careless. Living together will make me careless.

But Gabriel will be heartbroken. Just thinking about how he'll feel wets my eyes with tears and cramps my chest. It would have been so much easier if I had put off the wedding and continued our relationship as it was. Or I should have thought long and hard about living arrangements so that I wouldn't have to be letting him down after the fact. But I got comfortable. I forgot how easily I might touch people. And this time I got lucky. I don't think I will get lucky again. This was a warning. I have to listen to it.

My movements are heavier when I finally step out of the tub and start drying off. I think, if I can be calm and rational about this, Gabriel will agree, or at least give me what I need to feel secure. I know he wants to make me happy. So if I tell him this will make me happy, he'll do it.

I work to fight away the self-deprecating thoughts that now torment me in earnest. I have to remember what Gabriel said from the start: he wants me in whatever capacity I'll allow. *This* is what I'll allow. Gabriel will *still* want me.

But it still sickens me that we will be married people living separately. It sounds like the beginning of the end…

No. That's not what it is.

I take a determined breath. Gabriel will understand. Our situation is unique and it requires unique circumstances. There is nothing wrong with that.

When I come out of the bathroom in a luxurious bathrobe that Maris gave me, she's waiting.

"Here's your dress," she says, picking up a garment bag off the bed. "I had it cleaned this morning so you could wear it again. I think, Mija… that you might want a do-over. Am I right?"

"Do-over?" I ask, wondering if she's talking about redoing the wedding. I definitely do *not* want that.

"Yes. A chance to end things differently," she explains. "Gabe… well he kind of went a little loco last night, staying up late to take down the decorations. He said he didn't want you suffering any reminders of something that was obviously painful. So we can't have a do-over there. But I have a room—my personal space—that has a beautiful view of the sky—which is what I understand the rainbow theme was supposed to represent. My room should do for that…"

"You want to… redo the ceremony?" I ask.

"No, no, no," she says. "Obviously the ceremony was happy. Una ceremonia preciosa . As was the beginning of the reception. But the dancing was not. The ending was not. Those are things that need do-overs. And this time I think you might appreciate it *your* way—just you and Gabe? Sin distracciones."

"Maris, that's… perfect," I breathe, touched that she is attuned enough to know that I feel so badly for how things ended—though I guess I *did* tell her that last night. But that she would go through the trouble of having my dress cleaned in a rush and then dreaming up a way that I could make up that time to Gabriel… It blows me away that she would be so thoughtful.

Just like Gabriel. I guess I know where he got it from.

"If you like, I can do your hair again," she says.

"No, it's fine," I say. "I'll blow-dry it. I always feel more secure when it's completely down—and Gabriel likes it that way anyway."

She nods and smiles.

I step forward to pick up the dress to take back to my room, but I stop and look at her, wishing I could hug her. "Thank you," I say to her. I turn to go but stop again. "Maris, this is the nicest thing anyone other than Gabriel has ever done for me. I'm… really glad that I get to call you my mother-in-law."

Maris smiles widely. "Mija, the pleasure is all mine. I've never had a daughter. And I don't think God could have sent me a better one."

***

Maris leads me toward a room that I didn't know was above the garage. I only *thought* she showed me every room in the house yesterday. Apparently this was the exception. She calls it her 'personal space' so I'm guessing it's a room that's all her own. I'm moved that she's sharing it with me now.

When she opens the doors, sunlight hits me and my eyes are drawn upward. The ceiling has one huge skylight that gives a relatively unobstructed view of the sky. If I were to go into the colorworld now, the room really *would* look like the inspiration for the fabric-spangled ceiling of the room where the ceremony was held yesterday.

"Wow," I breathe, looking away from the ceiling finally to see that the room is a greenhouse of sorts. At least there are plants everywhere to make it *feel* like a greenhouse. It's air-conditioned though, so I'm not uncomfortable in my dress and gloves.

"*Your* space, huh?" I ask her, seeing that there is a desk on one side and several plush chairs that look like they'd be perfect to curl up in with a book.

"Yes," Maris says. "I've always loved the sky. And with those two boys around, I needed my own space that was devoted to just me."

There is more art here than anywhere else in the house. Several paintings and sculptures decorate the room, but as my eyes roam over the different pieces, I stop short, my eyes locked on one relief sculpture that's on the wall behind Maris' desk.

I gape at it, disbelieving.

"Wh—what?" I stutter, trying to understand what's going on. Did Maris plan this? How? Did Gabriel? Why? Why would they think I would appreciate this?

I stride forward. Maybe it's not the same sculpture. But as I draw closer, I can tell that it is. It's a cloud. Painted brilliant white on top, fading into darkness underneath—as if it is about to rain. Lightning bolts smelted from aluminum spring out from beneath the cloud. Only they aren't just lightning bolts. They are shaped to resemble people. One lighting-person is bent over, appearing to carry the cloud as if it's a grievous weight. Others are crouched over beneath the cloud as if trying to hide from its terrifying blackness. Others are being expelled from the cloud's dark underbelly. On top of the cloud, resting in its plush-looking tufts, are stars that have fallen out of heaven and they rest peacefully, at ease, oblivious to the chaos below.

I clutch my dress at my sides, stunned in disbelief.

I whirl around after a few beats. "How did you get this?" I ask, struggling to keep the demand out of my voice.

Maris looks from my shocked expression to the sculpture, confusion wrinkling the corners of her eyes. "Gabe and Mike bought it for me years ago. Why?"

Gabriel walks in just then, a wide smile on his face—here for the do-over I assume. But I don't even offer him a greeting. I'm processing what Maris said.

I turn back to the relief sculpture. Maris' feelings reveal she is truly oblivious. For several moments I ask myself over and over, *Could it really be?*

It doesn't seem possible.

I need to know how this piece ended up here. I turn slowly, suspicious that this is some kind of ploy. "Gabriel, is this the sculpture you said you bought your mother from the Detritus Benefit?" I ask straining to be impassive.

"Yes," he answers, bewildered by my lack of reception after our separation. I can't summon an ounce of regret right now though.

"What made you choose it?" I ask.

"Mike and I saw it and knew immediately that Mamá had to have it."

"You just… knew it? Both of you?" I question. "Why?"

Gabriel shrugs. "Mike and I are very different, personality-wise, but occasionally we can be precisely in tune. When we are, we never ignore it. This was one of those times… Why? You remember it from the benefit?" He takes a few more steps closer to me, deeply curious.

I nod slowly, utterly flabbergasted.

"Wendy, what are you not saying?" he asks.

I shake my head, trying to rack my brain, trying to remember seeing the person that bought the sculpture—did I actually *see* Gabriel there? If I did, I definitely forgot. In fact, I remember practically nothing from that night, just a few blurry details from the beginning. The entire event is surrounded by nothing but debilitating heartbreak.

I look up finally. Maybe Gabriel can figure it out. "Gabriel, this is *my* piece. *I* made it."

His eyes widen in shock. "Really?" he whispers.

"How in the *world* did you not only end up at the same place as me three years ago but you also bought the one item that *I* made?"

"I don't know," Gabriel says, taking one more step closer. "I had no idea there were student pieces there, otherwise I would have asked you the other night about what you had on display at the benefit, to see if I remembered it..."

I shake my head. "There *weren't* other student pieces on display. Only mine. At the beginning of the workshop we were told one person would have their work selected to be sold at the exhibition. Mine was chosen."

"El Cielo!" Gabriel breathes, working through the incredible circumstance of it. And we thought it was coincidental enough with us being in the same place at the same time, years before we would ever meet at the compound... This is... inconceivable.

"*You* made my Weighty Cloud, Mija?" Maris asks.

I turn to her. *Weighty Cloud?* "I did," I reply. "And I had *no* idea Gabriel bought it that night. I didn't know him, obviously."

Maris looks at me in thoughtful awe. "Such beautiful work... and from my future daughter's hands." Her eyes brim with tears. She looks heavenward, crosses herself, puts her hands together, murmurs a prayer in Spanish.

I turn back to the cloud. To me it is *anything* but beautiful. I know I went into that night wishing I could give the stupid thing away. Or put it in the trash. Either would have worked for me. But my instructor wasn't having it. She *loved* it. And the more she and her colleagues praised it, the more I hated it. As an artist you come to realize that the best art comes with the ugly moments of your life. So the more screwed up you are, the more *brilliant* your work is.

This cloud was inspired by the worst of me. I paid for that acclaim with my daughter's life. Disgusting.

But here it is. Somehow it found its way back to me... To torture me? That's what it feels like. But Gabriel is essentially the one who brought it back to me. So what does that mean?

I shake my head in aggravation and turn back to Gabriel and Maris—only Maris is nowhere to be found.

Gabriel hasn't moved from his spot. He keeps looking from the cloud to my face, stunned.

"What does this mean?" I ask.

His attention locks on me. "Mean?" he asks. "Are you asking… if it's some kind of sign? That's not really my area. I'm still bewildered by the fact that we were both there that night… I cannot *imagine* how on earth I managed to be so immediately drawn to your piece alone. It was like… gravity, Love. That is the one moment I remember clearly from the whole night. I saw it and had to buy it. In fact, Mike and I had to bid higher than the sales price just to get it. We weren't the only ones that wanted it. It's a stunning piece."

"This is… the biggest coincidence known to man," I say.

"I told you I don't ascribe to coincidence," he says softly. "And I wasn't joking when I told you I believed the forces of nature were trying to bring us together that night. That idea, in itself, is entirely new to me. I only… think I must have sensed your presence through your work? Honestly, Wendy, I don't have a logical answer. I—"

He looks up for a few moments. His warmth of gratitude has me drawing my arms around myself. His eyes are glassy with tears.

His gaze moves back to me again. "I only know it makes me want you more."

Gabriel steps forward carefully, testing. It occurs to me that he's afraid to come near me after last night. When he reaches my emodar range, his anxious questioning confirms it. He stops a few feet away, not reaching for my hand as I expected. He waits.

He's waiting for me to move toward *him.* To accept him.

"Why did your mother call it her 'Weighty Cloud'?" I ask.

"She said it represented the burden of love. I really don't know anything beyond that. I was just pleased that she loved it so much. The obscure metaphors of modern art are not my forte."

Gabriel considers it for a few moments though. "We normally think of clouds as weightless because their structure generates lift—that's why they float above the earth… But their mass actually causes them to weigh… billions of pounds. They are quite heavy in actuality… Interesting. They are indeed *weighty.*" He looks at me.

I turn back to the cloud. I never knew that about clouds. But it sure seems like some subconscious part of me knew that when I made the piece…

I have a moment then that I haven't had in a long time—that flash of light through my soul where I realize something I made is more than I intended it to be… that instead of me dictating the piece, the piece dictates *me.* And what it dictates is even *more* true. My instructors were right. It *is* a brilliant piece.

Brilliant as it may be, I still hate it. It still represents a time that cannot ever be made up for. I once sat on a cloud, selfish, oblivious to the reality I was creating. But I fell through finally, lost in the haze. But I didn't know which way was up. Finally the gravity of the struggle to find the light again pulled me down. Down into hell.

Maybe… this is supposed to tell me I can find the topside again. That my past is not a reason to deny myself happiness now. And I *am* with Gabriel. And whatever or whoever made sure this sculpture made it back to me is trying to… to keep us together?

I don't know… Maybe it's just the presence of the piece in general that is supposed to point me somewhere. Before, when I made the sculpture, the completion of it and the praise it got pointed me away from art. The problem was what I did after that, not necessarily the direction. I found Ezra after all. And that was the best decision I ever made. And now maybe it's pointing me away from where I intended to go, which was away from Gabriel—to keep him safe. When I gave my daughter up, it was because I was afraid that I couldn't take care of her. I wanted to keep her safe… from me. That was a mistake. Am I about to make the same mistake again?

I turn around.

"When I gave up art after my daughter died, I self-destructed," I say to Gabriel, unable to look at his face, but instead opting to look at the sky through the glass above. "I became an addict. Some people do drugs. I did emotions. In a crowd, I didn't have to touch people to know their vibe. It put me in a haze. So I went out *all* the time. Even better was when I found someone to touch *while* I did it. It was a way to escape myself entirely. *And* a way to find control."

I heave in a breath, crossing my arms as if to protect against the memory. "What I told you yesterday about being a flirt whore… it was all true. But it was a result of guilt that I couldn't handle."

I force my eyes to Gabriel now. "If you die because of my carelessness, I *know* what it will feel like. I… had planned to move back in with my Uncle… I'm terrified of getting comfortable in a space with you."

I hold his eyes with mine but his trepidation at my words lumbers through my body and I feel physically heavy. I push past it and continue, "But I see this thing that I did during the most harrowed time of my life, *right after* I made that decision and I… think it's trying to tell me not to make a decision out of fear again."

I bite my lip, thinking, trying to see how this new decision sits with me. At least it doesn't feel *wrong.* "I can't deny the stupidly unbelievable happenstance of it popping out of nowhere like this, in my *husband's parent's* house no less." I smile at him. It feels good to call him my husband. Thrilling even, especially now that the air rests a bit lighter on me. I look into his eyes again. "That piece represents the most awful time of my life. But to know my husband wanted even the worst part of me before he ever knew me…" Tears spring to my eyes. "I love you, Gabriel." I close the space between us and lay my head carefully on his shoulder which I realize for the first time is back in a tux.

He puts his arms around me in relief. He has gloves on and he brushes the hair from my face and wipes my tears.

"*This* is how we should have done it," he says. "I'm sorry I didn't listen to you more. I should have known you wouldn't appreciate fanfare… Especially with how things are."

"Gabriel, this marriage is not only about me," I say. "You do everything you do with earnestness. It's your style. It wouldn't have been right for you to temper yourself just to give me what I wanted. The mistake was mine. I'm just glad it didn't end badly."

"Me too," he says. And then he laughs. "I actually *did* temper myself. If it had been entirely my choice, there would have been a live band and every person I've ever met or known in attendance. Forgive that kind of chauvinistic side of me, but I want desperately to show you off as my wife to everyone who will listen."

I smile and roll my eyes. "Well it sounds like you did it just right then." I pull away from his shoulder. "It *was* perfect, Gabriel. Everything you did… It was the wedding I never knew I wanted."

His eyes gleam. "One thing will make it perfect for *me.* Let's have a redo of our first dance—one where you *haven't* just faced the possible death of your brother." He holds out a leading hand.

"Your mother is a genius," I say, putting my other hand on his shoulder.

"I can't believe she was actually right this time..." he marvels as he leads me over to the desk and picks up a remote. Music starts but I don't pay attention to the song. I look at Gabriel as he takes up my hand again and starts to lead me around the room.

"Gabriel, your mother is right about a *lot* of things. You should really listen to her more often."

He looks at me questioningly but doesn't speak. Instead he opts to watch me with that expression of oozing adoration that he always has when we lock eyes. With every step around the room, the air energizes and the future brightens.

I pull myself into the colorworld then because moments like this always have me wanting more of a connection with him. His purple cocoon of a life force swirls before me and I breathe him in, remembering all the reasons I want him as his essence overtakes my instincts. The love I have for him pours out of me and I press against his chest again, striving to be closer. He holds me against him, his heart completely open to me as it always is. He exhales in contentment.

I catch a glimpse of the sky in the colorworld as I peek up from his shoulder. The hues of it undulate like an aurora, blending, meshing, transforming as they mix and as we rock back and forth. I wonder then, what does a cloud look like in the colorworld? I've never seen one because California skies are almost constantly cloudless. And when they *do* show up, they swoop in overnight and darken the sky for days, sometimes weeks. What would the sky look like then?

I feel an unexpected dose of dread. Imagining anything in the colorworld being obscured, *especially* the sky...? I don't think I want to see that.

14

Because we plan on making a trip to Palm Springs to check in on Kevin Fowler on Monday, we decide to head back to Monterey for the night. We spend our do-over day driving and then enjoying an intimate dinner together at an extremely uppity restaurant that Robert paid for as a wedding gift.

Gabriel doesn't shortchange me on flirtation over our meal, offering me sultry emotions and telling me how stunning I look in my dress—I've kept my wedding gown on, and now that I'm nearing ten hours of wearing it, I'm looking forward to something more comfortable. Gabriel also tells me all about the planning process leading up to our wedding. I can tell from the way he talks and feels that he had been looking forward to his own wedding for quite some time. I could swear he's been thinking about it since adolescence—another interesting fact about him I never would have guessed.

As he talks though, I lament more and more how things played out. I respond eagerly to his flirtation, wanting so much to erase the memory of the cold shoulder and rejection I showed him only twenty-four hours ago. Even with the do-over, I really did ruin what might have been an intimate wedding night—probably one he had been anticipating. I spent it with his *mother* for goodness sake. There is so much I *can't* give Gabriel; the least I could have done was sucked it up and put aside my questions until later.

Who am I kidding? I tried that. It wasn't working. Admitting it still doesn't diminish the guilt though. I fool with the idea of seducing him in a more overt way than I have before. I want to make it up to him. I need to… give him something.

When we reach Gabriel's apartment, he stops after he unlocks the door and looks at me. "You've been a little distant, Love. Is there something on your mind?"

I almost roll my eyes. How on earth did he catch that I've been mulling something over?

"Oh nothing," I reply "Aren't you going to carry me over the threshold?"

His eyes widen in surprise. "Really?"

I look down at my dress and then up at him. "Well I'm pretty well covered. I think we can handle keeping you safe while I'm in your arms for a few feet."

"I'm certainly not going to argue with that," he says. He reaches into the back pocket of his slacks and puts on his gloves and then sweeps me up into his arms carefully. I can tell he is definitely pleased, giddy even at being able to satisfy one of the long-standing traditions of marriage. It puts a smile on my face.

Once inside, he sets me down carefully. "Welcome to your new home, Mrs. Dumas."

I look around the apartment, trying to adjust to the reality that it's now *mine* as much as Gabriel's.

"Surreal, isn't it?" he says, watching my speculative expression.

"Totally."

He reaches for my hand and kisses my palm before turning on a light and going into the kitchen. I go to the bathroom to test.

"Can I get you something to drink?" he asks when I return to the living room.

"No, thanks," I reply as I plop down on the couch. Gabriel turns the stereo on but turns the volume down low and then reaches for a glass. The bodice of my dress digs into me, reminding me again that a pair of flannel pajamas sound heavenly right now. Gabriel has brought our bags up and I almost get up to grab mine to change when I remember that I'm going to need help getting out of the dress.

I still haven't quite decided what kind of intimacy to safely offer Gabriel, but this seems like a good start. "Um, do you think you could help me out of this thing?" I ask, tugging at the back of the dress.

Gabriel turns to face me with surprise from across the room, holding a glass of ice water. "You want me to help you take your dress off?"

"I can't reach the zipper," I reply. "How else am I going to get it off?"

I enjoy the look on his face: confusion and a bit of anticipation battling with each other.

"Okay," he says with guarded enthusiasm. He doesn't know what to make of my request: whether I'm trying to seduce him or whether I simply need him for utilitarian purposes. I know he hopes for the former, but his face looks like he's worried of being accused of voyeurism. I think Gabriel genuinely hasn't expected any kind of seduction tonight—probably he was planning on interrogating me about what I've been thinking about. I like taking him by surprise; it solidifies my confidence.

He doesn't move toward me though, still working through what to make of it.

"Stop overthinking it," I say innocently. "I just want to be more comfortable."

I stand up and turn my back to him, waiting.

He hesitates only briefly before I hear his footsteps approach and his breathing accelerate. I hold very still.

Gabriel sweeps my hair, which hangs to the middle of my back, up over my shoulder. His hands move carefully, finding where the zipper starts almost at my neck. He tugs it downward slowly to avoid catching any of my hair. I shiver with anticipation. Gabriel is beside himself; his pulse erratic. His breaths deepen against my neck.

His strong and sudden physical reaction catches me off guard. I stand still, taking even breaths of my own, relishing our intertwined desire. A light touch strokes down my back where my skin is exposed. I jump briefly until I remember that he has gloves on. His hand comes to rest for a moment on the strap of my bra. I catch my breath as I remember I put on the ensemble he bought for me for the do-over. I didn't expect he was going to see it though. I thought I would be delivering sad news to him about deciding to live with my uncle and I just… wanted part of him with me as a reminder that I was still his.

"I guess you liked it," he says.

"I guess you must have been snooping in my underwear drawer to have gotten the right size," I joke, hoping my words can break through the heavy air between us.

I don't think it works. He strokes his finger up and down my exposed back, and I shiver with the contact. I'm deathly still, fright stalking in the background of my waning presence of mind. Passion is doing a good job keeping it at bay. But it's still hard to even breathe when it might cause me to come in contact with him.

His single-mindedness becomes overpowering though, pressing my fear away with insistency. He reaches around to my middle and pulls me toward him. I worry that he will lose control, but as I test his emotions I can tell he's measuring his actions with agonized focus. He's just pushing himself, probably to see how much he can take.

Delicately, he slips one of the sleeves of my dress over to expose my shoulder. He breathes heavily against my exposed back as he runs his hand slowly over my shoulder and down my arm. I close my eyes, the warm gust of his breath trailing goosebumps along my skin. I angle my head away, trying not to make a wrong move but not really able to think of anything but the taste of his scent and the sensation of his fingers spread wide as he grips my abdomen evocatively. The combination of fear and need creates an electric atmosphere only accentuated by the already-present magnetism between us.

Something about the danger makes every movement more erotic than any touch I've ever had. Just *knowing* there is more of him I can't have escalates that need to a level I don't think I've felt before. I would have expected it to be unbearable, begging me to fulfill it. But instead it becomes a static state of mind—a solid place that allows me to simply *experience* it rather than want for more. There is no more fear. There is simply this moment that I want to last for as long as possible. It's so compelling that my skin becomes hypersensitive, picking up even the slightest gust of his breath. The sensation of his gloved hand moving over my bare shoulder… I've never felt anything so intimate.

"Wendy," Gabriel groans, "Oh I want my hands on you… But I also want *this* moment to stay… How can I want two opposite things so badly at the exact same time? Tell me you'd give yourself to me if you could..."

My eyes have fallen shut and it takes great effort to think of what to reply. His physical need has taken over my body. Heat and chills, fulfillment and deprivation. I both love it and hate it. "I would," I whisper finally, leaning further into him because saying the words has me feeling a new level of vulnerability.

His hand moves back up and over my shoulder again. "Oh your skin… It's so beautiful…" He grips me tighter. "Wendy, Wendy. My Wendy," he sighs.

His all-consuming hunger has drawn me into its depths. The poignancy of the moment has taken over my ability to control my limbs—although I don't know if I would move even if I could. The anticipation has me waiting, *expecting* something to happen. I search it out, trying to figure out where it's coming from so I can experience it more fully—as if it's simply hiding under a mental blanket. I'm on the edge of an encore of some kind—I'm not sure what exactly.

Gabriel doesn't vary from his stance either, nor does he make an effort to quiet his delirium. With his arm still around my middle, his other hand strokes my back, moving under my dress. With the slip of his hand, my other shoulder is exposed, too. He caresses the length of my arm and then back up to my neck with slow, lingering movements that reach the roots of my hair and then back down to my shoulder and across my arm again. He takes measured breaths along the way, and I find my own breaths mirroring his exactly, intoxicated with the intimacy of our emotions sharing such a similar wavelength. But still I am starved for more.

The movement of his hands becomes more insistent then as they find my stomach beneath my dress. I melt into him, willing myself to stay upright. It's not so much his caresses that have me inebriated, but the air. I've never tasted it so well. I swear I can taste *him* in it.

The space between us—which isn't much now—has become so hot that it's starting to melt into a liquid. When it dissolves completely, I gasp. I no longer perceive the space that separates us. But nor do I feel his skin. The air has transformed into… an extension of our flesh. It binds us. And my skin has moved into some kind of hyper-alert state, like I can feel him with some sensation outside of touch: an acute awareness that reminds me of experiencing him in the colorworld, only I'm pretty sure I'm not there right now.

Some part of me has found some part of him. When I experienced Gabriel in the colorworld, it was one-sided. But this is a genuine moment of mutual connection. Every molecule of his breath as it gusts across my skin feels tactile. The movement of his body, even though it does not touch mine, feels as if it binds us.

The moment rises and falls, creating so many otherworldly sensations that are beyond my limited senses. I don't *feel* the connection as I would if it were our skin to connect us. I *know* the connection beyond the contact.

My body feels ill-equipped to withstand this kind of awareness. Energy has drained from my limbs. I think Gabriel might be holding me upright.

He inhales as if drawing me into him further, a surge of satisfaction flowing over and through him despite the ever-present need for more contact.

After a couple of minutes in the midst of the waves passing between us, we're both exhausted. And I can tell that we both feel intimately exposed. He takes several more deliberate breaths. He's calming himself. Finally, he releases me. His emotions retreat several feet away. I hear him fall into a chair, his pulse still in overdrive.

I sink slowly to the floor, my hands searching the fiber of the carpet to bring my senses back around and find a more familiar reality. I turn to see him sitting with his head in his hands. I can't do anything but blink and stare at him. I have *no* idea what just happened… It wasn't *exactly* like making love; it was… deep like that though. A definite connection… but more profound than I've ever felt with my body. It was *beyond* my body. My life force? I don't know. I halfway wish I'd been in the colorworld to see it. Only I'm pretty sure I wasn't seeing. In fact, I can't remember hearing, seeing, or smelling anything at all. Yet I felt bound to him. And I know he felt bound to *me.* Our emotions bonded in that same place—I don't remember being able to separate them.

He raises his head finally, a gratified smile slowly curving over his relaxed face. "I don't know what other people do to enhance the moment, but anticipation is its own form of love making, I'm sure of it. I feel as if I've run a marathon."

I definitely can't disagree with that. In fact, I'm entirely at ease because of what we just shared. So I stand up and step out of my dress completely. I deliberately remove the lingerie, laying it along with the dress on the couch and head to the bedroom to put some clothes on. Gabriel's jaw drops, and I giggle on my way down the hall.

15

Once I'm in my room—the spare bedroom Gabriel and I discussed would be mine—and my thoughts are free of Gabriel's consuming presence, my brain cranks back up. I sit on the edge of the bed and try to recall the sensation of connecting with Gabriel through the air. The taste of the moments we shared are still on my tongue. The experience was… complete.

Well, maybe not complete physically. My body, now that I'm really paying attention to it, feels jittery, like it has unused sexual energy. Now that it has my attention it is telling me that experience did not satisfy. I only just now notice this hunger for physical connection, but for whatever reason, it's easier to ignore. Like being offered a slice of decadent chocolate cake on a full stomach rather than an empty one. On an empty stomach, it's nearly impossible to turn it down. On a full stomach, hunger is satisfied enough that the thought of resisting chocolate cake doesn't seem like as much deprivation.

Right now, I am full.

Tears of happiness fall from my eyes and I smile with gratitude that I was able to share that with Gabriel. I replay the moments in my head, trying to pinpoint the hows, trying to dissect it to figure what exactly triggered it and if it can be duplicated.

But as I move through the details, one frightening realization surfaces: there was no fear.

I backtrack again, frantically almost, trying to figure out how it was that things didn't go further. Why did I stand so still? What kept me from giving in to my body's cravings? To *Gabriel's* cravings that were so overpowering? Except for the very beginning, before things had gone very far, not once did I stop to wonder or ponder or worry that the situation might be getting out of hand… *Not once.*

I grip the edge of the bed on either side of me. There was no restraint. Not an ounce. That I cannot pinpoint any moment in which I consciously held back is terrifying. I literally *forgot* during the most dangerous encounter we have ever had that my skin is lethal. And Gabriel… There wasn't a speck of worry from him at *any* point.

I run through the encounter again, this time remembering how desperately I wanted him. Imagining him putting his lips on my neck as I so desperately wished he would. How close we were to that actually happening… If *either* of us had given in neither of us would have resisted. And Gabriel would be lying dead on the floor right now.

Lifeless.

Empty eyes.

Gone forever.

I suck in a staggered breath. I was right—Gabriel doesn't take the danger seriously. He never has. Even after I almost killed my brother. Gabriel likes to push and push at boundaries because he wants to see how far he can go. That's who he *is.* He's going to push himself too far one day though. And it's clear now that I can be pushed to the point of letting him. How will we endure any kind of proximity if neither of us is thinking of caution?

Stupid, Wendy. I was the one who instigated it even though I knew where it would lead. My gosh, it's like I forgot how riled up he got by the pool. It's like I forgot how completely easily men can be ruled by sexual urges. I, of all people, have a *very* clear knowledge of this fact. You wind them up and they *will* to go somewhere.

Another near-miss. Another miraculous save. *Someone* is trying to get my attention and if I don't take a hint soon, this is going to end horrifically.

It's going to have to stop. I am *lethal.* My skin *kills* people. It is my reality. I have to stop flirting with the danger like this. To bring the message home I draw up the memory of killing Dina. It's not something I *ever* do, but I have to do it now. I need to *remember* so that my weakness for Gabriel won't win out over my need to protect him.

I grit my teeth through the images. I remember the walls collapsing. The darkness. The lack of sensation that allowed Nothing to take over and eradicate me. I conjure every moment I can and when that isn't enough, I draw up the details of the dreams that followed as Louise experimented with my lethal skin. I imagine Gabriel on the other side of an invisible wall, flailing and fighting against Nothing. I mirror the terror I know he would experience. I imagine his silent screams, his unseeing eyes as he is slowly… *erased.* I brand the image in my mind so I don't forget why I *must* protect him.

When I'm done, I open my eyes that have sprung tears. I look down to see I have wrapped my arms around myself. I'm trembling for a different reason now: terror.

Satisfied, I go over what to say, eventually deciding that straightforward is best. He says he wants me to talk to him when I reach my boundaries, and I'm positive I've found them. He can't deny that what we just did was perilous. He'll understand the necessity of backing off.

When I return to the living room fully-clad, Gabriel is in the dimly-lit kitchen, standing over the counter, wearing a white undershirt. His hair is wet and water droplets glisten on his face. His eyes have a gleam I haven't seen there before.

I pick up his glass that he left on the end-table to refill it, but Gabriel raises a hand. "You stay right there, you wanton temptress. I can't guarantee my safety if you approach me."

I plop down on the couch—I guess I should wait for him to calm down before diving in. I consider again how to broach this. I don't want to soil the memory of the experience but I don't want there to be miscommunication of my expectations…

"Cripes, woman. Where did you learn such enticing devilry?" asks Gabriel, still standing behind the counter.

"I didn't realize taking my clothes off would be considered a skill that needed learning," I reply.

"Taking them off the way *you* did does," he says, slowly edging his way around the counter, eyes on me as if trying to make sure I'm not going to jump on him or something. "Please tell me that your exploits as a 'coquetear puta' did not involve such displays. I don't think my insecurities can handle that level of jealousy."

I snort. "No way. I was a *flirt* whore. Not a whore whore. Besides, I think the fact that you had already partially removed my clothes might have clouded your perception. I wasn't trying to be seductive about it. I was only trying to get *out* of the suffocating thing," I say, smiling sweetly, but knowing I'm flirting to stall further.

"*Sure* you weren't," he says, rolling his eyes as he throws himself sideways across the easy chair. "Well you looked radiant in it… as well as out of it. You're breathtaking no matter what you wear—or don't wear."

"Thanks," I say, standing. I walk over to the sink and refill the glass. I really am thirsty after all that flaming sensuality. I rummage in the fridge even though I'm not hungry. I need to think, and the crisp air hitting my face revives my mental processes further. Then I pull my test kit from my purse even though I gave myself an injection earlier at the restaurant. Blood sugar normal, I have run out of things to do.

"We need to talk," I say finally. I've got to stop overthinking this and just *say* it.

My serious tone revives him from wherever his imagination has wandered to, and he looks over at me. "I agree. I knew you were stressing over something. I was trying to figure out a way to bring it up without ruining the… experience we shared." He sighs, remembering the moments in a cloud of amazement.

I nod, grateful that passion is stronger than sadness. I don't want to dwell on what I'll be taking away from Gabriel. I know it's the right thing to do. I come around to sit on a stool. "First of all, I'm really sorry I ruined our wedding day. I've been feeling really guilty about it—that's what was on my mind all night."

"You didn't ruin it, Love," he disagrees. "I really do regret that I made the event into any kind of production. I never should have invited people outside of immediate family."

I exhale heavily. "That's not my issue. And I could have behaved differently. That *was* my fault. It's not like I almost killed one of your relatives. It was my *brother,* who would have been there no matter what the size of the event was… Look, the point is I took away our wedding night. I felt bad about it and it got me wondering how things are going to move from here. And even though I decided that I would try to live with you after all, it doesn't erase *other* things that I'm not comfortable doing. I can tell we are *not* on the same page about my condition. Now that we're married, we need some ground rules about how this is going to work."

Gabriel looks at me with confusion and dismay. "What are we not on the same page about when it comes to your condition?"

His obliviousness unsettles me with apprehension. Gabriel obviously has definite assumptions about what our intimacy will involve now—especially after what just happened. And now I'm going upend those expectations. I gather courage though, remembering the abandon we both experienced. It was dangerous. It has to be stopped.

"The incident with my brother was proof that I am too careless," I say. "I'm getting too comfortable. I cannot expect to have caution when I'm comfortable…"

I close my eyes. Comfort is inevitable—*accidents* are inevitable.

This is impossible. If Gabriel would just… be afraid sometimes this wouldn't be so terrifying.

Gabriel's disappointment has deepened and he waits, knowing I'm not done. But I can tell he's got a full argument ready once I really *am* done.

I can't do anything but press forward more insistently. "Just think of tonight… Neither of us was thinking of the danger of my skin. And you *never* think of caution. So that means I have to. What happened between us tonight was only to make up for what I took away from you yesterday. And even *that* went too far. I'm sorry I started it. That was my fault. I can't take the risk again."

His disappointment sprouts tendrils of definite irritation that dig sharply into my chest. I try again, hoping to head it off, "We're begging for some accident to happen… If this goes on for a long time… If I can't… touch you ever, I don't want to get complacent. Complacency breeds foolishness and I won't be foolish. I can't afford to."

My words sound even more final aloud. I'm taking *everything* away from him. What will be left? The lump in my throat pushes up, and I blink back the wetness threatening my eyes. I look up at the ceiling to keep them from spilling over.

I am so tired of being such a leaky faucet.

"I'm sorry that you had to love me," I whisper, avoiding his face. "I know you expected more from intimacy than I'm willing to give. This isn't what you agreed to and I won't hold you to it. Whatever you want to do about… us, I'll get along."

Not knowing what else I can say, I close my mouth and continue to look at the ceiling, willing the tears to stop. They do as the silence continues.

Gabriel is disheartened and hurt, and it builds into outrage as he rifles through ideas. It burns from my chest up to my neck. It has transformed into full-fledged anger and my head is thick with it. I look over at him and see that his face is rigid. He doesn't look at me, but somewhere across the room, fighting to gain a hold of his upset.

Instinctively, I move to the next barstool over to escape it. But I forgot that my emodar has a far wider range for Gabriel than other people. I'd have to stand at the other end of the room to get away from his emotions. And right now he's so angry I'm afraid to do something that conspicuous.

I don't know what to make of his behavior other than to realize that I have angered him so much that it has suffocated his usually free-moving thoughts. His expression is like nothing I have ever seen on him. I thought Gabriel appreciated sincerity. I did my best to give him that. Why is he upset with my honesty?

The time I spend watching him is nearly unbearable. I consider several times fleeing to my room, but he'll follow. He doesn't balk from confrontation.

Finally, he stands up abruptly. "Let's go for a run," he says.

I furrow my brow. Is he serious? "Gabriel…" I say tentatively. "It's eleven o'clock at night."

"Do you have somewhere else to be?" he asks, avoiding my face.

He told me only a half hour ago that he felt like he'd run a marathon. And now he wants to *actually* run?

"But—" I say.

"Wendy, I need some fresh air. And I am *not* leaving you here after that. If you don't want to run, we can walk briskly. But I need to get out of here."

I don't have an argument for that, so I go back to my room to change. When I come back into the living room, Gabriel is already dressed in shorts and tennis shoes, stretching. He opens the door wordlessly when he sees me. I follow wordlessly. We cross the threshold he carried me over only an hour or so ago, this time with emotions that are completely opposite.

I have so much dread for what is going to eventually come out of Gabriel's mouth that springing into a run is *exactly* what I want to do.

We start off at a slow jog through the quiet darkness. Gabriel lives in Salinas, which is about twenty-five minutes from Monterey, but in this part of California it's pretty chilly at night, even in summer. A night run would be pleasant under normal circumstances, but to me the air is a little stifling. I can't get my brain working to analyze what I might have said to upset him so profoundly; I'm too busy imagining awful scenarios.

Gabriel seems to know the route well and for about ten minutes we jog past several blocks and around a golf course. He becomes less confused and more insistent. He *really* wants to talk and is restraining the urge to let loose whatever he's thinking about. I wish he would say it already. I want this over with.

We reach the crest of one of the rolling hills of the golf course and he slows to a walk. He works through a few ideas and then huffs in irritation and stops. "It's no use," he says, putting his hands on his hips with his back toward me "I'm going to have to start talking or I might just explode."

I take an instinctive step backward.

He turns to face me and plops on the ground, cross-legged. "I was hoping I could get my… anger under control before I said what I wanted to say."

I sit down as well even though I'd really like to run away. Thankfully my pulse is up and my lungs are burning a little from exertion, so the trepidation is easier to bear.

"First things first: for you to seduce me like that and then tell me it was… a strategy to alleviate your guilt is unacceptable," he says, glancing at me only once. "Don't ever do anything you don't mean. Don't ever be close to me unless it's *you* that wants it. I don't want to be someone you manipulate with your body. It isn't fair to either of us… to you for demeaning yourself that way, or to me by assuming that I am nothing more than a sexual animal with no need for intimacy to be mutual."

"Gabriel, that isn't— Of *course* it was mutual. I—"

"No. It wasn't," he interjects, holding up a hand. "Wendy, you believed you *owed* me something, so you decided you could make good on the debt by using your body. Don't you see what that makes you? What that makes *me*?"

I *do* see. And I struggle through the disappointment in myself to find a better way to express what I meant. But nothing I come up with in my head to rephrase what I said seems any better. I wish I could take the words back… I wish I could find a hole to hide in. "I didn't mean it that way…" I quaver as I keep my eyes on the grass in front of me. "I really didn't."

"Yes, I know," he sighs. "I'm sure your intention was to make me happy. I know I'm probably analyzing it a lot more than you did when you devised the scheme."

"It wasn't a scheme," I plead, putting my hands over my eyes that start to sprout tears in earnest. I *hate* this. I can't do *anything* right.

He sighs again. "Scheme is probably too harsh; words are often inadequate in expressing what we really mean. That's why I'm going to try my best to forget what you said because I don't want to remember what we shared that way." He takes a reassuring breath. "I'm going to let it go. I *have* to forget it.

Because what happened was *unrivaled* as far as I'm concerned. It wasn't a mistake to me… It could not have felt more sacred if we'd been actually touching. I'm still trying to understand it… How was such a profound connection possible that way?" He shakes his head in wonder. "It challenges everything I thought I understood about intimacy."

He wipes his eyes then and I see wetness there. His icy state of mind has melted finally, pooling in awe as he thinks about it. When he looks over at me though, self-doubt creeps up as he remembers how my words eviscerated a memory that was so perfect to him.

Shame strangles me. I've hurt him so badly.

"I am *so* sorry," I plead, wanting to reach out to him but not knowing if it's welcome.

"I know," he chokes, looking down. He doesn't move toward me at all so I stay where I am.

As the moments of silence stretch out between us, I berate myself over and over. *How old are you, Wendy?* Being honest doesn't mean saying the first thing that pops in your head. It means not being afraid to speak from a vulnerable place. I can't believe what I've done to Gabriel. He must hate me.

"Gabriel," I beg, unable to endure him thinking I valued those moments so little. "I… may have started it off wrong, but it transformed into far more than I thought possible. It was truly the most beautiful thing I have ever experienced. It took me completely by surprise… In those few moments, it liberated me… from *these*." I hold up my gloved hands. "It was perfect."

He manages a small smile, but there is still the tension of pain in his eyes and he works to push aside doubt. "Thank you for saying so," he says. "I told you I will let it go. I will. It will just take me a little time."

I slump where I sit, hoping he's right. I can't stand seeing that disappointment on his face and hanging so heavily in his thoughts.

"The second thing," he continues once he's evened out his aggravation again, "is that you need to stop acting like *I'm* the one who's going to leave *you*. It sounds more to me like *you* are the one who's undecided, and you're unwilling to make a call either way. You think it's ridiculous that I would want to be with someone who I can't touch. That's my problem. That's *my* decision. Don't try to tell me what I should think or how I ought to act.

"You said you made the decision to *try* and live with me. There is no *try* in this case, Wendy. There is only will or will not. Whether *you* stay is your decision and *you* have to make it whether you like it or not. I've already made mine. I married *you*, not sexual expectations you think I have. You can test my conviction in our relationship whenever you want just by being in the same room. Why do you still not believe it? I thought you told me this was what you needed before I proposed to you."

My face falls into my hands again. "I don't know," I reply.

He genuinely acknowledges my response, slightly disbelieving that I really wouldn't know why I behave the way I do. But he accepts it, and he starts on some new line of reasoning. Eventually, he arrives, almost suddenly, on something that melts his aggravation into compassion.

"Wendy, look at me," he says.

I obey, grateful that the sight of me doesn't disturb him anymore. His face is illuminated by the light from the moon and there I see tenderness wrinkle his brow and soften his mouth.

"You don't know because you don't believe what *I* see," he says slowly and deliberately. "You think you *owe* me for our wedding night because you don't think you alone are worth it." He looks away, contemplating something impatiently. Whatever conclusion he comes to bugs him. Then he looks back at me and shakes his head. "I can't give you that conviction, as much as I want to. I guess I can only show you how much I love you..." He looks away and somewhat to himself says, "Maybe if I tell you enough, you'll start to entertain that it's true." He exhales a long sigh. "It's not a conclusion that satisfies me, but it does take the sting out to understand your reasons now."

"My reasons?"

"Yes, for… earlier."

I struggle to understand what he's saying. My reasons for seducing him?

Before I can ask he says, "And now the third thing."

I look up. "There's a *third* thing?"

"Of course," he says, his brow creasing as he wonders why it wouldn't be obvious. "*Third*, this is a marriage, and we are two people. You don't make decisions by yourself that affect both of us. I respect that your body is yours, and you have the right to use it how and when you will, but you won't tell me how I will use mine. I will still push your boundaries, and you can feel free to push back. You have a right to say no. But don't set ultimatums for me. Don't try to control *me* so you can better handle your own uncertainty."

My eyes flash; I truly didn't expect his presumptions.

"*Push* my boundaries?" I ask, hoping that what he means isn't what I'm translating.

"Yes. *Push.* I won't stop trying to be close to you. I'm not willing to enable your fear."

I almost let loose on him. Almost. If I hadn't just severely wounded him, I would. I take several cleansing breaths to get my aggravation under control.

When I think I've got it, I search for the depth of sincerity and say slowly, carefully, "How do you not even consider how easily I could kill you? You aren't careful, so I have to be for both of us. That's why I have to shut that kind of intimacy down. I can't depend on you or anyone else to be cautious. Sure, tonight was... amazing. But I know you, and you will *always* push the limits. And one day it will be too far. I can't let that happen. How would I survive if I killed you?"

I've started to yank small handfuls of grass to neutralize my frustration. *Calm,* I think. I have to keep calm.

"Wendy, Love, if you stay too far in-bounds you'll miss out," Gabriel says. "Just imagine if we'd never pushed our boundaries as we did tonight, never found what we were capable of with each other. It saddens me to think of it. We'll both know the right boundaries when we meet them, but you can't make them based on fear."

I sit back and look at him, confused. "Then what *do* you base boundaries on?"

"Trust," he replies. "We've been given a unique opportunity to establish trust between us in a way that no one else has. Don't you want to explore that? That's why I'm not afraid. Fear doesn't bind. It separates. Trust is the only way to bind."

I don't follow what he's saying. "I'm not *binding* anything with fear," I reply. "I'm establishing limits. I'm sorry, Gabriel, but I cannot navigate my condition without some kind of caution. Only when I am afraid do I remember to keep my distance. That's what protects you. I don't know how *you* protect yourself, but for now I have to draw the line somewhere. Tonight I did not feel in control of my actions. So the line gets drawn."

Gabriel looks baffled. "Well that's interesting. I had no idea you operated that way... That sure gives me something to think about." Then he grins at me. My irritation with him, however, doesn't allow me to appreciate that this is the first genuine smile he's offered me since before our fight.

"As for how I navigate caution," he continues, "it's all about adapting. Deprivation makes us more aware of the thing we are deprived of. It's a natural consequence, and that in itself is what allows me to be confident and careful without being afraid. I'll always long to touch you and that longing is what will make me constantly aware and watchful… It will change the way I move and interact with you. So don't expect my advances to stop. You're upset now because of what happened with Ezra. But you'll change your mind when the shock wears off. I'm confident of that."

My face blanches. My head spins a little because of the about-face of my emotions. Where once I was sorrowful, now I'm furious that he has dismissed my concerns so readily. He gives them zero credence. In fact, I think he might be deliberately provoking me. How can he do that after how carelessly I behaved yesterday? Doesn't he get how hard it is for me to deal with something like this? It's not fair that I have to be the careful one all the time. He's clearly not going to *help* me be careful.

"Gabriel," I say tightly, "did you know that half of all car accidents happen within five miles of a person's house? Do you know why that is? Because when people are in familiar territory they let their guard down. Now we live together and I'm going to get comfortable in our space. Getting comfortable leads to carelessness and accidents. Why do you not get that?"

"Accidents happen because of a lack of proper habits," Gabriel says. "I am very much aware of the danger your skin presents. I don't think you give me any credit for being careful. It's when I'm closest to you that I am *most* careful. For the rest of the time, I think a few habits that we can both agree on would be helpful in alleviating your worries."

I bite the inside of my lip, hard. He acts like my concerns revolve around something as petty as one of us leaving the milk on the counter too often and letting it sour. Yeah, establishing habits are in order then. But nobody's going to suffer if we slip up. In this case, he will *die* if a mistake happens.

We've merely scratched the surface of intimacy. I wasn't even *undressed* when we shared that moment. We haven't established any boundaries or limits, nor have we discussed any precautions we might take to ensure his safety.

I don't get Gabriel at all right now. It makes me sad and desperate for some way to make him understand how wrong he is not to take the danger more seriously.

When I can't figure out another way to convey it, I get angry again. Which makes me defiant. I don't have to be part of his risky schemes. And he can't make me. I stand up. "I'm tired. Let's go home." Then I start jogging back the way we came.

Gabriel laughs as he catches up to me. "You should know I had another bed put in my room for you, but I can tell from your expression that you aren't ready for that. But I'll be waiting…"

I stick my tongue out at him.

"Very mature," he observes. "What's the matter?" he taunts. "You're afraid to sleep in my room? Too much man for you? I can understand that. I might not be able to sleep myself with your warm body so close."

I nearly stop right there and tell him what a jerk he's being. But I'm so tired of arguing. This has been a *long* day of ups and downs. I'm too emotionally exhausted to spar with Gabriel over something he is so set on.

"Hmmm, our first newlywed spat," he says, seemingly to himself as he jogs next to me through the empty street. "Somewhat sooner than expected, but I'd say that went rather well."

"Terrific," I reply drily. Maris was right. This *is* hard.

And we've only just started.

16

Gabriel is a tidy person. I hope I can keep my messy tendencies in check in his organized apartment.

His apartment. He said it's mine, too, but I wake up early in the morning with the distinct feeling that I don't belong here. I only slept over last night, just like I did a couple nights ago. I wonder if all marriages feel like this at first, especially the ones that aren't precluded by living together for a while. Of course, part of it's because I'm not waking up with my husband's arms around me.

I sniff. Yep, that is definitely why it's so weird.

I look around the room. A good first step will probably be to find some way to make the space distinctly mine. Sure, Gabriel told me his room is my room, but I have no intention of sleeping there. What if I sleepwalk? What if I get up at night to use the bathroom and trip over something and land on him asleep in bed? The proximity that now exists with us in the same apartment is bad enough without placing us even *closer,* and a bedroom is the place a person becomes the *most* comfortable.

I sit resignedly on the edge of my bed and ponder how this will work. How can I feel at home here but remain on edge enough to protect him from carelessness? How have I never thought of all these questions before? I bet Gabriel has, but I don't intend to ask him. He suggested we actually stay in the same room for goodness sake.

I have no idea where sure ground is in this relationship. I worry I'll never know and I'll be lost in unpredictability from now until forever. How can I be comfortable but not too comfortable? How can I keep him safe *and* satisfied at the same time?

This is daunting.

I guess I should just start somewhere… Maybe with my exceptional hearing. If I make listening habitual, I bet I can foresee potential accidents by making note of where other people are all the time.

As I listen now I can tell Gabriel is awake and moving about the kitchen. We are supposed to leave around noon for Palm Springs today. Robert is flying us out. The possibility of seeing Kaylen excites me so I hop out of bed.

I catch a whiff of what smells like peppers and onions as I get dressed in a pair of jeans and a light blue blouse. I smell *him* too, though, and my heart leaps at the possibility of seeing him first thing in the morning. But then my stomach churns in discomfort… I'm not sure what his expectations are. What are my responsibilities here?

I look around for inspiration and notice the bookshelf next to his desk. Most of the books are quite old. A lot of the covers are hard-backed canvas-bound. I even see one in cracked leather. And a lot of them look like they are in other languages.

There's one that catches my eye because of the author: Immanuel Kant. I think I remember Gabriel mentioning him once. *Kritik der reinen Vernunft* is the title. It looks like German maybe. I pull it out and thumb through it—I don't see a word of English and not one highlight or note. I end up at the elaborate title page and am amazed to find something written there:

I will always love Wendy for reasons a priori and never a posteriori.

I stare at it in open-mouthed disbelief. I have no idea what it means, but I am immediately taken back to that night Louise had us held in rooms that were side-by-side. The same night Gabriel proposed to me.

I was looking for something we could do that would help me feel more secure in our relationship. '*I'll settle for writing my name in every one of your precious books…*' I suggested when he asked me what I wanted from him. '*Then you'll read my name before you ever read a word of them.*'

I close the book and push it back into place. I pick up another one.

The Journals of Søren Kierkegaard.

On the title page:

Wendy is the welcome muse of my own subjectivity.

I continue this, taking book after book off the shelf. Each one is unmarked and in pristine condition except for the title page. On each one is my name and some short epithet dedicated to me. Gabriel has written my name on every one of his books… And not just *any* books. These are obviously books he has taken time to collect. Some first editions which I don't even want to guess at the cost of.

My cheeks are wet as I put the last book back in place, humbled and amazed that Gabriel actually carried through on doing something I was only halfway serious about. I only said it because I didn't know what I wanted. I was throwing ideas out. I would have assumed Gabriel would dismiss my requests once I made clear what I *really* wanted—which was marriage.

It's clear that these books *are* a prized possession of his and he hasn't marked up a single page of them until now. He *wrote* in them just for me. And he never told me he did it. I might never have opened one and seen…

I sink to the floor where I stand. It's so very hard to understand how I deserved someone as amazing in so many ways as Gabriel is. I can't comprehend that he's for real sometimes… And I wish I were like him. He's so good at thinking of me at every turn and he remembers everything I say—even the things I *forget* saying.

As I sit pondering how I can be a better wife to him, the bottom shelf catches my attention. It's full of CDs, not books. I have never paid attention to Gabriel's musical tastes. I only remember him listening to some kind of rock and roll on his mp3 player at the compound.

I read some titles I don't recognize and some I do: Nirvana, Prince, Michael Jackson, The Fugees, and Lenny Kravitz. I stop at one that surprises me and pull it out, a grin spreading over my face. I don't see any rap at all on the shelf with the exception of this album. I can't believe it's on the same bookshelf as fancy old philosophy books in other languages. It's almost like I've found some dirty secret of Gabriel's, but he is not ashamed of *anything*. Still, I check my glucose and then carry my post-meal insulin and the CD with me to the kitchen.

"Sir Mix-A-Lot?" I ask Gabriel's back. He's bent over the counter cutting something up.

He turns around, offering me an irresistible grin. "Hearing your voice first thing in the morning…" He sighs. "Heavenly." Then he looks at the CD in my hand. "I know it's before your time, but see, he wrote possibly the most famous rap song of all time. It's called—"

"Uh huh, yeah. I know what it's called," I interrupt.

"Really? 'Baby Got Back' came out in 1992. You weren't even born yet."

The words 'Baby Got Back' sound so funny coming out of Gabriel's mouth. He even enunciates it authentically; I can't decide if it would have been weirder to hear it in his unmistakable refined cadence or like this. But I roll my eyes. "Right, like everyone doesn't know that song. You'd have to be living under a rock to never have heard it. I'm just amazed that you actually *own* it."

He chuckles. "I love that song. I was eight when I first heard it. In fact, my brother and I even performed it for an audience."

I cross my arms and lean against the counter. "A talent show at school? I bet *that* one went over well."

Gabriel leans against the counter, a glint in his eye. "Actually, no. See my mother enrolled us in this children's poetry appreciation class through her church and—"

"You *didn't*!" I gasp.

"Well of course. At the end of the class everyone was supposed to do a poetry reading of their choice for all the parents. Mamá wanted us to do something cute like Shel Silverstein or Dr. Seuss, but we told her we wanted to do something a little more challenging. I've always had such a good sequential memory, and she was always careful to make sure she nurtured my talents, so she let us pick something out and prepare for it all on our own. Obviously she should have laid some ground rules."

"Oh my gosh. Your *poor* mother. You recited *Baby Got Back* in front of her *church congregation*?" I say incredulously.

"Recited?" he says, grinning widely. "No, we *performed* it. My brother is quite good at beat-boxing, actually."

I shake my head in amazement. "Ohhhh, Gabriel. I'm embarrassed *for* your mother and it happened twenty years ago!"

He chuckles. "She has it on video… well sort of. She has the first verse on video, but all through the rest of it she's wailing and flailing the camera around too much to really capture the full effect. She actually washed our mouths out after that. I told her they didn't place any stipulations on what work of poetry we could use.

"'That was *not* poetry, mi hijo. That was garbage that happens to rhyme,' she said. I protested, 'According to Sister Faxworth, it *is* poetry, Mamá. It has rhyme, meter, and rhythm. If that's not the case, I think they should hire a new poetry teacher since ours obviously didn't know what she was talking about.'"

I clutch my stomach to recover from a fit of giggles. Gabriel grins at me, his eyes alight with pleasure at making me laugh. "Wow, Gabriel. That's… Wow." I say breathlessly.

He turns to get a frying pan out of a cabinet, sets it on the stove, and then turns around dramatically. And then he starts rapping:

"I like big butts and I can not lie
You other brothers can't deny
That when a girl walks in with an itty bitty waist
And a round thing in your face
You get sprung, wanna pull out your tough
'Cause you notice that butt was stuffed
Deep in the jeans she's wearing
I'm hooked and I can't stop staring
Oh baby, I wanna get with you
And take your picture
My homeboys tried to warn me
But that butt you got makes me so horny
Ooh, Rump-o'-smooth-skin
You say you wanna get in my Benz?"

I roll with laughter. He doesn't just rap, he actually starts dancing to it, smacking my rear with a spatula like it's a prop in his performance. I squeal and swat him away. But he doesn't relent; now he's actually rapping *to* my butt. I laugh and back against the counter but that doesn't deter him. He goes through the whole song before saying the last line, "*Little in the middle but she got much back*!" with a flourish.

"Holy crap!" I gasp, my diaphragm actually in pain from howling so hard. I can't remember the last time I laughed so much. "You are too much, Gabriel."

He sidles up next to me and raises a sultry eyebrow. "Too much? Or not enough?"

I giggle again. "Oh baby," I breathe. "When you serenade my booty it gets me so hot. Stop, I don't think I can take it!"

Gabriel chortles and starts cracking eggs into a bowl. "Yes, well I'll take your luscious booty in my face *any* day because *that* is definitely hot."

Once I get a hold of myself, I say, "Really, I never would have guessed that about you. That song doesn't... I don't know, offend your refined nature or anything? Geez, Gabriel, you don't even curse. But that song is... well in *your* words, so *crass.*"

"I guess that's part of the appeal. It's *so* crass that it's funny," he replies. "Besides that, it *is* a fine piece of poetry. And it's a cultural icon. It made voluptuous women beautiful again. Plus, like you said, *everyone* knows that song. It's a rite of passage."

"Well it still sounds weird coming out of *your* mouth," I reply. "Although I'm amazed that you almost sounded... ghetto when you rapped it. I would have thought your… speaking habits would make it awkward."

"African American Vernacular English is its own language and *I* have a penchant for languages as you know. I always strive to speak a dialect as authentically as possible."

I chuckle. "If my brother were here he'd ask why you make up your own *English* dialect then." I smile at him. "But it's one of the things I love about you—among all the other odd things."

A knock sounds at the door then and I look at Gabriel. "Are you expecting someone?"

"Ezra and Robert," he replies and I catch the faintest bit of tightening in his thoughts. "They wanted to check on you."

I raise my eyebrows. "Check on me?" But I go over to the door and open it.

"Hey Ezra," I say when I see him standing there, and then I notice Robert behind him. "Robert, hi. What brings you guys all the way out here?"

"Gabe invited us for breakfast before you guys head out today," Ezra explains.

I glance over at Gabriel as I open the door wider and step to the side to let Ezra and Robert in. Invited them for breakfast? Why did I not know anything about this? Gabriel doesn't forget to tell me things. This smells suspicious.

Ezra comes through the door but stops in front of me. He's nervous about something, but before I can ask him about it, he reaches out and puts his arms around me, pulling me into a tight hug. Then he plants a kiss right on my forehead. He sighs, laying his cheek there.

The action is so sudden that it catches me completely off guard, and I blink for a moment before leaping away and giving Ezra a horrified look. "Ezra!" I gasp, my eyes darting over his body for signs of injury. "Are you okay?"

He stands there with his mouth twitching in amusement. He crosses his arms. "I've been wanting to do that for a while. When we rescued you from Louise, I cbouldn't even hug you in relief. Do you know how long it's been since we hugged?" Then he looks up at the ceiling and bites his lip. "I can't even remember. That's how long it's been."

He seems fine, standing there staring at me with a goofy grin while my shock wears off…

The relief doesn't last long. "Are you crazy?" I yell. "I almost kill you once, and you try to finish the job? What if it had been a fluke? What if my ability is sporadic? Geez, Ezra. Use that big giant brain of yours."

I'm about to look at Gabriel to back me up, but he's leaning against the counter with a stack of dishes in his hands, a *huge* grin on his face. One taste of his emotions and I can tell: he was *completely* in on this.

I glare at him, but he busies himself with silverware. Still, I can tell he's sheepish, which ignites me further. He knows I'm upset. I might have forgiven him if he had *any* sign of not foreseeing my reaction, but I can tell he *knew* I wouldn't like it. And then Ezra… I can't believe they would go behind my back like this… that *both* of them thought taking a risk like that was totally okay.

Ezra starts setting the table. Gabriel claps him on the back and chuckles. "Glad to see you're alright, hermano. It's a good thing someone's got some guts around here or we might never make any progress."

Fury rises up within me as I watch them. Heat floods my face. "Do I have to kill one of you before you take this seriously?" I fume. Hot tears spring to my eyes, and I stalk away, toward my room.

"Wen," Ezra calls. I can hear his footsteps behind me. I'm about to slam my door in his face but he catches it with his hand. "I'm not an idiot. I *did* use my brain. In my head, everything is mathematical: I live my life based on probabilities. Of course I considered the possibility that you might kill me. But I didn't see it happening."

"Oh, when you put it that way…" I say sarcastically, throwing my hands up. "Why the hell not?" I cross my arms. "Ezra, who *cares* what the chances are when death is involved? It was a completely unnecessary risk."

"To me, it was *totally* necessary," Ezra replies quietly as he leans against the wall in the hallway. "After Lindsey… you were so sad. You said it wouldn't be right to risk touching her—I guessed you were probably right. But I still asked myself, if I were in her place, would I do it? And the answer was yes. But I knew you never would. I wanted to give you hope, even if it made you mad for a second. Sorry. I won't touch you again if you want."

I can't argue with Ezra's face. I know how much he loves me. And this confirms it. And he knows me so well…

I sigh, wiping under my eyes to get rid of the few tears that have eked out. Ezra watches me apprehensively. "Please don't endanger yourself like that again," I say sternly, looking him in the eye. "Whatever happens or doesn't happen to me… it's not your job to fix it—let alone risk your life to fix it."

Ezra stares back at me and I can tell he wants to protest but he's keeping his mouth shut.

"I couldn't live knowing I'd killed you," I say.

"It wasn't that much of a risk," he replies earnestly.

I close my eyes for several moments, trying to pulse away irritation. But it doesn't budge.

Nobody understands…

The realization is devastating. Sadness seeps upward into my throat and burns my ears. Gabriel and now Ezra… neither of them grasp what this is like for me and they are so determined to push me into accepting this condition as if it's nothing more than a little handicap. I have no idea how to make them see things my way…

"I'll probably forgive you," I say, looking at Ezra finally, "but right now I need a minute to calm down."

I don't wait for him to answer. Instead I back into my room and close the door. I lean against a wall and sink down to the floor.

My thoughts swarm like angry bees. My face reddens and my hands ball into fists in my lap. I see red for several long moments as I replay what just happened over again. But eventually the frenzy of agitation dissipates and I reach a calmer place.

Although I still don't know how to navigate Gabriel and Ezra's persistent disregard for their own safety and I hate rewarding Ezra's stupidity, it would be ridiculous for me to not use this to my advantage just out of principle. I can't deny Ezra is immune, and as far as he is concerned, my ability is not sporadic. There was some kind of sensation I felt when he touched me besides simply the skin contact. It may give me some clues if I explore it more.

I push my palms firmly against the floor for a moment and then stand up. I find Ezra sitting outside my door. He clambers to his feet when he sees me, and without a word, I remove one of my gloves. I walk up to him before thinking can start burrowing a hole of doubt in my resolve. I reach up and put my hand on his cheek, taking him by surprise a little. I watch him carefully for any sign of… awfulness. But he stands there looking at me expectantly now. He really is okay.

I hold my breath as I explore the sensation of his cheek in my bare palm. It's warm and soft. I never paid much attention to skin before my transformation. When I touched people it was always about reading their emotions. But at this moment, his skin is *all* I focus on: it's temperature, it's texture. And something flows between us… Has skin contact always been like this? I never noticed…

"Do you feel that?" I whisper.

"What?"

"That… that hum, like static, or a current? I don't know. It's beautiful. You really can't feel it?" I ask, closing my eyes.

"I feel your hand on my face, that's all," Ezra replies dubiously.

"Shhh," I whisper. I want to focus. I cut off all the sounds around me: it's easy, like turning off a radio. There is nothing but Ezra's skin on mine and the flow between us, whatever it is, and the warm living sensation of his cheek.

It's a current, I decide. Sometimes it seems like I'm feeding it to him, sometimes it's the other way around—a back and forth movement.

I open my eyes and stroke Ezra's cheek. Then I reach for his hand instead. I look at it like it will reveal new secrets. I laugh.

"What?" Ezra asks.

"I must look nuts, staring at your hand like I found the Holy Grail or something." I laugh again and Ezra joins in.

"Well uh, I'm pretty hungry. Can we eat now?" asks Ezra, grinning at me with relief that I'm no longer about to bite his head off.

I sigh and release his hand. "Teenagers. Sheesh."

It's then that I notice Gabriel at the end of the hall, watching us.

I cross my arms and shake my head slightly at him. Aggravation resurfaces. I have so many words for him right now and none of them are nice.

Ezra, who has turned to go back to the kitchen, picks up on the tension. He stops and turns to me. "Wen, it wasn't his idea. But I talked to him about it because… he's really smart. I wanted a second opinion before I did it. And he just… let me come over."

I don't answer.

I decide silence will speak louder than words so I walk past Gabriel, avoiding his face.

He knows he's in trouble, and part of him is surprised by the intensity of my reaction. Even so, my cold shoulder doesn't bother him as much as I think it should. He *advised* my little brother to put himself at risk. I can't even fathom how I will forgive him for that—*especially* when he's not even sorry.

Robert is sitting at the table when we reach the kitchen, feeling awkwardly on the outside of a strained family moment. But I don't address it. I start eating even though Gabriel's relative indifference to my plight has given me so little appetite.

As the rigid moments wear on with Robert asking Gabriel about his new job, I start to pick up on a familiar vibe from Gabriel. He's leaping and somersaulting through a myriad of ideas. I know what it means. He's scheming.

If Gabriel were at all repentant about what he did, I'd know it. He can prostrate himself for forgiveness without the inhibitions of pride like no one I've ever seen. But Gabriel is thoroughly convinced he did the right thing. After all that, after seeing the look on my face and *knowing* how afraid I am of hurting people, he's determined to get me to do things his way.

I can't believe I was just lamenting how inadequate I feel as a wife to someone like Gabriel. I guess I should be relieved that he's revealing his flaws. But I'm too caught up in my fury at him to find that relief.

And how can I when he is plotting against me?

17

"How the heck does Louise fund that compound?" I ask Robert over breakfast once my irritation with Gabriel reaches unbearable levels. "That's got to be a way to track her, right?"

Robert looks at me in surprise as well as apprehension. I wasn't planning on bringing up Louise, but I need something to think about. Gabriel has been watching me while I've flatly ignored him. The more he schemes, the more livid I become. I am *so* glad we're going to Palm Springs today to find Kaylen. I just *know* she'll be able to help me find Louise. Everything happening to me right now is all Louise's fault. I'm going to find that woman and make her pay.

Ezra and Gabriel both look at me silently, wondering where I'm going with this unexpected topic.

Robert shakes his head finally. "Not sure. The compound appears to be funded by anonymous donations. It could be *her* money behind it, but I don't have a way to find out."

"What about Randy?" I offer, remembering the robotic woman whom I first spoke to after my hypno-touch transformation. "They were close. Randy ought to know where Louise is."

Robert shakes his head. "We've already questioned her. She hasn't been in contact with Louise since you were on the compound. Randy was never privy to Louise's real motives."

I throw my fork down with a little too much force. "I need to find Louise."

"Why the sudden interest in Louise?" Robert asks. "I thought you were against finding her?"

I shrug. "Things change."

As I sulk over my glass of water, I ponder Robert's reaction. Moby-Dick, as I like to think of Robert and his emotions, is in the midst of a deep dive. Down, down, down into colder and darker waters I'm unfamiliar with. I think it's at least clear that Robert does *not* like the idea of me going after Louise. I wonder… does he dislike it so much that he would *lie* to keep me from finding her? Why? Louise is dangerous, but I'm not stupid.

I look at Robert squarely. "One way or another I'm going to find her. Whatever she's up to, I am *sure* it's no good. I'm not going to sit by while she gets to do whatever she wants."

My statement is obviously out of place, but in response to Robert's emotional retreat, it's not. I meant my words for him alone. And I think Robert picks up on that.

The whale stops his descent, gliding smoothly but slowly once more. "Okay, Wendy," he says quietly. "You are probably right about that. I resist because I don't like the idea of her manipulating you. My brother..." Robert looks down for a long moment. "When I look at you, I see even more desperation than I saw in him..." He glances back up to my face and for the first time I feel a twinge of connection with him, as if Moby-Dick has come right up to the boat for a moment to look Captain Ahab in the eye. "I just don't want to see Louise take control of your life like I saw her do to him. That's why I hesitate."

It's hard to argue with that kind of sincerity. In fact, it takes me off-guard to see the whale up-close. For the first time Robert intimidates me, not in a scary way, but in a way that makes me believe that Moby has a lot more business going on in the depths of the ocean that I'm aware of—There's more to him. Besides, he's right that I *am* somewhat desperate. But mostly I'm ticked off. Louise is not someone I intend to *ever* be controlled by. "Robert, I'm not my father," I reply as I look back at him.

He sighs uncomfortably, submerging himself in the water once more. I swear I even feel the rocking of the boat from the force of it.

"Louise wants *you*, right?" Ezra says to me. "Seems like whatever she's doing, it's strategizing a way to get to you. So maybe you can use that to smoke her out."

"The only way I can think to do that is to figure out *how* she's planning on getting to me," I reply.

Gabriel becomes a little anxious all of a sudden. "What about Kaylen? She could very well use Kaylen if her father isn't being diligent..."

I turn to look at him with wide eyes. "As a hostage?"

"That's my thought."

"Wouldn't we have heard something by now if that was her plan?" Ezra says skeptically.

"True," Gabriel sighs. "Although it may be that she hasn't carried it out yet for some reason."

All of us fall silent as we consider it.

Gabriel clears his throat after a minute. "I think we may be going about this wrong. We're thinking about finding Louise based on what she has *done*. We need to think about what she'll *do.* Maybe her sights aren't on you at all anymore, Wendy. What might be her new angle?"

"Is there some *other* way to give people superpowers?" Ezra asks, sitting back in his chair. He looks over at me. "You know, besides what you can do and that sickness and hypno-touch combination? Any new idea yet why your ability increased? That might give you a lead."

I shake my head. A thread of worry moves through me, the same one I always feel whenever I imagine the possibility that my ability may continue to increase without my knowledge. I don't want to think about it. I can't. It's too terrifying.

I think about Kaylen instead. *She* has a powerful ability. How did she get it? If Louise found out about Kaylen, she'd want to figure out why, too…

I set my glass down abruptly. "Crap," I say, startling everyone.

"What?" Ezra asks.

"Oh no…" I say, shaking my head. "No, no... Why didn't I think of this before?" I look at Gabriel. "*Kaylen,*" I say. "Louise would want Kaylen!"

He furrows his brow. "I thought we agreed we didn't think so?"

"Not as a *hostage.* Louise wants her because Kaylen is powerful," I reply insistently, not caring that I am breaking Kaylen's confidence. This is far too important. "I caught her in the woods once, spinning ten-ton boulders around her head!"

"What!?" Ezra demands, leaning over the table.

Gabriel gasps. "I *knew* it," he says.

I balk. "You *knew* it? How?"

"I told you I had a guess when the subject of Kaylen came up last week," he says. "That was my guess—that she was more powerful than she let on."

I regard him critically. "How on earth would you guess that?"

"How she acted—the way she avoided using her ability. Supposedly salt shakers were her max. But I caught her once, saving a stack of plates that slipped out of her hands when she was on kitchen duty. She didn't know I saw. I never said anything though. What she could do was her business. I have to say though that I never suspected she could move *boulders.* That's quite a feat…"

"That's *amazing,*" Ezra breathes.

"I had *assumed* Louise didn't know what Kaylen was capable of," I say. "But even Kaylen wasn't so sure. And after all those years of Kaylen being on the compound, how could Louise *not* know?"

"Well that would explain why Kaylen had been on and off the compound for so long…" Gabriel muses.

"Wait, wait, wait," Ezra says. "If Kaylen is as powerful as you say, it sounds like she'd have no problem defending herself."

Neither of us has an argument for that, but Gabriel says, "*Boulders*? How big? How many?"

"Huge," I reply. "Fifteen, twenty? I didn't count them. She was spinning them around her head all at once though… But Ezra's right, Kaylen could bust through a door or wall with no problem."

"It doesn't explain why we've been unable to get a hold of her," Gabriel points out. "I've sent her at least three emails."

"Sounds like checking on her is the right move," Robert breaks in.

"Did Kaylen say how long she'd been having hypno-touch?" Gabriel asks then, propping his elbows on the table as he thinks.

"She said she didn't know," I reply.

"Is any part of her ability natural?"

I shake my head. "She didn't think so. She'd been having hypno-touch as long as she could remember. Her dad has known Louise for forever. Louise probably convinced him to let her do hypno-touch on Kaylen as soon as she realized she had a peanut allergy. What age could that have been? Three? Four?"

"Do you think it was so powerful because she started having hypno-touch so young?" Gabriel asks.

"Possibly."

"I'm with you that Kaylen could easily defend herself, but it makes me want to talk to her father more than ever," Gabriel says as he starts gathering up the dirty dishes. "That you and Kaylen both possess such powerful abilities is telling."

"So how did *you* end up on the compound?" Ezra asks. "You know, since you don't have allergies or anything."

"My brother told me about it," he replies, arranging plates in the dishwasher. "He knew someone who went there. And I was curious, of course. So it wasn't that hard to get into her good graces."

"Someone told your brother?" I ask, wondering why I've never asked Gabriel this before. "Who? That guy Louise had killed?"

Gabriel looks up at me. "What do you mean?"

"The guy…" I insist, racking my brain. "Kaylen told me there was a guy that blabbed about the compound. Louise sued him and then he disappeared. Kaylen insisted Louise had him killed."

"Oh…" he says pensively, leaning against the counter. "I never thought about that. I do remember hearing a bit about it—the suing, not the killing. But I'm pretty sure if the guy was killed, my brother would've mentioned something happening to his friend."

"And Louise let you in? What, did you knock on the door or something?" I ask, confused.

"Kind of. I showed up at her office in Pasadena—the same place you went—and started asking about their business." He shrugs. "I wanted to know about energy medicine anyway. There wasn't any mention of hypno-touch methods at the time, but they did mention energy medicine could enhance natural talents. My counting ability came up in conversation. They were intrigued and asked me if I'd be interested in participating. So I did. It was as simple as that."

I have no doubt it happened exactly that way. A couple weeks ago we went on a walk on the boardwalk and he pulled me into a tattoo parlor. He wanted to talk to the artist about the chemical components of tattoo ink. Simply because he was curious. I also noticed that Gabriel is really good at talking to people when he's fishing for information. It's almost like he has sway over their mood.

"Alright, let's say Louise knows about Kaylen…" I muse. "That means she would want to duplicate the effects, right?"

Gabriel's dismay pauses my thoughts where they are. "What if she's looking for younger subjects?" he offers. "What if she's looking for children to work on? To me that seems like the only explanation for why Kaylen's ability would be so powerful…"

That doesn't sit well with *any* of us.

I turn to Robert. "Do you think *now* would be a good time to find Louise?" I try my hardest not to be snotty about it, but I don't think I succeed entirely.

Robert turns immediately guilty and I regret my words. "I'm sorry," I say. "That came out wrong..."

Robert holds up a hand. "No, it's fine. You're right. I've been working so hard to abide by Leena's wishes... to protect you. I do feel guilty that I never came right out and warned you about Louise. I'll help you find her. If there's a possibility Kaylen could be in danger, you need to check it out and warn her father at the very least. I'll work the Louise angle."

I groan inwardly for being so hard on Robert. I've never been a nice person to people who are as guarded with me as Robert is. It's a residual side of my old self that has evidently stuck around.

"I shouldn't have been such a jerk about it," I say. "Sorry." And then, because I can tell Robert is a little uncomfortable with the spotlight on him, I hop up and say, "I'm going to go pack my stuff."

Once in my room I hear Gabriel say, "It would be nice to know what Louise and Carl were up to all that time..."

After a long silence from the kitchen, Robert says, "I wish I could give you more answers."

"Did Leena mistrust Carl?" Gabriel asks.

"It's possible," Robert replies. "Leena didn't seem to have much remorse after he died. Only concern about Louise."

"Mom did *not* like Dad," Ezra points out. "Wen told me once she thought Dad was why Mom didn't ever date. He totally screwed her with debt and she didn't trust guys... I don't know if that's true, but if he was involved with that head case, Louise, I don't blame Mom for thinking he was a loser... That old chick is crazy."

"Carl's precise involvement with Louise is definitely the question of the day," Gabriel says. "It would answer a *lot* of questions."

"Why didn't Mom just *tell* us?" Ezra gripes. "It couldn't have been such a big deal that we couldn't have handled knowing about it."

"She was only trying to protect you," Robert says. "Everything Leena did was for you and your sister. She was a wonderful mother and a wonderful person."

I zip my bag up and stop where I am. I could swear Robert sounds a little defensive. Was his relationship with my mom... more than what he says? Why else would he defend her? I loved my mom, too. But I can't deny she did a bad job of protecting me. Was it really easier for her to live a lie?

I hoist my bag on my shoulder and carry it out to the front door.

"You'll stay in my home in Redlands, I hope?" Robert says, standing when I come back into the room. "It's less than an hour from Palm Springs—should save you on hotel costs."

I had almost forgotten about Robert's other home. "Yeah… thanks," I say. "How many homes do you have anyway?"

"Four," Robert replies, glancing at me. "But I usually stay in Monterey. I'm thinking about selling the one in the northeast because it's been over two years since I've been there."

I try to imagine what that would be like—to own a home I never see. Just how much money *does* Robert have?

"We have about a half hour before we really need to leave, Wendy," Gabriel says. "Do you want to check out Ezra's life force?"

"Uh, sure," I say. "I saw it the other day, but I guess it couldn't hurt."

"I have an idea," he says.

"What's that?"

"Remember how much more you were able to see at sunset? How you said darkness makes the colorworld appear brighter?" Gabriel asks.

"Yeah… Oh, you're saying I should check out Ezra's life force in the dark?"

"Precisely."

"How are we going to do that in the middle of the day?" Ezra asks.

I look around like a solution might present itself.

"We have a walk-in closet," Gabriel says. "We can start there. If sunset is what's needed, we can try that later."

"Sounds like some good leads," Robert says. "I need to get to the office. Do you all think you could drop Ezra off on your way to the airport?"

"Of course," I say. And then, because I ought to be nicer to Robert, who I now remember is *flying* us out to Palm Springs on his private plane rather than us having to drive, I add, "It was nice to see you. Thanks so much for helping us out with all this."

"It's my pleasure, Wendy," Robert says.

I can tell he really means that.

18

"It is *soooo* hot," Ezra whines. "Wen, how do you *stand* wearing gloves in this heat? I think I'm going to pass out and I'm only wearing shorts and a t-shirt."

"Geez, you act like you didn't grow up in southern California," I say, opening the passenger door to the car and getting in. "And I *stand* it by not complaining about it. But you're making me hotter with all *your* complaining. Stop it or I'll make you ride with Mark and Farlen."

Mark and Farlen are the protection detail Robert sent with us. He says he's not taking any chances where Louise is concerned, so they've been following us in a separate vehicle.

With Ezra's constant griping since we've arrived, I've been wishing I'd left him behind. When I tried to look at his life force in Gabriel's cramped closet, he was too close for me to see anything at all. But the idea of seeing him further away in the dark, and possibly at sunset, excited me enough that I thought we ought to bring Ezra with us so I can do it tonight. He *is* on summer vacation.

Plus, I've been dreading being alone with Gabriel. Things are not resolved between us and I don't want to talk about them. Gabriel will probably make me angrier if he tries to prove that Ezra touching me was a good idea. I've had enough days of our bipolar relationship. Bringing Ezra should keep Gabriel from nagging me.

"Monterey has *ruined* me," Ezra moans from the back seat. "You were right, Wen. I've turned into one of *those* kids. Too much privilege—and good weather. I don't *ever* want to move back to southern California again."

"This isn't typical southern California," Gabriel says. "It's the desert. And besides that, it's pushing their record at a hundred and twenty degrees today."

"Really?" I ask. "I had no idea."

"How did you not notice?" Ezra says.

"Because, Ezra, I always expect to be hot since I wear gloves and long pants all the time. I can't accurately judge temperature."

"Well in that case, you should switch with me and sit in the back. Then you can take your gloves off and roll your jeans up to get some air," he says.

"No," I reply firmly. I am unwaveringly committed to keeping my gloves on if it kills me.

Gabriel gives me a long look as he puts the car in drive. He thinks I'm being irrational. I don't care. He can keep thinking that, as long as he stays safely away from my skin.

We've already been to Fowler's office. It was on one of the floors of a multi-story building. It was closed and when we asked the neighboring businesses about it, they said Mr. Fowler's not been around for a month at least that they've noticed. I guess if Kaylen really is on vacation with her father that jives.

Fowler's home residence is a one-story ranch in a nice suburb. When we get to the door, I don't hear any movement from within. I peek through the windows but everything is tidy and empty. Nobody answers our knocks. We decide to try the neighbors. It's late afternoon so we only catch one person at home, a woman with two toddlers. She tells us she doesn't know where the Fowlers are. They go out of town a lot.

"Have they been back at all in the last month?" I ask.

She thinks for a moment. "I think so… I saw Kevin… two weeks ago? We don't talk much."

"What about Kaylen?" I ask. "Was she with him?"

She looks at me with the beginnings of suspicion but says, "Don't remember seeing her. But she stays at that boarding school a lot."

"Do you have contact information for Fowler?" I ask. And then, to ease her distrust, I add. "Kaylen and I are friends from school. I've been trying to get in touch with her but haven't had any luck."

She shakes her head. "Kevin keeps to himself. He's gone more than he's home. Kaylen is here even less. She comes home for a week or two but she always goes back to that school."

I can tell as she says it that this woman doesn't approve of Fowler's actions in regards to Kaylen. That makes two of us.

One of her kids tries to push past her legs then and she picks him up, propping him up on her hip. I can tell the woman is intrigued with our conversation—it's clear that the Fowlers are a mystery to her. A mystery she'd like in on.

Utilizing her desire to be part of the gossip, and possibly her distaste for Kevin Fowler, I say, "I don't know much about

Kevin… but Kaylen always felt like her dad abandoned her at school. I always thought he was… a crappy dad. That's kind of why I wanted to check on her… To make sure she's okay since I haven't seen her at school all summer."

She bites. "Oh that's what we all think. No reason for that girl to be gone so much. And even in the summer? It's like he just wants to get rid of her." She shakes her head and then looks at me. "Poor girl. Well I'm glad she's got *somebody* checking up on her. Sorry I can't be more help."

"Oh that's okay," I say more comfortably. I think the woman has something else nagging at her that she's not sure about saying. So I press again to give her the opportunity to spill whatever it is. "Is Fowler friends with *anyone* in the neighborhood that might have contact information?"

She shakes her head. "Not that I know of. Like I said, he's not here much. In fact, I have no idea how he maintains his business being gone so much."

"Yeah, he's a CPA, right?" I ask.

She nods. "What do I know though? Maybe he has corporate clients all over the country."

There's something to think about. The business credentials that Robert's guy found didn't indicate Fowler was big-time at all. His company tax records indicate a modest income. And if Fowler was servicing corporate accounts all over the country, his office, in the very least, would stay open to field calls. He wouldn't be this hard to locate. I wonder if there is more to Kevin Fowler than Kaylen told me. Did he have more dealings with Louise than just Kaylen's staying there?

Gabriel, I can tell, has suspicions as well, but he remains silent.

I go out on a limb. "I always got the impression he was more than just a CPA though…" I say, taking note of the woman's emotions before continuing. She hangs on my every word. So I add off-hand, "In fact, Kevin used to bring this older lady with him to the school sometimes when he'd visit Kaylen. Long white-grey hair. I thought it was Kaylen's grandmother or something. But Kaylen said she wasn't related. She said the older woman worked with her dad. I thought it was weird. The woman didn't seem like business material to me…"

I'm just throwing it out there and I don't expect this lady to have ever seen Louise, but to my surprise the woman's eyes brighten with quick recognition. "Oh yeah. I've see her come around. I always thought she was Fowler's mother, too. You're saying she's not?"

I shake my head, stifling my eagerness. "Not according to Kaylen."

"Well that *is* weird," she agrees.

"So you've seen her come around here?" I ask, confident I've won her allegiance.

The woman nods. "Yeah. In fact, the last time I saw Kevin, I saw her with him."

I hide my surprise. "You said you saw him two weeks ago… That's when you saw her, too? You're sure?"

She leans on her door frame, her other toddler peeking out from behind her legs. "Yeah, I'm sure. I'd just gotten back from visiting my mom. Saw her come out of the house with Kevin while I was in my car waiting for my garage door to open."

"Hmm," I say, crossing my arms and looking pensive. "Thanks for your help. I'll check with his office again."

"Sure," she replies, smiling. "I hope you find her. If I see anyone come back to the house, I can give you a ring if you want to give me your number."

I gladly give her my information, thank her again, and return to the car where Ezra's been waiting in the air-conditioning.

"That was something," Gabriel says once we're inside.

"Yeah… Fowler with Louise two weeks ago *after* they supposedly parted ways?" I reply. "Something is up."

"No, I meant the way you schmoozed the information out of that woman," he says, shooting me a grin as he drives.

"Wen can get *anyone* talking," Ezra says from the back seat. "It's her mind-reading skills at work."

I sigh. I don't like that my manipulative proficiency is so obvious to my brother. And I don't like that it comes to me so easily.

"I do agree that something is up," Gabriel says. "The question is whether Fowler is working *with* Louise, or has Louise taken Fowler to get to Kaylen?"

"Sounds like holding her dad for ransom would be the only way to hold someone like Kaylen," Ezra says. "But why now? Louise has had access to Kaylen all this time without *needing* to hold her against her will. That douche bag dad of hers had her at that compound long enough. Seems like… odd timing."

"All good points," Gabriel replies. "I think we'll have Farlen and Mark do a search of Fowler's house to see what they can find."

***

Mark and Farlen don't turn up anything at Fowler's home other than a suspicious envelope in the trash. Instead of being addressed to Fowler, it's addressed to a Sally Stenworth to a post office box in LA. Langston believes that Stenworth is not a real person. She supposedly holds a lot of assets with no records to indicate where she got them. And he can't find her link to Fowler at all.

The home doesn't appear to be lived in much, confirming the neighbor's story that the Fowlers are never around. The kitchen is sparsely stocked, the office bare of anything but some books and CPA files—that at least confirms that he really is a CPA in some respect. There are only a few items of clothing either in the master or in the room that must have been Kaylen's. And there aren't really any photos to speak of. The only personal touch to the home is several pieces of artwork.

The only hope we have now is for Langston to dig deeper on both Stenworth and Fowler.

We're in Redlands for the night; tomorrow we'll fly back to Monterey. So just before sunset, we sit out behind Robert's Redlands home and I use Gabriel to enter the colorworld.

I sigh once I'm there. It just… makes life seem more manageable. With all of the issues I'm facing with my marriage, Kaylen, and Louise, I could use the stress relief.

In the fading light, Ezra, who sits some ten or fifteen feet away, does shine as brilliantly as Gabriel did in the sunset. I squint to adjust my eyes.

As expected, Ezra's life force looks exactly like anyone else's who hasn't had hypno-touch. Exactly like Lindsey's. But in this new light, where his life force is brighter, I make the same effort to spot anything that stands out.

After five minutes, I only come to one conclusion. "The energy vapor I saw at the Lone Cypress comes off of your life forces," I say. "It rolls off, kind of like steam from off a pot. But it has an iridescence to it… maybe like silver in gas form. I guess the darker it is, the more apparent it is."

"Anything telling about it?" Gabriel asks, his excitement growing.

I have to lean away from Gabriel to get a good look at him. Then I turn to Ezra to compare. "Actually…" I say, "it looks like it's coming off of you a *lot.* Ezra, not as much."

Still more of the vapor rolls off of Gabriel and it coincides with his growing excitement, as if it is a visual manifestation of his emotions.

I look at Ezra. "What are you feeling, Ezra?"

"Bored," he replies.

I look between them again. "It looks like… strong emotion makes it increase?"

"Fascinating!" Gabriel breathes as the vapor around him becomes even heavier.

I wave my hand through it but feel no sensation.

"How far away from the life force does it… dissipate?" Gabriel asks.

"Several feet at least. It's really gradual."

"Maybe it's the vehicle for your emodar. You pick up this steam out of the air that other people emit."

"That sounds about right," I say.

"Anything else?" Gabriel asks.

"The smells aren't any different," I say, leaning forward to sniff in Ezra's direction. "Not that I expect them to."

"You say the smell reveals the person's personality, right?" Gabriel asks.

"Yeah, they make me… experience. Like when you smell something associated with a memory and the memory associated with the scent pops into your head more vividly."

"It sounds like everything in the colorworld has to do with the essence of the thing or person…" Gabriel says. "What about the sounds?"

"You already know about the sound between life forces—like strings on strings." I listen without brushing through Gabriel's life force this time to see if there's anything I've missed.

"There's a… warbling," I say.

"Where's it coming from?" Gabriel asks.

"Everywhere. Everything is humming. It doesn't have a constant pitch though. It's so quiet… like a murmuring."

I close my eyes to focus on the sound, but everything is noisy—heartbeats, breathing, shifting of weight, crickets, people talking in the houses around ours, water running, a toilet flushing, music, a TV, footsteps, electricity...

I can usually ignore sounds easily. But I've learned this is more difficult in the colorworld. Something about the place enhances everything. I think it must be the hyper-alert state I have to go into in order to access the colorworld at all, but once there, I have to make a more concerted effort to tune the noise out.

I flip through the more obvious sounds, categorizing them and moving them to the back of my awareness, until I narrow them down enough to focus on the one very quiet, nearly imperceptible humming.

It's more like music, with up and down cadences, but not seamless like an instrument might be…

Then it hits me. My eyes pop open. "It could be voices," I say, shocked at the realization.

I'm hearing voices now?!

"Voices?" Gabriel asks in amazement. "What are they saying?"

"I don't know," I breathe. "It's like listening to a room full of people speaking at the same volume. I can't pick any of them out. But they *do* have a rhythm. Like poetry. When Louise put me under hypnotism that one time, I heard them, but I'd forgotten."

Ezra laughs. "Don't listen to them, Wen. Don't trust the voices if they tell you to do bad things."

I know Ezra's just trying to be funny, but I bite my lip. *I can hear voices*. Am I going crazy?

"Gabriel, am I schizophrenic or something?" I ask. The question sounds stupid, but the reality is that everything about my situation screams delusions and hallucinations. I'm pretty sure people that really are mentally ill like that truly do believe that the things they see and hear are real. "Please, tell me the truth."

"I was kidding, Wen," Ezra says.

"Wendy, don't be ridiculous," Gabriel says, almost like I've offended him. "You are not crazy and you know it."

I release Gabriel's arm to leave the colorworld though. Once it fades, my feelings of normalcy return even though I'm now blinded by the nighttime darkness. I exhale in relief. If I can *control* when I see and hear things, then I can't be crazy.

Gabriel can still tell I'm unsettled though and he says, "You and I have seen too many unexplainable things together to deny that even voices in a world of colors and lights shouldn't be considered bizarre. I wouldn't lie to you. You know that."

I *do* know that, and even as the honesty of his words cements my relief, I can tell he's also fervently focused.

"You doing a Rubix cube in your head or something?" I ask.

"That's an idea," he says thoughtfully. "I wonder if I could…" Then he shakes off the distraction and says, "No, I'm just turning over the new facts you've revealed. New mysteries are always enough to keep me up at night and you have surely delivered."

Ezra crosses his arms from where he sits, relieved that I'm no longer convinced I'm nuts. "You are so weird, man." He shakes his head and looks at me. "Wen, so no idea what the voices were saying?"

"No. It was hard enough to pick up on them, they're so quiet. But the sound is voices," I say, nodding confidently. "Voices definitely."

"Maybe things on that side are talking to each other," Ezra suggests.

"That's a fascinating prospect," Gabriel says, folding his arms and crossing his ankles.

"Fascinating, maybe," I say. "But hardly helpful. I don't speak life force language." I lean forward and prop my elbow on my knee. "It sure would be nice if I did. Then I could ask my life force why it likes to kill people."

Gabriel rolls his eyes. "I doubt your life force purposely does it. It seems like a natural consequence of something else."

"Natural consequence?" I say in disgusted disbelief. "There is *nothing* natural about what I do to people," I say darkly. "Trust me. If you knew what it… *felt like*, you would agree. It's not some natural chain of events with a logical origin that can make it *okay*. Imagine having your senses *erased* one at a time until your mind collapses in on itself. And then you are nothing. You are psychologically drowned. Slowly. It's *torture,* Gabriel. I *torture* them before they die. Whatever it is, it's not just death… they can't endure what I make them *feel.* In fact, every time it's happened, I'm amazed *I* even survived it. And once I get past the shock of *that*, I'm amazed that I'm still mentally stable."

Gabriel blinks at me in surprise and I huff in aggravation. "Stop calling it *natural* and *scientific.* It's neither. Sometimes I wish I could show you what it's like. But then I really *remember* it, and I can't wish that kind of horror on my worst enemy."

Gabriel looks at me critically now. Ezra is silent.

"Why have you never told me this before?" Gabriel asks finally.

I narrow my eyes. "Because I don't want to relive it. It sends me into a cold sweat just *thinking* about it. Because descriptions are inadequate and no matter how I describe it, you won't really get it. Not until you feel it. And when you do, it will be too late."

Gabriel sighs heavily. He thinks I'm laying it on thick to scare him, but I don't *have* to lay it on thick. No matter how thick it is, it will never be thick enough. I sit back in my chair, crossing my arms. The sweat I just spoke of has gathered on my forehead and I struggle to push the memories I've conjured away from me. It also doesn't help that it's probably at least ninety degrees out even though the sun has gone down.

There's no reason for me to endure the heat anymore so I stand up and go to the patio door. Ezra follows and soon after I hear Gabriel's footsteps behind him.

Ezra leaves us to go to his room and I hope against hope that Gabriel is going to let me be. Gabriel and I had a late night last night and I'm exhausted. I don't have the energy to talk to him.

I grab my bag from the front hall where Gabriel deposited it earlier and go to one of Robert's many bedrooms upstairs. Gabriel does not follow me up the stairs, to my relief.

I put my pajamas on and crawl into bed.

I've nearly drifted off when a knock sounds at my door, and then it cracks open.

"Wendy?" Gabriel whispers.

I almost pretend I'm asleep. But instead I say, "What, Gabriel?"

He comes fully into the room and looks for my form on the bed. Then he walks over and kneels down next to it. "I am sorry for speaking about things so flippantly," he says, truly repentant. "I didn't want to give your bad experiences too much attention because I didn't want you dwelling on them, but I can see that was a mistake. I was belittling a traumatic experience. And that is inexcusable."

I sigh. Gabriel is so quick to apologize when he realizes he's been wrong. However, it's obvious that his apology applies to his language only, and not necessarily his treatment of our risky circumstances. And not to his involvement in Ezra deciding to touch me again.

I can't figure out what to say. I don't want to accept a half-apology. But I also don't want a long-winded discussion.

"I'm sorry I didn't tell you sooner," I say, thinking those words accomplish both.

He's silent for several beats, deciding if he's forgiven. He seems to think so.

I really am tired, but all of a sudden the thought that Gabriel has misinterpreted my words as forgiveness isn't something I can accept.

"No," I say, disagreeing with his satisfied demeanor. "You're not just flippant in your words, Gabriel. You're flippant in your actions. I don't want to talk about this right now. I need to sleep. Maybe in the morning I can find it in me to forgive you for the things you aren't sorry for." Then I turn over and away from him.

That definitely unsettles him. He thinks about it, in a bit of shock over what I've said. He considers pushing the issue. I'm about to open my mouth to tell him in no uncertain terms that I will *not* talk about this right now, but before I can he changes his mind. He stands up and leaves the room.

The door closes behind him, the sound of it sealing me in the room with sadness that will not end here. I even whimper a few times, but I'm so tired that I don't have the energy to really cry. I reach up between the slats of my headboard and touch the wall thinking I haven't felt insecure like this since I was a child.

The solidity of the wall puts me to sleep quickly.

19

Worry over Kaylen helps my mood, ironically. I'm not nearly so irritated at Gabriel anymore. In fact, our mutual concern for her brings us together for the task. We spend the next couple days looking for records with Langston that have to do with Kevin Fowler, Sally Stenworth, and Louise. Unfortunately, it doesn't turn up anything of use. Langston says our best bet, from this point, is to monitor Stenworth and Fowler accounts to see if any money moves. He tells us we need to be patient.

When I hear that, I strongly consider begging Robert to use his ability to find Kaylen, but Gabriel says we should let Robert decide that. Robert gave us fair warning about the risks. And Robert should know better than anyone the right circumstances to use his ability.

I guess he's right, but I'm still antsy with nothing to do.

In the midst of worry, however, I also have another low blood sugar scare. I have no idea what to make of it but I get a little stricter about testing and I get some bottled juice to keep around the apartment and to take to work with me when I go back next week.

The next morning I wake up to the smell of Gabriel cooking breakfast. He's done that every morning since we've been living together. This time I think it's pancakes. I hop out of my bed in the guest bedroom, listen to make sure he really is in the kitchen, go to the bathroom, and then make my way to where he is.

Gabriel is moving to the stove to flip the pancakes when I get there. "You burned them," I say after one sniff.

"I did not," he replies, shoving his spatula under the first one. "See?" he says, turning and depositing it back on the skillet.

"Sure, I see. It's not burned if you *like* your pancakes dark brown. But I don't. Those ones can be yours."

"Fair enough," he says, smiling at me and completing the turn on each cake.

I sit on a stool on the other side of the counter and watch him.

"I forgive you," I say after a while.

He turns to look at me, questions running through his mind.

"It's just how you are," I say. "You drive me crazy. But all the things that drive me nuts are the same things I fell in love with you for. So unless I expect you to change the things I love, I can't honestly stay mad at you over them."

His eyes are wide, surprised. And then he melts entirely, striding over to the counter that separates us. "Wendy… You have no idea how the last few days have eaten me up inside…" His residual angst clenches my heart. "I've been trying *so* hard to determine how to comply to your wishes in the way you want without violating my personal convictions." He puts his elbows on the counter and puts his hands over the back of his neck like he's kneading out the stress. He looks up at me. "I *am* sorry for putting you through all that. I just… knew that I wouldn't take anything back even if I could—even though I hated hurting you." He sighs and stands up. "I've been so at odds with myself. And now you…" He shakes his head. "Wendy, you're so beautiful. How you can forgive me even if you don't agree with me… I hope I have that same capacity."

"Pancakes, Gabriel," I say. When he goes back to the stove, I continue, "Of course you do. You forgive quicker than anyone I know. You've forgiven me for awful words I've said. You've forgiven me for treating you poorly. You let me be me even though it seems irrational to you. You deserve the same."

After he pours more batter, he comes back to the counter, reaches for my hand, and exhales in relief. My world rights itself just by having Gabriel's hand in mine. I don't like fighting with him. I don't like being mad at him. He looks up into my eyes for several long moments. This simple act lifts a weight off of me.

"You should know that even if you intend to push my boundaries, I'm not planning on relenting," I warn. "I still think you're reckless. And if I let you have your way with me, I'm pretty sure you're going to get yourself killed—and the pancakes are burning again."

He scoffs and turns back to the stove. He flips the last of the pancakes over and turns off the burner.

"And if you ever advise my brother to endanger himself again, I'm going to have your head," I say, grabbing the syrup from the counter and taking it to the table.

He takes silverware and plates out. "For *that* slight, I truly am sorry. I shouldn't have gone behind your back. I know you don't want to hear excuses, but I knew that if you were in on our plans, you never would have allowed them. We both wanted you to see progress after so much disappointment. But I should have respected you enough to tell you of my intentions."

I roll my eyes as I sit down at the table. "There you go again. Half-apologizing. You should really just say you're sorry without all the explanation for what exactly you're sorry for. You dig yourself deeper that way. But like I said, I've already forgiven you regardless of whether you're sorry, so can we move on? I have a question." I've been stewing over it for days.

He furrows his brow, confused, but decides he's more interested in my question than my issue with his apology. "What's that?" he asks, bringing the plate of pancakes and sitting across from me.

"Do you think I'm being selfish? Trying to find a cure, I mean? You know, instead of trying to learn how I can help people with what I can see."

He looks at me with surprise. "You think looking for a cure is selfish?" He pours syrup over his pancakes.

"Well… maybe," I reply, slicing a banana. "These past few weeks have felt a lot like my time on the compound, when I focused on nothing but the limitations of my condition. I haven't really… made progress since I left and I don't really have a direction now."

"I take it you're still upset about Lindsey and Ezra?" Gabriel says, frowning.

"Forget them," I say, exasperated. I assumed Gabriel was going to go this route… although I had hoped he would wow me with something outside of my expectations like he usually does. "I want to know if I should be doing something I'm not. Maybe I have tunnel vision because of my condition. If what I'm seeing are… *souls* of things, then it's reasonable to assume that I have the power to understand things that could help a lot of people. Maybe I should learn energy medicine."

Gabriel tilts his head after he chews and swallows. "And you think that what you are currently doing is *not* helpful to humanity?"

"Well, yeah," I reply. "I'm not *looking* to cure sickness. I'm *looking* for a way to undo what's been done to me."

He smiles lightly. "Wendy, Love, there's nothing wrong with what you've been *doing*. It only sounds like you could possibly change your *thinking*. After all, if we discover the mechanism that brought about your ability to begin with, it will mean that we will have a definite understanding of how the body and life force collaborate. I don't think it's possible for you to *not* help others by what you manage to learn about in the colorworld. You can't accomplish one goal without accomplishing the other. They are interwoven." He pauses to take a few bites, thinking. "Don't worry so much. Learn everything you can from the colorworld and you'll find the opportunity to apply what you know to be of help to others. You'll see."

"You know," I say, pointing my fork at him, "this sounds a lot like what Louise said to me when I first got to the compound. Except she insisted that if I helped her meet *her* goals, it would help me meet mine."

Gabriel chuckles. "Well she was certainly right about that. From where I sit, there was never anything wrong with Louise's *goals*. She just went about achieving them in the wrong way. As astounding as the world she envisions would be—one where everyone has superpowers—you can't justify getting there by murdering people. The means are more important than the end-goal. In fact, if we will focus more on our means, the end-goal will work out. It's the journey, Love. The journey is what makes us, not the end-point."

"Okay, Mr. Philosopher," I reply, smiling, "that may be true, but this morning my end-goal was fluffy golden pancakes, and I can tell that your means suck; these pancakes are all too dry because you cooked them too long."

"They kind of are, aren't they?" he says, peering down at his laden fork.

I laugh. "You can memorize a book, watch a documentary, and listen to me talk without missing a word but you can't have a conversation and fry a pancake at the same time. I think I've discovered your weakness, Mr. Dumas."

"My weakness is you, Mrs. Dumas," he says, propping an elbow on the table and gazing at me in a way I don't think he's felt at liberty to do in days. "Your presence dulls my faculties."

I scoff. "A likely story. I think the truth is that you aren't so brilliant with things that require more than just your genius. After all, you were burning the pancakes before I ever came in the room."

"True," he says. "I was engrossed in my own speculations before you woke up."

"Care to share?"

"Not just yet."

"Not even a little?" I ask, disappointed.

"Let's just say I've been working on a theory ever since your ability improved that one time." I pick up a hint of excitement behind his words.

I haven't given that phenomenon much thought since I discovered it. People lose abilities. People increase them. As much as I wish it were so, mine does not seem to be going away so I've left off wondering about it. Leave it to Gabriel to not let *anything* fall through the cracks. "When you have a conclusion, I'll be glad to hear it. In the meantime, let me handle the dishes. I've been pretty useless around here with you cooking all the time."

He hops up. "All yours. I have a book on thermodynamic systems calling my name," he says as he bounds from the kitchen.

I shake my head in wonder. "Thermodynamic systems? Honestly," I mumble to myself, "if I can't figure out my problem with someone as brilliant as *him* around, then there simply is no solution at all."

20

In my dream I'm in the grocery store passing the aisles of produce, smelling different items. I reach a display of avocados; one variety is Haas and the other is the variety that I can never remember—the big green ones. The green one is only $2.25 and it's huge, easily three times the size of the Haas. The Haas is only $1.15 and the exact size I need for the salad I'm planning to make for dinner.

I'm torn. The big green one is a much better deal. However, it's much too large to use in one meal. There will be leftovers when I cut it up. How will I use the extra? Will it still be good when I get around to using it?

As I mull this over, the situation feels more and more dire. I'm all but sold on buying the green one and finding an additional use for it. But the Haas avocado is going to be upset at me for choosing the green one when it knows it's the perfect size. I'm selling out for a good deal.

"It's not personal," I say to the Haas as I reach for the big green one. "How can I resist a bigger one when it's obviously a way better deal?"

The produce doesn't speak back but sits there all forlorn. I hesitate. Maybe I should go with the Haas after all.

"It's just a vegetable," I say to no one in particular. "The Haas will never know."

Fraught with indecision, I rack my memory for other avocado recipes, but I draw a blank. Slowly, I lean toward the Haas. The green avocado is too good of a deal for me. The green one should be reserved for more savvy shoppers, true lovers of avocados, rather than occasional fans.

I know the green one is the right one to get. I can make guacamole with the leftover portion and serve it for lunch tomorrow. No big deal. I don't understand why the decision is so hard; I think I might break with the stress of it. I reject them both and push away from the dream, floating into darkness until I find a corner of wakefulness to grasp on to.

As my senses surface, I hear movement close by.

Someone is in my room. I stay very still, pretending I'm asleep. Adrenaline pulses through me and I squint through pinched eyes.

Darkness is no challenge to me and I easily see the figure sitting in the office chair next to my bed, legs propped up on the bed frame. He wears a white T-shirt and tan arms wrap around his knees. His head is tucked out of sight like he's sleeping with his head on his knees.

Gabriel.

I leap up and away from him, pinning myself to the wall behind me. "Gabriel!" I shout, looking frantically at my hands to ensure that I have my gloves on. Did he sleepwalk into my room? Did he fall asleep there? What is he *doing*?

His head snaps up. At first he's in shock, then he notices me plastered against the wall, bracing against an unseen danger.

He looks around with wide eyes, searching for the cause for my alarm. "What? What?" he says.

"What are you *doing* in here?" I say. "You scared the crap out of me!"

I sit back down on the bed, shuddering in relief.

"I'm sorry. I thought you were asleep," he says quietly.

"I was!" I say, still on edge. "I was having some crazy dream about avocados and it was making me sad because I had to choose between them. It was the strangest dream… I was sure the avocados were going to be mad at me. One minute I'm reaching for one avocado and the next I'm pulling my hand back like the decision is life or death. Geez!"

The dream is still fresh.

Gabriel looks at me in surprise. "You couldn't decide?"

"No… it was… weird. So real. I wake up because the stress is killing me… Then there's this figure in my room and I think I'm going to wet myself… Then I see it's *you* and—Why *are* you in here? Gabriel, I almost jumped you. I thought you were an intruder."

I settle down a little more now that my brain is back in reality and take stock of Gabriel's emotions. He's sad and slightly ashamed.

"What gives?" I ask. "Were you watching me sleep or something?"

It's not like Gabriel to be embarrassed over anything, let alone something like that, but I guess there's a first time for everything.

"Um… yes," he says with clear indecision. He's not lying, but he *is* holding something back.

"And?"

He looks up at me with a grimace.

"What else? I know that's not all." I cross my arms, looking at him expectantly.

Gabriel looks down. "You're going to be mad."

"It can't be that bad. What could you possibly have been doing that would render *you* speechless?"

I'm fairly sure it wasn't anything sexual. His emotions don't indicate anything remotely like that. The mystery puzzles me, and I look at him as he sits there with his head bowed, hands now clasped over his neck. He's trying to make up his mind.

"You know you're going to tell me," I point out, "so drop the tortured indecision."

He sighs then and says, "I was indecisive. You must have felt that in your dream. I should have guessed. It didn't occur to me you would feel that when you were sleeping."

"What were you deciding?" I say uneasily.

What could put such a look of distress on his face? I try… I *really* try to find an alternative explanation—especially after the other day when he made it clear he wasn't ever going to—but I can't help jumping to one conclusion. We've only been married a week and already he can't take it. I start to cry. "You were deciding whether to leave me," I say softly.

When I say the words out loud they sound so much worse, and I put my face in my hands.

"No, no, no!" protests Gabriel, leaping up to sit beside me on the bed, grasping one of my gloved hands. "Oh heavens, Wendy! Forgive me for making you even wonder at that!"

"Then what?" I ask, looking at him through my tears.

He watches my face for a moment. "I wish I could wipe your tears away," he says. "But what if your soul is more powerful than mine? What if I really am not worthy of you?"

"What are you talking about?" I ask, irritated that he's beating around the bush.

"I—" he starts. Looks up. Then down at the floor. His resolve solidifies.

"I have a theory," he says confidently. "Like I told you, I've been formulating it ever since your ability improved. I'm still not sure what caused it, but it got me to thinking about what it is that powers an ability in the first place. Hypno-touch can improve an ability that's either natural or has been manifested. And hypno-touch deals with the life force—the *soul*. Which means that souls must power abilities. They are a power source, perhaps pure energy themselves. When you touched Ezra you told me about the current and the energy vapor. That led me to thinking about how everything in the colorworld bears the essence of the person—the smells, the sights, the sounds even. I think—no I'm fairly positive—that you only kill people whose life energy is weaker."

Gabriel gets more and more excited as he speaks, but I remain confused. What does his theory have to do with his being in my room?

"Who have you touched?" he says. "There's Dina. Well I met her, and she was underhanded and manipulative. Purposely nasty and demeaning. Dishonest and an all-around unlikable person. She was Louise's closest cohort, much more than Randy. Derek seemed nice most of the time, but I watched him use his ability to con a woman into bed with him more than once. It was despicable, and I nearly entered into a physical altercation with him about it. That's when he started working for Louise outside of the compound.

"Louise's test subjects. I think they were most likely homeless or at least desperate individuals hoping to make a buck. I'm not saying they deserved to die, but how many homeless people do you know that are upstanding citizens? Most of them are addicted to some kind of substance, be it drugs or alcohol, and most would lie and steal to get it. Not all, of course, but a majority would be an accurate generalization. So again… not very strong 'souls' if I were to pass judgment.

"Then there was Don who obviously was intent on keeping you captive for Louise, who held a gun to you. He died. Again, another questionable soul."

Gabriel shifts to face me directly. "So what about the two who survived? Lindsey: someone who was only forced onto the streets because of her situation. She came across as—"

"Wait," I say. "What situation?"

He looks at me with confusion. "Don't you remember what she told Langston?"

I shake my head. "I was focused on her life force, not her life story."

"Oh. Well Langston found her at a battered women's shelter. She ended up there after leaving her boyfriend who had been abusing her. She was homeless for about a week after she left him. That's when Louise came by her. Lindsey seemed like a good person thrust into a bad situation."

"So… you're saying her life energy is…?"

"Strong enough to withstand yours," he replies as his eyes widen with excitement. "The same applies to Ezra… We know how good *he* is."

"You're saying good people have stronger life energy?" I ask, testing that idea.

"Exactly. It makes me believe that you only affect souls that are weaker than your own. Remember what you said it was like to touch Ezra? You said it felt like a current? And the energy vapor? We agreed it had to do with the state of a life force. I have to wonder if it would look different coming off of a person who was full of hate or malice. And a person's smell? It tells you about them exactly. The colorworld reveals the true substance of everything. Whatever you need to know about a soul can be found there. So I wonder, is my soul strong enough to hold up to yours?"

I follow his logic, but his purpose for telling me is obscure until the very end. Realization of his "indecision" hits me and I leap away from him and onto the floor.

"You wouldn't!" I exclaim in disbelief.

But I know he would. It's so *Gabriel.*

"What is *wrong* with you?" I shout. "Death odds of six out of eight aren't enough to scare you? What would I do if the test failed when you touched me? Wake up to find you dead on the floor, knowing I'd done it? I already see those people in my memory every day—and in my dreams!"

I shake my head and wring my hands. "The terror… Gabriel, you have no idea. I told you it was awful… I wasn't embellishing. Don't you remember how they had me restrained at Pneumatikon? I tried to bite through my own wrists to kill myself just to get the horror of it to go away."

I shiver at the memory, my head in my hands, willing him to grasp the seriousness of what he's proposed.

"If Don hadn't had a gun," I continue, desperate to make him understand, "I couldn't have gone through with touching him. I suffer guilt all the time knowing what I did to all those people—even though I wasn't aware. Because I know what they *felt* and what they went through. Soul torture, Gabriel. That's what it is. And you? My husband? The man I love, that I would die for? You want me to see you dead on the floor in my mind for the rest of my life? To feel *your* destruction? You would risk that?"

The thought terrifies me; his indifference chafes me so much I wish I could hit him, knock some sense into him.

"That's why I was undecided," says Gabriel quietly. "If I think I'm good enough for you, is that humility? I think not. So if I'm not humble then what does that make my soul? You see the problem? How can I accurately judge myself? How can I know for sure if my soul is as good as yours? If I'm wrong, then I'd leave you alone. I would injure you deeply. But then, I thought, you'd find someone who really is good enough, and it would work out. But all the hurt I would cause you? I don't know… I'm undecided on that."

"What?!" I yell, gesturing wildly. "How can you even think like this? You weren't going to do it because you didn't think you were *good enough*? *That* was what held you back? Are you freaking kidding me!? How about the possibility that your theory could be completely bunk? How about that? If I actually knew for one second that your theory was right, I'd have jumped you like *yesterday*. Your soul not as good as mine? Are you totally delusional? How about get your concerns in order. What if you're wrong? Huh? Did you even consider it?" Gabriel's line of thinking is so entirely out of whack I might have to question his sanity.

"I don't think my theory is wrong. Otherwise, I never would have considered it," he replies simply.

My jaw drops in surprise. "You know something I don't? Because it sounds like you have pretty circumstantial evidence as so-called proof. You're a scientist. Don't you have to have more to go on before you can go declaring scientific laws?"

"I don't see any evidence to the contrary, and we don't have the luxury of testing it out on people to get more empirical support. Besides, I'm *not* wrong on this," he says, getting annoyed at me.

A frenzied laugh escapes my throat. "You're *not* wrong? Oh excuse me, I didn't realize you were omniscient."

"I never said I was. But the theory supports the basis of what I have faith in," he says calmly.

I stare at him dumbfounded. His answers are completely absurd, and he talks to me like we're having a civilized discussion over tea. The more indifferent he is, the angrier I get.

"What does that even mean? *Faith*? Really, Gabriel, you can't make a few assumptions about a few scenarios and pop out with a solution that suits what you want. You can't be one hundred percent sure. You can't, and until you and I both are, you are not touching me. Forget it. No."

Gabriel looks at me with patient indulgence. "Wendy, calm down. I'm not touching you. I wasn't *going* to touch you. I told you, I was only thinking about it. Our reasons for hesitating are just different. As for faith? There are all kinds of things to have faith in, and I happen to have faith that there is good and evil in the universe and good always prevails. If I didn't believe that then I'd have no reason to get out of bed in the morning. I form every belief I have in my life on that understanding. You're telling me you don't?"

I cross my arms. "Good and evil? Really? What does that matter when I am here terrified that I won't be able to sleep at night because you might test out your theory? How am I supposed to trust you?" I ask desperately. Why is he getting philosophical when all I want is to keep him safe?

"Why would you not be able to trust me?" he asks. "Have I ever lied to you? I told you after the incident with Ezra that it was wrong to go behind your back. And I won't this time."

"So you're saying as soon as you *intend* to touch me, you'll do me the *courtesy* of telling me?" I say shrilly. "Then what happens? You chase me around and force me to lock myself away to avoid killing you? That's ridiculous!"

"I honestly haven't decided on that precisely," he replies calmly. "Because I don't yet have the intention of touching you."

"*Yet*!? Why are you doing this to me?" I plead. "This is insane!"

"Wendy," Gabriel says gently, "you aren't seeing the forest for the trees. You've got to stop looking at singular events as isolated things. I know I'm right because my theory and everything you describe about the colorworld fits into how I ultimately view reality, not because I have some kind of knowledge that you don't. Open your eyes! You've seen things that are invisible to the rest of us. You have to start drawing conclusions about what it all means. You have to piece it together to form a larger picture so you can make accurate deductions."

"Deductions? Gabriel, I deduce that my skin kills people. The colorworld is beautiful. My lethal touch is the exact opposite. You can't reconcile the two!"

"Can't reconcile them?" Gabriel asks, incredulous. "You *have* to. *Why* do you insist on seeing everything in a vacuum?

You touched your brother, Wendy! What does that mean? You've got to draw a conclusion!"

"There are only a million possible reasons why I can touch him," I say. "He's related to me."

"Name one that also applies to Lindsey," say Gabriel.

"I have no idea! That's the point!" I yell. "Too many possibilities to narrow down one theory. Come on, you're the scientist! You can't tell me you have absolute evidence."

Gabriel looks at me, surprised. "Absolute? Of course not. There's no such thing. In *any* scenario."

"Whatever, Gabriel. I don't care. What I do care about is that you don't endanger yourself by touching me. Please. Please. What can I do to get you to promise that?"

Gabriel is scaring me, and I already ramble through alternate plans in my head. Maybe my uncle will let me move back in. Maybe I should get a deadbolt on the guest bedroom door. *Holy crap, I'm going to lock my own husband out of my room? Is this a screwed up relationship or what?*

He shakes his head in amazement at me and smiles softly. "You are so obliviously moral. You do what you think is the right thing without even knowing why you do it." He sighs. It's like he's having a discussion with himself rather than me.

Then he looks at me. "How do you do that? How do you know what's right without even thinking about it?"

"Gabriel! I refuse to have any more discussion with you until you swear on our marriage and all that you hold dear that you will not touch me until I have agreed with you one hundred percent!" I snap.

Gabriel chuckles and shakes his head. "There you go again. Just can't let the moral rod go. It's positively riveting."

I don't think I have ever wanted to hit someone so bad. He's trying to *charm* me when I'm in the middle of a crisis!? He must be trying to sidetrack me from my question. He must think I'm a flimsy idiot. I am not falling for it. I give him a severe look.

"Okay, okay," he relents. "Let me think… I promise not to touch you until I am more sure of my theory."

"That's not what I asked—Hey! You just said you *were* sure of your theory!"

"Caught that, did you? Well, it's all about positive thinking, my darling. As your vision so beautifully shows, our thoughts influence our reality. But how would I be human if I didn't have some doubt?"

"Argh!" I growl, and stomp my foot. That doesn't help, so I grab a shoe and fling it at him, although he catches it easily.

"Can it already, will you?!" I say and then take several cleansing breaths to calm down. I look at him earnestly. "Gabriel," I say slowly, trembling, "can't you *try* to see things my way? What you're asking? It's not fair. You wouldn't just be risking your life. You'd be risking mine. I would not survive if I felt you die that way. I wouldn't."

His expression softens. "Of course I can see things your way. I told you I believed what you said about what it's like. Of course I factored that in. But I *also* told you that I wasn't willing to let you submit to fear. My feelings on that haven't changed. In fact, I am even more strongly committed to it."

Stymied by Gabriel's stubbornness, I shake my head in disbelieving awe. "Your mother was right… I mean, she was *totally* right. How on *earth* did she do it? It's a wonder she's still sane."

He's about to answer, but I hold up my hand. "No, that was rhetorical. The real question… or rather, *demand,* is that you do not touch me until we have *both* agreed to it."

"No."

"No?" I say, aghast. "You can't just say no!"

"Well I'm not going to say yes. 'No' was the only other alternative."

"But! What! You!" I sputter.

"Wendy, if I have learned anything from you tonight, it's that I have to do what's right on my moral compass. Furthermore, I have learned that you are never ever going to allow me to touch you, no matter what the evidence says. I swear, your own father could show up right now and tell you it's okay and you still wouldn't do it."

He shakes his head in wonder. "Your system of ethics is founded on something I've yet to pinpoint. But it seems to operate separately from what you see, hear, and smell. You label something as right or wrong without much agonizing or analysis. I don't operate that way. I don't deal in absolutes. Each situation is unique, and I don't think I have ever been one hundred percent sure of a decision the way that you seem to be. So if I agree to touch you only when you agree, it will never ever happen. I *will,* however, agree to postpone it until we have gained further evidence in support of my theory and I am more convinced that I am worthy to touch you. That is, after all, my real hang-up."

For a moment I'm stunned into silence. What do I say to that? He is devious and possibly the most pigheaded person I have ever met.

"You are manipulative and underhanded, and you may think I'm tied to a moral rod, but I can play dirty, too," I say, snatching a pair of jeans, a shirt, and my shoes, heading to the bathroom to change.

When I emerge, Gabriel is waiting in the hall. "Where are you going in the middle of the night?" he asks, slightly worried.

"To get some insurance," I say. "Where are my keys?"

"Wendy, if you would put them in the same place—"

"Found them!" I interrupt as I pull them from a drawer by the stove.

Gabriel is close behind me. "Where do you think you're going dressed like that?" I ask him as I open the front door.

He wears a white undershirt, red, white, and green striped pajama pants like the Mexican flag, and a pair of giant fuzzy purple slippers. The first time I saw him dressed down like that at the compound, I laughed so hard, the water I was drinking came out of my nose. He told me Einstein had once owned a pair of slippers just like them.

"With you, of course. What's wrong with what I'm wearing?" he says, delighted. He is enjoying this.

"We're going to be in public, that's what's wrong with it. And besides, I don't remember asking you to come with me," I say, folding my arms and blocking the door with my body.

"I'm coming whether you let me in your car or not. But it's not very environmentally responsible to waste fuel resources that way." Gabriel mirrors my stance with a stubborn look.

"Fine," I say. "Go ahead and embarrass yourself in front of complete strangers." Then I turn and stomp out.

"Why would I be embarrassed around strangers? I don't even know them," Gabriel mumbles from behind me.

I shake my head. He is completely serious.

Our car ride is silent. Gabriel is curious—big surprise—and I am exasperated but determined when I pull up to a 24-hour Walmart. I hop out of the car, not waiting for Gabriel to catch up.

He does anyway, of course, and then says with excitement, "I haven't had this much mischievous fun since we ransacked Louise's office. Are we going to ride a shopping cart around the store?"

I remain silent but hide a smile. Staying furious at him is incredibly difficult. He's like an endearing child who says things at inopportune times.

Once inside, I walk directly to the hardware department, searching through the aisles until I find the one I'm looking for. I carefully analyze the available selection. Gabriel watches me the whole time—he figures out my plan as soon as I reach the right aisle. Unfortunately he's not put-off like I thought he'd be. Instead, his intellect works overtime.

I finally settle on a purchase and snatch it up, heading to the front of the store to pay for it. The cashier eyes Gabriel's clothes, but says nothing. However, once she thinks we are out of earshot, I hear her laughing and talking about fuzzy slippers to her co-worker.

As we walk through the parking lot, Gabriel says, "If you think one measly deadbolt is going to force me into that promise, you are sadly mistaken. What exactly does that protect you against?"

I stop where I am. "It's not supposed to protect *me*," I say angrily. "It's *supposed* to protect *you* from that backward brain of yours. It's *supposed* to send you a message about how serious I am. It's *supposed* to make you stop and think about what you're doing. So help me, Gabriel, I will do *whatever* it takes to keep you safe. Don't push me, or I'll be forced to make this situation even more uncomfortable for the both of us."

I look down at the asphalt, my head still spinning at how *incredible* Gabriel's disregard for his safety and my sanity are. "I don't want to. But I will," I add.

When I reach the car finally, I throw open the door, and slam it behind me, shoving the keys into the ignition as Gabriel gets in the passenger side.

A big part of me is sad. But the other part is baffled. He doesn't get it. It's like he's incapable of comprehending my point of view. His conviction is mind-blowing. It's absolutely unrelenting, and if I don't find a way to breach it, our relationship is over.

I suck in a few breaths. I can't face that right now. There *has* to be a way to reach him. There has to be a way to make him see that what he's telling me is that I have to risk killing him or leave. That's not fair…

One week. We've been married for just a week. How have things turned upside down so quickly?

I become furious at him again. But at least it keeps my tears at bay until we arrive home. Gabriel falls asleep, almost immediately, in his room.

I cry myself back to sleep, thinking about and hating what he is forcing me to do.

21

On Sunday evening, while Gabriel is at the gym, I get the lock installed on my bedroom door. I purposely waited until he was gone because I knew it was going to result in a deluge. And it does. I feel like I'm screwing the thing right into my heart. Then I stay in my room the rest of the day just looking at it. I also have another sporadic blood sugar low which means I'm more angry than sad. Raging and low blood sugar go together. I think under normal circumstances, my diabetes acting up like this would freak me out, but I'm more concerned about Gabriel's life.

Gabriel comes home later, eyes my handiwork, but says nothing. His mental gymnastics are in full form. He has been thinking, hard. He stays silent the rest of the day, memorizing books in the living room. This continues the next day as well, which surprises me. I fret all day at work over what he might be strategizing.

After analyzing his emotions when I get home, I come to the infuriating conclusion that he is waiting for me to come around. He actually thinks that I'm going to move past what he deems as 'irrational behavior' and accept his theory.

The next day is the same. After work, I go for a run to escape the vapid air in the apartment created by our silence. When I come back, I start dinner.

I make puff pastry from scratch, getting some stress relief from rolling butter into layer after layer. Brush. Fold. Roll, back and forth, side to side. Repeat. Gabriel comes over to observe, asks me if I need help. I shake my head, say nothing.

He sighs and goes to sit on the couch, speed-reading another book.

I think about Kaylen then. With each passing day that we hear no word from Langston, I get more and more worried. I *really* hope Robert took us seriously when we insisted she was in trouble. I wish I could *do* something. My life is obstructed on every front.

After so many rounds with my rolling pin, however, I think I've ironed out my grievances enough and found my center. The serenity of controlling the dough in my hands—which have been ungloved as I work—gives me confidence. I can do this. I can outlast Gabriel. And we are *going* to find Kaylen. This stalemate can't last forever.

I stuff seasoned pork I'd slow cooked earlier into the pastries, one by one. I brush them with egg white. As they bake, I make a salad, rigidly committed to removing every bit of grit and residue on each leaf. I make a dressing from scratch while the pastries cool.

Once I've plated two portions, I take mine to my room, leaving Gabriel's on the counter. When I come back an hour later, he's waiting in front of the dishwasher, blocking it. I don't look at his face; I put my plate on the counter instead. He hesitates in indecision, deciding what to say to me. I don't stop. I turn my back to him and return to my room.

On the morning of the third day, frustration has finally stained the edges of his confidence. I smirk after I pass him on my way out the door to go to work. Now that he has his guard down a little, I start formulating some way to broach the subject with him again. I need something good. Something he can't argue with. All day at work I agonize over it. The only thing I can think of is to move out. That will prove to him that I'm serious, won't it?

I can't yet stomach that though. Whenever I think of it, my chest throbs. Maybe I should try talking to him again…

I go see Robert then because I can't take being thoroughly stonewalled. I ask him whether there has been any progress on Kaylen.

Robert shakes his head and watches me carefully. "I'm sorry. I know it's hard to wait, but it's all we can do right now."

I pause there for a moment, summoning my conviction to keep moving, looking down at his mottled grey carpeting.

"Are you alright, Wendy?" Robert asks after several moments.

I look up. "No."

"Is there something I can do?"

"Find Kaylen," I reply. And then I leave his office, back to the basement where my job is to open mail, date it, and get it to the right place... I may know where the mail goes but I have no idea where *I* go. I don't know what I'm doing and every day reiterates this point.

I make another elaborate dinner that night. Cooking is my method of sanity during idle hours. I decide to sit at the table to eat this time, a silent gesture to Gabriel that he can talk to me if he chooses. I know I need to out with it and ask him where we stand, but I really want him to start the conversation. Maybe then I can better strategize what to say to him. I have to convince him that he's being unreasonable.

He takes me up on the silent invitation, sitting across from me. I feel his eyes on my face periodically, and I also can tell he's wondering about this change of behavior. Confidence is slowly seeping back into him. It's maddening that he would consider this a sign of my relenting. I have to wrap my ankles around the legs of my chair to keep from stomping away in disgust.

"What do you call this?" he asks after taking a bite. "Some kind of… Mediterranean thing?"

"Falafel," I reply. "And it's Lebanese."

My answer surprises him—not the answer so much as the sound of my voice after so many days of silence. "You're talking again," he notes.

I rake in my irritation. He makes it sound like he's been waiting out a temper tantrum.

"I like it," he replies. "How did you learn to cook so well?"

"Practice."

"When did you have that kind of time on your hands? I thought you were pretty busy when it was just you and Ezra."

"When Elena died," I reply, still avoiding his face. "When I wasn't out, I was cooking. And when my mom was hospitalized, I cooked."

"Elena? That was your daughter's name?"

I nod, picking at a piece of pita bread. If I cared right now, I'd pat myself on the back for how good the bread turned out. It was my first attempt making pita from scratch.

"So you cook when you're sad?"

I don't answer. That should be obvious.

He sighs heavily and then shifts gears. "I've been wondering… Do you think you'd like to move to San Jose after this year? There's a job opening at the university starting in the spring and they've requested that I apply. The pay is more competitive and I figured since Ezra has to commute to school there every day, perhaps we could buy a house and have him live with us instead of Robert. You could go back to school if you want and you wouldn't have to be separated from Ezra."

I look at him for a moment, wondering what kind of ploy this is. It *sounds* like a great opportunity, but it's hard to imagine what my life will be like next *week* let alone next *year*. Back to school? I'm still adjusting to going to *work* and I don't have to encounter nearly as many unsuspecting people there. Plus, Gabriel knows how tenuous things are between us right now.

"Whatever you want," I say. "It doesn't really matter to me."

If he had brought this up a week ago, I would have been thrilled. But now? What does he think is going on between us? A simple lover's spat?

I expect him to delve into my frosty demeanor, but instead he says, "Sorry, Love. I know it's a big adjustment after we've just been married. It's silly for me to suggest that you uproot yourself when you've barely adjusted to your new circumstances. I take for granted that you feel unsure about your purpose now so much of the time. But I hate to think of you being stifled by your condition. You have so much to offer… I can be patient. Just know that whatever your hopes and dreams are, I will find ways to make them happen for you."

I sigh. Gabriel's obvious sincerity makes it hard to be irritated with him. "Gabriel, *you* are the talented one. If you have a good opportunity to do what you love, you should take it. I'm useless no matter where I am."

"Oh I merely talk loud and have an annoying enthusiasm for academics," he disagrees. "You have a grasp of life that relates to everyone, academic or not."

I control my breaths so they don't betray my aggravation, trying to decide if I should make an exit now. This is going nowhere and I am too cowardly to *take* it anywhere.

Gabriel, on the other hand, is looking into my eyes and I'm having a hard time not looking back, especially when his words are coupled with the softest affection—and wistfulness. He misses me.

When I manage to refuse the connection of my eyes, he closes his own, props his chin up, and inhales. "You smell so delicious. I can hardly keep my distance from you. It's a good thing I don't have your sense of smell. I would probably be unable to control myself."

He reaches across the table for my hand. I flinch away.

That simple movement strikes him with deep sadness. "Why are you being like this?"

"You know *exactly* why," I say icily. "The problem is that you don't *care* why. I told you that you would regret not promising me what I asked. This is the alternative."

I shove my chair back and go to my room. But Gabriel is hot on my heels. For a fleeting second, I worry what his intentions are. Is he going to touch me now?

No. He told me he would tell me first… but I don't know how that will work either.

When I reach my room, I don't bother shutting the door in his face. He's too close and probably won't let me.

"What do you want?" I say once I'm lying on my bed and staring at the ceiling.

"To be close to you," he replies evenly as he leans against the door jamb. Even at the edge of my emodar, I can tell he's getting irritated.

I give him a scathing look. "You are delusional. You think being in the same room and holding my hand is *close* to me? We couldn't be further apart right now."

"Why are you being so unreasonable?" he says angrily.

I sit up, furious. "*Me* unreasonable? Don't you get mad at *me*. This was *your* doing. Do you *honestly* expect me to want to be near you when I'm afraid that any moment you might reach over and touch me? I *have* been reasonable. But on this I will not bend. You've never taken the danger seriously, and as if that weren't bad enough, now you all but *force* me to endanger you!"

"I'm sorry I can't give you what you want, Wendy," he says. "I did make you a promise and I won't break it. I won't touch you until I have additional evidence."

"And how am I supposed to know when to be on guard? How do I know you won't read some message in the stars confirming your theory and then reach over and do it right then?"

"Don't patronize me, Wendy," he says bitterly, crossing his arms. "You'll know when I have the evidence I need, and then you can start running away from me, but doing it now will only hurt the happiness we have."

Tears flow silently down my face, and I say quietly, "How can I enjoy anything with you now knowing what you intend to do later?" I shake my head, my eyes closed. "You have given me no choice, Gabriel. None. So stop trying to make me feel even guiltier for pushing you away."

I turn my back toward him, lie down, and stare at the wall.

I pick up an edge of nauseating turmoil from him and I hope vainly that this is some kind of turning point. For at least a couple minutes he works through it, entertaining possible scenarios.

Eventually he leaps somewhere mentally that gives him assurance. "I love you, Wendy," he says softly. "I don't want to live without you. I won't."

His footsteps retreat.

His words have caught my attention though. They are the same words he said to me months ago right before he turned me over to Louise. Gabriel is always mindful of what he says. He said *those* words to send me a message. The first time, the message was that he was going to do whatever it took to keep me in his life. And what followed was him putting me into Louise's hands to rid me of the fear she took advantage of while I was under hypnotism.

Now? It sounds like he's going to do something equally drastic… But what? It stabs me with anxiety. And the depth of anguish. Gabriel has committed himself to a course of action. And I'm about to find out what that is.

***

At work the next morning, my cell phone rings. I don't recognize the number.

"Hello?" I say as I stamp a received by date on each piece of mail from the stack in front of me.

"Wendy?" says a female voice. I recognize it but I don't place it right away.

"Yeah?" I say, stopping mid-stamp.

"It's Kaylen!"

I set my stamp down. "Kaylen?" I exclaim, gripping the phone more firmly. "Oh my gosh! Where have you been?"

"Wendy, I need your help!" she insists.

"What is it?" I ask.

"My dad. He's been kidnapped."

"Really?" I ask, confused. "Louise?"

"Yes!" she says. "This morning when I woke up he was gone. There was a note from Louise left behind. She said if I want him back, I have to get you to give yourself up to her. I don't know what to do!"

Louise is using Kaylen after all…

"Where are you?" I ask.

"San Diego," she says. "And sorry. I only just got all your emails. I've been grounded from my phone and computer all summer… I didn't know you were trying to contact me."

"Geez, Kaylen," I say, stunned. I push away from my desk. "We've been worried about you. We thought this might happen, and we wanted to warn you. Looks like we were too late…"

"Wendy, what am I going to *do*? What if she hurts him? She says I have three days."

"Calm down," I say. "We'll figure this out. But first, we need to get *you* safe. I'll call my uncle. We'll come get you."

"Okay," she says, slightly relieved. "I really can't believe Louise did this. I mean my Dad *did* get mad at her for what went down at the compound but they've known each other for forever! It's like using your best friend as a hostage! That woman is so evil…" Kaylen's voice is pitched with outrage.

Best friends? Wow. Gabriel was right to think Kevin Fowler might know something about Louise.

"Kaylen, we'll figure it out. I am *so* glad you're okay. You have no idea how we've been worrying about you. I'm sorry my life is… screwing with yours. Louise is insane."

"She is going to *pay* for this," Kaylen says angrily, her voice laden with far more vengeance than fear. "And none of this is your fault. I have you to thank for getting the compound shut down. If it weren't for that, I'd still be there."

I sigh. "Man, I wish we'd gotten a hold of you sooner. We might have prevented this."

"Yeah. My dad is totally to blame for that one since he's the one that grounded me," she says with slight bitterness. "Although I bet even if you *had* warned him he wouldn't have taken it seriously. This is really just so weird. I never thought Louise would do something like this to him, not after how long they've known each other."

That's the second time she's said that. Just what kind of relationship do Fowler and Louise have anyway?

"How long *has* your dad known Louise?" I ask.

"Not sure," Kaylen says. "They knew each other before I was born. That's all I know."

A spike of anticipation moves through me. I wonder if there's any chance Kaylen's father knew mine. My dad would have died around the time Kaylen was born and if her father and mine both knew Louise at the time... What if Kevin Fowler knows something about my Dad's condition that might help me? I bet he does. I bet Louise has been watching us and knows we've been looking for Kaylen and that if we found her, Kevin might tell me something useful. I bet that's what this is. Louise is making sure she has the monopoly on any information that might help me. She's trying to make it so I have to go to her. *She's trying to back me into a corner.*

My eyes narrow. I'm not afraid of Louise; she's going to regret this. She obviously didn't learn her lesson when she kidnapped me before. If she's hoping to make me desperate for her help, backing me into a corner is the best way to ensure that *won't* happen.

"We'll get him back, Kaylen. She's not going to get away with this," I say severely.

Once I get off the phone, I feel a headache coming on. I test my blood sugar quickly before calling Robert, not expecting anything out of the ordinary, but instead find my glucose in the forties. I'm grateful I brought juice to work today, but I still wonder what on earth is going on with me. But more important right now is Kaylen, and what's going on with her father.

22

"I have to admit I expected something more creative from Louise," Gabriel says, pacing the length of Robert's living room. We're waiting for Robert to meet up with us here. Mark and Farlen have been sent to San Diego to get Kaylen.

"Threatening to hurt Kaylen's father unless you come quietly?" Gabriel continues skeptically. "Then what? How does she control you?"

Information, I think to myself, but I say nothing. I haven't shared my suspicions about what Kevin Fowler may know either. It's just a hunch anyway.

"That old bat is clever," Ezra says. "She could probably come up with a way." He looks at me critically. "You're not actually thinking of giving yourself up to her, are you?"

I don't want to answer that question. But when Gabriel stops and looks at me expectantly, I say, "Of course I'm considering it. But I haven't decided anything yet."

"Forget it," Gabriel says. "You can't do it. Ezra's right. *We* may not have imagined all of the ways she might control you, but that's because we aren't as ruthless as she is."

I raise my eyebrows defiantly. "Forget it? Until when? Louise sends us Fowler's body parts one by one? We have three days. Louise has no reason to bluff."

"I think the solution is to find her first," Gabriel says.

"We've been *trying* to do that, Gabe," Ezra says. "Now that she's almost got what she wants, she's not going to let her guard down and let us find her."

Gabriel groans. "There *has* to be a way to find her."

"We find her by turning me over to her," I say. "All we have to do is give you some way to track me down once she has me."

Gabriel shakes his head as he starts pacing. "She's too smart for that. She'll have devised exactly how to disappear with you once she has you."

"I'm not afraid of her," I say. "And I'll die going for her throat before I hurt anyone."

"That's exactly what I'm worried about," Gabriel says quietly, stopping to look at me. "Louise underestimates your conviction. She doesn't comprehend why someone would give their life simply to live morally. Therefore she discounts it. I believe she *would* expect you to kill someone. And when you defend yourself or attempt to escape, she'll be forced to hurt or kill you."

I don't have an answer for him that will assuage his doubts. He may be right. But he may also be wrong. Louise is using Kevin Fowler, someone I have never met, don't really like, and have no obligation toward, to blackmail me. She obviously believes I'd give myself up even for a relative stranger. She's demonstrated how well she *does* know my convictions—at least in part—just in her choice of hostage.

Robert appears at the front door then, slightly red-faced with wide eyes. We can tell by the look on his face that he's got news.

"Langston just picked up movement on Stenworth," he says. "An ATM in Riverside. Footage shows it's Louise."

I jump up. "Really?"

"That was fast…" Ezra says.

"With a location narrowed down, I'm going to try for a vision on finding her," Robert says. "Maybe she has Fowler there… In the meantime, go home and pack. We'll be staying in Redlands for at least a night."

"What about Kaylen?" I ask, weirdly suspicious. How did Robert find Louise so fast? How did Louise let herself get found like that?

"Farlen and Mark are still in the air. They'll meet up with Kaylen in an hour or so. But we don't have time to wait for them to get here. I've chartered a private flight to Riverside. Meet us at the airport."

"Gracias al fantasma de Einstein!" Gabriel says, throwing his hands up.

"Nick of time," Ezra says, shaking his head.

I don't argue. I grab my shoulder bag and head for the door, Gabriel behind me.

Nick of time. Yeah, I bet.

***

As I pull the zipper shut on my duffel bag, I stop and close my eyes, trying not to think about what finding Louise might mean. But it doesn't work. I want Fowler back for Kaylen of course, but I also want to get in front of Louise. She must know something about my condition. But Louise has never willingly spilled information unless it helps her. What's more, you can never tell what's truth. But still… I can't help hoping that all this is going to save my marriage somehow… *in the nick of time*.

When I come back into the living room, Gabriel is tying his shoes. I wait patiently by the door, worrying over his elusive plans again. We're about to do something that is possibly dangerous. I can't spend any time worrying about Gabriel.

He hops up, pulling a backpack over his shoulders. I open my mouth, figuring out what to say to get some kind of assurance from him.

He holds up a hand and rolls his eyes. "Wendy, I have more sense than you give me credit for. Why would I even *think* about touching you when we're about to do something that's probably going to require us working together?"

"No, Gabriel. You do *not* have that kind of sense," I retort. "Taking advantage of the situation is what you do. And this is just such a situation."

He tilts his head and nods slightly. "I guess I can see how you'd come to that conclusion…" Then he looks at me. "Wendy, I promise you that for the duration of this trip or until we find Kevin Fowler, whichever is longer, I will not touch your skin."

I sigh and turn to the door. As usual, Gabriel only gives me part of what I ask for.

***

"I'm so curious what it looks like from up here," Gabriel says, sitting down next to me on the plane. "Would you like a channel?"

A small smile forms on my face as I look over at him. "I guess you read my mind."

"Not exactly," he admits. "But you were staring out of that window so intently… and you were tapping your foot in the air—I've noticed you do that when you're impatient."

I fidget in my seat. "Of course I'm impatient. I'm ready to be on the ground so we can hunt down Louise."

"True. But I also saw you close your eyes and get that look on your face like you do when you're trying to go into the colorworld… Didn't look like you were successful in going there on your own."

"Wow, Gabriel. You're kind of a stalker, you know that?"

He chuckles. "I'm married to you now so I figure I can watch you all I want. I think it's one of the perks of matrimony."

I don't want to go anywhere near the topic of our marriage so I smile and say, "Okay, well give me your arm."

Rather than giving me his arm, he gives me his hand. He entwines his fingers with my gloved ones deliberately. I look down at our hands and can't suppress the butterflies his close proximity brings. It seems that no matter how at odds we are, he still has the same effect on me. It's helped by his mutual contentment that melts the parts of me that have been frozen for so long by indifference toward him.

I love him so much...

I have to force back the desperate want I feel for him. I have to choke off pleading with him to rethink this. I want to *beg* him to stop this and let things go back to how they were...

I turn to my senses instead, focusing them in the right way so I can pull myself into the colorworld quickly.

"I don't see the vapor here," I say, looking around the cabin. "That confirms it's only visible in the dark. And everything is back to its usual brightness..."

Gabriel is silent, but I know he hangs on my every word as he weaves the new facts in with what he already knows. I look to the window.

It takes a special kind of focus to see through glass or anything transparent. It has its own movement and luminosity in the colorworld. I don't quite know how it happens, but I have to relax my eyes just so in order to see past it with the same clarity that I would in the visible world. A screen over a window, for example, is easy to see past in the visible world. You choose not to focus, hardly thinking about it. But the colorworld moves so much that this is more difficult. I have to consciously focus.

"It's like... some kind of psychedelic aurora," I say in wonder, describing the view beyond the window. A human soul is the most incredible *experience* in the colorworld, but the sky definitely holds the most visual beauty. "It's kind of disorienting to look at for long because it's changing so quickly." I blink my eyes a few times. "It's like combining different colored oils of varying weights together and seeing the undulating ribbons mingle, never really mixing."

When the sky becomes too much, I look down. We're still pretty high up but we've been making a gradual descent. Since my eyesight is so good, I can already see buildings and cars and people below with ease. But their texture and movement isn't yet apparent.

Wait. I can see people*?*

"Oh my gosh..." I breathe. "The people... they're like... purple Christmas lights. They're obviously brighter than everything else."

I can't make out anything else about them, but it's clear from up here that their light has a reflective effect. "People light up the things around them," I marvel.

Gabriel is bursting inside. "What else?" he asks when I don't continue.

"It's like an animated world painted in all the wrong colors...but the people... I can't get over how they stand out... like beacons." Something about the people being so bright in a world that is already so bright and beautiful... It's mysterious and... heavy. To see them in the context of the surface of the earth fills me with a deep worth that I don't understand. People are... important here, though I can't place why exactly.

As I move my focus over to a park, I see quite a few flaming purple lights milling around, oblivious to their stunning beauty and impact. Tears fall from my eyes in awe. I wish they knew what they looked like.

Why? I can't say exactly. But I can't help wishing that they knew.

"What is it?" Gabriel whispers gently.

I shake my head. "I don't really know... Their life forces are just... significant." I look to Gabriel's purple life force and unfocus to see his face. "Do you get what I mean?"

He thinks, longing to see what I do. "People are... more?" he offers. I hear what he says, but I'm distracted by his life force. His scent has flooded my nose. It reminds me of a thousand moments I've shared with him. It reminds me of the intrinsic goodness within him, the unwavering dedication that only he possesses. The presence of his soul so close to me, permeating my senses, warms me through, as if circulating through my veins to reach every part of me. Connecting with Gabriel in the colorworld is always a memorable experience, but this time it's different. I think because I came here while so at-odds with him, his unique worth thrusts itself upon me, reminding me that all the negative things I've been amassing in my head about him are fleeting compared to what he is in actuality. His familiarity is new again, like everything I thought I knew about him is even more incredible than before.

The strings of my heart are knit with his; I want him near me always. I long for him through every strand of my soul—and that's what it feels like. My soul has missed his, and here in the colorworld, it's so much more profound than missing him with my fleeting emotions. It transcends my body. It reminds me when we made love with our souls. Remembering that reminds me of the bond we forged between us that night that I don't think can easily be undone.

Gabriel watches my expression. My attention melts him and he doesn't withhold the reverent affection he so easily bestows on me whenever I open myself to him.

I look back out the window; I can't go there right now with him. "Yeah… more," I say, at odds with myself. Like I can't reconcile my body and my life force.

I spend a couple minutes watching the people below, inviting amazement once more so I can stop thinking about how Gabriel's life force infiltrates me so fully in the colorworld. I articulate a bit more how the souls of the people below affect me. I have conviction that I know—*truly* know—the loveliness of each of them even though I can't see their faces. It's an intrinsic feeling rather than a perceived one.

All of a sudden something else catches my breath: their life forces definitely vary in brightness. I don't think I've been able to see it before because life forces are so bright up close. But this far away the differences are obvious. Some souls are clearly brighter than others by minute but detectable degrees—say seventy-five watt versus ninety watt.

I'm about to tell Gabriel, but stop. I know exactly how he'll take that piece of information. In fact, I worry I've already said too much, having just told him that a human soul illuminates the things around it. I'm actually afraid that he's going to ask me if their brightness varies…

Gabriel has picked up on my compounded wonder though and I struggle for something to say that will explain my reaction. And that's when I notice something else.

"Oh my gosh… I think I see the energy vapor. But from up here it's more like a haze over everything."

For several more minutes, I'm silent as I take it in, my eyes darting this way and that as I look for anything else I've missed. We are now much closer to the ground and the vapor is less apparent since we've descended into it. The texture of the buildings and earth becomes more and more obvious. I sigh and release Gabriel's hand.

"Wow," I say, watching the ground from the window, so still and… empty now of the lights that give it life.

"El Ceilo," Gabriel says. "The colorworld keeps giving and giving, doesn't it?"

I don't turn to look at him, not wanting to guess if there is double meaning in his words. I continue to look out the window. "This world is so dark," I lament.

"In so many ways," Gabriel agrees.

23

With all Robert's hired suits around, I feel like I'm in cahoots with a drug lord. There are at least a half a dozen of them all with wrist communicators, smartphones, and guns strapped to their hips. Everyone wears dark jackets.

Robert told us before we left Monterey that Farlen and Mark have Kaylen. They're waiting to hear from us about where to go next, whether to meet us in Riverside or go back to Monterey. First we need to see if finding Louise is going to pan out. And we're still waiting to hear whether Robert was successful in getting a vision.

When we're finally in a car, a spacious SUV, I lean forward from the back seat. "So what's the plan?" I ask eagerly.

"I need to focus," Robert says, loosening his tie a bit and sitting back in his seat as our driver gets us moving. "I didn't have much luck on the plane, but I'm going to keep trying. Things can change quickly."

I frown. That doesn't really explain *anything*. I want to ask more questions, but I don't want to disturb him. I sit back. I was really excited about this development, but now the whole thing seems really up in the air. Still, if Robert mobilized all these people, he must be confident that he can turn something up.

Gabriel and Ezra are on either side of me and we all remain silent, even afraid to whisper. Ezra watches the scenery speeding by; Gabriel is thinking, as always; and I concentrate on reading Robert.

I can't get over how quiet Robert's emotional currents are. Not that I expect them to be stronger now that he's meditating, but I've found that the more reserved a person is, the more they fade into the background. He is so easily overshadowed by others, like Gabriel. *His* emotions are so intense at times that 'listening' to him in deep thought, for example, is like a staring contest. With Gabriel, however, it's the "focus contest." I see which of us can focus our thoughts the longest. I always lose, of course—not that Gabriel has any idea I'm trying to out-focus him. The way he can shift from one intense line of reasoning to another is unreal. I never know exactly what he's thinking about, but I know his thoughts shift because the underlying emotion also shifts. It's a subtle thing that I only pick up if I've been around a person enough.

Robert is unusually controlled in a different way. Now, as I listen to him meditate, I realize that what I usually feel from Robert as emotional suppression is actually labored focus. It's not analytical like Gabriel's; it's concentration. I don't think I have ever felt anyone with so much mental discipline. As I finally articulate this, I think I get now how Robert has acquired all that he has. To be able to moderate your emotions that way would allow you to deal more shrewdly and objectively… I can't tell if this is a good thing or a bad thing. It sounds like the perfect recipe for corruption—the ability to disregard everything in favor of the outcome you want.

I don't have the energy anymore to labor over what to make of Robert. He hasn't done anything but help me. He deserves my trust. So instead I wonder what one idea he's settled on. Finding Louise I guess? I wonder if he uses words for his goal, or does he visualize something? Maybe he's focused on Louise's face?

I watch the back of his head for a long time, waiting for the exact moment he gets a vision, but the stillness of his mind gets tedious.

I look out the window and realize that we must be going well over the speed-limit. I see the sign welcoming us to Riverside; I think we just made a twenty minute trip in ten.

Robert's thoughts shift subtly just then and my eyes flit back to his head. He sits very still for about ten seconds and then relaxes. He takes a heavy breath.

"Did you get something?" I ask.

He turns in his seat with a look of uneasy surprise. "Yes…" he says tentatively. "How did you know?"

"I felt it."

"Oh…" he replies, slightly disturbed. "Good thing I didn't know you were mind-staring me so hard. I never would've been able to concentrate."

"She's always peeping at people's thoughts, even though it's none of her business," Ezra pipes up. "You get used to it." Then he grins at me.

Robert gives a little start. "You can do that?"

"No," I scoff, giving Ezra a look. "But it seems that way when I'm working really hard to read someone's emotions."

"Don't be fooled, Robert," says Gabriel from beside me. "Her ability makes her better at ascertaining thoughts than she lets on. Sometimes I would bet my mother's foot that she actually *can* read minds even though she claims otherwise."

I look over at him. "Since when is your mother's foot something to swear on?"

He shrugs. "I don't know; it just came to me."

I chuckle. Gabriel will most likely never cease to make me laugh, even without intending to.

Robert is still bothered.

"Don't worry," I tell him. "I really can't. If I could, I would be sure to let everyone know. It wouldn't be fair to do it secretly. That's rude," I say, making a face.

"Oh that endearing moral compass of yours. I'd like to take it to dinner sometime and ask it a hundred questions," says Gabriel, leaning back in the seat and crossing his arms behind his head.

"Focus, Gabriel," I say to break him out of what is surely going to be another attempt to get on my good side.

I turn back to Robert. "What did you find out?"

"Find out?" says Robert. "That's not really how it works, but I do have a lead. And I think it's solid. I'm thinking we should go find a particular psychic who's situated outside of downtown."

"What?" I ask, confused. "Is that where Fowler is?"

"I'm not sure," replies Robert. "I can't get a good vision on Fowler so we should treat it as it pertains to Louise. She could be seeing a psychic, staying with a psychic, living as a psychic, or it could be that she knows one. Or maybe there's a psychic who has seen her and will be able to point us in the right direction."

"So we go find this psychic and knock on the door and ask?" I say.

Robert shrugs. "Maybe. But the catch is we don't go until dusk."

"What?" I say, confused.

"Wendy, remember it's a right place and right *time* impression," he says patiently. "The time is dusk."

"But wouldn't it be a good idea to at least check this place out?" I protest.

"I have no idea what or who is at this place or how it correlates to Louise. If we go early and disturb the scene it could change things enough that we miss our mark. Trust me, I've learned that the hard way."

"Interesting," Gabriel says, speculative. "You have an example?"

Robert hesitates for some reason, but then he says, "Years ago, I wanted to hire a young man who was supposed to be an exceptional talent in server security. He was sought after though. I used my ability and got a vision that I should be at a particular restaurant at a certain time. I paid a big tip to get a table at the last minute. My intention was to watch and wait to figure out why I was supposed to be there. I assumed it was something like the man showing up there where I could make a pitch when I saw him.

"Nothing came of it. At the end of the night, when I had seen no one I recognized of import and heard nothing of interest, I asked the host to see the reservation book. I learned that *my* reservation had actually taken the place of another one: the very young man I had gone there hoping to see. As it turned out, he had discovered that I had bumped him and refused to negotiate with me after that."

"Yes…" Gabriel muses. "Timing is obviously important."

"Correct," Robert says. "It's a tricky business, trying not to manipulate the ultimate outcome so much that my own agenda is disturbed."

"Okay," I say, impatiently resigned. "So tell me something. What did you focus on in order to get a vision about a psychic?"

"Wanting to find the person who could give me the most information on life force ability manifestation in Riverside."

"Why not Louise specifically?" Gabriel asks.

"A few reasons. For one thing I don't want to limit the vision to just Louise. If she is in Riverside, I have to guess she's here to meet with someone who works for her, or for other business. Chances are they practice energy medicine. Louise is the best. She trains the best. So finding the best narrows it down to her as well as those who are associated with her. It would be just as helpful for us to find someone who could help us find her."

"A specific person would probably make you have to do that compounding vision thing like you did with Wen, right?" Ezra says, referring to what Robert explained to us after he rescued Gabriel and me from Louise. It means he has to use a vision to narrow down a previous vision.

"Exactly," Robert says, smiling. "What's more, limiting my goal to one person also limits the possible ways to achieve it. The key is to insert myself in the right place, in the *path* of events, rather than directly affecting them. It's a constant balance of being specific but not *too* specific."

"Fascinating," breathes Gabriel, his eyes unfocused as he thinks about it.

"If your ability is about achieving specific goals that pertain directly to you, wouldn't it have been better to think something like wanting to find someone who could help you develop your ability in Riverside?" I say, still skeptical at his method.

"That would be a lie. It actually has to be something I want. You can't really lie outright to yourself, you know," Robert replies.

I nod, pensive. At first Robert's ability seemed like a dream come true, but now it sounds like a guessing game.

"What's your success rate?" asks Ezra, who has been silent up until now. He takes the words right out of my mouth.

"On a first go like this? It's improved over the years. I would say fifty-percent," says Robert.

"You're saying we only have a fifty percent chance of actually finding Louise, or whoever she's working with?" I ask, incredulous.

"Fifty percent is better than zero isn't it?" asks Robert. "We have to take advantage because if this fails, a second chance will be unlikely. Remember, Louise knows about my ability and she has been working to avoid me. Usually, when I have a goal, I focus on it over and over every day to narrow down a plan of action. In fact, I often get multiple visions that I piece together to get information about how to go about a goal in the first place. I don't typically get one vision and jump on it like we're doing now."

I guess that makes sense. There are only a million variables that affect how one course of action affects an outcome. It really is like predicting the future. And if you were going to predict the future, you'd want to tap into it multiple times until it settled on something more permanent you could depend on to get decent results.

"Wendy, it's essentially predicting the future. What's more variable than that?" Gabriel says.

"Yes, that just occurred to me," I say.

"Of course it did," he sighs. "I always discount your—"

"Yeah, yeah," Ezra interrupts. "Wen's amazing and brilliant. So what do we do in the meantime?"

"We have to figure out exactly where this psychic is," says Robert.

"You don't know?" I say.

"No, I only know what the building looks like," he replies. "I'll know it when I see it."

"How do you know when to be there?"

"Because of where the sun is. Context clues in the vision give me the time. Sometimes I simply wait around an area inconspicuously until I get an idea as to why exactly I'm there."

"How do you know we're supposed to go there today?" This sounds more and more like inevitable failure.

"I don't. But the vision was very clear. If it's farther in the future, it doesn't usually settle easily. I'm almost positive it's today given how specific the goal is and the fact that we *know* Louise is in Riverside or at least has been recently. We got very lucky, actually, that I saw such a definite vision so quickly, and it's something we can carry out today," he says. "I'm confident, although it's unusual to have such quick success like this."

"I'll say," I reply, only halfway sarcastic. I don't think it's lucky at all, but I have to have faith in what Robert knows about his ability.

The car decelerates and Robert instructs the driver on which part of town to drive through.

"Eyes open, everyone," he says to us. "We're looking for an unobtrusive sign in a window with a woman's head beneath the words 'Psychic Reading.' It's kind of shabby, two stories, with a tree in the front. Let's see… the sun's position would indicate that it should be on the west side of the street."

"Can't we look up all the psychics in the phone book?" I ask, looking for a way to make this process more efficient. A sign in a window? How will we ever find such a thing? There must be hundreds of thousands of buildings in Riverside.

"Yes, but 'Psychic Reading' isn't very specific, and the place doesn't look like it merits a listing in the phone book," Robert says.

"You never know," I say. This is getting sillier by the minute.

"How are we supposed to find something we've never seen?" Ezra asks, more to himself than anyone else.

Doubt nags everyone but Robert. I'm outright annoyed; I don't even know what to look for which is a shame since I have by far the best eyesight…

"Wait!" I shout.

Everyone jumps and looks at me and then out the window, thinking I've spotted the sign already.

"Where?" Gabriel asks.

"No," I reply, "I mean stop looking. Robert should *show* me what he sees."

Ezra and Robert look confused, but Gabriel readily understands, and his eyes glow with zeal.

"I could kiss you right now!" he says enthusiastically. "What could be better than you seeing what he sees? You could spot it a mile away!"

"Exactly!" I say.

"Could you please explain what you two are going on about?" Ezra says.

"When I'm in the colorworld, the person I use to access it can send me thoughts and images. Gabriel and I discovered it by accident at the compound. Robert, you can *send* your vision to me so I know exactly what to look for. I should be able to spot it anywhere as long as it's unobstructed," I explain, not bothering to contain the huge smile on my face. Nothing feels better than being useful at a time like this.

Robert is stunned. "But you said you couldn't read minds."

"She can only see what you direct to her," Gabriel says, giving me a knowing look. "That's how I won her over, you know. Planted thoughts right in her head when she couldn't get away. A rather genius idea, I think."

I roll my eyes. "He's right, Uncle Rob. I can't get anything you don't send me, and it has to be while I'm in the colorworld, and you have to be my channel."

"You are such a freak, Wen," Ezra says.

I kick him in the leg and look expectantly at Robert, who seems hesitant. What is his problem? Is there something up there he doesn't want me to see?

Fortunately, it doesn't take him long to decide. "Alright," he says. "What do I do?"

"Gabriel?" I say, looking at him now. "You're the expert on this."

"It should be simple. You *will* the visual to her, like you're talking to her mentally," Gabriel explains. "If you imagine she can hear you, she will."

I scoot forward and put my hand on Robert's shoulder. Then I pull myself into the colorworld.

Robert is still slightly nervous, but I ignore it. There's no time to dwell on his apprehension.

"Okay, I'm there," I say, closing my eyes to the colors and waiting for something to come. I don't know that it helps, but I focus on Robert's mental current as much as I can.

The picture reaches me in pieces at first as Robert gets the hang of directing his thoughts to me. But it finally comes together, gaining more and more clarity with every moment. When it finally settles in my mind, I'm aggravated with how blurry it is, although I suspect that it only seems that way because my vision is so detailed. I want to ask him to focus more, but I don't want to break his meditation, and I'm sure he is already doing his best.

With a little more concentration on my part, I think I might actually be pulling the vision right out of his mind. Small details move into focus, although the picture is still extremely cloudy.

Once I've got it firmly, I say, "You're right about the time. The horizon has a stream of receding light and the front is really dark. It's hard to see clearly, but I think there are three numbers in the address—only I can't make out what they are. They aren't ones or sevens or fours. They're rounded numbers—eights, zeros, threes… I guess that's not super helpful. And the symbol on the sign is pretty distinct. It's not just a woman's head. It looks like a Medusa's head or maybe a woman with unruly hair. That should help. And I wouldn't say the building is shabby. It's old. The grass is well-kept, so I think it's probably in a decent neighborhood."

I open my eyes. Robert looks at me appreciatively. "That was perceptive of you with the address number. I can see what you mean, but even I can't make out the numbers enough to see that they're rounded. And then the sign and the age of the building… How did you do that—see more than I can see?"

I shrug. "I don't know. I guess I'm *used* to seeing more and I expect it, so I see it."

"Well that's not really helpful except that we can start a block in the triple digits and rule out a block once we hit the quadruple digits." Ezra says.

"Still amazing, however," Gabriel says.

"It is," agrees Robert, "I don't often get the outside of a building like this so it didn't occur to me to look for address numbers."

"If it's the inside of a place how do you have any idea where or what it is?" I ask, focusing on the passing buildings.

"I work harder to narrow down a good goal—that's the challenge. A good goal will almost always deliver a workable vision. And if I want a good one, I have to do my research beforehand."

Gabriel nods. "True omniscience is in knowing enough about the now to determine the most probable future. The power of foreknowledge is granted by perspective. Anything else would mean predestination. And I am not interested in having my future written in stone."

Ezra sighs exasperatedly. "Is there anything you *don't* have an opinion about?"

Gabriel is unperturbed by Ezra's tone as he considers it. He opens his mouth to reply and Ezra shakes his head and says, "Rhetorical, Gabe."

We spend a half-hour driving up and down every street before I decide this is a waste of time.

"You aren't utilizing the fact that I can see easily down any street without actually *driving* down it," I say to Robert. "You need to stay on main streets. We'll get through town much faster if we narrow it down."

"Narrow it down?" Robert asks.

"We need a map."

He thinks for a minute but doesn't argue. He passes instructions to the driver, and we stop to get a detailed city map.

"Help me work out a route, Gabriel," I say once I have it in my hands. I smooth it out on the seat of the car. "I can see about five blocks, so work in the cross-sectional routes that way."

Gabriel is delighted with the mental task and looks at the large paper eagerly. "The sun is setting behind the building so we only want to look at buildings facing east," he says. "So we stay on east/west main streets. We don't care about anything that's north/south."

"Yes!" I say, bobbing my head excitedly. This will definitely narrow it down. "You are a genius."

"Not without your encouragement. I say, get you focused on accomplishing something and you are pertinacious!"

Gabriel marks out certain areas with a pen and circles others. He then highlights the exact route to take.

"Impressive," Robert says appreciatively.

"Freeeeaks," Ezra whistles. "You two are so made for each other."

"Okay," Gabriel says. "We've got a working schematic. It shouldn't take long at all to cover."

I look nervously at the time which reads nearly five o'clock. We have, at best, three hours to find this place.

Robert changes seats with me and, still unhappy with my vantage point, I decide to sit on the armrest and poke my head through the sunroof. I'm sure I look silly, but I don't care. I'm not missing this opportunity to find Louise.

At least an hour passes while I look from side to side, resting my hands on the top of the car. I think I must be pushing my eyesight to the max by looking at every house and building on every street. Since I know exactly what the building looks like, and since I know that I'm only looking for places with triple-digit house numbers, I can easily disregard streets with numbers that don't qualify.

It seemed like such a good idea, but with each street we pass, I become less and less confident.

After another half-hour, however, I spot it. I catch my elbow painfully on the edge of the sunroof pulling myself through with such speed, but I breathlessly collapse in my seat and say, "I saw it! Turn around. The last stoplight!"

Everyone cranes their necks at once as the driver gets the car turned around. We pull down the street I indicate while I point enthusiastically.

"There! See it?" I say, plastering my face to the window.

"Where?" asks Ezra. "Be more specific."

"One… two… three… four blocks down. Right *there*!" I exclaim.

"Ironman's underwear, Wendy! I really thought you were stretching it with the five blocks thing," Ezra says. "You know we can't see it from here, right?"

"Sorry, I always forget."

"That's barking crazy. Four blocks away? And look at the sign. It's like two-feet wide! We never would have seen that," Ezra says in amazement as we get closer to the building.

"Agreed," says Robert as we pass by. "I doubt I would have tried this street. I had no idea it was a converted garage."

It *is* a garage, detached and remodeled long ago to look like a shop, and the neighborhood consists of residential older homes. It looks exactly like Robert's vision with the strange Medusa-like symbol beneath the words 'Psychic Reading.'

The building is aged, but the house next to it is stucco-finished with a welcome mat in the front. It's unobtrusive, and I wonder how this so-called psychic gets any clients.

"Okay, so we found it. Now we come back later?" I ask as the place passes out of view.

"We need to come up with a plan," Robert says. "I think we should arrange for a couple of us to take a walk, maybe on the other side of the street as the time approaches. I think our best bet is to observe, and then hopefully we'll understand why we're supposed to be there."

"Can we talk about it over dinner?" asks Ezra. "I'm starved."

"Absolutely," Robert replies and then pulls out his phone to issue orders.

"So which of us could possibly take a walk without being recognized?" I ask after he hangs up.

"I think we should have my people do it." Robert replies.

I grimace. "I'm sure they're skilled and all but I don't like leaving Louise's capture in someone else's hands."

Gabriel speaks up then, "Well I think a better use of your talents would be long-range surveillance, Wendy. You could obviously see what's going on. You could even hear what's going on, couldn't you?"

"Yep," I say, smiling. "That should be no problem." I relish the knowledge that my usually useless abilities are serving a real purpose today. That's it. I need to join the CIA.

"We'll station people around the neighborhood and have someone walk by close to dusk," Robert says. "In the meantime, we'll find a place for Wendy to watch. I'll get Dean to set you up with radios, and then we'll decide what action to take once we know why we're there."

24

Branches are digging into my back and my knee is cramped from staying in the same position for so long. I'm starting to rethink climbing this tree; I feel like a peeping tom. I would have opted for a roof somewhere like Ezra suggested, but getting off of a roof is a lot harder than getting out of a tree in a crunch.

"Anything yet?" asks Ezra through my earpiece.

"Ezra, I will tell you as soon as I see anyone," I say into my wrist. "Stop yapping."

"Sorry, Wen. These communicators are so cool!" he replies back. "They're like spy gear. Uncle Rob is the bomb!"

"I'll attempt to control his exuberance, darling," Gabriel's voice adds. Gabriel and Ezra are positioned together a block closer to the psychic, behind a garage in an alleyway.

I continue watching the building for any signs of movement. From what we can tell, it's empty, but I'm not letting it out of my sight. Still, the sun is swiftly setting, and I don't see anything at all. I haven't given up hope yet though—the lighting is not quite right. Maybe we're waiting for Louise to arrive.

There hasn't been much movement along the street either. Sometimes people come home. Sometimes they leave. I hear everything going on in the homes around me. I'll more likely hear something before I'll see it. I'm starting to gauge distance better. I can push easily past the voices in my immediate vicinity, taking note of which sounds are farther and which are closer. I have been practicing this for a while now, pulsing out my auditory sense to get an idea of my surroundings based on sounds alone.

I pick up Gabriel's voice then, *not* through my communicator, and it grabs my attention. "Ezra, honestly. She'll tell us when she sees anything at all."

"I hate sitting here. Can't we have at least hidden somewhere where we could actually *see* the street? We're going to miss everything!" Ezra hisses in annoyance.

"The point is to *not* be seen," says Gabriel. "I don't like leaving Wendy out there with no one to protect her, but she has to be there, and *we* have to be here. Now can you be quiet and wait? Do some math problems in your head or something. Cripes. Wendy, if you're listening, your brother is now behaving his age."

I smile and whisper loudly over my radio, "Shut it, Ezra."

I continue to reach out with my ears, moving further away, toward the psychic's office. I can't be sure if I'm tuned in at the right distance, so I fluctuate my hearing in the area I think the building lies in. I still can't match what I hear with what I see, and I'm mad that I've not perfected this skill sooner.

"She can *hear* that far? Holy Batman, Wen, you're like Superman!" Ezra says. I'm stretching my senses out so far, it sounds like he's right next to me even though I know he's a block away.

I hiss over the radio again, "Ezra, could you please shut up? I can't concentrate with you yelling at me!"

"That's amazing!" says Ezra.

"Ezra, quiet already. Did you forget your Ritalin or something? Why are you so hyper?" says Gabriel.

"I don't take Ritalin," grumbles Ezra. "I'm just jumpy. I can't take the suspense."

I am about to tell him to shut up again when he says, "Okay, okay. I'm quiet now, I swear."

I wait a moment, and when I hear nothing from him I focus on listening toward the psychic's building again. Still no movement there, but the sun has just set. We have only minutes before dusk officially becomes night.

I listen intently again, and all of a sudden Louise's voice hits me like a bad dream, "Yes, this morning… I'll be staying in public areas as much as possible. It shouldn't take them too long. I'm on my way to a music festival. I think that's a good place to start. If you don't hear from me, you know what to expect."

"She's there!" I hiss into the radio as I leap out of the tree, rolling my ankle a little in the process. I curse as I stand back upright and limp to the sidewalk.

"Wendy! Do *not* move from your position. We need eyes and ears," says Gabriel's voice in my ear.

"You gotta head to the psychic. I swear she's there. I just heard her!" I say back.

"Everyone move in on the building," orders Robert's voice in my ear. I know he has about five other men positioned around the area.

I do my best to shake off the pain in my ankle and run as fast as it will let me. Now that I'm on the ground, the distance that seemed so short to my ears is now a ridiculously long expanse to my eyes and legs. It's disorienting.

I see two other figures running in the distance: Gabriel and Ezra. That's not surprising. They were positioned a good hundred yards closer to the building than I was.

My ankle throbs insistently; it's all I can do to focus on moving my feet through the pain. It seems like forever, but I'm nearly there. Robert's men emerge from all sides of the place looking confused. They have their guns drawn.

"Wendy!" says Robert, out of breath. "There's no one here! I thought you said you heard her voice."

"I did!" I say, looking around like Louise might jump out from behind a bush. "You checked inside?"

"The entire place is locked and dark. There's no one here," Robert says, confused.

Gabriel comes up to me then. "You heard her but she's not here. Are you sure it was from this direction?"

"Yes!" I say. "I heard it like it was right next—" I stop. Louise must have been closer. I heard her voice right after I listened for Gabriel and Ezra.

I shake my head. "No, she was closer to the tree I was in. It couldn't have been this far away. Stupid! I jumped to conclusions. Quick! We have to head back the other direction!"

I start forward only to be reminded of the state of my ankle. At the same time, I recognize that dusk has blackened into night, dashing any hope in Robert's vision.

"Are you alright?" asks Gabriel, catching my arm as I fall forward.

"Yes, I just twisted my ankle when I fell out of that stupid tree," I say. "I'm not going to be able to run back there. Go. I'll be fine. Hurry."

Robert and his men have already headed back in the direction I pointed out. Gabriel hesitates but he runs off after them.

Ezra is about to follow, but I grab his arm. "Hold it. You are hardly old enough to be chasing after bad guys. Someone's got to keep me company."

He groans in aggravation but doesn't argue.

I sigh at the sky; it's becoming velvety black. Why did Robert see this stupid psychic sign in his vision? Louise doesn't have anything to do with the place.

Several things happen in quick succession: I look up to watch Gabriel's back as he runs. He's about fifty yards away. Then I see a pair of headlights pull out of a driveway beyond him and turn in my direction. Gabriel stops mid-stride, nearly toppling over as he turns back toward us and yells, "Run!"

I'm confused. Then I see the car again. It must be Louise. I push Ezra toward the side of the building and jog out to the end of the driveway. I want her to see me and slow down. Maybe it will give Robert's men time to catch up with her.

It works. The car jolts to a stop in the middle of the street about twenty yards away from me. Only then do I see two other vehicles approaching from the opposite direction—Robert's men I think. The door opens then and Louise steps out carrying a gun. She glances toward the approaching vehicles and then back at me. To my left Gabriel is running with a few of Robert's men. Ezra is next to me now, placing himself in immediate danger. Louise won't hurt *me*, but she won't hesitate to hurt Ezra. Or Gabriel or Robert or anyone else. I need to distract her.

I make another split-second decision. I am *not* going to lose Louise.

"Stay here," I order Ezra. Then I run for Louise.

25

Louise raises her gun. Fear shoots through me. But I don't stop. I close my eyes and bolt for her. I don't want to kill her. I need her alive.

I hear the click of a chamber, and then a shot.

I shuffle to a stop, expecting the bullet to have found me. But when I open my eyes, Louise is on her knees, cradling her arm. There's blood near her shoulder. Her gun lies on the ground a couple of feet away from her. Someone must have shot her before she could shoot me.

Louise looks up at me now, and I swear she's annoyed, like she can't believe we had the nerve to send a bullet her way. But she also looks relieved that I've stopped coming at her.

Ezra comes up beside me. Gabriel moves past us, kicks Louise's gun further away from her reach, and then grabs her hands and twists them behind her back. He pulls her to her feet smoothly. His movements are surprisingly practiced. Louise cringes, blood staining her yellow shirt where the bullet struck her.

At that moment I notice that Louise is not alone. She has a driver. And he's raising his gun toward us.

"Look out!" I shout, leaping between Ezra and the shooter.

But as soon as I say it, Louise whips her head around. "Oh for Pete's sake, Stiles, do you really think that's a good idea?"

The guy hesitates, lowers his gun and drops it to the ground. One of Robert's guys comes up behind him, and grabs his arms, cuffing his wrists.

"We've got to get out of here," says Robert.

I look around. He's right. People have turned their porch lights on. A couple brave ones are peeking around their doors and through their curtains to see what's going on. They must have heard the gunshot.

Robert begins issuing orders and everyone finds a vehicle. I end up behind the wheel of Louise's car with Ezra in the passenger seat and Gabriel with Louise in the rear. He has her expertly pinned into the seat. I hear her muffled groans.

"Uh, have you done that before?" I ask as I drive, surprised at his skill again.

He glances up. "I've taken extensive self-defense classes."

"No kidding," remarks Ezra.

Before I get to the main road, Robert comes over the radio, "Take the 91 freeway north."

I search for the sign, refraining from speeding so I don't capture the wrong attention. After a few stoplights, I find the freeway, edging into the steady but uncongested flow of traffic.

"Where's Fowler, Louise?" I ask, breaking the silence, keeping my eyes trained on the road ahead.

"Let me go and I'll tell you," Louise says calmly, her voice muffled against the back seat.

It's not like I expected her to answer my question, but asking is a good place to start. She's as unreadable as ever though. Louise is in pain, but underneath that she's so serene that I'd think she considers this a vacation.

"So… your life for his?" I say to her.

"No reason to complicate it," she says easily.

I wonder that Louise isn't upset that her plans have been foiled. And she's not even afraid at all… But that is not something I've ever felt from her. In fact, the only time I've ever seen Louise afraid was when I ran for her only ten minutes ago. Now that I think about it, she was probably intending to surrender herself. With Robert's men prepared to block the road in front of her, she had to stop and give herself up. She only waved the gun at me because I was attacking her. Louise does *not* want me dead.

"Why aren't you disappointed?" I ask.

"I never look back," she replies.

Her indifference worries me. She's like a lion, stalking patiently, waiting for the right moment to pounce. I shiver involuntarily. She's probably thinking up some *new* way to manipulate me.

"Maybe you should start," I say. "So far your methods aren't working very well."

Louise chuckles. "You imagine you know what my goal is. What's more, you imagine success can be had without failure along the way. You imagine a lot of false things, dear."

I work hard to not read into or wonder about her words. She knows how to give away just enough information to drive a person crazy and I need to be clear-headed now.

"A pair of cuffs are in the glove box," Louise says. "It would be more comfortable for Gabe. He doesn't have a seatbelt on, you know. Safety first."

"You're always so practical, Louise," says Gabriel. "I would like you a lot more if you weren't always trying to kill people."

Ezra reaches into the glove box and I say, "Gabriel, make sure she doesn't have a key or something on her. She might be practical, but she's also a liar."

Ezra hands the cuffs back, and I hear Gabriel snap them on. Louise's unruffled expression appears in my rearview mirror. I feel violated having her delusional mind flooding my own.

Robert's voice comes over the radio again, "Head west on the 10. We'll go to my home in Redlands. I'll pass you once we get closer, and you can follow me there."

"Copy," says Ezra into his wrist, grinning.

I roll my eyes at his apparent glee.

"These things are so cool," he replies defensively. "I can't help it."

"It's so *good* to see you back with your brother," Louise says warmly. "And congratulations on your marriage. And you've been managing your condition… That's such good news."

I glance in the rearview mirror to eye Louise who is looking out her window. Of course.

"Thank you," Gabriel says cordially. "You know, Louise, I think since we won this round *and* the last one, we deserve some information. We'll consider it a wedding gift."

Louise smiles sweetly at him. "Oh Gabe, Wendy is so lucky to have you, unafraid to champion her cause. She might come around yet and be of some use."

"Murder is not a use," I say. And then I grip the wheel tighter. "You know what? Never mind. I don't even know why I'm explaining morality to someone like you."

"And your brand of morality *is* a use?" she questions. "How is that working for you? Since we're talking about effective methods and all…"

I grit my teeth. "It's working great. I have you, don't I? All I want from you now is Kaylen's father and then everything will be just peachy."

Louise laughs lightly. "Is that *all* you want from me? You aren't a very good negotiator, dear."

I keep my mouth shut. I'm not going to spar words with her when all she'll try to do is get under my skin.

"You know what we want from you," Gabriel says though, disdainfully. "You've taken Wendy hostage, tried to coerce her into murdering her own brother, and then you kidnapped Kaylen's father. You know, your aspirations might be better met if you'd tell people what you want instead of trying to manipulate things out of them. Just a word of advice. You catch more flies with honey."

Robert's taillights pass me and I pay closer attention to the road to make sure I don't lose him.

"Yes, I know all about flies," Louise replies. "And they aren't much use next to the honey pool. And *this* one would hang out by it all day if given the chance. She sees nothing beyond the blinders of her own problems. Fear is the only thing that feeds her, *moves* her. This I know. She is *just* like her father was."

"Fear?" I snort. "I'm not *afraid* of you. I don't *need* you, Louise. No matter what you say or do, that will never change."

Ezra reaches over and puts a hand on my arm. He sends me an invisible current of warning; I'm letting Louise get to me.

I take a cleansing breath and concentrate on the road for a while.

"I'm willing to wait until the fear ripens," Louise says several minutes later as if she's talking to herself. "Patience: another ingredient of success."

Louise isn't giving anything away. And she definitely has plans.

I sigh; I'm tired all of a sudden.

Robert has led us off of the freeway and into the ritzy gated neighborhood of his Redland's home. The neighborhood has been landscaped with copious vegetation so that it's reminiscent of being in the woods. Massive houses poke up through the trees periodically.

We pull in front of Robert's home, an intimidating monstrosity that is much nicer than the one in Monterey—which is saying a lot since that one is impressive all by its self. We stop in front of the garage around the back.

Two men come forward to take hold of Louise. They pull her inside while the rest of us follow. They handcuff her to a heavy piece of workout equipment in Robert's home gym.

I walk up to her and put my hands on my hips, watching her. I finally have Louise…

What now?

"Can we get her bandaged up?" I say, noticing the crimson stain on her shirt again.

"Of course," Robert says quietly, not moving his eyes from Louise. I don't think I've ever seen Robert look at someone so intently. He uncrosses his arms and waves a hand behind him. One of his men appears out of nowhere with a first aid kit.

The man examines Louise's injury and declares that it's a flesh wound. Louise doesn't react or respond to anyone while she gets taken care of.

Meanwhile, about a thousand questions run through my head, but I bite my tongue. I don't want to give her the opportunity to exploit my insecurities.

I want this over. I'm sick of this. Of Louise. Of my situation. Of everyone. I find it hard at the moment to be incensed at her. I want answers too badly. And Louise must have them. My marriage and the rest of my life depend on the information she's been harboring.

I lied.

I *do* need Louise. And needing Louise is never a good place to be in.

26

"Robert, dear," Louise says as if she's just now noticed him in the room. "How *are* you?" Her shoulder is now bandaged, which changes her mood all of a sudden from close-lipped prisoner to Grandma come to pay a visit for the weekend.

Robert stares at her, undaunted. This is a side of him I've never experienced. It's kind of intimidating. After several silent beats—just like Robert is known for—he says quietly but with conviction, "You will not trap her like you did Carl, Louise. I won't allow it this time."

Louise laughs delightedly and it's eerily out of place. She looks back at Robert with a smile. "If I wanted to *trap* her, Robert, I'd find a far more… *clever* way to do it."

Robert doesn't flinch at what I'm sure were meant to be laden words. Instead he leans toward Louise slightly and says with an authoritative voice I've never heard him use, "Yes, I *do* know how to trap people if the need arises. As *you* can see. So whatever your plans are, you should bear that in mind."

"I will," Louise replies with a bizarre tone of gratitude that I doubt is genuine. "Impressive, indeed, how quickly you can work when you really want something. I'd say you've been holding out on people all these years." She glances over at me briefly.

I can't deny that riles my suspicion. And I want to ignore it because Louise is nothing if not manipulative in her every word. But I don't like how familiar these two seem to be with each other. What's more, I've never seen Robert speak with so much audacity. This new side of him adds to his mysterious nature, further aggravating me.

"Let's get on with business," Louise says. "I'm much too busy to spend any more time than necessary chained up. You want Fowler and I want freedom. I'd say an exchange is in order."

"How do *you* envision that happening?" Gabriel asks.

"Wendy and I meet up with my people in a secluded place," she replies. "We carry out the exchange there."

Gabriel snorts but before he can speak I say, "Kaylen has to be there. She's the only one that will know if it's her dad."

Louise nods with a bit of anticipation. "Sure, why not? I've never been privileged to see Kaylen operate at her full capability. It should be quite entertaining to watch her hurl things at me telepathically."

I can't tell if she's joking. She seems unperturbed by that idea—and if there is one person Kaylen would gladly hurl objects at, it's Louise.

I still haven't given up hope of getting some information from Louise—though I know I should. Because even if I got her talking, I'd have no way of discerning truth from lie. They both fall effortlessly from her lips.

I restrain a groan. Everything Louise says is convoluted. And in fact, the only time I ever remember Louise expounding on things was when I first met her and she explained hypno-touch theory. I remember wondering why she went through the trouble of explaining so *much* to me. I think it was because I didn't act like I needed her. I had made it clear to Randy that I was ready to walk away from Pneumatikon unless they gave up some information to help me. And maybe if Louise thinks I'm going to walk away now, she might give something up eventually.

So I shrug. "We'll see what Kaylen says." Then I turn on my heel and walk away from her.

"Did you watch Don die on the other side when you touched him?" Louise asks before I reach the door.

I pause and suppress a smile. She fell for it. I decide whether to address that; I desperately want to. Trying to make me kill someone in the colorworld is the one thing Louise did while she had me captive that fails to make any sense.

When I don't turn, Louise sighs to herself. "Like father, like daughter. I could have guessed… I give you the perfect opportunity to explore your ability and you waste it. Let me guess, you were more concerned about Gabe's safety than taking the opportunity to see what you are capable of?" Louise scoffs. "You are so blind to what you are, Wendy."

"Which is what, Louise?" Gabriel speaks up, turning back to her. I can tell he's been as baffled as me about everything Louise has said so far.

Resolving to ignore everything Louise puts into my head so I can keep the upper hand, I touch Gabriel's arm. "Don't waste your time. She only wants us to *think* she has information. But she doesn't. She had every opportunity to play her hand and she didn't. She doesn't *have* one. We'll let Kaylen decide what to do with her."

He looks at me with confusion for a moment before allowing me to pull him out.

Once we're in the living room, I plop exhaustedly on the couch and Ezra says, "That woman creeps me out."

"Wendy, I'd advise against meeting her demands for an exchange," Robert says, sitting in an armchair.

"It's not up to me," I point out. "But even if it were, what choice is there with Kaylen's father in danger?"

The lock on the front door sounds just then and Gabriel and I stand up. Farlen appears, and right behind him a dark brown head.

Kaylen steps out and her eyes light up. "Wendy! Gabe!" she squeals, bouncing forward.

Gabriel strides forward and throws his arms around her, picking her up and setting her back down. "Kaylee!" he booms. "Seeing you is like a breath of fresh air."

"Kaylen!" I say excitedly, though I feel awkward standing here, unable to demonstrate the same excitement without hurting her.

She walks toward me, a smile on her face, her porcelain cheeks flushed. She reaches out slowly, carefully, drawing me into an embrace which I return, keeping my exposed skin away from her.

She pulls away and exhales.

"I'd ask you how you are but... well, you know," I say.

She laughs. "Just another day for you, huh?" Then her eyes narrow. "So you have her? How did you find her? I would have thought for *sure* she'd be too careful to get herself caught."

I step to the side to reveal Robert and Ezra behind me. "This is my Uncle Robert and my brother, Ezra," I explain. "Robert is... skilled. Supernaturally. He's the one that found Louise."

Robert steps forward and offers Kaylen his hand. "It's nice to meet you, Kaylen. I know Wendy and Gabe are both glad to have you safe."

Kaylen takes his hand, somewhat awed, also slightly confused. "Thanks," she says, observing his face for a long time. She wonders about something before asking, "Supernaturally talented? Are you one of Louise's experiments, too?"

Robert withdraws his hand and steps back. "No. I was born with my gift."

That baffles Kaylen, but she dismisses it. Then she puts her hands on her hips, looking around at all of us. "What's the plan?"

I recount Louise's demands to her.

"Let's do it," she says easily. "I'd like to see her *try* and double cross us. In fact, I *hope* she does. Then I can vent on her without suffering any guilt."

"Yeah, that's what I was thinking," I reply. "The exchange part. Not the double crossing."

Gabriel sighs. "I don't like it."

"Neither do I," says Robert. "I've known Louise a long time. Just because we caught her doesn't mean she has given up. She's going to use this opportunity."

Kaylen crosses her arms. "Then how exactly do you propose we get my dad back? She's not going to let him go just because you threaten her."

"Let me make an attempt to locate Kevin Fowler first," Robert replies.

"I agree," Gabriel says. "Louise is a slippery Termagant. Everything she does is more than what it seems. She only wants us to *think* there's no alternative."

"Dude, can't you say, 'she's a slippery bitch' and move on?" Ezra snorts.

"Heavens, Ezra, there are ladies present!" Gabriel says. Then under his breath, "His manners are as uncouth as his sister's…"

Ezra and I both roll our eyes and I say, "Now that we've had a vocabulary lesson *and* a manners lesson, can we get back on topic?"

Kaylen giggles before saying, "Look, I don't deny that Louise may have plans, but the only way to win is to be ruthless. Because that's what she *doesn't* expect."

"Louise knows we won't resort to torturing her," I add. "What does she have to lose? We can't mess around with her."

Gabriel sighs. "Can we at least sleep on it?"

I look at Kaylen.

"Fine," she says. "I don't want to do an exchange at night anyway. But I'm telling you, we can't go about this afraid of what she's going to do."

Kaylen is right. We have to go at this with guns blazing. Timidity and second-guessing are what Louise wants *and* what she expects.

I am not second-guessing myself. And if Kaylen agrees with me, nobody here is going to stop us.

***

"What is it?" I ask Kaylen, shutting the door to the room Robert showed her. She whispered to me earlier that she wanted to talk to me alone so I came back to her room to see what she wanted.

She sits on the bed cross-legged. She props her chin on her hand, consternation spelled out clearly on her face. "I'm not sure. It's just… you found Louise so easily. You said your uncle did and I… Well how did he do it?"

I give her a quick explanation of how his ability works.

"Oh, I guess that would do it…" she muses, though a bit of uneasiness still nags at her.

"Kaylen?" I whisper. "What?"

She thinks about something for a few moments and then whispers, "It's just that Robert seems really *familiar* to me… I don't know why… I thought maybe I'd met him on the compound once, but then he said his ability was natural—which is kind of hard to believe anyway. I don't know… There's something about him that rings a bell, you know?"

I widen my eyes in surprise. "Really? That's crazy… I felt him a little when he introduced himself to you, but I didn't get any recognition from him."

She shrugs. "It's probably nothing. Anyway, when I heard you'd caught Louise, I swear, Wendy, I was *sure* she must have *let* herself get caught. She's too smart to slip up and get found right off the bat like that, you know? And then I see your uncle and I think I must know him from somewhere… had me suspicious… But if he can do what you say, I guess it makes more sense."

As I speculate on Kaylen's words, I recall something, "Well it wasn't *all* his ability. She *did* slip up. She used an ATM in Riverside under her alias. Robert has to have a location narrowed down to make his ability work right."

Kaylen furrows her brow, uncomfortable once more. "Louise let herself get caught on camera? *Right after* she kidnaps my dad?" She sits up and shakes her head decidedly. "That reeks, Wendy. She is *not* that dumb."

I think Kaylen gives Louise too much credit. Even Louise can't devise a fool-proof plan, and it sounded like Robert was telling Louise he can find her if he wants to… She even said she was impressed—not that I can trust *anything* she says. I bite my lip. I need to trust Kaylen's instincts. The last time I doubted her intuition about Louise, she *did* catch me.

"Why would she do that?" I ask.

"I'm not sure… to get your guard down? Make you too confident? Get you to an exchange in the middle of nowhere where she can ambush you? It could be anything."

As I search my memory for evidence of Kaylen's theory that Louise *allowed* herself to be caught, something leaps forward almost immediately: the words I overheard her saying when I was in the tree. She was telling someone she'd be staying in public areas… She knows how Robert's ability works, so public areas would make it *easier* for Robert to find her. Why would she do that unless she *wanted* him to find her? And then she said, 'It shouldn't take *them* too long.' Is *them* us? And then finally, 'If you don't hear from me, you know what to expect.'"

My jaw drops.

"Oh my gosh!" I breathe. "You're right. She *did* let herself get caught!" And then the words tumble out of me as I tell Kaylen what I overheard Louise say. "She must have planted the Sally Stenworth letter at your house," I finish, "knowing we'd be trying to track her after she took your dad. And then she was going to *let* herself be found…"

"She *did* plan this," Kaylen hisses, her eyes flashing. She looks at me directly. "So what do we do?"

"We tell no one," I whisper. "Because if they know, doing the exchange the way Louise wants is never going to happen. And we let Louise *think* she has us fooled."

Kaylen nods adamantly. Then she straightens and folds her arms. "I have no idea why they'd be so nervous about us going anyway. I can take anyone Louise would throw at us."

There *is* that. Louise has made it clear she knows what Kaylen can do. Yet she *still* consented to have Kaylen at the exchange…

What would make Louise so confident?

***

"What are you doing?" I ask when Gabriel sits down on the bed I'm lying on. Robert directed us to the same room earlier and I almost protested but Gabriel whispered to me, reminding me of his promise that he wouldn't touch me for this trip. I relented when he insisted he would sleep on the couch that the room is also furnished with.

"Shhh," he says quietly, leaning closer to me. Then he whispers so softly I'm sure normal ears wouldn't hear it, "I don't know if this room is bugged and I don't want to take the chance of being overheard. Just listen and don't say anything. I am not sure I trust Robert."

I turn my head to look at him with confusion. First Kaylen, now Gabriel?

I move my gloved hand to his arm and pull myself into the colorworld.

He recognizes my unfocused look and he thinks to me, '*Why didn't I think of that? That does simplify things.*'

"What is it?" I whisper, wishing I could speak telepathically to *him* as well. I try, but it doesn't work. "Elaborate."

'*Seems like there's something going on between Robert and Louise. They are saying things to each other without saying them. Louise knows Robert. Really well, I think. More than he's let on. And I've never seen Robert so up-tight. I get that he doesn't trust her. None of us do. But it's like he's afraid of what she's going to say...Think how reluctant he's been to help us find her. He all but told Louise he could have found her at any point if he'd wanted to. I could be paranoid. I don't know. But the entire situation has me on edge.*'

I nod, unsure of what's safe to say out loud. I agree with him, to an extent, but I think it all has a reasonable explanation. We already *knew* why Robert was reluctant to find Louise. He told us as much.

"She came between Robert and my dad," I whisper. "Carl died without the two of them making amends—I think Robert blames Louise for that. If Louise had had a hand in *my* brother's death…?" I shake my head. "Besides, Louise knows how to plant ideas in your head." In fact, I think everything Louise said was an attempt to make me question the trust I have in the people around me… make me more desperate to go to her for help.

'*Yes... But that whole situation in the car this afternoon with him asking about whether you could read his thoughts…?*' Gabriel continues. '*Why would you get upset about someone reading your thoughts unless you had something to hide?*'

“Privacy,” I whisper. “Everyone likes privacy. Except you.”

He furrows his brow. ‘*But how well do you really know Robert? He just showed up in your life at the right moment and offered you everything without asking for anything in return. I appreciate his generosity as much as the next person, but he seems so... aloof. I just want you to be careful.*’

I know all these things Gabriel is saying. But I’ve held on to trusting Robert because he has never once come across as malicious. If he really isn’t what he claims, he is unlike any villain I have ever encountered—not that I have that much experience. Louise demonstrates a lack of emotion, too, but in a way that had me mistrusting her from the beginning. Her selfish tendencies were clear. But Robert doesn’t demonstrate that. He has always been genuinely concerned about me and about Ezra. I’ve overlooked his distance because of that. But I can at least agree to be cautious.

Gabriel is still lying next to me, watching my face.

I raise an eyebrow. “Something else?”

“Sorry Love,” he says aloud, grinning. “I was seeing how long it would take you to kick me out of your bed.”

He hops up to go to the bathroom that adjoins our room and shuts the door.

For a fleeting moment I wonder if I have to worry about Gabriel tonight…

It doesn’t last. Despite his complete disregard for my feelings, he is nothing if not honest and trustworthy. If I can’t believe that, how can I live? If blatant deception was in his repertoire, he could have promised me what I asked in the very beginning and then turned around and broken his word.

No, Gabriel is someone I trust and will continue to trust.

Robert? I have no idea what to think about him.

27

I wake in the late morning to the sound of Gabriel showering. My ankle is still tender and it's a little swollen. But I'm convinced it's probably just a minor sprain. Nevertheless, the stiffness of sleeping makes it especially painful and I cringe when I put my weight on it.

I pin it on Louise. Then I remember Robert. Gabriel and I didn't even discuss how we're going to handle this newest development. What exactly does 'be careful' mean? Do we go about our business like nothing is happening? What about Ezra? He lives with Robert.

The shower is still running and that gives me an idea. After testing my glucose, I make a production of opening and closing the bathroom door so Gabriel knows I'm here.

"Care to join me?" he asks from the shower, which is nothing more than a fancy contemporary glass enclosure. I was expecting at least a shower curtain between us.

I look around. It's a very spacious bathroom with double sinks and a full-size window that frames the back yard. The floor, counter, and tub are granite. The fixtures are bronze—the real kind—and the mirror is gilded in it. And this is a *guest* bathroom? I shake my head in wonder as I test my glucose. It's a bit high—strange since I just woke up and haven't eaten anything since dinner last night.

I can see Gabriel's form behind the foggy glass and I swallow, rethinking my plan. I've never actually seen him naked before. I try to ignore my sprinting heart as I move next to the door. "So what are we going to do about Robert?" I whisper—which is stupid. There's no way he's going to hear me over the sound of the shower.

Stupid normal human ears. I don't know how much louder I can safely get.

He sees me standing there next to the glass after he finishes washing shampoo out of his hair and says with amusement, "If you want, I'll stand in the corner and let you have all the water. There's plenty of room in here, you know."

He's right. The shower is easily three times the size of a regular one. But I have no intention of putting my bare skin in there near him.

I pull open the glass door, peeking around the edge. That surprises him, but he smiles anyway and starts soaping up. "I need to talk to you!" I hiss. I can't help watching him standing there under the water though. "Very nice." I nod appreciatively.

It's more than nice, but I do my best to find his face with my eyes and concentrate on it. It's a little surreal to be so close to his naked body. It doesn't *feel* wrong, although intuitively it seems like it *should* feel wrong. Experiencing his life force in the colorworld is deeply intimate. Then there was our wedding night… It's kind of silly to be uncomfortable around him while he's undressed—for me anyway.

Gabriel is watching me. "Are you certain you don't want to come in?" He looks up for a moment and then adds, "Under normal circumstances I don't think I could keep my hands off of you, but I *did* promise…" He chuckles then as he notices my eyes wandering. "*You,* however, didn't make any promises… Wouldn't it be wicked fun to resist?"

I swallow at the thought, forcing my focus back to his face. Why am I here again? Just then, he turns his back to me. It's a long minute before I find my words again. "Stop it, Gabriel!" I hiss. "You know I am *not* getting in there with you. I'm just trying to talk to you!"

He turns around again and chuckles, giving me a look of innocence. "I'm not doing anything except taking a shower. You're the one *spying*."

"I'm not spying! I'm trying to have a conversation!"

Unable to focus enough to articulate what I want to say, I close my eyes. "What are we going to do about Robert?" I ask into the darkness of the back of my eyelids.

Gabriel laughs again, delighted. Then he clears his throat and says, "I can't talk to you when I can't see your eyes. I can't read you at all. It's not fair if you can read me and I get nothing."

I wrinkle my nose. Even though I know he's doing it to manipulate me, he's kind of right. But how am I supposed to have a conversation with him when he's standing in the shower all casual like a model for an art class?

I open my eyes and look up at his face, determined to keep them locked there.

"Okay, my eyes are open. Tell me what you think. We can't go about our business like sitting ducks. We need to find out some info on him," I say as loudly as I dare.

"Agreed. But research is going to have to happen when we get home. I don't know how he would fit into this whole thing. I don't think he works *with* Louise. He obviously doesn't like her, and Louise enjoys making him uncomfortable.

"Maybe he's some kind of third party. Maybe he worked with your father. But that wouldn't explain why he's kept it from you. I just don't know," Gabriel says. "We probably shouldn't let him in on any further discoveries pertaining to your colorworld sight. And we watch him more closely. I don't know if you've noticed, but he avoids being in your range—like he doesn't want you getting a read on him."

I furrow my brow. I actually *haven't* noticed.

"Watching and researching may be the only things we *can* do at this point," Gabriel replies. "Unless you have another idea?"

I don't like not having much of a plan of action, but he's probably right. Robert really might be exactly what he says. Confronting him and being wrong could be disastrous. Confronting him and being right could also be disastrous.

My eyes are wandering again, so I say, "That sounds like a plan." Then I shut the door, turn away, and head for the sink. I reach into my toiletry bag and pull out my toothbrush to have something to do with my hands.

The shower turns off then and Gabriel steps out. I can't see him through the fog on the mirror and I keep my eyes trained on the sink.

When he appears next to me, he's got a towel around his waist, but water glistens on his rippling, muscular physique. Gosh, I want to put my hands on him. I spit out my toothpaste, rinse my mouth, and make a hasty retreat.

As I close the door behind me, I hear Gabriel say "She totally wants me." He knows I can hear. And then he chuckles at no one in particular.

Stupid hot husband. I am still in my clothes from the day before and I want to change, but I am not going to do it right now. Instead, I wait until he's done so I can take a shower next.

I shake my head and exhale. I asked for it. I could have waited until he was done, turned on the shower, and then spoken to him *outside* the shower. I knew *exactly* what I was doing, and it was stupid. The problem is I really *do* want him.

I should ask Robert for a separate room today. I need to avoid every temptation.

Gabriel exits the bathroom looking refreshed and positively pleased with himself, like he's just won a gold medal. His short-sleeved, fitted brown shirt and excellently faded blue jeans hug all the right places and none of the wrong ones. His dark hair is styled and he smells delicious in his usual alpine cologne, which only accentuates his natural smell.

Fierce yearning knots my chest. It's like I've been saving up my feelings during all this time we've been at odds. Now that we're on speaking terms again, those emotions are breaking through more forcefully.

But it's not just that. I know Gabriel is a good-looking guy. But *not* being able to have him in any physical way makes him that much more tantalizing. Or maybe my fury at him the past few days has fueled my desire. It's as if he gets more good-looking every day.

"My turn," I say, grabbing my bag.

"I'll bring up breakfast for you in the meantime," he says, flashing me one of his excellent grins.

Ugh. I'd better make it a cold shower.

***

The lukewarm water should feel nice but it's strikingly lonely instead. Where I had originally woken up in a decent mood, I now have my thoughts alone and they start wandering. I start thinking about things I don't want to think about.

I wonder about the colorworld sights from the plane yesterday… Life forces shine at different wattages and that *means* something. I want to pay attention next time I'm in colorworld to see if I can differentiate the brightness of the life forces around me like Gabriel, Ezra, and Robert.

Gabriel always has good insights, but this time I don't want to hear his ideas. He'll align it with his own theory, and then… I'll have to run away? Lock myself up? I don't know. He hasn't been clear about what extremes he'll take in order to touch me.

I groan. What is *wrong* with Gabriel? If I didn't read his intentions so clearly, I am *positive* I would think he was crazy.

My body feels even heavier now. The constant fear of an unknown future has drained me. But I still need to think about it even though the anxiety over it has me nauseated.

The only way to translate Gabriel's actions are as an ultimatum. He leaves me only two choices when all I want is the middle ground… But he won't take it. And he isn't going to give up either. He will push and pull and manipulate until he gets exactly what he wants. Just like when we first met.

I can continue this pretense—live with him and be constantly on guard. But one day he'll decide to touch me.

I shake my head. His daring is unreal—unbelievable. But I know how real he is. Gabriel is an anomaly. He adheres to a strict personal code, but within that code, all other bets are off. He *does* have it in him to take this kind of ridiculous risk.

I know it's not that he can't live without touching me. Somehow, *because* of his commitment to his theory, I now understand and believe that Gabriel would stay with me no matter the conditions. I finally grasp the depth of his audacity. And now he's latched on to this idea and he isn't going to let it go.

There is another option: let him touch me. I warm at the possibilities. I daydream briefly what it might be like to find that he's immune to my touch, just like Ezra.

Darkness creeps into the middle of my daydream, however, the slow but inevitable Nothingness paralyzing me. Paralyzing *him.* Gabriel's eyes go blank, unseeing. He scrambles for unseen walls. He doesn't hear his own screams… His heart thuds for the last time and goes silent.

I press my hands to the side of my head and shake it vigorously to dispel the images. I start gasping.

"No!" I say firmly. I will not let that happen to him.

Frustration overwhelms me. It's so harsh that it constricts my throat and rattles my thoughts out of order. I pace the shower space, looking for some kind of escape. But there is none.

Except Louise.

Without her, my life with Gabriel will be over. I will have no choice but to leave him to keep him safe. I need what she knows. I *have* to know what she knows.

I stop pacing abruptly, my head clearing. There is *nothing* stopping me from going with Louise. If everyone I love is safe and aware of the threat Louise presents, she won't have any way to force me into doing anything. I can at least *entertain* the possibility, can't I?

I sigh. I shouldn't even be thinking about it. But with everything I may lose, how can I *not*?

28

As promised, Gabriel brings me breakfast. I manage to create within myself the illusion that my happiness will extend indefinitely. I do a pretty good job lying to myself about the situation, especially with Gabriel's positivity around. I smile genuinely at him when he comes in bearing a tray with pancakes, fruit, and a flower in a vase.

Ezra and Kaylen both pile into our room right after I finish so we all head downstairs.

"So you guys are married now…" Kaylen says after swallowing a mouthful of cereal. "Sorry I missed the invitation. But congratulations!" She beams at me.

"Thanks," I say, smiling mildly.

Kaylen doesn't miss my expression, but she doesn't voice her questions. Thank goodness. I refuse to think about my problems with Gabriel right now.

Instead I think about what Kaylen and I discovered about Louise last night, questioning whether doing the exchange is the best idea. I slowly turn my glass of water around and around on the table in front of me.

"You know what I don't get?" Ezra says, plopping down next to me with a bagel and a tub of cream cheese. "How is it Louise ended up being there at the psychic's way *after* the time in Robert's vision?"

Gabriel sits down on the other side of the table and his eyes glint with excitement. "I was confused by that at first, too, but as soon as I saw that car back out of that driveway, I knew it had to be her. I looked back and saw Wendy standing in front of that psychic sign. At that moment I knew it wasn't Louise that Robert *thought* he was locating. It was you, Wendy," says Gabriel, somewhat triumphantly.

"What?" I say. "I don't get it."

"Remember what Robert said he made his goal? He said he wanted to find the best person to give him information about life force ability manifestation. We initially thought that person would be Louise. But it's not. It's you. We should have guessed that. We already know you can work with life forces in a way Louise can't. Forget Riverside. You are likely the best in the *world.* Robert saw a vision of where *you* would be in Riverside at dusk," replies Gabriel.

The pieces click into place one by one as I wrap my head around that. "Gabriel, you are such a freaking genius," I say in disbelief. "How did you figure that out so fast?"

"Wait," says Ezra as Robert comes into the kitchen. "But you weren't even *in* Riverside when he concentrated on that goal. That should have left Louise as the only alternative."

I shake my head. "When he *started* visualizing his goal that was true. But I remember feeling him concentrate. I was looking out the window and seeing the sign for Riverside as soon as I felt his vision settle. Plus, I was already on my way there. I think that counts as far as predicting the future."

Gabriel smiles broadly, eyes alight. "No doubt if Wendy had put any effort into it, she would have figured it all out without my help." He shakes his head. "Isn't her intellect riveting?"

I snap my fingers. "Focus, Gabriel."

"Yeah man, we're all mesmerized," says Ezra, rolling his eyes.

Kaylen giggles.

"So if it was me in the vision, how the heck did Louise end up there?" I ask.

"Because your goal was to find Louise," Gabriel replies. "Robert says specific people are hard to pinpoint. But if they are settled on a goal, they probably *would* be easier to locate. Where *she* would be was where *you* would be. Your future in Riverside would have—"

"Been affected by wherever Louise was. So we essentially located Louise by locating me," I finish. *Not to mention Louise* wanted *to be found...*

"Yes!" Gabriel exclaims. "So the only way to solidify Robert's unwitting goal of finding you was to give you a static location. And the only way to accomplish that yesterday was to give you *your* goal to find Louise, which gave Robert *his* goal. It's absolutely boggling, isn't it? It's like you willed Louise right into your hands, just by thinking about her so hard."

"That's fascinating," Robert says, impressed.

"My brain hurts," Kaylen says, her mouth twisted with the strain of trying to wrap her head around it.

"Gabe, I cannot deny that you are one brilliant S.O.B." Ezra says. "Makes up for everything else."

"So are you, hermano menor. Though how you've managed it on such a regular diet of fictional fantastical cartoons in print is beyond me," Gabriel fires back.

Ezra laughs sarcastically. "Yeah, I *am* brilliant. But reading fictional fantastical *literature* keeps me from becoming an S.O. B. like you."

Gabriel smiles and stands up to take his bowl to the sink. He ruffles Ezra's hair on the way like he's a little kid. "Quite a weisenheimer today, this one," he says. "Must be something in the air… Or maybe it's the effect of having a certain young lady in the room?"

I can tell from Ezra's sheepishness that Gabriel has hit the nail on the head with that one. But Ezra tries to deflect. "No, Gabe. I'm pretty sure it's having *your* ego around using words like *weisenheimer* that bring it out of me."

"Okay, everyone," Kaylen interjects. "The morning banter and rabbit hole lesson have been fun, but I think Wendy and I can both tell you're stalling the real issue. We talked about it last night and we're doing the exchange."

Disappointment all around: Gabriel is frowning; Ezra's upbeat attitude sinks; and Robert shifts his feet apprehensively.

"No argument," I say when I feel Gabriel on the verge of objecting. "Unless one of you have Kevin Fowler's location right now, we're doing it. We can't afford to waste time."

The room may be silent, but my head is crowded with all their respective emotions tumbling around as they search for new arguments. Robert sighs finally. "Okay. But let's be smart about it. GPS locators, bullet proof vests, the works. This whole situation is too simple. Simple is not Louise's style. I could be completely wrong, but I don't want to take chances."

Robert isn't on my list of trustworthy people right now, but given what I know about Louise's plans, I think Robert is exactly right on this one.

He seems to know her M.O. almost as well as Kaylen does… Yet the last time he dealt with her was fifteen years ago?

That mystery is going to have to wait until later.

29

Kaylen looks and feels like she's doing a hard math problem in her head. I'm driving but she still concentrates intently on the road in front of us.

Louise is handcuffed in the back seat with her ear pressed to a phone, telling her people where we'll be meeting. We decided to wait until the last minute to inform them where the rendezvous point would be to decrease their preparation time. Louise didn't seem to care one way or another.

I want to ask Kaylen what has her so focused, but I don't in case she's working on some kind of backup plan. We're on our way to carry out the exchange in a valley east of Banning. There are no buildings in sight of normal human eyes out here. I have no problem, however, seeing the nearest town with mine.

The rendezvous point is something Kaylen and I spent an hour talking about. Louise's only stipulation was that it be away from civilization. Kaylen wanted a less open area with more rocks, boulders, and trees, but I wanted some place really open so I could see what was coming.

Eventually we agreed on the valley near Banning because the mountains to the north and south have plenty of fodder for Kaylen's abilities. Kaylen reminded me, however, that not only can she not move people, but her range is pretty limited; she can only manipulate objects that are within about fifteen feet of her. The closer they are, the more she can lift. The farther out, the less mass she can move.

The plan, if we do get in trouble, is to get as close to the mountains to the north as possible and find cover.

The road we travel, a narrow two-lane, eventually peters out into dirt that leads into the scorching desert. Meanwhile, Louise's continued indifference bugs me more and more with every mile we leave behind. I still can't guess what she might have planned, but I know there's nothing she can say or do to change my mind. I will never trust her. I will never let her use me to hurt others. And a cure to my condition will never be worth human life. If I could resist killing people even when she was torturing Gabriel, I am confident I have the ability to hold myself grounded in what I know to be right. The only explanation for Louise's confidence is that she underestimates me.

We finally reach the agreed-upon GPS location and I stop the car. Now we wait for Louise's people. I like that I'll be able to see them coming.

I send Gabriel a quick text to tell him we're in place—that was one of the other requirements of the drop point: cell phone service.

After about five minutes of sitting in the car, craning my neck to look in every direction for approaching vehicles, I become too agitated to sit still. Louise's calm is driving me crazy. I don't know what I expect, but Louise's confidence is growing by the minute. Things are going exactly as planned for her.

I take a bottle of water and say, "I'm going to step outside and keep a lookout."

Kaylen nods at me, her jaw rigid with stress. Whatever she's thinking about, she isn't going to share. I guess if Kaylen wants me to know, she can step out and tell me.

Outside the car, I scan the horizon in every direction back and forth, a tiny bit relieved with my unobstructed view outside the vehicle.

Inevitably, I become hot. There are absolutely no clouds in the sky to hide the sun. It glares down on me with insistence. Kaylen and Louise both enjoy sleeveless shirts and shorts while I'm smothered by long pants, a Kevlar vest, a t-shirt, and gloves.

I had planned to take the gloves off when Louise's people arrived, but I don't see any reason not to do it now. It might keep me from passing out from heat stroke in this upper-ninety degree weather.

My exposed skin instantly cools and I sigh with relief. The gloves are damp with sweat, but I have an extra pair in the car. I roll my jeans up to my knees, feeling terrifyingly free. Since Gabriel found me by the pool that day, I haven't exposed my skin to fresh air like this. It's exhilarating.

After about thirty-five minutes, I hear a roar to the south, down the road we just travelled. I turn to see the approaching car. At least two people are inside it, in the front seats. As it gets closer, I make out a third person in the back.

I hastily roll my pants back down and tap on the window. Within moments, Kaylen emerges. I take a step back at the sight of her. Her steely expression is frightening. Under the blazing sun and in the wildness of our surroundings, Kaylen looks like a destroying angel. Her hair floats so subtly that it could be easily missed by less scrutinizing eyes and her own eyes flash with an unknown but evident power. Her skin glows with a sheen that is faintly luminous. I wonder, for a brief moment, if I have unknowingly channeled into the colorworld, but I see no tell-tale colors here.

"What?" asks Kaylen, looking around when she notices my alarm.

"You look like, like... I don't know... Otherworldly," I answer.

"Oh. Well I didn't know it made me look any different," she says.

"What do you mean?"

"I've been saving up. You know, not expending my ability so I would be more powerful for today. I wanted to make sure I was strong enough to handle whatever they throw at us... That's why I've looked like I've been constipated. Containing my energy is mental work," she explains.

"You look... Well *I* wouldn't mess with you." I give her another once-over, intimidated. She's only about my height, but her presence right now makes her seem a lot taller.

She nods and smiles, noticing my exposed arms. "I guess we're both prepared now."

We both look to the south. I can easily see the car approaching, but Kaylen squints at what, to her, looks like a miniscule dust cloud in the distance. "Is that them?"

"Yep," I say.

She opens the door for Louise while I keep my eyes on the approaching vehicle. I check our perimeter regularly but don't see or hear anything suspicious. It really is pretty barren here except for the scraggly-looking shrubs and craggy landscape.

The car draws closer. Kaylen looks like she might snap at any moment and cause an earthquake or something. I cross my arms rigidly, listening and staring so hard my head hurts.

I don't recognize either of the men in the front seat. Maybe they're just for brawn, but it's possible that they have some kind of ability that might present an obstacle to us.

Kaylen can't yet tell whether her father is in the car, so we wait. Louise stands off to the side. It's Kaylen's responsibility to maintain control of her and keep her close until we are sure we have Mr. Fowler.

The car stops in a cloud of dust about twenty feet away. Adrenaline courses through me, and I find myself wishing I had even *more* skin exposed. Viewing my ability as helpful this way is surreal.

"Whatever happens, Kaylen, don't get near me," I say. On the other side of the car, it's unlikely she'll be anywhere close enough to me to be in danger, but I want to make sure she remembers.

The two men in the front get out. One carries a gun. Kaylen is like a loaded weapon, so we agreed to one person being armed. It isn't a guarantee that they don't have more guns under their clothes, but at least if they do, it will take them some effort and time to get to them.

The armed man opens the rear door. Another man emerges. He has dirty-blond, slightly disheveled hair. He wears a suit that looks new, but no tie, and he is clearly older, probably in his late forties.

Nothing about him stands out much except that I have the distinct impression that I know him from somewhere. *Did I ever meet Kaylen's dad?*

"Is that him?" I hiss at Kaylen, scanning the distance to be sure there isn't anyone else coming.

Kaylen nods and I can tell the strain and the heat are getting to her. Her forehead beads with sweat and her muscles tense like she's ready to spring. My own nerves are so worn I think I might collapse from exhaustion.

We both expect Louise to double-cross us one way or another, and neither of us has realized how sure we have been of that prospect until this exact moment. I glance at Louise, and the cursed woman is looking off in the distance, not even watching the approaching men. Her complete indifference to the situation is beyond irritating. I want to shake her into showing some kind of normal human reaction.

The three men stop about ten feet away and I look at them, analyzing their every movement. I don't know when I should say something. I'm about to tell them to send Kaylen's dad forward when Louise speaks up in an amused voice, "You two look like you're expecting an ambush."

I look over at her in surprise. She seems genuinely entertained.

"Send him forward," I say loudly, trying to ignore my apprehension that things are going exactly how Louise would like.

The men look at Louise and she nods. Kaylen's dad steps out, his head bowed as he looks down at his feet.

Holy crap, I know this guy! But I can't *place* him. Everything about him is familiar, even his walk—the way he holds his hands clasped behind his back as he moves.

"Are you okay, Dad?" asks Kaylen, worry creasing her brow.

He looks up then and smiles briefly at her. Why do I know that smile? My brain works overtime, trying to place this man that I am sure is a stranger but whose every nuance strikes some chord. I know I should be worrying about this later and concentrate on getting us safely out of here, but the man is so *familiar* that it unsettles me.

"Stop," I command. I don't know what the heck is going on, but I'm sure this is why Louise allowed herself to be captured.

Kaylen and her father both look at me then. Kaylen is confused, but her father is… tentative.

He knows I know him.

Behind Kaylen Louise is impassive, but she's watching me carefully.

"Who are you?" I ask Kaylen's father.

"Wendy, this is my dad," says Kaylen, perplexed. "What are you doing?"

He turns his head slightly to the side and his eyes crinkle a tiny bit like he's in thought, his bottom lip drawn slightly into his teeth.

That small movement of his eyes and mouth is all it takes for me to find a name: *Ezra*.

That is Ezra's face. But it isn't Ezra. It's…

My head spins, and I place my hands on the top of the car to steady myself.

"Who *are* you?" I repeat. This time the demand is clear in my voice.

Whoever this man is, he's Louise's *real* bargaining chip. This is the reason she was captured. This is who she *brought* me here to meet.

"Wendy! What are you doing?" Kaylen says, at a loss. "I told you, this is him; this is my dad. Can we go now?"

"He looks like Ezra, and I want to know why," I say firmly to Kaylen, but I'm looking angrily at the man whom she claims is her father.

"Hello, Wendy," says Kaylen's father. "It's been a long time since I've seen you. You're looking well."

"You didn't answer my question," I say through gritted teeth.

Kaylen keeps looking back and forth between me and her father, clearly agitated. But not nearly as inflamed as me. Louise has pulled one over on me. I just don't know what it is yet.

"There now," says Louise, clasping her cuffed hands together under her chin. "Isn't it lovely to see families reunited again? Carl, you wouldn't believe how like you she is."

30

Carl?

No. It can't be.

"Carl?" I say, my eyes wide. "As in Carl *Haricott*?" Even the words don't feel real.

"Yes," the man says tentatively. "But Kaylen knows me as Kevin Fowler."

I close my eyes for a moment and ask, "My… *father*?"

I search his face, like I might see some indication of myself written there. And now that I have entertained it, he looks more and more like Ezra. And then Robert. They're brothers…

"Yes," he replies firmly.

I can't think. Shock sweeps away coherency for several moments.

When I look up again I catch Kaylen in my peripheral vision. "So Kaylen and I are sisters?" I ask.

Carl looks calm but sure and says, "No. Kaylen is adopted."

I glance over at Kaylen but I don't process her expression. I can't get my brain to work right, so I ask the first thing that comes to me, "Did Mom *know*? That you… didn't *die*?"

Carl's eyes narrow. "I assume you are talking about Sara. That woman was not your mother. *Your* mother died when you were very little. Her name was Gina." His expression softens and his voice gets lower as he says her name.

I have no words. My mouth is full of cotton. My mom is not my mom?

You never did look like her. I hold my head in my hands, fighting the swarm of questions gathering.

Carl shifts his weight and his face hardens again. "And yes, Sara knew. She knew and she kidnapped you. Which makes her a criminal, not a mother."

I close my eyes again and the ground seems to shift. I put a hand on the top of the car to steady myself again. I scramble in my head for some way around these lies he's telling me, but they sound too feasible. The so-called Carl looks like Ezra. They are *definitely* related. And Ezra and I resemble each other, but I do not resemble my mom. She had blond hair—like Ezra—and she was short with petite features. I have a thicker build and I'm taller than she was. I never questioned it. But now that the doubt has been introduced, I feel like intuitively I knew it all my life.

And the file… the one that Gabriel found on the compound said my mother was Regina Walden. *Gina.* She had an empathic ability like me…

But he's also telling me that the woman I called Mom was a baby-napper? No. That can't be. She may not have been my biological mother, but she was *not* a criminal.

But she lied. About so many things. Her real name… My dad… My ability…

I put my hands over my ears and shake my head. This can't be happening.

Carl sighs. "Seeing you brings back so many memories. You are the spitting image of Gina."

"Ezra?" I finally ask, wondering how he plays into this. Mom was pregnant with him when our dad supposedly died.

"Sara was his mother. A son I never knew I had," Carl replies bitterly.

Kaylen has been watching our exchange silently. She gawks at her father, sometimes glancing at me but always moving her focus back to him. Speechless. If I was worried at all that Kaylen was in on this, her face and stupefied thoughts are enough to prove otherwise.

"Are you… working *with* her?" I ask, my eyes flitting over to Louise who doesn't look like she's paying our conversation much mind. She might even be a little impatient.

Carl scowls at Louise. "No." He turns back to me. "Can we go now?" he pleads. "I can explain everything on the way."

"No." I shake my head. "You explain *now.*"

Kaylen looks at me incredulously.

Carl shifts his weight again and when I don't give any sign of relenting, he's a little surprised. "Louise and I have been friends for years, yes. And I've been looking for you ever since Sara took you. I learned Louise had found you, and I was afraid of what my brother had told you. What *Sara* had told you. I didn't know what you'd think of me appearing in your life all of a sudden. Louise was supposed to… find all these things out. But instead she was exploiting you. I had no idea what she was capable of until…" Carl takes a staggered breath. "I'm sorry she put you through that. I never would have allowed it. And all I want now is to know you. To know Ezra. And to be with Kaylen. The four of us. We're a family."

I stare at him for several silent beats. "Why haven't you tried to contact me since my stay at the compound?"

"Because Louise threatened to expose me for fraud if I contacted you. I took Kaylen away to protect her. I was afraid Louise would use her to get to you. But Louise knew where we were all along."

I don't look at his face. Instead I eye the distance between us. I need to feel his emotions.

"Please, Wendy. I've been waiting your whole life to be reunited with you," Carl pleads. "Whatever you've heard about me, I beg you to just give me a chance—find out for yourself."

"Oh, for heaven's sake," Louise says impatiently, crossing her arms. "You all got what you wanted: Kaylen's father. If you have doubts about his character, work them out on your own time."

I don't move.

"Come on, Wendy," Kaylen pleads, seeing the look of heavy skepticism on my face. "I'm as in shock as you are. But can we get my dad and hash this out later?"

I nearly give in. It *can* be hashed out later. But I am pretty sure that's what Louise wants and expects. If she *planned* this, that means she *wants* me to trust Carl. Or maybe she wants me to *think* that's what she wanted, just so I'd doubt him…?

I shift my feet and cross my arms, frustrated.

I look over at Kaylen and then Carl. "No," I say firmly. "Louise planned this whole thing. She *let* herself be caught so she could get me in front of you. We are not going anywhere or doing anything until I have the answers I want." I turn back to Kaylen. "You know you can disarm them right now if you want. But this wasn't about guns or force. This is about Carl. And *I* think it was to make me trust him. But I don't trust anyone who has ever been that heavily involved with Louise."

Kaylen, I can tell, is battling her own confusion and disbelief. She looks from Carl to Louise and then over to me.

But I watch Carl. Now that he knows I don't trust him, will he change his angle?

His brow is furrowed for a moment. He is definitely bothered but he finally shakes his head. "Whatever Louise led you to believe about me, it was manipulation. That's what she does. She wants you not to trust me. She wants you to be alone so you'll go to her."

I steal a glance at Louise. She looks off into the desert, but her expression is blank. Too blank. I think she's working hard to keep it that way. I think I've upset her. I think my first assumption was correct: Louise wants me to trust Carl.

I'd be more smug about ruining her plans if my whole world weren't rocked at the moment…

I move my eyes back to Carl and then step toward him.

He takes an instinctive step back—I *am* ungloved—but I say, "I just want to read you."

I have to get within five feet of Carl before I can pick up on him. Once I do, his agitation unsettles my stomach and I have to adjust myself to it. It's going to be hard to decipher anything through it.

I cross my arms and look at Carl. "The floor is yours, *Dad.* Wow me."

Carl takes several deep breaths to soothe his dismay. Finally, he sighs and crosses his arms behind his back, just like Ezra does when he's standing still for a long time. I grimace at seeing that mannerism on this stranger. I don't like it.

"Louise and I have worked together on a number of occasions," he says, not looking at my face. "We share the same goal, but we obviously have different methods of getting there. She's desperate to have you. That's why she kidnapped me—to get to you. Whatever doubts you have in your head about me, *she* put them there."

Carl is a pot of emotion: anxiety, irritation, desperation. I hate feeling people when they are this stressed, but I need to feel him long enough so I can start picking up the finer nuances.

"Not good enough," I say. "Start at the beginning. Tell me about Leena or Sara—my mom. Why did she take me away from you? Did you fake your own death?"

Carl sighs grudgingly. "Gina and I loved each other. And we had you. We wanted you to have advantages in life. So when you were an infant, I instilled you with special life force abilities using hypno-touch. Your mother passed away shortly thereafter." He holds himself in reserve as he says that.

"Wow, Carl. Kind of sounds like a speech you prepared. Why so rigid?" I demand.

He tilts his head slightly. "It is not a time I welcome remembering," he replies. "If you lost the love of your life, you wouldn't want to remember it either."

He takes a breath. "Then I met Sara. I thought she was a good woman. I thought she'd make a wonderful mother for you. And she did for a while. But I put too much trust in her. And I had no clue at the time how against our work she was."

"Why was she against it?"

"She didn't think it was a good idea for people to have such powerful abilities. She didn't believe humanity was capable of being responsible with it."

That makes me resentful for some inexplicable reason. As I work through it, determining its origin, I realize that it's not really *my* anger. It's Carl's. We feel anger almost exactly the same way…

This is insane!

"She probably had a good point," I say, holding my stance. I want to convey to him how dead serious I am about not trusting him. "Just look at Louise. She thinks she *owns* human potential."

"Then Sara should have come to me instead of taking you!" Carl insists, throwing his hands up. "How does any of that justify her *stealing* you the way she did?"

"I don't know, *Carl*," I challenge. "Why *would* she do something like that? Maybe because you were just as nasty as Louise and still are?"

"Wendy," Kaylen begs from behind me. "You're asking for answers and then you're attacking everything he says! Your mom *stole* you from your family. That doesn't upset you?"

I turn to look at her as I answer. "No. It doesn't. Because my mom was a *good* person who revolved her life around my brother and me. So *forgive* me if I'm not willing to take this *stranger's* word for it. This *stranger* who dumped *you,* his *daughter,* at a compound with a psychopath for *years*."

Kaylen has her mouth open slightly and she looks from me to her father. She opts to be silent and then stares at the car with a look of annoyance. Then the car lifts up, levitating a few inches above the ground where it stays.

I turn back to Carl. "I'm waiting to hear about how you loved me so much you faked your own death…?"

Carl sighs, putting his fingers on his temples. His irritation bubbles back up. I should probably stop purposely ticking him off. I'm never going to be able to read him outside of my own emotions that way.

"I ensured you were gifted with powerful abilities that would change the landscape of life force abilities," Carl says.

"And yes, it was going to push my work forward. But I'd sacrificed a lot financially to my research. I had a lot of debt. I had to disappear. So I planned to fake my own death. Sara was supposed to keep you safe until I could resurface under a new name. But she took you away instead. Robert ensured her ability to disappear entirely. Sara not only stole *you* from me, but she stole *Ezra* as well…" His jaw tightens and I have a hard time not reacting to his bitterness.

This cannot be real.

I don't trust the man, but everything he's saying… It explains too much to dismiss as readily as I'd like. Like how he says my mom didn't believe people should have abilities beyond the norm. I keep thinking of how she treated Ezra's talents… Brushing them off and downplaying them *and* mine. She even stifled her *own* gifts when they could have saved her so much financial stress.

And I wasn't her child… What if she took me because she didn't want Carl to be able to use me to bring *more* abilities about? We already suspect I can gift abilities well above what Louise can do. If that's not true, why else would Louise want me?

And Robert… Maybe *this* is what he's been hiding. That he helped my mom steal me from my dad. That I wasn't really Leena's daughter. It explains why he didn't want to find Louise. He didn't want me knowing the truth.

"I was so torn over losing you and your mother," Carl says, his voice breaking through my conflict. "I was so lonely. Everything had been taken from me. So I adopted Kaylen. I gave her special talents as a baby as well. To me she is as much a daughter as you are." He looks at Kaylen when he says it.

Then he looks back at me and it feels like he's foisting his desperation on me. "I have searched and searched for years, Wendy." He gives Louise a reproachful look. "But Louise was a step ahead of me. I never should have trusted her. I am so sorry…"

A loud, creaking *whump* sounds from behind me. I think Kaylen dropped the car. I hear her footsteps until she appears a few feet away. "You're *sorry*?" she seethes. "You dump *me* at the compound for years and never once have you been sorry about *that.*"

"Kaylen, you always saw it as a prison-sentence, but that's not what it was," Carl insists. "It was to protect you. Look how powerful you are. You're barely more than a child. How could I take the chance of having you out among people who would never have understood?"

Kaylen's face goes into her hands and her anguish twists my stomach. The disappointment of betrayal moves through her, but she struggles against accepting it.

I remain silent, battling my own indecision. How many times have I wished that I could have Carl to speak to for just a few minutes so I could ask him how he controlled it? Why would I drive him away like this?

I don't buy Carl's supposed rift with Louise for one minute, not because of his emotions, but because I know all this was in Louise's plans. I want what Carl knows. But I know that Carl is with Louise. One way or another, Carl Haricott is *not* a good guy. He's not to be trusted. And Louise *wants* him to go with us. I can see it on her impassive face, as much as she wants to hide it.

"I'll take you back with us under one condition," I say.

Carl looks at me expectantly.

"How do you control it? Tell me how you are able to touch people."

31

Kaylen's head snaps up. "What?" Her eyes flit from me to Carl.

I guess Kaylen didn't know about that… How? But I guess if she had known, she surely would have mentioned it at the compound when she met me.

"Yeah. Louise's file said my father's ability was the same as mine," I tell her. "Louise confirmed it. Even my uncle said so. Carl killed his baseball coach with his death-touch when he was a kid." I bore my eyes into Carl's now bewildered face. "Robert said you learned to control it. How?"

Kaylen is reeling. "That's just not possible," she whispers.

Carl, on the other hand, has drawn up an emotional wall. It's reminiscent of Louise's self-imposed meditation. "Very simple," he says. "But without your trust, I can't tell you. You're too powerful. I can't give you information you can use against me."

My jaw drops in disbelief. Is he for real? "Too powerful?" I say incredulously. "Use against you? What are you *talking* about? Telling me how to control it is ensuring I don't kill people. How on earth is that *using it against you*?"

Carl shakes his head. "You've never seen your ability for what it really is. It's much *much* more than you think. I know what you're going through, but this is bigger than you alone. You believe I've had a hand in harming people. You could destroy my work. I can't let that happen. I have to be able to trust you."

Kaylen scoffs. "Oh yes. Of course. Your work is more important than anything. You know what? You're just like Louise. I don't know why I didn't see it sooner. I just… always wanted to give you the benefit of the doubt. But I'm done being blind when it comes to you. You're a lying piece of crap. I don't even know you. I don't even *want* to know you."

I cross my arms and glare at Carl. "So that's your move? You're holding my happiness for ransom?"

"It's not like that," Carl says.

"Oh I know exactly what it's like," I snap. "You and Louise want to own the monopoly on making superheroes and you need *me* to do it."

Realization has been washing over Kaylen gradually, growing in increments as we stand there. It reaches a peak and she can't contain it. "*That's* why you grounded me from my phone and computer, isn't it?" she says "You purposely concocted that *stupid* fight all of a sudden about my grades, saying I wasn't working hard enough to earn the *privilege* of the internet and my phone... You only wanted to take away any means of having Wendy contact me, didn't you? So she'd start worrying about me and about Louise? And then you could spring this trap for her, huh? Get her to trust you?"

"Honey, I told you I was protecting us from Louise," Carl chides. "I couldn't have you contacting Wendy and giving away our location. It would ruin us."

"Why couldn't you tell *me* the truth then?" she demands.

I can tell Kaylen is right because Carl fidgets internally, running through various responses.

"All these years..." Kaylen breathes when Carl doesn't answer. "I've been nothing but an *experiment* to you. You lost Wendy, and you adopted me in hopes of making another one just like her, didn't you? All this time I've thought you felt so *bad* for allowing Louise to do hypno-touch on me when I was little. I thought you regretted it because I overheard you tell her once that it was all a mistake. That you never meant for me to have the powers I did. And I forgave all those years you kept me there... You were just keeping me from being exploited, right?" Kaylen shakes her head angrily, her cheeks wet. She all but collapses against the trunk of our car.

"But what you really meant was that *I* was a mistake," she continues. "You didn't mean for me to be telekinetic. You meant for me to be like *her*. Like Wendy. Because you're just like Louise. All you care about is life forces. And you want Wendy because she can see them. You don't want me at all. I didn't work out like you wanted and putting me at the compound was your way of putting me in the garbage."

Carl has grown angry again, and I can't stand feeling *myself* coming from him so I back away a few steps to escape it. His ears are red and he crosses his arms now, fighting for the right words to say now that he's been exposed for what he is.

Kaylen has climbed out of the doldrums of sadness though. The fury of betrayal rules her as she comes to accept what this man has done to her. A few rocks pick up off the ground and travel around her in a tight cyclone. I have to step away from her to avoid being hit.

As I replay her words, I look back to Carl, and something clicks. "Oh my gosh," I breathe. And then a bit louder, "*Instilled* me with an ability using hypno-touch? You weren't kidding, were you? Kaylen and I both have food allergies. And *I* have Type 1 Diabetes… *You* did that to us, didn't you? You made us *sick* as *kids* so you could screw with our life forces!"

Kaylen puts a hand over her mouth, and the rocks around her drop to the ground at once.

Louise looks from Carl to me. "Oh yes, *such* a burden," she sneers. "Your diabetes barely registers and a nut allergy is a dietary paper cut. Such a small price to pay for what your abilities can offer."

Carl looks like he's stewing over my rejection. And though he may not be in my emodar anymore, I can see ire move like a storm cloud over his face.

It unsettles me—not that the whole situation isn't unsettling—but to imagine that Carl's emotional patterns are so similar to mine fills me with disgust.

Carl appears to calm himself finally. He looks up, more confidence in his face than I've thus seen. "You help me and I'll help you," he says with a note of insolence.

Kaylen lets out a high-pitched groan. Maybe she was holding out some doubt about Carl. But now he's just admitted whose side he's on.

"Help you?" I say incredulously, taking a few steps closer to him again. "Do what? Kill people in the colorworld? You're out of your mind."

"Of course not," he says. He stares at me for several beats, coming to some conclusion before shaking his head in disbelief. "Why are you so antagonistic all the time? You could have made this so easy… You should have taken me with you. Now you've alienated any chance that I would help you short of your coming with me. What have you done with your ability outside of trying to get rid of it? That's exactly why I can't give you the information you want. How do I know you won't abuse it?"

"Really?" I reply snottily. "You're lecturing *me* on misusing information?"

"This isn't just about a few people with life force abilities," Carl says impatiently, *earnestly*. "I *created* you so you could help people. You have a responsibility. Can you *please* step outside yourself and see that your so-called death-touch is only a pinprick compared to the suffering going on in the world around you?"

"Suffering?" I fume—or maybe Carl's getting angry, too. His emotions are so similar to my own, though his are far more consuming. "You and Louise… you always give me piss-poor explanations and expect me to trust you because you say so. And then you turn around and lie through your teeth about *everything.*"

Carl runs an aggravated hand through his hair. "You necessitated it!" he insists. "You were *never* open. *Never* willing to explore what you could do. *Never* willing to take risks." Carl shakes his head, spreads his feet, grounded in defiance—another emotional tactic uncomfortably similar to my own. "You want the information that will fix your problem? Then you have no choice but to work with me."

"Why can't you just tell me what you really want?" I ask, trying not to beg. "To create superheroes? Is that what you think will *help* people?"

"There's more to it than that," Carl replies in a quieter voice now that I'm asking genuinely. "You see the energy world. I've never been able to see it in as much detail as you. I've only ever seen blurs of it, and I can't hear or smell it like you can. What I can do doesn't matter though. The point is that you are able to observe the energy world in a way that no one else can. And our energy is the invisible part of ourselves that will allow us to solve problems *here,* in *this* world. Energy theory is true. What you do to the life force, you do to the body. Physical ailments can be eliminated. Death can be staved off. Suffering can be ended. This is what I have dedicated my life to. It is the reason you are here."

I look away and hold my breath. Why am I still standing here listening to him? Why am I trying to talk to him like he's a rational human being?

Because I believe him.

I look heavenward, recognizing how true that answer is. The colorworld, to me, is a place that makes sense of so much of my life. I'm not one to ascribe greater meaning to things, but intrinsically I think the colorworld is an important part of who I am. So much about my life in the last couple months has been… impossible. But the colorworld remains. And despite Gabriel brushing me off the other day, I feel I'm supposed to be doing something more with it than I am.

I believe in energy medicine theory. And if someone as capable as me can manipulate life forces to give people astounding *superpowers,* imagine what I could do to help sickness? With my plans for a cure halted, I am confronted, head on, with the possibility of a life stuck like this.

And if this is my life, then what is my purpose?

Someone like me, with my history, *needs* purpose.

My daughter, Elena, proved that. I have owned fault for her death over and over. But no matter how much I think I have accepted it, it never goes away completely. A sudden heavy and unbearable guilt can weigh me down at the worst times. The only antidote is staying busy. Like when I took care of Ezra. And then in my efforts to nurture a relationship with Gabriel. But I have to face it: that may very well be over. And when it is, everything that I've screwed up in life will haunt me and I'm going to find myself desperate for an outlet.

Elena died from RSV, something babies get often but rarely die of. Is it possible that I have the ability to help prevent things like that? My eyes start to sting. I shuffle my feet, gripping my crossed arms tightly, trying to breathe normally.

I chose myself over Elena all those years ago. And chances are she'd still be alive if I hadn't. And now I have the chance to make up for some of that mistake by helping people via my abilities. But all I've cared about is getting *rid* of what I can do—because I can't live with the consequences. Just like Elena: I couldn't live with *her* as a consequence, so I got rid of her…

Carl is being genuine right now. I can tell his claims are real. I don't know whether what he envisions is possible, but I can *feel* his conviction that it is. He is either delusional or a hundred percent right.

Am I willing to give up the chance that he's right?

I put my hands on the back of my neck and touch my bare skin… skin that keeps me from a real relationship with my husband. I need to stop trying to *fix* it. I need to let it go, move forward.

I am so sick of screwing everything up.

I just want to do *something* right for once.

"Carl…" I whisper, looking up at the blue sky to keep my tears in. "Just tell me straight. What do you want from me? Why *wouldn't* I want to help you if it's a good cause?"

"It doesn't matter *what* their cause is," Kaylen says from somewhere behind me. "They're killing people. Did you forget that, Wendy?"

"You won't have to hurt anyone," Carl interjects, excited by my desperation. "That was the wrong direction, and both Louise and I know it. You can help so many. No one knows what you're going through like I do, so let me help you. My way. I just can't help you like you want. Not like this. Some things are more important than our own happiness."

He looks down, conflicted. "I'm sorry you feel betrayed by me, but I have always placed the good of humanity over all else. It's why Sara took you away. She believed you shouldn't have that responsibility. It was too much. But look what has happened? Your destiny came back to haunt you. All this struggle you feel? It's fate's way of pointing you back in the right direction. Don't ignore it."

"You know what *I* don't get?" Kaylen says, stepping forward, next to me. "The way you've gone about this. You could have helped Wendy with her problem right off the bat and she would have done whatever you wanted—no matter *what* her mom or her uncle had said about you. It doesn't add up, Dad. You and Louise murder all those people and make Wendy hate you. Why would you do that?"

I snap my head up and look from Kaylen, whose tears have dried, to Carl's face, which he struggles to keep impassive.

He's nowhere near as good as Louise at controlling his emotions though. Kaylen has definitely asked the one question he hoped I wouldn't ask. He looks from Kaylen to me, and I think he wonders if he's expected to answer.

Carl's hesitation speaks volumes. He struggles for a response. For a good lie. For the right thing to say.

He settles on an excuse, but he also knows I have been experiencing his struggle. He can't lie his way out of this. He shakes his head finally. "No. You are not in a place to bargain. You either come with me, or you live like you are. And mark my words: you will not ever solve your problem without me."

I glare at him as the lion within me reemerges. Carl may think his words scare me, but he doesn't know me very well. A breeze of relief clears the last of the confusion from my head and I see him exactly as he is: desperate and hopeless. He's been working for what? Twenty years at least trying to… do whatever it is he's doing? No, I don't need him. He needs *me.*

"I will not go with you," I say confidently. "Not now. Not ever." I like the way the words sound coming out of my mouth. Even with what may happen after I leave here, it's still freeing.

Utilizing my ability for something other than a cure doesn't have to include Carl and Louise and their completely amoral methods. Of that I am sure.

Carl looks at me shrewdly and backs away slowly. "You'll come looking for me sooner or later. We are at war, Wendy, and you have just chosen the wrong side." He holds out a hand, "Come on, Kaylen."

She laughs mirthlessly. "Yeah right."

"You are my daughter and you will do as I say," Carl says firmly, authoritatively. "Now come along."

"I'm not going *anywhere* with a sick bastard like you," Kaylen says, easing a step closer to me until she's only a couple feet from my side. It makes me nervous, but I'm not going to put up a fuss right now.

"Kaylen. Now!" Carl orders.

Kaylen's countenance grows fierce; her hair swirls around her face, and she holds her hands out to her sides like she's summoning energy from the earth.

She looks at Carl with wide, taunting eyes and says, "Make me."

32

Moments after Kaylen issues her challenge, a slew of rocks rise up and fling themselves toward Louise and Carl.

"Car!" shouts Kaylen.

I leap for the driver's-side door, and Kaylen dives for the back seat. I don't pause to see what Louise and Carl are doing. I throw the car into drive and punch the gas.

Just then, I hear the popping sound of a gun and the shattering of glass. "Kaylen!" I shout.

"I'm fine!" she yells.

I will the car to move faster; my foot is all the way to the floor. It would probably work better if I had accelerated a little more slowly and given the wheels time to find purchase. As it is, we aren't in motion for a few seconds. The tires spin and the engine screams in protest. I'm too terrified to think, and I duck my head to get it out of range of any flying bullets. I turn the wheel wildly, fighting for control. The tires spin out from under me, fishtailing and sending us off the road and into the craggy desert.

More shots. I hear Louise's voice beyond the dust cloud that our tires have kicked up, "Don't kill her, just aim for the tires!"

I accelerate and jerk the wheel again to circumvent the other car and head back the way we came.

I swerve this way and that, trying desperately to move in one direction, and then I hear Kaylen scream. I glance behind me just long enough to see her being flung out of the car. She rolls into the dirt at the same time that I slam on the brakes. I throw my door open and launch myself toward her instinctively, but in the same instant wonder what it is I think I can do for her. I'm not gloved.

I turn back to get my spare gloves out of the car but there are more shots. I have to duck to the ground instead.

I peek beyond the car to see that we're only about fifty yards from Louise, close enough for a gun to still be deadly. Sure, she doesn't want to kill *me*, but she might kill Kaylen to get to me. I wish I'd gone off on the other side of the road; at least then my car would be between us and the figures approaching through the thick cloud of dust.

I turn back to Kaylen who, thankfully, looks like she's coming around. She sits up, looking a little bewildered. She glares in the direction of Louise and Carl, fire building in her eyes once more; her hair starts floating again.

"This is for you, *Dad,*" she says quietly.

All of a sudden the ground beneath me shakes and I hear a rumbling like thunder. A great wave of dirt flies straight up in front of us. The force of it pulls me forward and I tumble down a very steep hill. It feels like an earthen undertow.

The dirt forms a wall in front of us and then launches itself forward and away. The force of the retreating wave leaves a vacuum behind it that sucks me forward and my head slams into the rock-strewn ground.

Pain explodes from my forehead. My awareness starts dissolving until all I can see is darkness.

***

Someone is yelling my name.

And I'm absolutely terrified with no understanding as to why I'm so scared. Underneath the terror I'm in confused awe, like I've been surprised by something I did not imagine was possible. I neglect the surprise for distress again. Someone calls my name once more. Whoever it is, they are very close to me. Too close.

Instinctively I try to get away. Whoever it is should keep their distance from me, especially when I'm unconscious. And I know I am, or at least in the place between sleep and awake. I can't find my senses. My head is too hazy.

But I don't think I have full control of my arms and legs. Someone is yanking on my leg, jostling me, making me more aware. And whatever I'm lying on is not very soft. It's hard and rough. My shirt has ridden up and my spine is scraping rocks.

I open my eyes and see the blue cloudless sky above me. Pressing more firmly against the veil of fogginess, I fight for my legs. When I reach full awareness, I fling my arms out to stop myself from moving. Finally, my legs are free and I see Kaylen.

"You're awake!" she exclaims, standing near my feet, her eyes wide. "Get in the car. We've got to go!"

We are right next to the car. I think Kaylen has been dragging me by my denim-clad leg into the back seat and has obviously not gotten very far with it.

I still haven't fully processed the situation, but the look on Kaylen's face moves me into action. I stand up as quickly as I can, but then grasp my head, still woozy, and sink back to my knees.

I scramble on all fours for the driver's seat, but can't shake the dizziness from my head. "Can you drive?" I gasp.

"Uh—um, I don't think—and you—" she stutters.

"Forget it," I say. "I'll drive. I don't have gloves on so get in the back."

She scrambles in while I scan our surroundings. Some fifty yards in the distance I see freshly turned-over earth. People are pushing through it, standing. One sits up, looking disoriented.

It's Louise.

I need to get us out of here. Fast.

I throw the car into drive and accelerate, this time more slowly with the terrain in mind. I'm still recovering from unconsciousness, and I shake my head and blink several times. I glance at Kaylen in the rearview mirror. She's sitting with her knees tucked up, her eyes wide. She's lost in bewildered panic.

Not wanting to miss a threat, I look into the distance again and catch sight of a hole, about ten yards away, maybe twenty yards across, and several feet deep. I look from it to Louise's position amid the mound of earth in the distance.

"You did that?" I ask in amazement as I maneuver over and around the rough terrain.

She doesn't answer. I focus on getting the car back to the smoother road. Once I hit it, I glance in the back again, expecting that Kaylen will relax now.

She doesn't.

"Kaylen!" I say firmly and loudly, trying to calm her. "We're okay! We're getting away, see? It's going to be okay."

Kaylen whimpers a little at the sound of my voice.

I don't have time to analyze what's going on with her. I keep checking my rearview mirror for our pursuers. It looks clear so far. I have to press myself against the headrest to keep the fogginess in my head under control, but at least I can see okay now.

Kaylen's hysteria hasn't left though, and it's making it hard for me to concentrate when I already feel so out of it. "Kaylen, why—"

"I touched you!" she wails suddenly. "Am I okay? How long does it take? Am I going to die?"

She clings to the shoulder belt, her knuckles white, tears springing to her eyes.

I look at my bare arms. “Kaylen, no. You didn’t touch me. Why do you—”

“No!” she insists. “In the hole, when you were unconscious! I touched you. Please, tell me! Am I going to die now?” she sobs, beside herself.

“You—you touched me?” I ask, looking at my arms again as if I might see her fingerprints.

Kaylen is silent but for her quiet sobs. I look at her in the mirror again, take in her fear, which is nowhere near the kind of horror someone experiences when they are dying from my skin contact.

I know she’s okay. But the disbelief that yet *another* person has escaped my death-touch is simply too good to be true.

“Kaylen…” I start, and then hesitate, wanting to be sure I say the right thing. “You’re fine, Kaylen. You would be dead by now, or at least knocked out. You must be… You must be immune,” I say, disbelieving my own words.

“Really?” she says, catching my eye in the mirror. She gasps a few more times and wipes her tears away briskly, sniffling.

“Yes. But why would you touch me? Did I fall into you? Oh my gosh, *why* did I take my stupid gloves off?” I bang the steering wheel in aggravation.

“I forgot because everything was crazy,” she says pleadingly. “But I remembered right after I put my hands on you and I let go. I saw Louise and my dad coming around, and I just panicked. I needed to get you out of that hole. I was depleted. I didn’t have enough energy left after throwing that much dirt so far—which I still can’t believe I did. That has *never* happened before. Of course, I’ve never saved up that much energy before either and I was so *mad…*”

Her face darkens, and then she shakes her head. “Anyway, I figured I was going to die anyway, and I wanted to get you to the car, so I grabbed your arm and pulled you. But it was so crazy, Wendy. When I touched you… I swear, it was like a current passed from you to me and I had energy to power my ability again. I didn’t hesitate. I cleared an incline up and out that I could drag you up. I even lifted the car up and closer to us so I didn’t have to drag you so far.

“I couldn’t get you in the car though so I called your name. I thought, if I was going to die, you should at least get out—Wendy, am I really going to be okay?”

"Yeah..." I say, thinking about the strangeness of what she just said. *I powered her ability?* "Touching me that long should have knocked you out on the spot."

I amaze myself with how easy it is to say, like I'm an exterminator discussing the effectiveness of a particular pesticide spray. I must be in shock.

"Thank God you're alright," I breathe.

"I guess I really am immune to you then," Kaylen says, testing out the words, significantly calmer now.

I check the rearview mirror and see the clouds of dust still in the distance. No vehicle is behind us... yet.

"But what happened?" Kaylen asks then. "I was totally leeched-out, I could hardly lift a pebble when we were in that hole. How did you do that? How did you pass energy to me?"

"I have no idea," I say, wondering the same thing.

My thoughts jump to Gabriel then. I know exactly what he'll make of Kaylen's immunity. I don't, however, know how he'll link the energy transference to his theory, but I'm confident he can and he will.

"Kaylen..." I start, hesitating to lie to Gabriel yet again.

"Yeah?" she says, concerned by my tone.

I adjust my hands on the steering wheel nervously. "Please don't... tell anyone you touched me... or that I uh, jump started you."

The words sound so deceitful out loud, much worse than they sounded in my head. I hate it and I bite my lip, reassuring myself that I'm doing it to protect Gabriel.

Kaylen is obviously confused by my request, and I continue, "Gabriel thinks I only kill the bad people I touch. But he only has a handful of evidence to support it. I'm afraid that if you tell him, he'll take it to support his theory and touch me." I search for her eyes in the rearview mirror, pleading with my own to convey my desperation. "I couldn't take it if he was wrong. I can't take the risk of killing him. Please."

She gets over the surprise of my request quickly. "So that's why you guys have seemed so... on edge. He wants to touch you?"

I swallow back the misery that's building now that our recent catastrophe is behind us. "Yes. He's dead set on this theory of his. He won't take no for an answer. I don't know what to do... I *know* he's going to test it if you tell him what you just did."

Kaylen's eyes are wide with amazement but not disbelief. She knows Gabriel's drive pretty well, too. "Oh Gabe…" she says to herself, shaking her head. Then she glances up at me. "Okay, if that's what you want. It was my own fault anyway. I didn't realize how much of the ground I was going to pull out from under us—I really didn't expect to pull so much. And then I didn't think about the kickback when I threw it and you got knocked out… Sorry about that."

"No harm done," I say. By yet *another* miracle.

Well, I probably have a concussion, but that's way better than any of the alternatives. Things could have gone so wrong…

"I just miscalculated," she says, still apologetic. "I can only move things within my radius, and there was nothing there except dirt! I was sure I was skirting our position but it collapsed under us anyway. I've never done it before—and did you see how big of an area I affected? Holy cow! It was *yards*! No wonder I got worn out. I didn't know what I was doing. And then I threw everything I had left into flinging it at them and… oh man, did you feel how fast it was?"

Kaylen babbles through her own awe, but I don't mind. It's fascinating, and I'm finally getting over the shock of not killing her.

Thankfully we hit the paved road and I can pick up speed. Then I feel sadness, which I find is coming from Kaylen. I glance back at her again. She's staring out the window.

"Hey, I'm sorry about your uh, dad," I say, making an assumption about her melancholy.

Kaylen takes a slow breath. "Yeah… you too. I think I might be in denial. It's not bothering me nearly as much as I would have thought... Or maybe I'm too angry at him right now to care. The way he tried to manipulate you…? How he refused to help you even though he *must* know what you're going through?" Kaylen shakes her head and grits her teeth. "I had no idea. *No* idea he's been working with Louise so closely. He's a *CPA*! How did I miss it? Everything about him was a lie!" She throws her hands up and then looks at me. "I've never seen him wear gloves, Wendy. *Ever.* And his vision? He wears *reading* glasses! Unless that was just another act…" She crosses her arms. "I have no idea."

Resentment consumes Kaylen. Carl may be my father, too, but my only desire is to never see him again. Just noting our similarities is enough to make me squirm internally. I don't ever want to be him, and I guess, considering my past, I worry that I'm not so far off the mark…

But my mom… More lies from her… If Carl told me the truth, and I believe he mostly did, Mom lied to me about my dad, about my abilities, and even about being my mother. I wonder what else she kept from me. And *why*? So many *lies* she had to maintain. Was it really so important to her that Ezra and I not know anything that was hard? Did it really give us the *unburdened* lives she imagined for us? I think not. I think she made things *harder* by not telling us anything. Just look at the mess I made of my teenaged years. And look at the mess I'm in now because no one bothered to tell me the truth about myself.

Kaylen emerges from her own reflections then. "Were you really considering going with him?"

I sigh. "Yeah, for a few moments. Because desperation made me forget everything I knew about him and Louise."

Kaylen is amazed at my declaration of weakness, but at that moment I see a car approaching us head-on.

I remember then that while Carl was talking I heard my phone ring in the car. Gabriel checking up most likely. He must have worried when I didn't answer or call back. That must be him and Robert and whoever else heading our way.

I check behind us again but see no one. After another minute, I see there's more than one car headed toward us. I bet they're all Robert's vehicles. When we finally reach each other, I slow to a stop and stick my head out.

Gabriel's head appears from the first vehicle. His face is blanched and worried until he sees both Kaylen and me. But then his brow furrows as he eyes my naked arm on the door frame. "You're alright?" he asks. "Where's Kevin Fowler?"

Ezra peeks around Gabriel with a similar look of concern.

I bite my lip. "Kevin Fowler is really Carl Haricott. And he works with Louise. We can tell you about it when we get back."

Gabriel and Ezra's jaws both drop. Gabriel is close enough to me that I can feel the questions jostling for position in his head. "Let's just get back where it's safe," I say.

Without another word, he pulls forward. He turns around and gets behind me.

As I exhale and drive down the road, I'm amazed at Louise's cunning. She almost had me. If I hadn't overheard her while I was in that tree in Riverside, would I have questioned Carl's coming with us? I have no idea.

"Now I get why Robert was so familiar," Kaylen remarks. "He looks a lot like my dad."

"Yep," I say. "And now we get to find out how much of this Robert actually *knew* about. Gabriel and I have felt like he's been holding something back."

Kaylen snorts. "I'm still trying to figure out how my dad kept his secret career with Louise from me my whole life…"

After a few more silent moments, she says, "So we both climbed out of the pit and hopped in the car?"

"That's exactly what happened," I reply, nodding.

33

"Wendy, I had no idea my brother was still alive," Robert says emphatically. "If Leena knew, she never told me. And I had no idea you weren't Leena's biological child. But it explains why she refused my protection and opted to just disappear."

I sigh. I am never going to know the truth about anything. Robert, from what I've sensed in the few times I've been near him since we got back from the desert, is in turmoil. It's not really something I can translate.

"This family is a freak show," Ezra says for the second time since we got back and explained what happened. "I need to start my *own* comic book. This stuff is better than fiction!"

"I'm going to take a shower now," I say wearily. "I'm filthy."

Then I heave myself to my feet and leave the room. Everyone is still in shock except for me. I'm in resignation mode. To me there are bigger problems than whether Carl is still alive.

In the shower, I expect to start crying my eyes out about what is to come. Our trip is drawing to a close which means Gabriel's promise is about to expire. I need to cry about it before I confront him and possibly make our separation official. But the tears don't come. I stay in the shower for forty-five minutes waiting for it. But indifference remains.

I opt for thinking since my brain has chosen to behave so rationally. I like to imagine that if I don't address Gabriel's ultimatum, it will go away. But I know it won't. Thanks to my near-miss with Kaylen so recently, the lethal nature of my skin is in the forefront of my thoughts. I can't be a passenger in this. Gabriel's life is on the line. I have to decide. I have to *act.* And there are only two solutions: allow Gabriel to touch me or leave him.

So I'm leaving.

How ironic that before, I thought what I wanted was to find a solution to my condition. The prospect of being unable to touch people for the rest of my life seemed unbearable. That possibility now looks like a blessed reprieve. If only the impossibility of a cure was the only thing I had to contend with. I would gladly spend the rest of my life with Gabriel, not touching him, as long as I had the assurance that he would keep well away.

I could tell Gabriel to forget a cure altogether. He asked me that once—whether I wanted him to stop looking. He said if I told him to stop, he'd never look for a cure again. I don't doubt that he would have kept that promise if I'd asked. But I don't see that happening now.

And the truth is I don't think I ever *can* give up on a cure. So even if he *did* agree to stop looking, telling him I don't want to find one anymore would be a lie. I can't live so many lies. I can't repeat my mom's mistakes. So I can't be with him.

I know what I need to do. But I can't find the courage in me to do it.

***

"You're looking well," says Gabriel from where he sits cross-legged on the bed as I come out of the bathroom. It's dark outside and there is only one lamp on in the room. The dimness of the room matches my mood.

"Thanks." I stuff my toiletries in my duffle bag, purposely avoiding his eyes. I'm carrying so much guilt right now that I'm sure he can see it. I can't live like this. It feels worse than the impending loss. I start searching for some way to do this. Something to say to start the conversation. But my mouth is immobile. My convictions are in an upheaval now that he's in front of me.

"Are you going to speak to me in one-word answers from now on?" he asks. I see him grinning at me out of the corner of my eye.

"I haven't been back for more than an hour, so how can you make a distinction about my conversation habits so quickly?" I ask. "Kaylen did the story telling, and the rest of the time I just spent taking a shower."

Why are you stalling? Get it over with so you can go cry in a closet somewhere.

I throw my sore body on the couch. Kaylen did a great job with the story. I'm grateful I wasn't conscious for the part she had to lie about. For all I know, it happened exactly as she said.

"I can tell," he says, watching me.

Stupid over-perceptive husband.

I stare at the ceiling, hoping to find what to say next.

"You took off your gloves I saw…" he says.

I do my best not to react and maintain a cool tone. "I told you I was going to. Besides, it was hot as Hades out there. I worried I might die of sunstroke."

"Understandable," he says thoughtfully. "Perhaps we should move somewhere where the weather is cooler year-round."

I don't respond.

"Where would you like to go?"

I look over at him briefly. "Why are you so intent on moving somewhere?"

"I'm not intent on moving. Only on making you happy. If you need to move to Alaska to be more comfortable, I'll do it."

I stare at him for a long moment. He's willing to drop everything to move somewhere where the temperatures are more bearable for me, but not willing to make me the one promise that *will* make me happy?

"You suck at making me happy," I say simply, turning away from his face to look back at the ceiling. It was harsh, but it needed to be said. This all has to end somewhere. And soon. His safety depends on it. I pick up a spasm of regret from him in response to my words. He's on the edge of my range, so I don't get much more than that.

"How do you feel about your dad being alive?" asks Gabriel after a moment.

I wrinkle my nose. What's he getting at? I expected him to respond with some comment about my pessimism and close-mindedness. Then we'd get in some fight about how I can't live with his ultimatums and then I'd tell him I'm leaving. He'd get upset, and I'd dissolve in a puddle of sobs. Yeah, that's how this is supposed to go. But instead he asks me a totally unrelated question like I didn't just tell him he's a crappy husband.

I look at him with a bit of confusion and answer, "He's not my dad."

"Well, not as a father *figure* but in a biological sense..."

"I never knew my Dad so I didn't have any beliefs about him. Mom didn't talk about him much."

I stare at the ceiling again. If he is going to ignore my controversial remarks about our relationship, it's going to be really hard to break this off.

Break this off. That sounds really final. My breaths shorten.

"You must have had some idea of him in your head. Your mother must have told you things about him. You know, like what he was like. Kids always want to believe their parents are superheroes."

"Not really. Like I said, she didn't talk about him much. Now that I've met him, I can see why."

Where is he going with this?

"So why did you push so hard from the get-go that he was on Louise's side?"

I sigh. I can come clean on this lie at least. "Because when we were doing surveillance on that psychic's place and I heard her voice, I overheard her planning her own kidnapping. So I knew she was behind the whole thing. And if she was behind it, the only explanation was that Carl was too."

"You didn't tell me that."

I shrug.

"You could have ignored that and brought him along with you, maybe gotten some answers. He could have helped you."

I snort. "He can't help me."

"How do you know?"

"The way he's gone about this whole thing… I can tell. Why has it taken *this* long for him to come forward? He couldn't tell me *anything* I don't already know? Louise knew how badly I wanted to figure out my condition. They could have gone about this a million other ways. It doesn't compute. He doesn't know anything."

"You don't know that for sure," Gabriel says. "You can't know he doesn't have a cure. What would you have had to lose? How *does* he touch people?"

I shake my head. I have no clue. "If my mom worked so hard to keep me away from him, I wanted to keep Kaylen away from him, too. I didn't want to let him in like I did Louise and get screwed. It was too risky."

I think about it for a few moments, surprised to find practically no regret over that decision.

"Besides," I continue, "I'm starting to suspect he lost his ability like Dina. Kaylen said he wears glasses. And if not and his ability is like mine, that must mean he can manifest abilities as well as I can. So why do they need me at all? Why else would he try to duplicate his abilities in Kaylen after he lost me? I think it's because he can't anymore. I think his plan was to come with us and earn my trust, but when he saw that I wasn't going to allow it, he tried to make me believe he still had his ability so he could hold it over my head…" I shrug. "Maybe life force abilities wear off."

"That's a fascinating lead for you," Gabriel says. "I'm especially intrigued by how he managed to give you diabetes. I suppose it's possible, and he *is* a doctor. But that would still be quite a feat. I guess that's why your disease has never been as unpredictable as most individuals with juvenile onset. I'd love to know precisely how he did it… Do you think you'll lose your ability like he did?"

"I have no idea. So far it's not looking that way—especially since my ability already improved once." I heave a sigh. "And whether or not I lose it in twenty years doesn't really matter. It doesn't change things as they are right now."

I roll over and grab a throw pillow to tuck under my chin as I stare across the floor. I trace the pattern of the wood planks with my eyes. It's cherry probably, expensive surely.

Gabriel is quiet for a long time, and I think about what Carl said about his eyesight and the colorworld. He can't hear or smell it. To me, that means there is no one out there with any more knowledge about my condition than me. I'm alone, on my own to figure it out by myself.

"Do you love me, Wendy?" Gabriel asks then.

I look up at him, concentrating on the sound of our breaths, matching mine to his. *It's coming.*

"Yes, Gabriel. You know that."

"Under what conditions would you be willing to stay with me?"

"I don't want you to touch me."

"Ever?"

"Until I say so," I answer, quelling the vain hope that somehow Gabriel will comply with my wishes.

"And if I disagree?" he says.

I sigh and focus back on the floor. "I can't stay with you."

I glance up quickly to see him nodding pensively, looking past me. I partly wish he was closer so I could tell if there is any hope that he's considering giving me what I want. But when the time comes, I don't think I can stand to feel *his* emotions fully as well as my own.

"I have put you in an unfair place, I realize that. I *want* to promise you what you ask for. You know that, right?" he says, focusing on me.

"No, Gabriel. If you wanted to promise me, you would have done it."

"It seems that way to you, doesn't it?" he says.

I don't answer. My silence is my reply.

"You know how you just *know* your dad doesn't have a cure?"

"Yeah…?" I reply, confused.

"You don't really have any solid proof, you know. In fact, you have so much evidence to the opposite."

"So what?" I say, getting aggravated that he's jumping around so much.

"I bet part of you even wants to believe he has a cure, but you reject it so it will fit into what you want, which is to have nothing to do with him."

I roll over on my elbow to look at him more fully. "Whatever method of control he may or may not have, I would never trust him enough to try it out. So it doesn't matter. He's delusional."

Gabriel is not looking at me again. He's looking down. And I barely pick up on him agonizing over something. "Yet you still made the decision on what you *believe* to be true... It's the same for me," he says quietly. "I can't explain why I believe so strongly in what I do about your condition, but I had an idea. It was reasonable."

I shake my head. "Just because it's reasonable doesn't mean you act on it. Especially not where death is involved. There are too many alternative explanations."

He looks at my face, his eyes pleading with me. "There will *always* be alternatives. *Everything* is refutable."

Several moments of silence pass between us as we look at each other. Unlike when we usually connect this way, now we beg each other. I wish Gabriel could see things the way I do for just a moment… then he would understand. But he doesn't. I can see it in his eyes. He is going to take this as far as it can be taken.

"I can't do it," I say finally. "Don't ask me to take that risk with you. It's not fair. How can you love me and try to force my hand like this?"

"It's *because* I love you that I refuse to watch you driven by fear. You want me to let you be unhappy. *That's* not fair."

"It's not fear. It's reason," I say, my voice starting to catch. "It's caution. It has nothing to do with my happiness, which you seem to think you know better than I do. Why don't you get that?"

"I told you I'm going to do whatever it takes to keep you happy," he says softly. "I'm willing to put my life on the line to do it. Why can't you let me?"

A few hot tears spring forth and my head spins. "Because if you die, I will never *ever* be able to endure the memory."

"Why are you always so afraid of your emotions?" he asks gently.

This is going nowhere.

"Some decisions are just made on faith that what we see is what is," he continues. "You have to make them based on what you know, not on what you feel or what you *fear* feeling."

"You don't know *anything* about real fear," I say angrily, brushing my eyes and bringing my knees up into a fetal position to squeeze the knots in my stomach. "And you don't care at all how I feel. You only care about what you think you know."

His head is bowed, his eyes closed. "No. You're wrong," he whispers. He opens his eyes and looks at me. "I only care about your happiness. You insist you would be happy if I would drop this, but everything you do shows me that's not true. You pushed me away because you're afraid of exploring any kind of intimacy, and that was before I ever revealed my theory. What do you expect me to do? Watch you waste away in misery? Let you push me away further?"

I don't have an answer to that. And every word he says makes me believe more and more that this marriage was a mistake. We will never see eye-to-eye on this. Gabriel will never respect my condition like he ought to.

"I could make the promise you ask for," he says, watching my face. "But I can't be sure that if the right circumstances presented themselves, I wouldn't break it. If I said the words, it would only be temporary happiness. And I won't settle for less than the *real* thing for you."

I can't bear to look at him, but there is so much sincerity in his voice. Even with my constricted anguish threatening to surface, his earnestness tugs at me even on the edge of my emodar. That and the sound of his calm and kind voice that I hear every day makes me long to be with him forever. I can't comprehend how he can love me as much as I know he does yet do this to me.

I want to hate him. It would be easier. Maybe if I wasn't an empath I could. But it's hard to be bitter when his love for me can touch my heart even through my own pain.

My tears are falling in earnest now. They drip onto the blue upholstered pillow tucked under my chin. But it must be water resistant because the droplets don't soak in. They shoot down the incline, leaping off of the edge. I don't see where they land. The floor probably.

I have the sudden urge to look to be sure, like this small assurance of the law of gravity will make this moment less out of control. I lean forward a little, but there is no puddle on the floor.

Where are my tears going?

"I won't ever break a promise to you, Wendy," he says quietly, deliberately. "Too many people have let you down. I won't be one of those people, even if it divides us now. I never want you to look back and see that I let you down like that."

My chest is throbbing. A couple more tears leap off the side of the pillow.

"So you're leaving," I choke out in a whisper.

"No. But you're asking me to leave," he says solemnly, the darkness of his sorrow compounding my pain so much that it's unbearable. I can't move. It hurts so much.

"Yes," I whisper, wishing he would go away already. I can't stand this. I pinch my eyes shut, and then hear the rustle of his bag and his footsteps as he walks out the door and down the stairs.

I sit up as soon as I hear the front door open and close. I need to figure out where my tears went. I don't know why I care. Maybe I want to distract myself from what just happened.

As soon as I lift the pillow, there they are: they've gathered together into a tiny puddle. With the pillow now out of the way, the tears stream down the water-resistant couch cushion where my weight has made a depression. The puddle reaches my jeans and slowly wicks into them as I watch.

And then I slink to the floor.

They say you shouldn't bottle up your sadness. But I don't know if I believe that. No matter how many tears I've let out over the years, they always manage to return to me.

Part II

34

"Wen? Wendy!" Ezra says loudly.

I turn to him standing by the counter across from me.

"Do you want some eggs? I'm making some for me and Kaylen," he says, holding up an egg carton.

His purple life force swirls around his face, glowing luminously, flowing and feeding into the swirl of his chest. It's so lovely.

"Kaylen and *myself*," I correct.

He rolls his eyes. "Yeah thanks, grammar queen. Do you want some or not?"

I shake my head.

Ezra scrutinizes my face, and even though he's not in my emodar I can tell he wants to say something but doesn't know what. He sighs instead and turns back to the counter.

I'm in the colorworld—I've spent a lot of time there over the last couple months. This morning I use Kaylen as my channel to access it. She reads a magazine, not oblivious to my use of her arm, but unconcerned by it.

As I sit with my chin propped on my hand, I stare at the glazed, terra cotta tiles of the kitchen floor. They're handmade and vary in hue in the visible world. In the colorworld they range from sky blue to lavender to pale pink. If I move my head a little bit, the colors change along that scale, and in a coordinated way so that the tiles appear to be part of one entity.

I'm enthralled with phenomena like this in the colorworld. Living things have more static hues while inanimate objects are more dynamic. If I stand at one end of a room and then switch to the other end, the colors are never alike. Nothing is exactly as it first appears in the colorworld.

The perception-dependent nature of this mysterious place makes me believe that these moments of stagnancy cannot possibly go on forever. Somehow, one day, I'm going to find a different approach to my life. I'm going to move forward and things will finally look different.

Besides coming here for comfort, my regular visits to the colorworld have revealed that if conditions are right, I can tell the difference in brightness between life forces—confirming what I saw from the plane that day. I can only tell when two people are far enough away from me—at least ten feet—and if they are nearby another person for comparison purposes. But not too close. If they stand too near one another, their light seems to reflect off of one another so that they appear the same. But if they are several feet away from each other, I can pick out which of them is brighter as long as the difference is significant enough. Kaylen and Ezra, for instance, are too close in 'wattage' that I can't tell if one shines brighter than the other. In the few times I've looked at people out in public, I've become more frustrated than intrigued because I have been unable to establish a scale to gauge what I see. It's exactly like trying to determine the wattage of a lightbulb in broad daylight. I also have no idea if someone's wattage changes throughout the day or if it remains static. Robert, however, is one exception so far. He is clearly brighter than anyone else I have observed since I discovered there is a difference in such things, and I don't need a basis of comparison to know—that's how much he shines. But I don't know what any of this means.

I don't share my insights about the brightness of life forces with anyone. I don't want anyone to tell me how this evidence supports Gabriel's theory—which they all think is valid. After Gabriel left, Ezra even tried to tell me he thinks Gabriel's smart enough to have looked at this from all angles. "Just give him a chance," Ezra said. "He only wants to make you happy."

"A chance to kill himself?" I asked him. "This isn't a mathematical theorem that needs testing. This is life and death that *none* of you have *ever* taken seriously."

Ezra has kept his mouth shut since then, but emotions don't lie. He and Kaylen both feel sorry for me in a way that leads me to believe they think I'm being unreasonable. Neither of them are in my shoes though; people always feel at liberty to advise others on when and what to risk. I can't possibly expect them to really get it.

I've been apart from Gabriel for almost two months. To my bitter-sweet surprise, I am getting used to it. I'm staying busy. Robert has promoted me to mail room supervisor because of my voracious work-ethic. Every week I plan out a dinner menu and spend a lot of time locating hard-to-find ingredients, prepping, and cooking. I focus on each day because I don't think I can bear to imagine the future. And it's working. I'm making it through each day without being too tempted to turn to the emotional highs of my past.

I stand up and leave the colorworld because I'm thinking too much. My butt is starting to feel like lead in this chair. Whenever that happens, I know I have to get moving. I go over to the sink, change into a pair of rubber gloves, and wring out a rag. I start wiping down the counters and putting away Ezra's breakfast things. I find an all-purpose cleaner and start spraying the table.

Ezra lifts up his plate. "Geez, Wen. I'm not even done yet."

I spray under his raised arms and wipe. "You're making a mess," I say. "Why can't you eat *over* your plate like Kaylen?"

Ezra sighs heavily and he thinks about something *else* he wants to say. I'm sure I don't want to hear whatever it is so I don't even look up. I finish my meticulous back and forth movement across the table, admiring the wet snaking pattern I leave on the table.

I take the rag back to the kitchen sink and shake out the crumbs from Ezra's toast. Then I find a dry towel and start buffing the stainless steel sink. This has become one of my favorite things to do—I love the look of spotless metal.

When I'm done, I lean against the sink and wait for them to finish eating.

"In the name of the Guardians, Wendy, how long is this anal cleaning fetish going to last?" Ezra complains, noticing me watching him.

I raise a questioning eyebrow. "Weren't *you* the one always telling me what a slob I was before?"

"I prefer the slob to this Stepford homemaker routine," he replies.

Kaylen elbows him. "Stop it," she says. "Cleaning is cathartic."

"Nothing's wrong with cleaning," Ezra says, cringing away from her, "but I can't eat when she stares me down like that, just waiting for one crumb to fall out of line."

I roll my eyes. "Fine, I'll go away and change for my run."

I switch into my other gloves and push away from the counter. I walk out of the kitchen, but as soon as I hit the stairs, the phone rings.

I pause for the briefest moment with my hand on the banister. Grip it firmly to steady my heart that leapt at the sound. Like it always does. Then I walk carefully up the stairs. Since my incident with Ezra, I've made it a habit to take stairs slowly, pausing every few steps to look around. I do the same thing at work when I walk down a hallway. I stop at each doorway like it's an intersection on the street. I've developed some pretty effective habits that have allowed me to feel more comfortable in public with people around.

I only make it about halfway up the stairs when Kaylen's voice sounds from behind me, "It's for you, Wendy."

I pause on the step. Turn slightly to look at her. *He* is the only one that calls me. And he tries every day at some point. Robert, Kaylen, and Ezra know not to even ask. When Ezra picks up the phone, he just hangs up. I never ever answer the phone. Sometimes he calls me at work, but I always hang up when I hear his voice.

Kaylen looks apprehensive.

"I'm not—" I start.

"It's not him," she interrupts, though there is still hesitancy in her voice.

I sigh and walk carefully back down the stairs to take the receiver from her.

"Hello?" I say.

"Hola, Wendy!" says a familiar voice. My instinct is to hang up on her, but that would be childish. It's not Gabriel. I can handle his mother, can't I?

"Uh, hi, Maris," I reply, unsure.

"Feliz cumpleaños!" she says. "Happy Birthday!"

I'm confused at first. *It's my birthday?* I totally forgot. *What kind of person forgets their own birthday?*

"Thanks, Maris," I reply, not offering further small-talk. I want to get off the phone. I've not spoken to Maris since my wedding.

My wedding. My wedding. The memory is surfacing and repeating the words over and over keeps it from playing.

A long sigh emanates from the other end of the line and then, in true Dumas form, Maris says, "I won't pretend I'm calling for polite conversation. But I've been praying for you this morning and felt impressed to call. Dios, dame la fuerza… I know it's not my place to intervene in this whole business—at least not aside from telling my son he's not welcome in my home until he brings you with him—but I thought… well… you might be able to use some words of encouragement. Tú eres mi hija."

Wow. She won't let him in her house?

"Encouragement for what?" I ask, swallowing to gather my stoicism.

"For putting my obstinato hijo through his paces, of course," Maris says. "I'm proud of you for holding your ground. Tan orgulloso. But I'm sure it's not easy. I should know."

I catch my mouth hanging slightly open; I'm not sure how to respond. What exactly does she think this *is*? Some kind of mind game Gabriel and I are competing at? The one who outlasts the other in the separation wins?

"Maris, I think Gabriel has been misleading you about… well about the situation."

"Ah sí? You didn't leave him because he refused to not endanger himself?"

"Um, yeah," I reply. "But I'm just trying to…" I stop because I can't honestly say *what* I'm doing. I'm still married to him. I still wear his ring. And *he* still lives here in Monterey even though better opportunity is available to him in a hundred other places.

"Wendy, nobody knows better than me exactly how stubborn my Gabriel can be," Maris replies. "He will stand by what he believes. It's a blessing and a curse. I told you that."

"Yes, but what exactly are you expecting? He's committed to this separation. He doesn't want to be with me, Maris. Not like this. And I can't be with him if he disregards my feelings." I try to say the words as evenly as possible, but they still catch in my throat as I speak.

"Oh, Mija," she says affectionately. "Of course he does. He's stuck between his convictions about your condition and his commitment to your marriage. Eventually he's got to give up one. I daresay it will be his convictions if you continue to show him he can't force you into doing something by his ridiculous terquedad. Chico estúpido." She huffs.

The line goes silent but for our breathing as I figure out what to say.

"I'm *so* proud of you," she continues when I don't reply, "and so *grateful* that my son managed to marry someone he so desperately *needs.* I don't think he yet fully realizes just who he married. Aye yi yi." She takes another deep breath. "He does not see it. So stubborn. But he will. It's a rare occasion to see him make an about-face on something he is committed to so strongly, but he will. You stick to what you know, Wendy, mi hija. Don't give in."

Silence again.

Part of me wants to believe her and rally my own convictions. The other part wants to tell her she's mistaken. It's over. But how can I honestly say that? So I say the only thing I can think of, "Thanks, Maris."

"Anytime," she replies. "You call me *anytime*, okay, Mija?"

"Okay. Take care, Maris," I reply.

We hang up and I see Kaylen still watching me from the doorway of the kitchen with wide eyes. I step forward and hand her the phone. Without a word, I head back up the stairs.

Instead of changing into running gear like I intended, I sit on the edge of my bed.

I usually avoid letting my mind wander to Gabriel at all costs, but a phone call from Maris is not something I can ignore like I do the other, more regular reminders of him.

And Maris' call is forcing me to reexamine what it is I've been up to in the last couple months.

The answer is avoidance.

The doorbell rings then but I don't acknowledge it. Instead I'm thinking about what I'm going to do if Maris starts calling me regularly as well. Actually, the question applies to my whole life. What *am* I going to do now?

But I don't think I can answer that. Just toying with the edges of the question makes my lungs burn and my head spin—things I have avoided since the few days after Gabriel left and I moved back in with my uncle.

A little more time, I tell myself soothingly. I have too many other adjustments with my condition to expect myself to *also* adjust to the finality of my relationship with Gabriel. I can't do both right now…

I stand up and change out of my pajamas into stretch pants, a long-sleeved T-shirt, and running shoes. Then I start stretching in my room, holding and pressing long into the resistance in my joints and muscles, breathing out the frustration of my problems.

I make my way carefully back down the stairs when I'm done. Before I head out for my run, I stop by the kitchen so I can finish cleaning up after breakfast now that Kaylen and Ezra are done.

Instead of crumbs on the table, I see something else: flowers and a 'Happy Birthday' balloon.

I know who it's from.

I don't set one more foot in the kitchen.

"We didn't forget your birthday, Wen," Ezra says, capturing my attention from the other side of the kitchen where he's putting detergent in the dishwasher. "We have plans for you. So I hope you're up for it later."

My eyes wander back to the flowers, resting on the white envelope I see attached to them.

I haven't given up on you, Love. Yours always, Gabriel.

I close my eyes. I know that's what the card says. That's what it *always* says. Gabriel sends me something every week: flowers, a card, some kind of wrapped gift. At first I dissolved in tears every time this happened. But within a month, I began to view it as a challenge. I had to prove that I could control my outpourings, that I could *manage* myself without Gabriel. Once I started seeing his gestures this way, I tried really hard to read his words stalwartly. He always wrote the same thing. But it didn't matter. Seeing his handwriting always led me to imagine him writing the words, feeling their meaning as he wrote them. So I stopped opening the notes. Once I conquer the latest gift with indifference, I give myself permission to throw it away.

Maris' unexpected phone call has thrown me off my usual routine though. I turn around with practiced caution and head for the door, my legs already twitching in anticipation of a run.

35

I talk to myself about dinner for almost my entire run. I'm making roasted Cornish hens. I read an article the other day about how to remove the skin of poultry in one piece, debone it, and then re-stuff the skin so that it's still shaped like a whole bird again. That's probably a bit much to do for four small individual birds, but it's my birthday. I deserve to spend as much time on meticulous tasks as I want to, right? I probably ought to start as soon as I get home though, to give myself plenty of time since I've never done it before. Good thing Robert's office is closed today and I don't have to work. It should allow plenty of time. Looking forward to the upcoming job has me in much better spirits by the end of my run.

When I come into the vacant kitchen later, ready to get to work, the flowers are still on the table. I stop at the entryway again, eying them like the threat they are. And with my mind on methods of re-sculpting chickens in their skins, sans-bones, I'm ready to win this stand-off.

The color of the flowers knocks me off my determination for a moment. I know Gabriel picked them out. They are the Mexican flag colors: red and white with green foliage arranged in stripes across the bouquet—cheesy, but totally him. Just like his pajama pants. I hold my breath, refusing to process that or conjure any memories of him so they don't thrust me into a place that will only wound me.

There now, that wasn't so hard.

I walk purposely to the table, put my hands on my hips, my eyes drifting to the sealed card. I'm annoyed that I lost it so easily this morning when I first saw them. The card now beckons like a dare.

I pluck up the envelope and tear into it without another thought.

When I open the heart-shaped card, a few small slips of paper fall out and flutter to the table. I gather them up and examine them in amazement.

It looks like a letter. But it's written in the tiniest print imaginable.

I can't help the wide grin that spreads over my face or the belly-laugh that bubbles out of me so easily.

I have no idea why Gabriel wrote this letter in such tiny scrawl, but imagining him bent over these four inch pieces of paper and writing so small that I'm sure his eyes were tired by the end of it brings such soothing warmth to my ailing heart. I remember exactly why I love him so much and I can't really think of anything else but that at the moment.

I arrange them back in order and read:

Dearest Wendy,

Happy Birthday, my Love!

I wish I was there to celebrate with you. I miss you. I love you. Lest you think me unfaithful, know that our separation has done nothing but make me want you more. The harder you push me, the more committed I become. It's beyond my understanding. Every day strengthens the connection I've felt with you since the first time we met. I need you. I feel like an ionized atom. You, the electron I'm missing to be stable.

FOCUS GABRIEL. That's what you would say. It makes me laugh to think of you saying it.

Back to what's been on my mind. If you've been reading my other letters, you'll know I've remained suspicious about Robert. As I said I would, I've been doing some digging. Here's what I've found: Aside from strict software development, he's a software contractor. He connects corporation and government needs with various software companies. He's very well-connected, even and especially beyond his niche. He specializes in discovering talent not just in his field, but also in every other business sector you can think of. He seeks talent and then finds a place for them. I have found article after article showcasing individuals he has "discovered." It's not even limited to a particular area. I've found things like a young actor that managed to score a leading role in a box office hit. A talented young chemist placed as lead researcher in a chemical engineering company. A physicist prodigy attains a spot as a NASA recruit. A promising mathematician scores a coveted analyst position at an investment bank. The list goes on and on. And Robert has been the head hunter in each case.

I'm sure you are following my drift. I wouldn't say his work is pro-bono either. He's likely receiving a massive broker fee for his services in locating individuals that are often described as being 'bizarrely gifted.' Imagine how much an investment bank would pay for someone who can analyze and properly predict market trends?

So, mi encantadora doncella, eyes open. Your uncle is not what he seems. Your brother is still attending that private school that specifically utilizes his mathematical talents, right? Kaylen is still living there. And while I can't imagine her telekinesis being useful without exposing it, I would bet that Robert's hospitality is due to more than purely benevolent intentions.

Now, allow me to take another direction, that of your condition. I have a new idea. As I told you in my last letter, I've been studying Collision theory because I was thinking there must be some chemical reaction going on with your skin contact. I've been looking for someone I can trust to analyze a tissue sample of yours to look for anything unusual. That you only affect people when you physically touch them is telling in itself—it indicates a biological catalyst.

One of my colleagues from UCLA, a geneticist, is a possibility so I've started looking at his work more closely. I was memorizing one of his books on mutations one evening as the sun was going down and I started to get annoyed at the lamp in the living room because it wasn't bright enough. See, I installed it with LED bulbs recently because they are more efficient and environmentally friendly and last longer. Except the blasted things aren't nearly as bright as an incandescent bulb. So I was rethinking my decision to replace them in the first place. Of course you are always on the edge of my thoughts and I remembered with a smile that you would have no problem at all with the light sources in the room seeing as how you can read a book in the dark just as well as you can in the light.

At that moment, in thinking about you and incandescent lights at the same time, I had a moment of enlightenment. A light bulb moment, if you will... literally. Funny, right?

Incandescent light bulbs use electrical filaments. Electricity heats the filament to a particular temperature, causing it to illuminate. Most of the electricity is emitted as heat, however, making incandescent bulbs the inefficient pieces of technology they are. The telling part is that when you send too much voltage through an electrical filament, it disintegrates or 'burns out.'

So where am I going with this? Well, I think our life force must operate like a filament. Actually, every substance in the universe acts like an electrical filament if heated to the right temperature. My guess is that some life forces are more efficient filaments. Consider life forces like light bulbs. Some are 120 watt, some 60 watt, some 45, and so on. A 120 watt light bulb can handle more voltage passing through the filament than a 60 watt. I remember what you spoke about with your brother when you touched his skin—how a current passed between you. I think this is a good indicator of what you really do. I think normally life forces do not pass energy to each other. They are probably closed systems, existing on their own circuit, so to speak. Your ability must involve being an open circuit so that whenever someone touches you, they tap into your circuit. So if you are, say, a 120 watt life force, touching someone who is a 60 watt then they are receiving the same voltage as you. And what happens if a 60 watt light bulb gets as much voltage as a 120 watt? It burns out. It tries to send it to ground. In this case, I think this must be the body. I think this is why the heart stops. It gets an energy overload on the circuitry. In your thinking-box technological world, you might equate this to "frying the motherboard." Morbid as this sounds, it explains why there are only certain people who you can touch.

Here's where it gets a bit more metaphysical. Stay with me. If someone's life force is already accustomed to emitting large quantities of light, then they are unaffected by the extra voltage. How do we then stand to endure higher voltages? We often equate goodness with light and there may be more truth to this idea than we grasp.

The thing I'm not sure about is if it's possible for you to know if someone runs on the same voltage as you. Maybe the "energy vapor" you talked about is a clue. My other guess is that maybe some life forces emit more light than others and this is a way you might tell. Did you ever notice a difference? I'm sure you would have mentioned it. It may be that the difference is indistinguishable—

especially with how bright you always say everything is—but perhaps you should see if you can tell.

I wonder what you would say to my gesticulations. You would probably tell me my theories are not proof and you would be right, but it sure does give you something to think about, doesn't it?

Farewell, my lovely wife. I think of you almost every moment of the day, wondering what you're doing, devising schemes to get you back. I will have you back, my Love, doubt not.

I remain forever yours,
Gabriel

With my lips parted in disbelief and my eyes wide with amazement, I stand for several moments marveling over Gabriel's most definite genius. How does he do it? I'm no doctoral student, but even I can tell that the current I experienced when touching first Ezra and then Kaylen—and actually powering her ability that way—supports Gabriel's idea of energy transference as it relates to light bulbs. I remember looking down on people below the plane and describing them to myself as being different *wattages*. And Gabriel came up with the exact same analogy when he hasn't even *seen* what I've seen?

A wave of guilt gives me a fresh dose of self-loathing—but it doesn't last long. I obviously did the right thing by lying to him. Just because my experience fits with his theory doesn't make it fact. Despite how badly I *want* to tell him what I know, there's no guessing what he'll do with it. I can't risk having him… chase me down to touch me.

How can I risk his life like that?

Ironically, this beautiful theory of his starts to twist into more prison bars. There is still so much we *don't* know. Why, for example, do I only affect people when I touch their skin? If souls conduct energy, why am I able to touch someone's life force without harming them? They are obviously interacting, as evidenced by the musical sound my life force makes against theirs and the way our strands bind. Theories of energy healing, such as hypno-touch, are *founded* on the idea that life force energy can be transferred *without* skin-contact.

With his theory in mind, however, Kaylen's immunity is logical. She has an outlet for the energy I channel into her. But so did Dina and Derek—if their abilities used the same type of energy as Kaylen's—yet they died.

And what does this have to do with my super-senses? Like me, Carl has both a death-touch and colorworld sight, so the two must be correlated somehow. Gabriel's energy theory doesn't explain *any* of that. And he told me once that all of my abilities must be related somehow.

And goodness as life force energy tolerance? How exactly does that translate? People are a fluctuating mix of both good *and* bad. How *bad* can a person be and still be considered *good* enough to touch me? How easily can that change? Still, if he knew what I knew, he'd probably be breaking in to Robert's house some night to get his hands on me…

I feel a momentary twinge of fear at the thought. I'd like to think that Gabriel wouldn't really do something like that, but he has surprised me too many times in the past for me to discount it. He's unorthodox. And he does whatever it takes to accomplish something.

However, his discoveries about *Robert* shouldn't be ignored. It's undoubtedly suspicious. I dropped my earlier doubts about Robert after my encounter with Carl and Louise. While he remains decidedly aloof, Robert did nothing but help us during that fiasco despite not wanting to. He willingly and graciously took me in after Gabriel and I separated. He has given me a good job—promoted me even. I want to be grateful without being skeptical. But now, knowing what I do, I ask myself once more if Robert knows more than he says.

Brokering of people happens all the time though. Talent scouts, agents, and employment consultants are perfectly legitimate professions... But if the individuals he brokers are supernaturally endowed, that presents sinister possibilities. Is it just his ability that gives him above average results? That's entirely possible…

The real question is whether these talented people he brokers are actually products of Louise's research, thereby connecting him to her in some way. I should be able to tell, if I ever see one of them, by entering the colorworld and observing the pattern of their life force.

As I move through the possibilities, I hear footsteps. I quickly stuff the letter into my waistband, grab the flowers and toss them into the trash quickly. Then I pull some bread from a cabinet to make toast since I haven't had breakfast.

Kaylen appears, which is no surprise. I've become adept at recognizing footsteps. I don't look up when she enters, but I hear her pause in the doorway. I put the bread in the toaster and open the fridge for butter.

After a few moments, Kaylen says, "Are you up for doing something tonight? Ezra and I want to take you out for your birthday."

"Sure," I say, turning around and forcing my mouth to curve into a smile. I guess I won't be stuffing Cornish hens after all…

Kaylen isn't fooled. "You know, if you aren't up to it, you don't have to go for our sakes. It's *your* birthday after all. You should do what you want."

Yeah, right. I won't be able to do what I really want to do for as long as I live. I haven't been able to do what I want since… well I can't remember the last time. Tonight won't be any different.

I'm undecided about telling her and Ezra what Gabriel found on Robert, but if I decide to, an outing will be a good opportunity to do so.

"I need to get out." I reply. "I'd like to take a look at some other people in the colorworld, so I hope we're going somewhere populated."

"I think we can manage that," Kaylen says as she smiles brightly, pleased with my response.

I used to be afraid of crowds, but I've realized it's silly to be so paranoid when every inch of my skin with the exception of my face is covered. I've pondered over the last few months how it is I've come to be so much more comfortable with my condition so quickly. The conclusion I've come to is that Gabriel was the source of my uncertainty. I think it's because he was always pushing boundaries. That's why fear was always near the surface. But without him around, life is more secure and predictable.

Someone like Gabriel and someone dangerous like me are a bad combination. He will probably never understand that.

There I go again. Thinking. I pull the lid off the butter and open the silverware drawer for a knife.

I don't like the arrangement of the drawer so I start pulling things out. Forks should be to the left, ordered by size. Butter knives should be to the far right because they are rarely used. Soup spoons go up top and don't get mixed in with the regular spoons…

Why is there a vegetable peeler in here? That goes in a different drawer…

"You okay, Wendy?" asks Kaylen loudly through the metallic clanging of the handfuls of silverware I deposit on the counter.

I stop and look at her. "Yeah. Why?"

Kaylen thinks about something while I grab a rag to wipe out the bottom of the drawer.

"Have you really never been this much of a neat-freak?" Kaylen asks.

"Nope," I reply, placing the silverware tray back in the drawer.

"Is there something I can help you with?" she asks.

I place the knives in first, their edges all pointing the same direction. "Yeah," I reply. "Butter my toast before it gets cold while I finish this." I hold out a knife.

She shakes her head but walks over to me to take the knife. "No. I meant is there something I can do for you… about Gabe? I know you don't talk to Ezra, because he told me so, and I thought maybe you'd like… a listening ear?"

She turns her back to me and starts spreading butter, but I can tell she's nervous about asking me that.

I stare at her, touched that she wants to do something for me even though she has no clue how or what I need. Her desire is genuine and non-condemning, full of nothing but love. I've worked so hard to tune out emotions over these past months, afraid of falling into addiction again. I think I've been missing people's concern… mistaking it as pity or disapproval because… I don't know.

I look across the room, remembering the colorworld from this angle, how that wall looks yellow from over here, but sitting at the table I know it looks orange-brown. Different perspectives…

I sigh. I need a new perspective, especially today with Maris' phone call and Gabriel's letter. Fresh misery looms over me like a heavy black cloud, ready for a downpour. It obviously hasn't moved as far away as I have imagined it has during this time.

"I feel… *trapped,*" I say finally, leaning against the counter and wrapping my arms around my middle. I look down at the tiles at my feet.

Kaylen turns around and hands me my plate of toast. But I'm not hungry anymore. I set it on the counter next to me.

She waits.

"I stay busy so I don't have to think," I say. "I don't know how to move forward." I look up. "How do I move forward?"

Kaylen furrows her brow. "Move forward? Like… with your condition?"

Instinct has me rebelling against thinking about this. I've been resisting it for so long…

"Yes," I whisper.

New perspective, I remind myself.

"Um. I gotta admit, I have no idea," she replies. "I'm not married and I don't have a death-touch."

I look up and she shrugs. "I'm only sixteen." She smiles.

That makes me giggle. "Yeah, I guess you are. But you know, I'm only… well twenty. But I was a teenager only yesterday."

Kaylen backs up and hops up to sit on the island countertop. She looks down for a moment, pulls her hair over her shoulder, twisting it a few times before saying, "I don't really have any advice on that stuff, but maybe I can help you look for a cure?"

I raise my eyebrows. "How's that?"

"I've thought a lot about the energy transference that happened between us," she explains. "I've been waiting for you to ask to try it again—maybe you can see it in the colorworld this time? I could deplete myself and then we can see if it happens again… Nobody knows what to do or say around you, and when you didn't ask I wasn't sure if it was because you didn't think you *could* ask or because you didn't see it as relevant."

I shake my head. "No way. It could have been a one-time occurrence. It could have been that you survived because you didn't have any energy. It could have been the heat. There could be a thousand reasons. I don't want to take that chance."

Kaylen looks slightly alarmed but calms quickly and wrings her hair again, this time more forcefully. She takes a deep breath. "Wendy, have you ever considered that you might be a tiny bit too skeptical for your own good?"

"How do you mean?" I ask.

"Well you know, you take every bit of evidence that might give you hope that you aren't lethal, especially to Gabe, and you throw it out like it doesn't matter. I mean, shouldn't you be clinging to every bit of evidence you can get your hands on?" she asks.

She's apprehensive and her heart pounds nervously. Obviously she doesn't know how welcome her comments will be.

Since her intentions are completely sincere though, I manage to avoid being defensive. Maybe she can help me organize my dilemma in a way that isn't so torturous. Ever since I met her, Kaylen has been someone I have been able to confide in. Come to think of it, there is no one I have ever been as honest and open with aside from Gabriel. Despite being 16, Kaylen carries a certain maturity and experience—probably from being surrounded by adults all her life on the compound.

"I know it seems that way," I sigh. "And I guess I do. Every time I find out something new I can't help but be hopeful. Then I consider all the things I *don't* know and I remember how many gaps there are. The big picture has big holes in it, and I can't be sure of what the picture *is*. If I look at it the way I wish it was, like that I could touch Gabriel and he would survive, it lines up; I believe it."

I cross my arms tighter about my waist. "Then I see Dina's eyes. I see those homeless people. I try to get my head around the fact that I *killed* them just by *touching* them!" I sputter. "Do you get how… screwed up that is? There is *nothing* out there that has the same kind of instantaneous ability to literally *slaughter* another human being with the same kind of… *torture* that I can inflict. There *is* no precedent for something like that. The picture becomes distorted then. Nothing adds up and I can't take the chance. How can I really? How can I take the risk of killing him?"

I blow out a few calming breaths. I've gotten worked up just thinking about what touching someone feels like. When I look up, Kaylen's face is drawn in concern and her compassion washes out the uneasiness I once felt from her. "The picture will probably never be complete. That's life, isn't it? And the chances are good that he'd be okay. Isn't it worth the risk especially if he's willing to take it for you?" she asks, her tone almost pleading.

"If I did… if I took the chance," I say, "it would be the equivalent of holding a gun to his head with one bullet in the chamber, not knowing where the bullet is. It's Russian Roulette, Kaylen. Sure, the *odds* are good, but the risk that the one bullet is lined up with the hammer is still solidly real. Could *you* do that?"

Kaylen shivers internally with the image. "When you put it that way, I don't know. But there will always be that chance. If you really think you can't take it no matter how good it is, then it doesn't matter if you find a so-called cure, because you will never test it out. It's one way or the other. You have to be okay with taking a chance, or you have to be okay with never touching anyone again."

I stare at her blankly for a moment, the truth of her words ringing loudly in my head. I've spent so much time looking at individual pieces of the problem. She's looking at the whole picture. I'm not fighting with hope. I'm fighting with whether or not to pull the trigger of the proverbial gun. The realization is depressing. Beyond depressing. Tears spring to my eyes.

You asked for it.

"Oh my gosh, Wendy. I'm so sorry. I didn't mean…" she says, distressed.

"No," I sob. "I needed that." I hold my hand up to stop her from coming over to me.

"Going upstairs," I say as I head out of the room.

Kaylen is taken off-guard by my reaction. I'd like to assure her that I'll be okay, but I can't speak, and if I don't find my bed soon, I'm going to lose it right here. I don't see the stairs as I ascend them, and I feel my way to my room and sink to the floor by my bed, dissolving in a torrent of tears.

As I lie there gasping for breath, I beg myself to find the courage to pull that trigger so I can be with Gabriel. But there isn't a speck of bravery to be found anywhere. If the "gun" were in my hand right now? There is no way…

I remember Gabriel saying that he wished he could promise me he wouldn't touch me, but he knew in his heart of hearts that he would break it. Well I know I will never be able to take the chance no matter how many times hope springs up and makes me think I can.

My cries increase as that reality sinks in. My life finally inches forward for the first time in months.

I cried a lot after he left. Once I figured out that staying busy could help me avoid the pitfalls of feeling sorry for myself, I stayed on top of it. I held off wondering what to do with myself because I wanted a purpose first, and *then* I would go back and assess what to do about Gabriel. I wanted a backup plan. Instead I've kept myself in a self-imposed limbo. I could have come to this conclusion so much sooner if I'd ever allowed myself to think about it.

Instead I've spent the whole time torturing myself by refusing to move on, and I've allowed Gabriel to build hope and conviction. I'm so good at perpetuating the consequences of my mistakes.

My cries grow more insistent. My hands have balled into fists and my stomach contracts so painfully I imagine it's drawing my life force in with it. It hurts to breathe and my head pounds. I hold my arms about myself and draw my knees up into a fetal position.

My body feels like such a burden. It's too big for this suffocating, toxic space. It's like getting in a hot car in the dead of summer. Everything you touch is scorching: the steering wheel, seat belt nylon and buckle, even the seat itself. You breathe and your lungs fill with broiled air. There is no ready relief from heat. It can only be endured. No wonder I've opted for cold for so many months…

I wish I had never met him. I wish he had left me alone. We would both be better off now if our paths had never crossed.

I want to wipe him from my memory. Frantically I tug off my left glove. I yank the rings from my finger and search for a place to put them out of sight. I clamber to my knees and open the drawer to the bedside table and throw them in. I slam the drawer shut, but it doesn't do anything to chase away the emptiness that threatens to swallow me.

There is *nothing* on the other side of this. It's just as I worried: no purpose, no plan.

I lie back on the carpet, drawing into myself, flexing my muscles and pinching my eyes shut. My insides burn, so I hold my breath because breathing feels like fanning the flames of torture.

Please, I beg, *just burn it out of me already.*

36

Somehow, when the tears dry, I am able to reach past the darkness and grasp something. I don't know what. But it's solid and I'm pretty sure I'm going to be able to leave this room at some point. I stare at the ceiling as the hard, painful knots in my stomach loosen.

I sit up, extending my legs in front of me and leaning against the side of the bed. Inhale. Exhale. Brush my hand over the blue chevron-striped comforter on my bed, straightening it. I look closer at the individual threads, noticing that some of the fibers escape the threads. It's this phenomenon that gives fabric a soft texture and depth, and I don't think I've ever looked at it this closely before. My own vision can really blow me away when I explore it, and it gives me something to do, which I'll need to fill the upcoming days. But first, I need to take care of something more important.

I look around for my purse. I intend, while my heart is subdued, to go right now and file divorce papers. Then I remember Ezra and Kaylen who have plans for me this evening. Will I be in a state to get out of the house once the deed is done?

It can wait for tomorrow. I don't want to spoil their plans. And then I will go somewhere far away from here and hit the reset button on my life.

Ezra and Kaylen are my family, though… I can't go live alone somewhere and expect to be happy without them. I have to be a grown-up about this. I can't just react like I always do. I have to use my brain.

What about Robert? What if his motives *are* sinister?

That idea is actually exciting, not because I *want* Robert to be bad, but because uncovering the truth about him will give me something useful to do with myself. I cling to this new task like a life line.

Hopefully I'll find out that he's good. Then, I can leave. Not forever, but for as long as it takes Gabriel to move on—he won't have a choice if I'm gone.

Robert floats into my mind again. His life force is actually brighter than Kaylen's and Ezra's… Far brighter. Does that mean that the brighter a life force, the worse the person? That doesn't align with Gabriel's theory, and I'm not going to take it as proof of Robert's true intentions. But it does indicate that there is something different about him. And if Robert truly is bad, it blows Gabriel's theory up…

What are you doing, Wendy?

I can't go there. Trying to align Gabriel's theory with what I see in the colorworld is only going to make me indecisive. The search for a cure is over for me. It has to be or I will *never* be at peace.

So I'll do my digging the old-fashioned way: Robert has an office in the house. I'll search the place, see what I can turn up. Tonight, after I go out with Kaylen and Ezra.

I'll have to tell them about my plans, too. If Robert is malicious, I'll have to take them with me.

But I barely afforded taking care of Ezra on my own… And now Kaylen, too?

I sigh. I can't leave them with Robert who might exploit them. The only way I can see is to stay here *with* them where I can watch over them until I can support us.

But so close to Gabriel? It will put him through more suffering. He's going to keep calling me. Sending me gifts…

I take a deliberate breath, expelling the air of frustration clouding my head. I'm getting worked up again. But this is the worst kind of unfair. I'm being tied here. Just when I've finally gotten the courage to turn my back on Gabriel for good, to distance myself from him, my efforts are blocked.

If I leave Kaylen and Ezra here, they may be in danger. If I take them we could all end up homeless. If *I* stay here, I will be inflicting Gabriel and myself with more injury.

Those aren't choices. Unless you think choosing your punishment a choice. But I guess I should be *grateful* for some choice in that, right? I scoff.

I lean forward, put my elbows on my knees, my chin in my hands, hot with aggravation. I need to calm down; I make dumb choices when I'm angry. I *really* need to make the right choice for once. The three people I love the most are on the line.

But I can't focus. Instead, I uselessly question the unfairness of it all. Do *other* people face the kinds of decisions I've had to face in the past three years? Or is there a demon out there with a personal vendetta against me?

Kaylen appears in my open doorway just then, a look of expectant concern on her face. "Want to go riding?" she asks, smiling tentatively.

I lift my head. It sounds like a spectacular idea.

"Let's do it," I reply.

***

Robert provided Kaylen with a place to ride—a barn that rents horses. Although she's happy to be able to ride whenever she wants, Kaylen has been fretting over Morgan, worried that Carl let him go to some stranger and that she'll never see him again.

If only my concerns revolved around finding my missing pet…

I'm itching to get on a horse, maybe go really fast and leave my problems in the dust. Aside from riding at the compound a number of times, I've been riding with Kaylen several times since I moved back in with Robert. I have a measure of comfort on a horse now.

I hop in my car just after noon, waiting for Kaylen who is having trouble finding her riding boots. I tap the wheel impatiently as pangs of resentment toward every aspect of my life beat insistently inside of my head.

I think again about my commitment to go file divorce papers tomorrow. I placate myself with those plans and it gives me the first twinge of triumph. At least there's one thing I *can* control about my life.

Anticipating progress becomes uncomfortable though. I need to do it *right now*. I need to accomplish something *today* so my head doesn't explode in the meantime.

"Do you mind if we make a stop on the way?" I say to Kaylen once she gets in. "It might take a little while, but we should still have time to go afterward."

"Uh, sure?" Kaylen says uncertainly. "But we're picking up Ezra at four-thirty."

"Should be fine," I say, throwing the car into gear and speeding away.

I have no idea how to file for divorce except that the courthouse is involved. It's probably a more lengthy procedure than going down there and signing a form, but at least I can start the process.

As we pull into downtown Salinas, the Monterey county seat, I pick up on Kaylen's wondering. When I park in front of the courthouse she says, "What are you going to do?"

"File for divorce," I reply simply, the same way I would say I'm running into the grocery store to get bread. I don't really hear the words as they come out of my mouth.

I unbuckle my seatbelt. Kaylen sits still in disbelief. I don't know how much more I have to do to prove how serious I am. Maybe she will want me to bring a copy of whatever form they give me out to show her.

When I open the door she says, "Wendy, wait."

"I have to do this Kaylen. I *need* to do this. You can understand that, right?" I say, pausing with my door open, waiting on her.

She doesn't budge, only sits and looks at me in amazement.

"Are you coming?" I ask, getting desperate to be on the move.

"But Wendy, it's Columbus Day. The courthouse is closed," she says, furrowing her brow, distressed by having to point this out to me.

"It's... Columbus Day?" I ask. It's now my turn to be in disbelief.

"Yeah, that's why you're not at work?"

I tilt my head to look at her. Of course I knew that... didn't I? Wasn't someone at work *just* mentioning the other day that Robert closes his offices for Columbus day because he contracts government work so often that he usually tracks their days off? Geez, have I been a zombie or what?

But why isn't Kaylen at school? "You have the day off, too? I don't remember having Columbus day off in high school," I say to her. I can't believe I didn't think to ask this morning when she and Ezra didn't leave.

"Ezra and I are in private school... They have different days off."

I look up over the top of the car, my hand on the door as I stare at the courthouse beyond. Of all the days... Of all the days I have had in the past month, I pick *Columbus Day* to file for divorce? Well, in my defense, I'd have to get off work on any *other* day to do it. But still... This is like a slap in the face when I'm already so beaten up.

"What is *your* problem?!" I yell at the courthouse.

To speak *to* the building seems fitting, because beneath each of the ten windows of the two-story courthouse are stone busts. Heads literally protrude out of the side of it in relief. They could easily be laughing at me. Right above the door is a huge and menacing relief sculpture of a woman with long wavy hair, wielding a sword above her, as if prepared to take the heads of evildoers. Beneath her are two much smaller people, a man and woman, kneeling with obeisance, their heads bowed under the weight of the offerings they carry on their shoulders.

Justice personified?

I don't care what it's *supposed* to mean. It's art. It means exactly what *I* say it means at this exact moment. And right now it's telling me that justice will always prevail. It will *always* find me and distribute the fruits of my mistakes swiftly and without mercy. Even as I bow in regret and guilt, always trying to make things right again, I will never gain forgiveness and I will never find peace. Consequences are eternal, inevitable.

Maybe out there somewhere is a path I was intended to be on, but it's long gone. I have no hope of ever finding my way back to it. I fell beneath the cloud long ago and have had nothing but the confusing noise of thunder as I run back and forth beneath the gloom. Whenever I think I might have found a place to stay, the lightning comes, violently striking my path. Life has lost all gentleness.

I stare down Lady Justice with her giant sword, my eyes flashing as I look between her and her subjects who so dutifully attempt to earn their way back into her good graces. I will not be them. I refuse. I am done trying to appease Lady Justice. I may be below the cloud, but thunder and lightning don't scare me anymore.

I sit back down in the car in one quick motion. I put the key in the ignition and start it again. Then, without a word, I backtrack, heading in the direction of the barn.

Kaylen is silent but scared. I'm probably driving way too fast, but I don't care. I have excellent reflexes thanks to my superb senses. And staying within the bounds of the law is no longer a personal rule.

I stop in front of the barn in a cloud of dust, and I say cheerfully to Kaylen, "Let's go!"

Kaylen unlocks her death grip on the door handle and follows wordlessly.

37

Tacking up takes an extraordinarily long time. Pepper, the horse Kaylen arranged for me, is not one I've ridden before and he looks like he might not be up to the kind of action I am. That's disappointing, but I won't be deterred. I'm going to get on a horse and ride, and the only thing that will stop me is Armageddon.

Once we're finally mounted, I take the lead, starting off at a brisk trot. I always remove my gloves for riding, and I do so now as well. My gloves, which have always been about protection, feel like punishment again and I will *not* yield to the universe's vendetta to keep me in submission.

I brush my hands through Pepper's mane, reveling in the coarse texture against my fingertips—*any* texture is preferable to the inside of my gloves. I miss more than just the feel of human skin. And I'm safe from harming Pepper. Animals are immune to my ability. Apparently residing among the animal kingdom is where I belong.

No way.

I kick my legs, and Pepper starts cantering. I didn't mean to kick him to move faster but to vent my aggravation. It's cruel, but it does make me feel fractionally better. The speed sends a thrill down my spine, so I lean in and squeeze my legs, urging Pepper to pick up his pace.

I obviously misjudged him. He seems to be enjoying the freedom of speed as much as I am. I'm no expert rider, but I'm decent enough to stay on. I don't have much interest in controlling *where* he goes, only in how fast he gets there. I hear Kaylen's horse behind me, far behind me, and I smile, adjusting my body to accommodate the pitching motion of Pepper's gait and imagining that I can reside in this moment forever.

We ride up a hill and back down to a straightaway. The woods are close to us and I'll have to guide Pepper around a curve soon if I don't want to run into the trees. As I consider this, a flock of birds rise from the thicket to my left. Pepper notices, too, but his abandon must have him off-guard. He shies to the right, away from the movement. But I stay left, losing my seat. Terrified, I reach out, but find only air. I expect to hit the ground, but instead I see Pepper's rear legs moving in front of my face. Somehow I'm dangling from his side.

Panicked, I reach up with frantic effort, searching for something to pull myself up with. I need to get away from his powerful and thundering hooves. Pepper seems terrified too; his pace is erratic. He slows for a moment only to take off again, always moving to the side in an attempt to get away from me. The reins hang loosely, but they are too far away to grab. I have no idea how to get him to stop.

I use all my strength just keeping my head away from his legs, but exhaustion is beginning to win out. I hear more pounding hooves then, rapid ones, and they come up beside me, keeping pace with Pepper. It's Kaylen's horse.

I see Kaylen's hands reaching for some part of my clothing. I stretch my arm out to her, trying to get my hand on her leg, her saddle, anything close enough to grip to help me stay away from Pepper's hooves.

Kaylen grabs for Pepper's reins instead. I hang on to her stirrup leather and she pulls our reins together, slowing both horses at the same time.

We come to a stop finally and Kaylen dismounts. She heaves me upright until I get my free leg on the ground. But still I cling to her, trying to overcome the terror of having nearly been trampled to death. Holding me up awkwardly with one arm, she grabs my boot with her other, freeing it from my stirrup. I can't let go of her though.

Only after a moment do I become aware that her skin is touching mine, but I'm too frightened to care. She's in some shock, but she's standing and alive. She's fine. Kaylen holds me as I find strength to hold myself upright. We're about the same height, but I'm pressed into her, cowering in her arms, just trying to breathe.

I hear more hoof beats from somewhere over the pounding of my heart, but I don't look up. I'm so relieved to be unharmed and alive that I just rest on Kaylen's shoulder as the panic slowly eases from my muscles and is replaced with a jelly-like feeling. Kaylen strokes my back but doesn't say anything. My teeth start chattering as the shock catches up to me.

"Here, sit down," she says, lowering me to the ground.

The hooves I heard moments ago approach us and slow. Then an alarmed voice says, "El cielo, Wendy! Are you hurt?"

I know it immediately.

Gabriel.

I leap to my feet, amazed that my muscles are cooperating after their lifelessness only moments earlier.

He has already dismounted and is coming toward me. I dart to the other side of Pepper and away from him.

"Don't touch me!" I warn, searching frantically in my back pocket for my gloves.

Stupid, stupid, stupid. Removing these things has gotten me into constant trouble.

Gabriel comes around the side of Pepper. I back up in earnest, trying not to fall over my rubbery legs while I fumble with my gloves.

"No!" I say, trembling. "Stay back!" Tears spring to my eyes then, different tears. Tears of fright, not relief, and they're starting to blur my vision.

"Will you relax, Wendy? I'm not trying to touch you," says Gabriel, stopping finally.

Relief that he's not going to touch me—at least not right now—relaxes my muscles briefly, but it's short lived. His face... I see everything I want there. It's not fair. It just isn't *fair*. I have to get away. I can't take this.

"I have to go," I say, looking at Kaylen who holds both our horses' reins. She glances with wide eyes between Gabriel and me.

I squeeze in next to her, take Pepper's reins, and lead him away.

"Wait, Wendy. I promise, I am not trying to touch you. Won't you even talk to me?" Gabriel asks, his voice desperate.

"There's nothing to talk about," I say, not turning around.

I hear their footsteps scuffing the grass behind me and I walk faster. Gabriel just saw me touch Kaylen. He said he isn't trying to touch me *now* but how long does that promise last?

This is ridiculous. Why is he here? Did Kaylen plan this? I have to get away…

"Stop following me, Gabriel," I say sharply. "I'm not kidding."

"Stop being childish," he says, obviously irritated now.

My throat catches when I hear his tone and I walk still faster to get him well out of range. He doesn't get it. He never has. Why do I have to love him? At this point, I can't remember the reasons. Whatever I know about him, whatever qualities he may have that I fell in love with, they don't trump the fact that he continually trivializes my feelings. He doesn't ever respect what *I* believe or what *I* say. It's always about him and his brilliant ideas. And when I don't agree, it's because I'm immature and unreasonable.

As I walk, collecting up the pieces of my heart and super gluing them into place, his face no longer in my view, I reclaim my rage from earlier. I find conviction once more that separating myself from Gabriel in every way I can is the right thing to do. And I'm relieved that even with him so close, I have the presence of mind to stick to my guns.

When we finally arrive at the barn, I tie up Pepper several yards away from Gabriel. I throw the tack in the barn, give Pepper a quick brush, and lead him to his stall.

Gabriel seems to be ignoring me as well, but he takes greater care with his horse, and so does Kaylen. I sigh. I can't leave until Kaylen is done.

"I'll be in the car," I say to Kaylen as I walk past her. I don't even look up when I pass Gabriel.

Once I'm in the car, I allow myself a little breakdown. Not too much, just a few desperate whimpers before binding up my wounds with indignation again. Sure that Kaylen had a hand in planning this, I think of a million different things to say to her and a million different things she could say back.

Finally, the door opens, and I'm about to let one of my accusations loose when I see that it isn't Kaylen, but Gabriel. I fumble for the door handle.

"WENDY, STOP!" he yells in the loudest tone I've ever heard him use.

I freeze. That his command should make me immobile is silly, but it does. I stare at him wide-eyed, my hand on the window, my breaths coming erratically.

His stern expression melts immediately, and pain moves over his features. He stings me with full-fledged despair. It's so strong that I feel it even over my own frenzied panic.

He laces his fingers over the back of his neck, squeezing as if to force his unusually disorganized thoughts back in line, and then says quietly, "I'm not trying to touch you. I only wanted to speak for Kaylen. She is understandably upset and scared."

Then he wipes his face with his hand, sick with turmoil. I see redness in his eyes, and I look away, unable to endure that visible sign of internal pain.

"I ride with Kaylen sometimes. That's why I'm here. Today though, I decided to come by myself because... well it doesn't matter. I swear, I had no idea you would be here. And Kaylen had no idea *I* would be here. This wasn't planned."

I'm looking through the windshield at nothing, my hands now resting awkwardly in my lap. I become painfully aware of them, specifically my ring finger which is now bare. I fight with feeling afraid for him to see and wanting to tuck my hands under my legs to hide it. As much as I know I need to convey finality to Gabriel, a large part of me doesn't want to hurt him even though I know that's impossible. As I fight to hold my hands still, I think Gabriel finally does notice. In my peripheral vision his eyes have fallen from my face to my lap. I cringe and my left hand involuntarily moves under my right.

But it's too late. I've stabbed him right in the heart. I know it because I feel it. It's all I can do to simply sit here and not react to his pain. I feel his eyes on my face again. Gabriel's emotions are usually so purposeful and easy to translate; they move as if they've been choreographed. But this is the first time I've felt them stagger about incoherently. Like trying to walk a straight line while drunk. He takes some train of thought only to find that he has ended up in a place he didn't intend. It's making him crazy but he's having trouble shutting it down. The inability to move his mind in the direction he wants is frightening to him, and out of the corner of my eye I catch him gripping his head in his hands as if trying to purge the confusion out physically. After an unbearably long time—maybe a few seconds, maybe a few minutes—Gabriel opens the door and steps out, shutting it behind him.

Once he's finally out of range, my gridlocked thoughts inch forward again. I work to translate what I just felt. It felt like he was considering giving in, like he was rethinking this whole separation. For a few fleeting seconds, I daydream a reunion.

But then I freeze that vision abruptly. I shove it back. Hard. This is always what it's like when Gabriel is around: uncertainty, bitterness, second-guessing, *fear.* Intimidation even, because he's so much better at articulating himself than I am. I can never win an argument. And he always labels my actions as fickle and groundless. My words are always invalid.

What's more, the uncertainty of my life with him seems to have agitated my diabetes. I've had several more low blood sugar episodes since Gabriel left. I've even had a few stubborn highs that required multiple injections to bring back down. I've nearly doubled the number of times I test myself throughout the day.

I guess Gabriel is unhealthy for me in more ways than one.

It's clear that he still loves me. But I *know* Gabriel can tell how he's hurting me, yet he chooses to do it anyway. I just felt him completely at odds with his own feelings, with his own guilt over hurting me, yet he ignores it in favor of *logic.* He *chooses* to hurt me simply because he thinks I'm doing things wrong. What kind of love is that if he *purposely* inflicts me with pain?

I think Gabriel doesn't know how to love a person without imposing his will on them.

I snort. I called it, didn't I? I told him when I first met him that he was arrogant. I think that was a fair assessment. The more I think about Gabriel and how he thinks his reasoning skills are superior to everyone else's, the angrier I get. With myself mostly, for not seeing that side of him sooner. For not recognizing the problem it would become later. How ironic it is to remember how worried I was when I found out my ability had increased, thinking sooner or later I couldn't even be *near* people without hurting them. But instead the real threat was Gabriel and the way he'd choose to react to it. I was *so blind* to what he was. I was too smitten by everything else about him that was so refreshing and amazing.

I've already had a good cry today. I don't want to again, but the realization that Gabriel, whom I have loved and respected and admired for so long, has completely let me down in the most profound way, just adds insult to the injury he has already caused me. No matter the seemingly innumerable talents he possesses, they are almost perfectly matched by the deepest of flaws.

I am a churning sea in the midst of a storm: despair and anger and pain and consuming disappointment. I already decided to let him go. But now the reasons go beyond the necessity of preserving his life. Now I choose to leave *him,* not merely the situation.

Tears spring to my eyes for the second time today. It feels like all the water in my body has pushed to my tear ducts. It can't get out fast enough. But unlike earlier today, I don't spend any time resisting my cries. I don't even resent them. I made a mistake in marrying Gabriel. Now I pay. And when I'm done, I move on. And considering how quickly this cry of acceptance and understanding has followed up the other one of finality, I can tell I'm getting better at this tragedy thing.

I lower my head to the steering wheel and weep openly. I let the storm rage. Experience tells me there are clear skies and still waters on the other side.

I hear the door open and immediately smell Kaylen's scent—an aged sweetness like perfume lingering on clothing that's been in an attic for years. She places her hand on my back and I sob under it, letting the tears flow. They ease more quickly than the last time—I *am* getting better at this. I lift my head up. Kaylen hands me a bottle of water. I don't know how she knew I would need it, but I down it in seconds.

When I finally have my bearings, I put the key in the ignition, start the car, put it in reverse, and back out.

Then I drive—at the speed limit this time—back home to Robert's.

38

We lean over the Sting Ray exhibit as I trail my hands in the water, hoping to brush the back of one of the graceful rays. Ezra has a familiar look on his face. His brow is scrunched and he's biting his lower lip. It's what he does when working out a problem in his head. It's kind of funny usually, but there is nothing to laugh about here.

Evidently the Monterey Bay Aquarium, with dinner to follow, is my birthday surprise. After Kaylen and I got home from our disastrous ride, she asked me if I was sure I was up to going out. When she revealed the destination, I couldn't think of a better place. Fish and water are soothing. And I need to be around people to remind myself that I'm not alone, especially now that I have made a definite decision about Gabriel.

I figured if I couldn't pack my bags, jump in the car, and drive until I felt like stopping, the least I could do was go somewhere unfamiliar in town. Plus, I love aquariums and Monterey's is world-renowned. The tanks are like bottled tranquility.

I took the opportunity to tell Kaylen and Ezra about Robert, and about my plans. It's like I'm living on the compound again. Only this time it's more subtle. Robert is *allowing* us to develop our talents rather than actively facilitating it, hiding behind the guise of benevolent uncle to gain our trust. And like the compound, I've begun to feel dependent and secure under his shadow. Plus, I don't get reprieves in my life like uncles who really *are* what they claim.

But I think as long as he doesn't know I'm onto him, he'll continue letting us all live there, biding his time until one of us becomes a valuable commodity. It should buy me time to get my life straightened out and figure out a way to support myself and two teenagers.

I'm also hoping that if I can get a little time in as a supervisor at Robert's office, it will earn me a comparable job somewhere else. I need to get out of California completely. It's notoriously expensive.

After a while of me trying to gain the trust of the passing rays, Ezra biting his lip, and Kaylen sitting on the landscaped stone edge of the tank watching the both of us while she slowly twists her hair, Ezra finally says, "Okay, but we help you. I'm not going to be out on this; it affects me even more than it does you so don't try to convince me otherwise." He's referring, of course, to my plans to inspect Robert's office.

"Me too," says Kaylen, looking stern.

I'm not going to argue. More people shouldn't make it any more or less dangerous.

"I think you should wait 'til Thursday," Ezra says. "He'll be in San Francisco overnight."

I'm loath to wait even those three days to get answers, to *do* something, but it *is* safer. I need to not be reckless.

"Fine," I agree. "Thursday then."

I put my glove back on and stand up, deciding what to do with myself between now and Thursday. Get a divorce and research places to move, I guess.

A huge blue tank brightly illuminated from within greets me once I'm back inside, contrasted by the surrounding darkness of the room. At first I can't tell what it is, but as I draw closer I see a massive school of shiny silver fish. Sometimes they pass in front of the glass. Sometimes I have to press my face into the glass to watch them. In all, it appears to be a boring exhibit, but I'm mesmerized by how they all move in unison, like they're yoked together. There must be hundreds of them.

Stupid fish. It's like they lack a will of their own, just going with the crowd.

But as I watch, I think they look rather content with their lot, not caring that everywhere they look there are other fish, just like them. Everyone moves together. I don't know what their goal is, but they seem to know, and they look happy.

I wish I could be happy like that.

I don't know how long I stand there, but I hear Kaylen and Ezra come up behind me. I've felt for weeks now that they have a thing for each other, but I've been too invested in my own problems to delve into it. Neither of them have pursued it, and I think they both still wonder what the other one thinks of them, especially given the awkwardness of their adopted sibling status.

I know the truth, and right now, they are both wondering if their feelings are reciprocated and whether they should make a move. Well… *someone* should be happy, even if it's not me.

They stand next to me so I turn and bring their hands together until they're touching.

"You're both thinking the same thing so stop second-guessing yourselves," I say. Then I turn back to the exhibit.

I don't watch their expressions, but I get satisfaction in their surprise, which is followed by the lightening warmth of happiness. I don't realize how tightly I've been holding my chest until I experience that with them.

I've even been stifling my intellect, apparently, because my thoughts feel more viscous all of a sudden as they move in and out of my consciousness. The difference is night and day. Now, as I watch the fish, deep wonder fills me up that I didn't experience before. I'm struck by the sheer mystical nature of the school. The fish turn *exactly* in unison. Unbelievable. It's like they choreographed it. But fish don't choreograph things. They live in a fish-eat-fish world, striving for survival. Yet here they are, moving together, cooperating in a way that you rarely see people do unless it has been planned and practiced for hours.

It's like the fish know each other's thoughts—like they're telepathic. How else could they synchronize their swim so well? I watch, perplexed with not understanding it. I look at the placard next to the exhibit. It explains "schooling" as a little understood phenomenon. Fish appear to have some instinct that allows them to coordinate movement. It all sounds very bland and scientific, hardly describing what, to me, is fantastic—supernatural even.

I'm moved with an inane desire to see their interaction in the colorworld. I glance back at Ezra and Kaylen. They look so content, catching each other's eyes, not caring that I'm standing right here. I don't want to ruin their moment, but I need a channel, and I'm not about to ask a stranger.

I turn back to the fish, twitching and fidgeting, unable to satisfy my curiosity. I think I can finally understand Gabriel's ill-timed inquisitiveness, which is ready for any occasion, no matter the seriousness.

It's too much, so I turn around and find a place on the other side of Ezra. "I need a channel," I explain as I close my eyes and put my gloved hand on his arm.

Once in the colorworld, I look for the fish. The first thing I notice is the water though: dots of color are interspersed throughout it like miniscule fireflies. It would be enough to hold my attention if I wasn't more interested in the fish right now.

I spot them easily, a green mass, exactly how I expect life forces that close together to look. But this is not what holds me breathless: the green mass looks like *one singular life force*.

Only in larger animals like dogs and horses have I seen swirling life forces so similar to humans. The smaller the animal, the less swirling is apparent until they don't really have a life force at all—they simply glow in an odd color. I expect something as mindless as a fish to have no apparent strands. But they appear to share one life force here, a beautiful conglomeration of strands interwoven and swirling together like they are one. I can't even make out individual fish.

I unfocus my eyes to find them underneath their green singular life force. They swim so close together that they almost touch. But in the colorworld they appear as one singular organism; it looks as if it can't be separated. To my further surprise, however, every now and then one of the fish, or a small group of fish, moves away from the group. The ones that break off phase back into luminous green lights, no form or flow or strands, just static little dabs separated from the body of the beautiful swirling green school.

It's absolutely enthralling to watch. Singularly, the fish are separate entities, low level intelligences, swimming by themselves, disconnected. Then they join back into the mass and become part of it, moving again in perfect unity with one another. I don't know how long I stand watching this exchange, but eventually Ezra shifts his feet, distracting me.

"Oh sorry, you must be getting tired of standing there…" I say, clutching Ezra's arm. "But you wouldn't *believe* what this looks like!"

"You could fill us in maybe. Give us something to think about while we stare at a boring school of fish," he says.

I laugh with delight; the feeling I get from watching the fish is pure awe. Their communion with each other is nothing short of divine. What I see before me is pure truth, a semblance of what people strive for individually but never achieve. But even if people don't know *what* they are looking for, here it is, plain for all to see. Yet they never realize it, thinking it's some kind of biological instinct, shoving it away in a textbook as merely another unexplained mystery in the world.

I describe it to Kaylen and Ezra, my voice full of wonder, wishing more than anything that they could see it the way that I do. Words don't suffice. I fall silent finally, resigned that I can't properly share this with anyone.

"It sounds beautiful," says Kaylen appreciatively. "I wish I could see it."

"So their individual souls make up one higher soul—if 'higher' is the right word," Ezra says. "It's like a human's? With the strands and the swirling?"

"Are life forces really souls?" Kaylen asks before I can answer.

"I don't actually know what a soul *is,*" I reply. "But I'd say, yeah. I think you could call it that. It bears the essence of a person… What else could it be?"

"We should all call them souls then," Kaylen says. "Every time I hear the word 'life force' I think of Louise. I don't want to associate her with anything that's beautiful, let alone something as important as a soul."

"I guess I've always used 'life force' because it's less… controversial," I explain.

"It's not like you're speaking to a crowd about the colorworld," Kaylen says. "It's just us and I think we can all agree that soul and life force are synonymous."

"Okay," I say. "Soul then." I look more closely at the school's 'soul' so I can answer Ezra's question. "It's definitely like a human's. But the fish soul is a little looser. The strands aren't as tight and directional. In fact… it kind of looks like they're connected by thousands of strands." It occurs to me that if many fish make up this one soul resembling a human's, what must *our* souls be a combination of? Are we made up of individual pieces of a whole, just like the fish?

Maybe we are of higher intelligence because we *aren't* made of individual pieces… But that doesn't seem right. I can't quite find the right explanation so I tuck the question away to think about at a later date when I can handle thinking about other things I don't understand.

I sigh and step away from Ezra, back into the real world. The fish still swim together, a beautiful silvery mass, reflecting the lights shining on them from above. Even here it's still beautiful, still mesmerizing. I can't believe that people walk by the display thinking there is nothing interesting about a school of fish.

But I almost missed it, too…

An announcement comes over the intercom telling the stragglers that the aquarium is nearing closing. Begrudgingly, I turn away from the display, walking with Kaylen and Ezra to the exit. I pause and take one last look behind me but I can no longer see the fish; the glare on the glass of the overhead lights from this angle makes it impossible.

I don't know what it means, but it's what I needed. It feels like the whisperings of peace. It gives me confidence in myself again. I am going to survive, and somehow I will be a fish again, happily swimming in the sea of life, likely nowhere near as synchronous as those fish, but content. I will make that my goal: contentment. I will find a way to be okay with what I have.

39

It's a good thing that I decided not to invade Robert's office tonight. I don't realize how exhausted I am until I catch sight of my bed. I fall asleep fully clothed after finding a birthday card from my uncle with two hundred dollars in large bills, in celebration, it says, of my being twenty years old. Twenty dollars makes more sense but what's two-hundred dollars to a person like Robert? He is generous with his money, which is fine with me. I need money right now.

I awake the next morning to my alarm, groggy but with a renewed determination that today will be much better than yesterday. I listen but hear no other sounds in the house. Kaylen and Ezra must be at school by now, and Robert leaves early and works late on most days. The man is a workaholic.

As I stand in the shower, I wonder what it's going to take to convince Gabriel that this is over…

That smarts a little. If I just focus on the task, though, I think can manage.

I called Robert last night and told him I need to come in late so I can take care of personal business. The courthouse is in my sights again. Divorce papers should send a clear message to Gabriel, because I'm not sure I can handle a face-to-face conversation or even a phone call right now. Hopefully my distance yesterday at the barn revealed the finality also.

Finality: another depressing word. It infuses me with a different sadness: long and low and lasting, not turbulent and choppy with stabs of pain like yesterday. I'm grateful for it because it means I no longer have to be tortured with indecision.

I'll start with divorce. If he needs further encouragement, hopefully I'll have had time to recover enough to… tell him to go away.

Out of the shower, I rummage through my closet for some clothes. Green is lively, and I need to feel like a person again. I pick out a tunic blouse with a green and brown retro paisley print and wear it over a pair of white skinny jeans. I accessorize with a belt and pull on a pair of leather boots.

I wish I had the courage to wear my hair up, but I need the security of its length to hide my neck. So I clip part of it out of my eyes and look at my reflection in the mirror.

For the briefest moment, I think to myself how Gabriel would love this shirt—it's exciting and eye-catching. It's outside my usual taste of fitted shirts in solid colors with interesting cuts, but I bought it shortly before Gabriel and I were married because I wanted to dress more mature. He is nearly eight years older than me and I didn't want to be mistaken for one of his students.

My mind is wandering again. I take the clip out and decide to blow dry my hair. I take a very long time. I like the task though: brushing it out in one smooth motion while moving the blow dryer over the length. I repeat this over and over until my arms hurt. My hair has grown so long in the last year and a half that it has become a real chore to manage. I'd probably cut it if I didn't actually *need* it now.

When I'm done I look at myself in the mirror again, turning this way and that. My gloves are on as usual and I have to admit I look pretty classy.

With my purse and keys in hand, I'm finally ready to go. I open the front door. As I step out into the driveway, I stop.

Gabriel's car parked near the garage.

I tense when I spot him in it, his head leaning against the steering wheel.

I don't wait for him to see me. I run for my own car. As I wrench the door open, I hear Gabriel's voice, "Wendy, wait!"

"Stay away from me!" I shout, throwing myself into the seat and yanking the door closed. I press the lock and shove my key in the ignition. I look in my rearview mirror as I throw the car in drive. He's standing outside of his car, looking on in bewilderment as I speed away.

I grip the steering wheel with trembling hands. Gabriel has not once come to Robert's house since we've been separated. That he's shown up now, only one day after seeing me touch Kaylen, can only mean he was planning on touching me. I bet he went to my work and found out I was at home. Alone.

This is not going to work. A divorce doesn't keep him from pursuing me. I should know better. Once he's served papers, Gabriel will do something drastic to get me back before the divorce can be finalized. He knows where I live and where I work. I have to get out of here. Like today.

Desperate times call for desperate measures, so I put a visit to Robert on my list of errands. Right after my trip to the courthouse.

***

When I sit down in Robert's office and tell him what I want to do, Moby-Dick strokes his salt and pepper goatee and trolls the waters for a long time. Then he asks me a question that surprises me, "Wendy, have you ever heard the phrase, 'Better to reign in Hell than serve in Heaven?'"

"Uhhh, yeah," I reply, confused.

"It's a line from *Paradise Lost* that warns of the attitude that leads to hell which, in essence, is self-imposed misery. C.S. Lewis sums it up beautifully in *The Great Divorce,* a story about heaven and hell."

I wonder where this literature lesson is going. It sounds like a lecture, and Robert has never offered one before. He's always so busy and rushed whenever I see him. And *The Great Divorce*? Gabriel mentioned it once when he was telling me about his new ability to memorize books.

When I stare at him dumbly, Robert continues, "In the book, hell is a place where everyone has exactly the things that they want—*things* being the operative word here. The occupants of hell are allowed free and uninhibited passage on a bus to heaven whenever they want, but it's never what they expect when they get there and most of them don't actually believe that it's heaven. In fact, most of them don't even realize they live in hell. Notwithstanding being told by the heavenly beings where they are and where they came from, the lost souls can't seem to believe it because they can't let go of the material glory that hell offers. But even so, they all recognize that what they have there is still not quite what they *want* only they are unable to pinpoint what that is."

I still don't know what the point of this is. Afraid of coming across as… ungrateful by hurrying him along, I wait as Moby logs in the water for a bit.

Taking the cue, Robert folds his hands over his desk and says, "The most interesting part of this story is that most of the damned that visit heaven *choose* to return to hell. They are never forced to leave. They leave of their own accord, and all because they have chosen to hang on to something that they believe brings them the *promise* of happiness rather than the *reality* of happiness. And so Lewis refers to this line in *Paradise Lost* in which we understand that misery is centered around control rather than submission.

"I'm sure you are reading this as me telling you what to do in your relationship with Gabe, but I want to assure you that I'm not. I don't know you enough to pass judgment. I simply want to present an alternative way of thinking, to be sure that you consider your actions carefully. I hate to see you in such misery."

That was a lot of words. I haven't heard Robert speak that much in months. What's more, I'm floored that of all the books he could have given me a lesson from, Robert chooses the same one Gabriel once did.

I sit in silence and confusion for several moments as Robert looks on calmly. Moby-Dick approaches the boat, making his sincerity readily apparent.

Is this coincidence supposed to *mean* something? What? That I'm supposed to go back to Gabriel?

No way. I admit that part of me is hoping for a different outcome to all of this. But I've already made my decision. I can't handle any more ambiguity. I'm done being tortured by regret and guilt and I'm done having what I feel marginalized by everyone.

What part of 'death-touch' do these people not understand? Is he telling me I should let go of concern for the lives of other people so that I can be happy? That's stupid. Dina had no fear, and look what happened to her. And Derek. And all of the other people who touched me and died. A little fear might have saved them. Gabriel has *no* fear. I'm protecting him from that hitch in his reasoning.

But I need Robert. And from what I can tell, he's only trying to help. So I hold back the scathing words I would like to say.

"Thank you, Uncle Robert, but I *have* thought this through. It's *all* I've thought about. I *have* to do this."

Robert sighs in clear disappointment. But without further complaint he says, "Okay, Wendy. If this is what you feel you need to do."

So Robert and I work out where I'm going to go. I'll travel to the east coast where he has a friend that will agree to give me a job. Robert has a branch of his company there as well, but I need to be untraceable to Gabriel whose relentlessness is sure to bring him to the ends of the earth looking for me.

At first I think it ill-advised to depend on Robert for everything like this, but I'm reminded of the old adage that states: keep your enemies close. And if Robert *is* my enemy then making him think I trust him so fully is a great way to do that.

I tell Robert I'd like to take Kaylen and Ezra with me eventually—probably at the end of this semester—which he agrees to as well. Robert seems like someone who avoids contention, so his quick acceptance doesn't surprise me. I hate that he's so likeable and easy-going about everything. It's hard to *not* trust him.

"When would you like to go?" Robert asks.

"Friday," I reply. I filed divorce papers right before I came here. I did it without tears too, still hyped up and jittery after narrowly escaping Gabriel. He will be served papers early next week, so I need to get out of town before he does.

Robert raises his eyebrows. "So soon?"

"I have to get away from him," I insist. "He's going to kill himself if I don't."

I look up to the ceiling and then prop my elbows on the end of Robert's desk as my lingering sadness spasms momentarily. It has stuck around since yesterday but I'm already starting to accept it as background noise.

"Just… whatever you do," I say, "when he comes around here looking for me, do *not* give him any information about where I am."

"I'll keep you hidden if that's what you need." Robert sighs. "I'm sorry this is how things are turning out for you. I wish I could do something."

"You are," I reply. "I wouldn't be able to do this without you." I'm a hundred percent truthful about that. I look at Robert and hope that Thursday's search will reveal that he's truly benevolent. I really do.

"Okay, I'll get it all arranged. Why don't you take the rest of the week off? I'm sure you need time to pack and prepare. Also, spend some time with Ezra and Kaylen before you go?"

I stand up. "Thanks, Uncle Robert. That'd be great."

I head for the door but stop, turning around, wanting to make another request but hating that I am asking him for yet another thing.

"What is it?" he asks, seeing the indecision on my face.

I look down and bite my lip. "Do you think that… you could maybe have your men keep Gabriel away from me? Friday is three days from now. That's plenty of time for him to corner me or something. I could file a restraining order I guess, but that doesn't actually give me much assurance…"

Robert's face deflates even more. He looks as harrowed as I feel, but he says quietly, "Yes, Wendy. I can do that. We'll make sure he doesn't have the opportunity to approach you."

I sigh. "Thanks."

I leave Robert's office relieved and horrified at the same time. It's so backward that I have to take such extreme measures against the person I trust more than anyone else. Because I *do* trust Gabriel. That's *why* I have to do this. I know that what Gabriel says is exactly what he'll do, what he'll commit himself to no matter the consequences. Ironically, it is one of the reasons I love him so much.

I slow to a stop in the hallway, baffled by my ability to both love and detest him for the exact same reasons. How is a person ever supposed to work with someone like that?

I start walking again, pausing in front of each doorway I meet, thinking about Gabriel. Getting disappointed all over again that he's not what I thought. He *was* too good to be true. And in a way I never would have guessed...

I take the elevator down. I walk into the mailroom, the underbelly of Robert's daily operations where I greet the staff absentmindedly. When I reach my small office to gather my belongings, I sit in my chair and wonder: *If Gabriel isn't what you really want, then what* do *you want?*

A less maniacal Gabriel. Someone without a death wish. Someone who doesn't make me feel... unsure of myself all the time.

It sounds like I want to have my cake and eat it, too.

I shake my head. It doesn't really matter. I still kill people with my skin. No sense in figuring out what I want but will never have.

Another blip of sadness. I adjust my grip on my heart, squeezing a little tighter to make sure it doesn't spring a leak.

Three days. And then I can put all of this behind me.

40

I don't leave the house for the next two days. And there is no sign of Gabriel either. I've not even gotten his customary phone calls, notes, or gifts. I think Robert had his number blocked. I fight not to care or think about it. Which is hard. I have nothing to do but wait and worry. And endure questions from Ezra, who thinks I've gone crazy.

"Wen, I think you're blowing this way out of proportion," he says.

Kaylen defends me, "Ezra, this is what she needs to do. You don't know Gabe like we do. He gets carried away, and the only way to get past him is to get carried away yourself. If he's intent on touching her against her will, what do you expect her to do?"

Ezra grinds his teeth. "What is *wrong* with that dude?" Then he looks at me. "Wen, I think you kind of suck at picking 'em. Each one seems to get more nuts than the last. Maybe you should opt for an arranged marriage next time."

I try not to take it as a dig, but it smarts anyway. Ezra can only be referring to the guy I dated in high school as 'the last.' The one who got me pregnant. And I don't like him talking about Gabriel in the same camp. They are *not* the same. They shouldn't even be considered the same species.

Even now when he's driving me to these extremes, I can't help but admire him. I know it's totally screwed up from an outsider perspective, but Gabriel is *good.* I know that with every fiber of my being. It's the only reason he's doing this. *Because* he's good. His methods are just… flawed. And Ezra's just a kid. I can't expect him to understand.

"Ezra, he's just driven and convicted," I sigh. "The only reason I'm doing this is to protect him from himself."

Ezra, I think, recognizes the pain in my voice and his expression softens. "Sorry, Wen. That was messed up. Of course you don't suck at this. I didn't mean that the way it sounded. I just hate that you're hurting."

I hug him then, thinking that the pain hasn't really begun. I'm about to leave my family to be alone, and right after breaking it off with the love of my life. It's frightening. I have a long road ahead of me. I'm going to have to discover a new meaning to my life. I'm going to have to cope with my condition. Searching for a cure is irrelevant.

***

Thursday brings with it indecision. I'm not so sure I want to snoop in Robert's office now. He's been so kind this week. So understanding and supportive, even coming into my emodar of his own volition. I have felt his genuine sympathy. He is mourning for me and the loss of my marriage nearly as much as I am. I am about to leave the two most important people to me in his hands. Do I really want to start off that trust with an act of *distrust*?

Even Kaylen broaches the topic, reluctant to do something so underhanded to someone so kind. She tries to make comparisons, saying that Robert doesn't resemble Louise in any way. There's no way he could be pulling the wool over our eyes *this* thoroughly. And I want to take a leap of faith against the evidence and trust him. I need someone to trust right now.

So I think about it all day—we are planning on carrying out the deed tonight. I have nothing better to do *but* think about it. By the afternoon, I am nearly set on letting my questions about Robert go.

I am perusing the internet for colleges and universities in Virginia where I might be able to finish my degree when the doorbell rings. I freeze.

The doors are locked. I've been checking them incessantly. As well as the windows. So I force a calming breath and go to the door.

I peek through the peep hole but don't see anyone. I'm expecting Gabriel of course, so I don't look down at first. But when I adjust my sights lower, I see a short Hispanic girl.

It's Letty.

That's a surprise…

I peek through one of the windows, checking that this isn't some kind of ambush, but I don't see anyone else. I ease the door open carefully.

"Letty?" I say through the crack. "What are you doing here?"

Letty looks me over with incredulity. "Uh, coming to see you. Are you going to let me in?"

I glance around again but it looks clear.

Once she's inside, I deadbolt the door behind her. Letty watches me with slightly parted lips, confused. "Are you alright, Wen?" she asks. "You look like you've seen a ghost."

I lead her into the kitchen, drawing my nerves back in. It's just Letty. She's going to get really suspicious if I keep acting so jumpy.

"I'm fine," I say dismissively. "I just didn't expect to see you here. You live like nine hours away."

I plop down in a chair.

Letty follows suit, sitting across from me, but I can tell that she doesn't yet buy my explanation. But she's more curious. Letty likes to be in on all the gossip.

"So what brings you here anyway?" I ask. "Were you just… in town?"

My casual tone settles her and she gets more comfortable in her chair, drawing a leg up underneath herself. "Yeah, I was actually. I'm doing an internship up here for the capstone class for my marine biology degree."

"Oh, that's awesome," I say, slightly jealous that Letty is finishing up her degree. I should have been taking classes this semester…

"Si…" Letty says. "It was kind of out of the blue, actually. I didn't think I was going to get it. I was put on a waiting list in case someone bowed out at the last minute. And someone actually did. At the *very* last minute. Anyway, I only got here yesterday. I would have come to see you as soon as I got here, but I've been running around nonstop. I thought you were living in that apartment—the one you gave me the address for—and I went by earlier. Only you weren't there…"

Letty waits expectantly but my mouth has gone dry and I start cycling through things to say. I can only assume, by the way she's looking at me and by the tenor of her mind, that she must have spoken to Gabriel. And he must have told her some semblance of what's going on. I'm not sure what to say since I don't know *what* he said.

"Yeah, I live here now," I say, hoping my reluctance will get her talking so I can figure out what story to spin.

"I know," she says, watching my face, plotting how to get more out of me.

I don't reply, only wait expectantly for her to continue.

Letty furrows her brow, irritated.

She throws her hands up. "What the hell, Wen? Are you getting *divorced* now? That dude is like *all* messed up over you. He spent the entire time *begging* me to come see you and talk to you for him. And then when I finally managed to get out the door, he made me promise like *over* and *over* that I would call him and tell him I talked to you and tell him every word you said. It had me pretty freaked out actually. And the only thing I can think of is that he's one of those wife-beaters who hits on his woman and then starts begging for forgiveness because he knows he's a douche."

Letty puts both feet on the ground now and scoots forward to the edge of her chair, putting her elbows on the table. "If that's not why you left him, can you *please* explain to me what on earth made you leave someone that devoted to you? Is he like that all the time or something? Does he smother you? Is he a serial killer? Holy mierda, Wen, what? Because he said your uncle had pretty much barred him completely from contacting you in any way. I can't imagine why you would have your uncle do that unless he was dangerous. But I just… and he doesn't… I just didn't get that impression from him, you know? But then, I guess it's always the ones you least expect…"

I'm grateful for Letty's endearing quirk of going on and on when she talks, because it has given me some time to concoct a response. Finally, I say, "Why did *he* tell you I left?"

Letty watches me for several long moments.

"He said he abused you," she replies, testing. "Not like hitting you. Or calling you names. But because he 'backed you into a corner'?" Letty shakes her head. "He said he didn't want to lie to me but he couldn't tell me the whole story. I really didn't get it. All I know is he's messed up. Like *really* messed up. And he told me to give you a message. Begged me, actually."

"What message?" I say, knowing this ought to be my natural response. Even though I really don't want to hear it. I need to point Letty's questioning in a different direction.

Letty doesn't respond though. Instead she puts her chin in one hand and asks a question of her own, "Did you know I got stopped at the gate out there? They asked me like twenty questions about why I was here. Where I came from. Who I was. And then they called somebody to get permission to even let me into the driveway. This is tonterías! What is going on?"

I sigh, my shoulders slumping. I have no idea how to answer her questions now.

At least Robert has definitely been taking my request seriously…

"Okay, look," I say. "I really can't get into why I'm separated from Gabriel. But just know that it has nothing to do with him being a bad guy. Because he's not. We just… aren't going to work out. And it also has to do with keeping him out of danger. I'm really sorry you had to endure his… desperation. Really. I promise you nothing is going on with me that you need to worry about."

I can't help my shoulders slumping as I say the next part, "He's upset now, but he'll get over it eventually. Just like I will."

Letty tilts her head, weighing whether she believes me and also if there's any chance she's going to get more answers out of me if she keeps pushing.

Finally she sighs and shakes her head. "Okay, I believe you that he's not a bad guy. Gracias a Dios. Like I told you, I didn't get that impression. Mostly he was sad. Desperately sad. Like you'd died or something. I actually thought that's what happened when I first got there and saw the look on his face."

Letty sits back in her chair. "After the whole tercer grado to even get up to your front door, I was really hesitant about giving you the message because I didn't know if he was telling the truth or not. If that hijo de puta was trying to joder with you, I didn't want to be part of it. But if you say he hasn't abused you or anything, then I guess there's no reason I can't tell you."

She waits, the glimmer in her eye as well as her anticipation revealing that she has some juicy piece of news to share. Letty *loves* delivering gossip. In fact, whatever it is, she's kind of in disbelief about it.

I roll my eyes. "What is it, Letty?"

She leans back casually. "He said he's had a private investigator on your uncle and he has a photo of Robert talking to your dad. He said you needed to know. He's been wanting to tell you, but Robert has blocked off all communication with you. He said he went to the police to get some kind of escort in here to talk to you but he found out Robert filed a restraining order against him, and that you had filed for divorce. The police thought Gabe was some kind of danger to you. There has been absolutely no way he could get in here to talk to you legally and he's like… aterrorizado that your uncle's going to have you carried off somewhere and make you disappear."

My eyes are wide with shock and my pulse accelerates. I need to get into Robert's office. Like right now. Which means I need to get rid of Letty.

"Thank you for telling me," I say.

Letty's jaw drops and her hands fall to her sides. "Qué demonios?" she says. "Thank you? Wen, is he for real? Is your dad actually alive?"

I nod.

Letty becomes flustered. I know she's going to blow up at me any minute for holding out on her.

"And why would him being with your uncle be a bad thing?" she asks slowly and deliberately to convey her annoyance at having to drag the details out of me.

"Because my dad is not a good guy," I whisper. Then I lean in conspiratorially because I need to scare Letty, get her out of here so I can deal with this. "I don't want my uncle finding out you were here to warn me about him," I continue to whisper. "That you know anything about this. Just leave as casually as you came and don't worry about me. I'll be fine."

Letty's eyes almost bug out of her head. "There was one other thing," she whispers.

I raise an eyebrow. "What?"

"Gabe said to tell you the thing you wanted him to promise is yours. What did he mean?"

I suck in a breath. My heart hammers so hard that my face flushes. For several beats I am elated. I want to go to him right now. I want to be in his arms again and feel the assurance of emotions; I want them to wipe away the sadness of the past weeks.

But it only takes looking back on those weeks to make an about-face. I'm now furious. *Now*? He makes me the promise *now* after all that crap he put me through? It took two months, divorce papers, a restraining order, being entirely cut off from communication with me, and finding out I might be in trouble with Robert to give me what I asked for?

The promise is practically meaningless now. That such a thing could even move me as easily as it just did—even if it *was* brief—is proof positive that Gabriel still has far too much sway over me. I'm not going to let him jerk my emotions around anymore.

I guess my face must reveal my anger because Letty unconsciously scoots back to get away, cowed. "I take it that's a bad thing then…"

I take several calming breaths. "His promise means nothing," I say tightly. That's pretty much the truth.

"What should I tell Gabe?"

I close my eyes. What *should* she tell Gabriel?

I only know two things: I need to get away from Gabriel and I need to find out what my uncle is up to. I have no desire to see Gabriel and give him another chance to take advantage of my emotions. Promise or no, I want him to stay far, far away from me. I will get Ezra, Kaylen, and myself out of here one way or another. If Robert doesn't know I'm on to him I can continue my current plans.

"Tell him I'll meet him tomorrow at the Del Monte mall to talk about it. By the fountain at two."

I have no intention of meeting Gabriel. But it will keep him out of my hair until I'm in the air and on my way to Richmond, Virginia at noon. Once I'm safely away, Kaylen or Ezra can call him and tell him I'm safe. I might even make that call myself and make it abundantly clear to him that we are over.

41

Kaylen kneels on the floor, her hand resting on the wall as she peers through the crack between the door and the jamb. She and Ezra showed up from school as soon as Letty left.

Ezra and I both stare open-mouthed. I had no idea Kaylen could unlock things with her mind. There's a click and then Kaylen grasps the handle and turns, opening the door to reveal the darkness of Robert's office beyond.

"That was the freaking coolest thing I've seen in real life," says Ezra.

"You think that's cool, you should have seen her with that giant mound of dirt in the desert," I say. "It was straight out of one of your comic books."

"You gotta show me that one someday," he says excitedly. "I bet it was like Sand Man in Spider-Man!"

I chuckle. Ezra can't help his nerdy side sometimes. He is especially funny when he's stressed, which all of us are now.

We walk into the room; Ezra and Kaylen head for the bank of filing cabinets while I sit at the desk in front of the computer. I need to see what I can get off of it.

Kaylen sits down on the floor and opens one of the bottom drawers. Ezra takes the top of another.

We work quietly for some time, and I find Robert's computer to be much more of a challenge than Louise's. He obviously has more concern for security, and that's worrisome.

I'm sure I'm overly paranoid though. He *is* a businessman after all. You can never be too careful, and living in such a nice home must make you concerned about break-ins. You wouldn't want to leave any personal information vulnerable in that scenario.

I have to bypass his whole boot-up process and hack into his hard drive through a partition that is, thankfully, already established. I hope I can find something really useful on here, because it's an intensive process. And I'm a little rusty.

"Dang, Wen," says Ezra who's been watching me as he rifles through files. "I might be smart, but my smarts are pretty specialized. I can't pick up stuff like you do. How do you get past the passwords?"

"It's called working hard, Ezra," I say. "It's not a talent. If you have the right thing to motivate you, you can do anything. And I had *you* when I took up my degree. Anyway, I rewrote the boot protocols outside of Windows. It allows me to boot up under the guest user with access to the administrator files."

"You're freaking the coolest sister ever," Ezra says. "I'm going to miss you like crazy when you leave tomorrow—because I can't find anything bad on Uncle Rob. Just a bunch of charitable donation files, real estate stuff, business associate information, client corporation details..."

Kaylen cuts in then, "Um, I think *I* found something."

I spin around and look at Kaylen who sits on the floor, crossed-legged, a stack of files on her lap.

"What is it?" asks Ezra.

I can easily spot the words from where I sit. "Energy Phases Research Project," I say, reading the file label. "Karen Spilter, telekinetic. It's some kind of hypno-touch file?"

Ezra moves next to Kaylen and leans over her shoulder so I can't see anymore.

"Okay, okay," I say. "Give her some room. Kaylen, why don't you read it?"

Ezra sits on the floor then and Kaylen speaks up, "It looks like a file detailing her abilities... mid-level telekinesis, kind of like mine I guess. It gives a date though, for her first energy session. It looks like that's when she gained her abilities. July 23rd 19—" Kaylen's brows pinch together. "92? That was 20 years ago. She was developing her ability with some place called Four Winds Energy Touch. It doesn't say anything about hypno-touch. It says the method was visuo-energy touch. That's a mouthful. Then... oh my gosh, she died in 1998. That's not helpful."

"Does it list any contact with Robert? You know, jobs she had, anything?" I ask.

Kaylen shakes her head. "Just that she was working on controlling her ability. It looks like a medical file after that." She flips through more pages. "Pancreatic cancer—that's what she died of. How sad. She only lived a month after she was diagnosed."

Kaylen hands the file to me. I look through it but don't see anything that links it to Robert.

"There's more here. It looks like it's this whole drawer," says Kaylen, "There must be like fifty of them in here..."

"Maybe we can each look at some," I say. Kaylen hands a stack to each of us.

Intrigued and anxious at the same time, I open the first one: Garret Chaumers. He possessed an ability that allowed him to encode messages on radio waves with his mind. The date for his transformation was August 15th, 1989.

I read on and see that he's dead too. He passed away in 1993 from hemophilia.

Wait. *Hemophilia?*

"Um," I say. "I'm not a doctor, but don't you *not* die from hemophilia? Isn't it one of those things they can treat?" I look up at Kaylen and Ezra who are engrossed in their own files.

Kaylen answers, "We had someone with it at the compound once—that's what gave them their energy kink. I guess it's genetic. They usually diagnose it early on, when the person's a kid, because the child gets a cut or something that keeps bleeding. Then they get stitched up and they have to be careful after that. It's not a huge deal but life threatening to kids if they aren't watched carefully."

"What about an adult dying from it? Say… forty-five years old?" I ask.

Kaylen shrugs. "I don't know… Seems like it would have to be a freak incident where the person didn't realize they were cut or something. Or internal bleeding."

I look down and flip the page. "It says here he cut himself, bandaged it, and fell asleep. They found him bled-out and dead the next day."

I turn another page. "*Undiagnosed* hemophilia?" I shake my head in confusion. "Tell me, how do you go forty-five years and never know you have hemophilia? And it says here the man had no family history of it. Are you sure it's genetic?"

"This one is dead too," Kaylen says, not answering my question. "Cancer. Wow, he had some kind of limited mind-control thing with skin-contact. He could put people to sleep almost instantly just by touching them. Same place for their energy work, Four Winds in 1989. He died three years later."

"This one's not dead," says Ezra. "Or, at least not that this file shows. It doesn't look like any of these have been updated in a long time. This is from 1991. Oh, but he has diabetes. Not like yours though, Wen. Type 2. Holy crap though, this guy is a professional triathlon competitor. His ability is extreme photographic memory. He can remember pretty much anything he can see."

"How does a triathlon competitor get Type 2 Diabetes?" I ask, sensing an ugly trend.

No one answers the question, but Kaylen says, "Here's a woman. Her ability is listed as truth discernment—like Dina, but refined. If someone told a lie, she knew exactly what they lied about and could tell you the exact truth they were hiding."

"She died in 1990," Kaylen continues after a moment. "Congenital heart defect? And according to the medical records, one she should have died from as a baby. Wow, it was a miracle she lived until… age 50? Her ability was only manifested in 1987." Kaylen shakes her head in disbelief.

"This man died of cancer, age 29," I say, having moved on to my next file. "He could create detailed hallucinations in others. But he died within five years of gaining his ability. Lung cancer. Non-smoker, no family history." I look up. "How do you die of lung cancer at age 29 with no family history and no smoking history?" My anxiety is now in full-force. What is going on here?

"I guess it could happen," Ezra says. "But obviously the correlation with these abilities is too coincidental."

I know what Gabriel would be saying right now: he doesn't believe in coincidence.

"Does everyone have this Four Winds Energy Touch place listed on their files?" I ask.

"Yeah," Ezra says, thumbing quickly through his stack. Kaylen nods.

"And visuo-energy touch?" I ask.

"Yep," Ezra says.

"Mine too," Kaylen says. "I wonder what the difference is between hypno-touch and visuo?"

"I don't know," I reply, "But all of mine are dead."

"So what if… what if Robert runs this Four Winds place?" Kaylen offers in quiet horror. "What if he's doing something to these people to manifest their abilities, something worse than Louise… and it's killing them?" She looks at me, her eyes drawn together in worry.

"Yeah…" Ezra says, still rummaging through his files.

I furrow my brow. "These are all really old files. I wonder if he's still doing the same thing?"

"These are crazy," Ezra says, shaking his head. "Mental numerical manipulation for hundreds of digits at a time, musical memorization, echo-location that worked over miles, light wavelength manipulation, wind control. This is comic book stuff. It looks like these people get these crazy strong abilities manifested from this visuo voodoo and then they die within a few years. Are we sure they weren't sick *before* they got abilities? Didn't you say the more sick someone is, the stronger their ability?"

"Well, yeah…" I say tentatively, crossing my legs. "But the illnesses themselves are bizarre. And none of these files indicate they were sick *before* they got abilities."

Ezra gets up and starts opening more drawers, searching, I guess, for any files we missed.

"So maybe Louise does hypno-touch and Robert does this visuo thing," Kaylen says. "But if he was talking to my dad, do you think that means they're working together somehow?"

"If Carl is working with him, doesn't that mean Louise is, too?" I say. "I don't see how they could be, unless the entire Louise kidnapping thing was an act. Which I guess is possible... But I'm just having trouble wrapping my head around Robert being that kind of dirt bag. His mind is just… nothing like Louise or Carl. Plus, he got me away from Louise that first time. What was the purpose of that charade? Why would Robert help us with pretty much anything? It doesn't add up."

Kaylen props her chin on the end of her stack of files. "So maybe they're competing… They obviously know about each other, and even though Gabe saw Robert with my dad doesn't mean the meeting was friendly. The files are old, but that doesn't mean Robert's not still doing it. Who keeps paper files anymore? Other than Louise—That woman does *everything* on paper. So if he's still practicing—whatever it is he's practicing—then he must keep those files somewhere else."

"Maybe the computer," I say, wheeling my chair back to the desk. "Whatever he's doing, it's *something* not right," I say firmly. "And he's lied—on more than one occasion. That can't be—"

"Here are some hypno-touch files," Ezra interrupts. "Not as many as the Visuo ones…"

I decide not to wait while Ezra thumbs through the files. Instead I get to work on the computer again. I finally make it into the operating system, but when I try to access the files, which are on a file server somewhere, I can't get into them. I'm good with operating systems, but not file servers. They are a lot more heavily protected.

"Dammit," I say. "There's no way I'm going to be able to access his files."

"Wendy, here's... your um, biological mom?" says Kaylen, handing me the file. "Regina Walden. Manifested abilities in 1990 with visuo-touch."

I turn around in surprise to take the file from her. Kaylen and Ezra are both looking at me, so I read it aloud, "Ability was 'acute empath in a max range of twenty feet.' Wow. That's way farther than me. She died in December 1994 from some kind of aggressive leukemia."

I'm silent for a minute, thinking, before I say, "That was fourteen months after I was born."

"These hypno-touch files are even older than the visuo ones," Ezra says. "But from what I can tell, none of them are dead. And the abilities aren't as fantastic. They're run-of-the-mill stuff like you described from the compound."

I slump in my chair, thinking. "So I think it's safe to say that my biological mom died from visuo, which is what gave her the powerful ability she had—she wasn't born with it. And if Robert was the one who did it, and Carl was with her at the time, that probably means Carl would have been mad at Robert over it? Then Leena—Mom—wanted to get us away from *both* of them. Not just Carl. Then that doesn't explain how Carl got so... morally backward. It looks like Robert is the one with the real issue." I puff in frustration. Gabriel would probably have a really good theory right now.

I'm reminded then of the warning Carl gave me about a war. Could he have been referring to Robert as the 'wrong side?' From what I'm seeing right now, possibly.

"Okay," Kaylen says brusquely, slapping her stack of files back on the floor. "I'm getting pretty irritated with all these people who think manipulating life forces for profit is okay. We have what we need. My dad is a bad guy. Robert is a bad guy. So what do we do now?"

I lay my head back against the chair and sigh heavily. It's clear that I *cannot* leave Kaylen and Ezra behind as I planned. It looks like I need to get the three of us away from *everyone.* We need to disappear completely. But with Robert's guys supposedly protecting me from Gabriel, that means my every move is being watched. Letty's experience at the gate to the house surprised me.

I have been able to come and go, oblivious to any surveillance, but obviously they are good at being inconspicuous. How will I get away?

There is the tiniest sliver of light in all this. When I had Robert make the flight arrangements, I asked him to get me a ticket with a public airline. At the time I did it because I knew that leaving was going to be really hard on me. I wanted a nice overly-crowded airport and flight with other people whose emotions I could leech off of to get me there.

And that means that there will be a small window of time in which Robert will not have tabs on me. Once I'm through airport security, Robert's guys will lose track of me. If I can get Kaylen and Ezra to go with me past security then I can have them disappear *with* me. I'm pretty sure the airport allows that if you get clearance. And knowing Robert, I bet it would be a piece of cake if I tell him I want Ezra and Kaylen to stay with me until I board.

Once we're beyond security, obviously I won't board the plane. And Robert won't know about it until much later. We'll have plenty of time to get away.

I nod to myself. This can work. I have no idea where we'll go next, but it's just like I told Ezra: if you have a big enough motivator, you can accomplish anything. I have a motivator alright. And to my great relief, I have no time in all this to feel sorry for myself and my lost relationship with Gabriel. My survival instincts have taken over. I grasp my newfound purpose with gusto.

I'll make it work. Just like when I first got custody of Ezra. I will do whatever it takes to take care of Kaylen and him.

42

Our plan could *not* be going better. As we wait in the terminal for my plane to take off, Kaylen, Ezra, and I sit, holding our breaths almost in disbelief over what's happening. We are about to be officially on the run.

We're well-prepared though. Ezra even knew where Robert kept a stash of cash in the house, which meant that we'd have enough money to subsist for a while until we figure out how to live under the radar. We took all of the money—some five thousand dollars—and we packed my carry-on carefully last night so we could have two changes of clothes for each of us since Kaylen and Ezra couldn't very well come with me toting suitcases. My plans with Robert were to ship the rest of my things, so I couldn't bring large suitcases with *me* either.

Robert's hired protection followed us, as expected. Kaylen, who got her license last month finally, drove us to the airport. I called Robert this morning under the guise of thanking him before I left, but really it was to tell him I didn't need Gabriel kept away from Kaylen and Ezra once I'm in the air. In fact, I told him the two of them would be going to go see Gabriel right after I leave. My hope was that Robert would withdraw his security detail so they wouldn't wonder why Ezra and Kaylen don't turn up immediately after my flight takes off.

It wasn't until the three of us got through the security gate that I saw Robert's two men, Farlen and Mark, turn around and go back the way they came. I heaved a great sigh of relief, watching their retreating backs go through the glass doors toward the parking lot.

"I've never been to Arizona," Ezra says, referring to our destination. "But I guess it's like California if you stuck it in an oven."

"I've been there," Kaylen says. "Actually I've been a lot of places. When I wasn't stuck at the compound I travelled with my dad a lot. He always had business all over the place." Kaylen twists the thick dark hair she's pulled over one shoulder, wringing out her nerves. "We always stayed in hotels, but do you think there are other compounds that he was travelling between if he wasn't doing CPA business?"

I prop my chin on my hand. "After what we've seen, I don't doubt it."

"There it goes," Ezra says as my plane taxis down the runway.

"Well let's go," I say, standing, pulling my gloves up farther, and straightening my shirt.

Kaylen and Ezra follow suit. They are both nervous. So am I. There are a lot of unknowns ahead of us.

We navigate the small terminal and exit the arrival gate. We walk through baggage claim and out to the curb where we see the taxi I called for earlier. I glance around quickly as Ezra and Kaylen get in, specifically looking toward the parking lot where I know Mark and Farlen should have left already.

I don't see their sedan anywhere but I stop with my hand on the door when I see something else: a black SUV. I don't know why it captures my attention other than that black SUVs are always telling in movies and my paranoia is at an all-time high. It's parked at the far end of the loading zone some hundred yards away. I look around, not yet alarmed, searching for more. I count two others. They aren't nearby. The second one is moving slowly away from us, about two hundred yards away. Another is in the parking lot, cruising slowly up a row which happens to be the same row Kaylen's car is parked in. I catch my breath and sink quickly down into the back of the taxi alongside Kaylen and Ezra.

I try to tell myself that I'm being paranoid, and truly, three black SUVs aren't unusual. I instruct the driver to take us to the bus station, but on the way there I glance periodically through the back window to watch if any of the SUVs are following us.

Kaylen and Ezra are distracted by the relief that we're getting away, oblivious to my plight. I don't want to alarm them so I keep cool. After all, I could be seeing things that aren't there. Without my vision I never would have noticed them anyway.

I keep checking behind us but can't see a thing because a semi is following us for at least a mile. But when the taxi changes lanes, I see it about five cars behind us: a black SUV.

I face forward abruptly but feel stupid immediately. *I* may be able to see that far, but they definitely can't see me looking for them out of the back window from this far away. So I turn back around slowly, ensuring that I'm seeing what I think I'm seeing.

Sure enough, there it is, still maintaining a good distance from us. The cab takes an exit off of the freeway and I slink back, peeking carefully over my headrest.

Ezra, who is sitting next to me, hisses, "What are you doing, Wen?"

He turns to see what I'm looking at, but I slap his arm. "Turn around!" I hiss back. He does, sitting rigidly, his nerves blossoming into alarm. He knows something's up.

My stomach drops when I see the SUV take our same exit. I turn back around. "We're being followed," I mumble to Ezra.

Just to be sure, I lean forward. "Excuse me, I'd like to make one more stop before the bus station. Can you swing by Cannery Row?"

"Sure," the cabbie says, unconcerned. He's humming along to some country music emanating from the speakers in the front.

"What do we do?" Kaylen says in a high-pitched whisper.

"We'll stop off for lunch and keep our eyes peeled. And *I'm* going to keep my ears tuned in."

They nod and commence staring nervously ahead. I instruct the driver toward a fish and chips restaurant near the boardwalk. Once there I get out, pay him, and tell him we'll meet him in thirty-five minutes at this spot.

Then the three of us walk into the restaurant, which is filled. It's a cool, breezy, and cloudy day. Still, Cannery Row, one of the biggest tourist sections of Monterey, has plenty of people at lunch time. We take a seat outside, and while we wait for our food, (which I don't think *any* of us is hungry for), I start to glance around like I'm taking in the scenery.

When the cab dropped us off, I saw the SUV pass right by our position out of the corner of my eye. I don't know where it ended up. But I'm sure that if they really are following us, they're nearby.

There are so many people. And I'm not practiced at spotting 'suspicious.' I'm not sure what it looks like. And I don't *see* any of Robert's men so instead I listen. I want to close my eyes while I do it, but in the interest of not looking suspicious myself, I keep them open. There are so many voices around, but I dismiss the ones that are obviously not from people concerned about our little group. Bubbly, excited, conversational—these are tones I ignore. Instead I listen for low voices. Voices trying not to capture attention. I can perceive a visual of our surroundings based on the sounds. I must speed through hundreds of voices, overlook a thousand other sounds, until I have focused my attention in the right way to be able to pick out the tenor I'm looking for. I listen to about ten voices that sound like what I want. Then I find it.

"*—spreading out our perimeter to make sure we don't lose them.*"

A pause.

"*Yes sir. I wouldn't advise that. I'd recommend waiting until they reach their final destination. We won't lose them. The telekinetic is with her. We don't want to draw attention here. If they're hoping to drop out of sight, they're sure to be on guard.*"

My eyes widen but I quickly resume a blank expression. It doesn't stop my heart from speeding on, however. The voice stops talking for a long time and I hunt for it desperately, hoping I haven't lost it entirely.

And then it bursts back into my ears—probably because I was searching for it so hard, "*Brecken here. Report?*"

A pause, during which time I don't let my attention waver.

"*Why would he be going to Del Monte?*"

Another pause.

"*Tail him. Do* not *lose him. We need tabs on* all *assets.*"

I grip my legs as fear grips my chest. I see a clock tower across the way: one-thirty. I know what I've just heard. Gabriel must be going there to meet me. Closing my eyes, I reach for calm.

Our food arrives. Kaylen and Ezra look like they're going to be sick. "Eat. Now," I say firmly. It is more important than ever not to let these people know we are aware of being followed.

As I chew fried chips mechanically, not tasting them at all, I listen and I think. Brecken occasionally makes his presence known, giving orders to check this or that, noting what we're doing, how long they think we'll stay in our position, and so on.

He eventually gets a call again and he answers the same way as before, "*Brecken here. Report?*"

I don't want to pause what I'm doing, which is chewing a bite of fish, but I'm afraid to miss any of his words. So even though I haven't swallowed, I stop and pick up my glass like I'm about to take a drink.

"*Waiting? He must be meeting someone. Maybe them. Keep me updated on his status.*"

The clock tower reads one-fifty now. I'm pretty sure the cab is going to be waiting on us if we don't go now. So I check my glucose, annoyed to find it really elevated even though there is no way what I just ate could have already affected my blood sugar that much that quickly. I discreetly give myself an injection and leave money on the table. "Come on," I say to Kaylen and Ezra.

They don't reply but get up robotically and follow me. I wish they'd at least talk, and not *look* like we're in trouble. I slow down and link arms with Ezra. He's holding hands with Kaylen more for comfort than as a romantic gesture.

"Don't look so miserable," I mumble. "Talk about something. Don't you have a project at school or something you want to tell to me about?"

"Um," Ezra says, unsure. "Yeah… I really liked the work I was doing for Uncle Rob on voice commands. So I was paired up with this other dude who does software development. We've been collaborating on writing a data retrieval algorithm. I've been analyzing data about common…"

I let him prattle on while I listen and watch for our pursuers. I hear Brecken again, "*Headed your way, Smith. Probably back to the cab. Outer perimeter, head to the street.*"

Sure enough, our cab is waiting. I breathe a sigh of relief once we're back inside; we don't have to put on smiling, carefree faces anymore. But that doesn't mean I have time to relax. The bus station is really close to where we are; we'll be there any minute. But now that I have discovered the sheer magnitude of the operation Robert has unleashed to keep track of me, I wonder how we'll manage to lose them at the bus station. But more importantly Gabriel is at Del Monte right now, unsuspecting of any danger. I have no idea how Robert caught on to our plans to leave but I don't have time to guess.

Considering Louise had no qualms about using people I love to control me, I'm convinced that Gabriel is in very real danger. Brecken made it clear that they are waiting for the right moment to capture us. And that probably means that as soon as they do, they'll have Gabriel as well. I have to figure out a way to warn him. Except I have no way to contact him. I left my phone at the airport in case it could be tracked. The only way is to go to Gabriel in person. I hate the idea of bringing the fight to him but I have to count on Brecken's patience. Del Monte is sure to be busy enough that he won't risk taking us there. I still don't know how we're going to evade them, but if I don't go to Gabriel myself, they are sure to use him to get me.

"We're going to Del Monte mall instead," I say loudly to the driver. Then I turn to Kaylen and Ezra and speak more quietly, "Gabriel thinks he's meeting me there. Yesterday I gave him a message so he wouldn't be on my tail. But their guys are waiting for the right opportunity to take us, and if we don't warn Gabriel I know they're going to use him to get to me. We might have to… fight our way out, Kaylen." I look at her. When it comes to a fight, Kaylen is our asset. Even Robert's men want to avoid provoking her.

"But what about Gabe? Won't he—" Kaylen starts.

"He already promised me," I interrupt, knowing she's asking how I'm going to keep Gabriel from touching me.

Kaylen looks at me critically, several questions running through her head at once.

"It doesn't matter anymore," I reply flatly to convey that I'm not interested in talking about it, especially not right now.

Nobody says anything for the rest of the trip, but when we arrive, Kaylen leans over suddenly, grabs Ezra's face, and kisses him. And not simply a peck on the cheek. It's a long kiss and she's wrapping her arms around his neck and straddling him while I stare on in dumb amazement, my hand on the door.

Ezra, at first confused and unsure, finally relents to her persistence and puts his own hand on her cheek, clasping his other hand behind her neck.

What on earth is she doing? Maybe she needs to gather her nerves or something. The climate in the car is definitely shifting from alarm to hot passion.

After what seems like an unbearably long time, Kaylen releases Ezra, her cheeks flushed and her hair in disarray. Ezra, meanwhile, sits back, amazed. He's a little confused but mostly he's really pleased. I haven't had the opportunity to feel my brother ever *turned on* before, and feeling it now in my own head is just plain weird so I open the door and extract myself from the car.

I hand the driver some cash and he smiles at me in amusement.

Kaylen and Ezra finally step out of the car and I reach into the trunk for my suitcase, securing my backpack at the same time.

As we walk toward the shopping center, I say, "What on earth was that for, Kaylen?"

Kaylen flips her hair back and her confidence grows. "Energy," she says nonchalantly. "I told you high emotions make it gather. I needed a refill."

I glance over at her as we step up onto the sidewalk. "Well then. You just got totally used, little brother."

"And I am *so* okay with it," Ezra says dreamily.

Kaylen pulls her hair back into a ponytail as we round the corner. "Let's do this," she says.

43

My heart bounds forward when we round the corner and Gabriel comes into my view. My steps quicken without my notice. Warning anxiety surfaces though, and it conflicts with the anticipation. I'm a primordial ooze of indecision again. How does the sight of him disarm me so quickly?

As soon as he looks up I see devastation ground into his features. I falter in my step and my heart sinks so swiftly I put my hand there to catch it. It feels like being in an elevator that has had the cables cut. You plunge toward the earth, perceiving that you've left your organs behind. My instinct is to reach out, to comfort him. But at the same time, I wonder what his face means? It should not matter to me, but it does. I wish falling out of love was as easy as falling *in* it.

If Gabriel is at all happy to see me, his face does not reveal any inkling of that feeling. He remains where he is as we come nearer. He looks like he has melded with his seat by the fountain.

He hates me.

My heart is hemorrhaging.

Please, I beg myself, *you have to keep it together.*

Remembering the situation helps. It burns the wound closed with fear. We reach him quickly but I keep him just outside of my emodar. If his face is any indication, I won't be able to endure his emotions even though his unique thought processes are something I have sorely missed these last few months.

I can tell that Kaylen and Ezra have no plans to do the talking. They wait on me, nervous about what's going to happen.

Gabriel avoids my eyes. He looks down at a spot somewhere halfway along the cement space that separates us. He sits so still that if I couldn't hear it, I'd worry that he wasn't breathing.

Confronted by the problem of my much farther emodar range for Gabriel, I resign myself to moving closer because I don't want to speak to him from this far away. As I take several more steps, I exert all of my effort to push his presence in my mind into a deep, dark place so I don't have to acknowledge him.

"Gabriel," I say, surprised by my own composure. My insides feel kind of empty, calm, and alert. Maybe I'm wound up about the danger closing in on us and it's giving me clarity.

He doesn't look up but he does shift his feet ever so slightly. "I'm not going to touch you. You didn't have to bring Kaylen and Ezra in order to defend yourself," he says with a hint of bitterness.

I look to either side of me at Kaylen and Ezra. They both look like they're ready to jump someone. Yeah, I guess he could easily draw that conclusion. "I know. That's not why I brought them."

He looks up at me but avoids eye contact. "Then can we get this over with? A phone call would have sufficed."

For a moment I don't understand what he's talking about. But then I realize he thinks I came here to officially break things off with him. It surprises me that he seems to be allowing it without a fight. My heart throbs painfully and I swallow to keep it from rising up. I should be glad that he's as ready for this to be over as I am. But I can't find that relief. I can only feel my heart breaking again. I wish the dumb thing would *stay broken* so I don't have to keep feeling it.

"Thank-you for warning me about Robert," I say, crossing my arms and trying to focus on the dire straits we're in at the moment. "I'm only here because you're in danger. We found out some really damning info on Robert and now he's having us followed. He's got people here right now who want to capture us *and* you and we need to figure out a way to get out of their sights."

Gabriel readily switches emotional gears. He even glances at me briefly with alarm.

"I'm sorry to put you in this position but I have no idea what to do and we need your help," I say. "My plans are on hold until all of us are safe."

He looks from Ezra to Kaylen, adjusting himself to this new situation that was obviously not what he expected from this meeting at all. Still he doesn't reply so I take a step closer. "What do you say? Can we have a truce?"

He really looks at me this time, his heartache returning in full force for a moment. I wish I could have left today like I planned. Interacting with him when he's in so much pain is hell.

"Robert has had you followed?" he asks finally. "Do they know you know?" he whispers.

I shake my head.

He looks pensive and then says, "Okay. Ideas?"

I sit cross-legged on the ground about four feet away from him. Kaylen sits next to him and Ezra sits next to me. I'm expending so much effort on controlling my own thoughts that emotions start to break through: Gabriel's. He's analyzing various solutions, but in the background is anguish waiting for him to give it an audience. I have to concentrate on breathing just to endure it.

"Well, we've got Kaylen," I say in an effort to regain control. "We can create a diversion of some kind."

Gabriel looks up and glances around us. Then he bows his head again. "How many do you think there are?"

"There were at least three SUVs following us," I reply. "But I know they had someone on you as well. So that means at least four vehicles. The one that I got a look inside at the air—I mean the one I was able to see inside had two people. So that makes somewhere between eight and sixteen guys? I'm not sure."

"We need to like… draw them into one place and trap them," Ezra says.

"The only way to do that is to have them actually *try* to contain us," I say. "Make them think they have us and then surprise them?"

"Wen, can you hear them now?" Ezra asks.

"Good idea," I say. "You guys keep talking so we don't look suspicious while I listen."

Focusing on the ground, I stretch out my hearing once more. Knowing what Brecken's voice sounds like, I listen for it specifically now. I do this for a long minute, searching amongst the many voices for his.

I'm about to start listening for some other voice—thinking maybe Brecken isn't here—when I hear it. I repeat what he says quietly so that Gabriel, Kaylen, and Ezra can hear, "I'm not sure what they're doing, Sir. They appear to be conversing… No sir, I don't advise it. It's still an open area. I'm starting to suspect they know they are being watched. That's why they keep congregating in public areas. Maybe they're deciding what to do… But I think we should wait them out. I'd recommend the parking lot. We can station men there, hidden. They have to leave eventually and their cab left so I bet they'll take Dumas' car out… Yes sir, we'll make sure to station some men behind in case they take another route.

Our first priority will be to take out the telekinetic. Then we'll close in on the others..."

I don't hear anything else after that although I keep my ears open.

"Dang," Ezra says. "Do you know where the voice is coming from?"

"Pretty sure he's dead ahead, around the corner on the other side of Williams-Sonoma," I reply.

Ezra wrinkles his nose. "Freak, Wen. That's far."

"The parking lot would be the perfect place to ambush them," Kaylen says. "Lots of cars to throw around."

"If we can actually *get* you to the parking lot safely," I say. "Where are you parked, Gabriel?"

"The parking deck," he replies. "It's on the north side of the shopping center near the movie theater. I say we walk to the theater, turn the corner, and then take the entrance into the parking deck there. I don't think we'll be vulnerable until we reach Macy's. There aren't as many small shops so there aren't as many people that congregate outside there. It should make it easier for them to do something about Kaylen. If we can get past there and to the parking deck, Kaylen can take care of the rest. Am I right, Kaylen?"

Kaylen nods, a severe look in her eyes. "Should be a piece of cake. Once we hit the parking deck it will be impossible for them to get anywhere near us, let alone chase us."

I heave in a breath. "Well, no time like the present. Let's go. Kaylen, as soon as you see us getting into an area with few people, you need to start raining down rubble or throwing trees around. Anything to protect yourself from being shot at—I hope they only mean some kind of tranquilizer but I have no idea what these people want. And I stay next to you. I'll cover you with my body if I have to."

Everyone stands up then and I grab my suitcase. Somehow I doubt it's going to make it all the way to the car once we start running, but leaving it right now will definitely give us away.

We walk close to the building on the north side of the walk. Gabriel and I flank Kaylen on her right and Ezra on her left. We pass between a building and a little grove of trees. I look ahead: from here to the movie theater looks like one massive glass storefront, perfect for an ambush on Kaylen. Dreaded anticipation weighs me down with every step.

"I don't like this," I mumble. "I'm afraid to look around because then they'll know we're on to them. But I want to see when they strike..."

Kaylen's alarm aligns with mine. Then she says in a low voice, "I need to get us cover *now.* There are lots of trees along here. I'll pull them all out and give us a moving shield."

"But all these people," I say quietly. "You're going to lift full-grown trees out of the ground with everyone watching?"

"I'm pretty sure, Wendy, that Robert's guys aren't going to expect us to expose ourselves like that," Kaylen replies. "Plus, these people will probably be so afraid when they see it that they'll start screaming and running. A frenzied crowd seems like a great way to lose thugs who are after you."

"Good point." I nod. "Okay, what do we do?"

"Just start walking again," she replies, pulling us along with her. "As soon as you hear screaming, keep pace with me exactly. Stay as close as you can. I don't want to hit one of you with a tree."

"This is going to be so cool," Ezra says, grinning.

No sooner does Ezra say this than I hear groaning earth, snapping wood, and whooshing leaves. The air becomes clouded with dirt and dust, but amid that is a sudden calamity of plant life. And then the screams begin.

Trees, branches, shrubs, and a couple wooden benches swirl slowly around us, gaining speed little by little. My suitcase even joins the mix. Dirt and twigs are raining down on us from above and when I glance up I can see Kaylen has us covered from all sides as we walk in tandem down the center of the gully between buildings. Any time we encounter a tree or a shrub or a bench, it gets wrenched from its place to join the rest of the objects orbiting us in a slow-moving whirlwind. There is no way anyone is going to be able to penetrate this kind of barrier.

My hand found Gabriel's at some point and I'm gripping it so tightly that I think I've begun to cut off his circulation. But he doesn't seem to notice. The sentiment in our moving bubble of debris is one of pure, intimidated awe.

Kaylen is on my other side and I start to feel her strain: this kind of concentration is hard work and soon she's going to get tired. I know she'd like us to walk faster but there are literally people everywhere. It's like they have no idea what to do with themselves and they don't get out of the way fast enough. We're in a tight space, too. Kaylen has to keep our spinning shield close to us without hitting any of us or anyone *outside* of us. The wind flings my hair around my face. Soil and mulch fall from the roots that whip through the air as well, and I have to squint my eyes to avoid getting stuff in them.

Kaylen doesn't speak. Sweat beads her forehead and she's getting worried. We're only about two thirds of our way to the movie theater and I don't think she can keep this up much longer. She drops a couple of trees and they crash to the ground, making our bubble a lot less impenetrable.

I'm a little frantic by now. I don't think Ezra or Gabriel know how much trouble Kaylen is having keeping such rigid control. She becomes distressed, her concentration cracking. One of the trees above us nearly falls, but she catches it at the last minute.

If only there were some way to refill her energy tank right now...

An idea comes, but I'm afraid. It worked before. It should work again. I haven't touched Kaylen since the day I fell off the horse, but if I really did power Kaylen's ability that day in the desert, *I* should be able to refill her tank.

I swallow my doubt. I let go of Gabriel and yank the glove off of my left hand before I can start talking myself out of it. Then I grab Kaylen's hand with my bare one.

The effect is instantaneous. I'm drained suddenly, causing me to stumble slightly. But my hand feels glued to Kaylen's and she pulls me upright. Surprise leaps into her thoughts. And then renewed determination. Our shield regains its integrity. A few more bushes even join in.

Kaylen starts to walk more swiftly. We can't see much in front of us, and all of us are hoping that people are safely out of the way and that we can get to the parking garage before Kaylen runs out of juice.

The screams have moved farther away. We don't slow. Kaylen even manages to swipe the eaves of a few shops as her trees spin faster and catch on things. She starts running then, and we keep pace. I haven't once let go of her hand. It feels like my energy is slowly being drained from me.

I catch sight of the movie theater through the rubble around us. Relief propels us faster.

This happy recognition distracts Kaylen though, and she grabs Ezra abruptly with her free hand, jerking him out of the way just as a tree branch swipes the small space to her left.

We finally stop in front of the movie theater. Gabriel points to our left. “Over there. The entrance to the parking deck.”

“I want to save some of this energy for the parking deck so I’m going to drop everything and we’re going to run, okay?” Kaylen says.

“Go for it,” I say.

Kaylen doesn’t merely drop the trees. She flings them outward and away from us. I don’t pause to survey the damage. I run.

We hit the door to the parking deck in about three unprotected seconds. I pile through the door behind Kaylen. Ezra is in front of her. Gabriel is behind me. In our rush we forget to check the door before we go through. That is a major error on our part. Because beyond it are about ten armed men. And they are all pointing guns at our position.

One of them shoots. Right at Kaylen.

44

My instinct is to shield Kaylen. But I'm behind her. At the same time that I hear the gun fire—it's much quieter than I expected, like maybe it has a silencer—I see Ezra's form flash in front of Kaylen. Almost simultaneously, a car sweeps in front of us from the left and across the row of men before us, knocking every one of them to the ground or across the parking deck. The flying vehicle crashes into a cement column.

I blink once, twice, and then recover and look down.

Ezra.

He's on the ground in front of Kaylen. Fear stabs an icy knife into my chest when I see him lying there, unmoving. But I don't see any blood. My eyes finally rest on a dart that's lodged in his shoulder through his sweatshirt. *Tranquilizer?* I had no idea those things could work so fast. But I'm more overcome with relief that it's not a bullet.

"More men?" Kaylen says then.

I realize I haven't let go of her, and I can tell she's entirely depleted now. My own legs threaten to buckle beneath me. But she's right. I can see figures moving in on us between the parked cars.

Just how many of these guys are *there?*

"Stay behind me," Gabriel orders, darting past me and picking up two guns that must have flown off of the men that Kaylen took out.

I do exactly what he says, pulling Kaylen behind me and hovering over Ezra. And then Gabriel starts shooting. He looks completely skilled at it. I was expecting the quieter sound, but the booms echo loudly through the cement-enclosed space. He has guns with real bullets. And he's sending a volley of shots into the parking deck as the men duck and take cover behind vehicles.

While Gabriel is shooting, I try to lift Ezra to get him to safety. But he's too heavy.

Kaylen crouches next to me and puts her hand on my bare neck.

"I'm empty," I say. No sooner do I say it than I realize I *do* perceive an energy flow. Not out of me though. *Through* me. I can't figure out where it's coming from right away. But I look down where I'm gripping Ezra and get that it's flowing from *him* where my bare hand touches his. My mouth opens in surprise. I'm feeding Kaylen from Ezra?

I don't ponder it long because energy suddenly pulls through me from Ezra swiftly, like having the breath knocked out of me. Right after that, I register that the cars in front of us—somewhere around ten or fifteen of them—get flung outward with the force of a bunch of wrecking balls crashing at the same time.

Gabriel stands in front of us and stares at the scene in numb surprise for about three seconds before moving into action. He turns back to us. "I'll get Ezra. Follow me. Eyes open in case that didn't catch all of them."

I stand up and back away as Gabriel picks up Ezra and puts his body over one shoulder. He starts walking with Kaylen and me behind him. With his free hand he starts shooting again, sending a few shots into the parking space where the cars are all smashed against the parking deck wall. I doubt any of those men are conscious. The carnage of the scene is incredible.

Fortunately, Gabriel's car isn't far—and thankfully intact. He opens the back door, lays Ezra down inside, and moves to the driver's seat.

"You take the front, Kaylen," I say, stumbling into the car and crawling over Ezra. I can't move with any grace because of my shaky limbs. Even my mind feels lethargic.

Once we're all in, Gabriel throws the car in reverse and punches the gas. Luckily, Kaylen's car-smashing extravaganza cleared the way to the exit and we speed through without braking even a little. The open air hits us and relief washes over me, giving me enough energy to stay alert. It's a bizarre sensation—being energized by my own emotions when I thought I had no energy at all.

Gabriel guides the car through the traffic easily, weaving in and out, while I look around, searching for any of the SUVs that followed us here. Gabriel doesn't relent on the gas, running several red lights and blowing through stop signs. He drives on highway 1 for about a mile before getting off on Monterey road, this time slowing to the speed limit.

"I think we lost them," I say.

"Well I'm not stopping until we're at least twenty miles outside of Monterey."

"Good idea," I say. "Maybe Kaylen's energy will have built back up by then. Too bad Ezra's out or he could fill her tank up himself."

Kaylen shoots me a weak grin. I can tell she's as tired as I am—maybe more so.

"I take it that has something to do with what you all did back there?" Gabriel says, glancing at me through the rearview mirror. "That was incredible."

"Totally. Too bad we couldn't feed off you too, Gabe," Kaylen says, slurring her words a little. "I probably could have demolished the roof and *flown* the car out of there."

Gabriel glances at her with amazement and a little confusion. But he doesn't ask her to clarify. That's not like him. In fact, he's not been like himself at all since we met up with him back at that fountain—reserved mostly. Gabriel is never reserved.

"So where do we go now?" I ask the car, not expecting anyone to really answer.

"I'm thinking somewhere north of Salinas," Gabriel says.

"Can they track us?" I ask.

"I don't think so..." Then he sighs. "But I have no guarantees. I suppose it's recognizable, but this car isn't GPS-enabled in any way. I'll drop you off somewhere. Then I can drive elsewhere to draw them away from you just in case."

"What?" I say. "How does that help? Then they'll be after *you*. And from the looks of it, they'll probably catch you. We'll be right back where we were."

"They won't," he says quietly. "I'll lead them on a wild goose chase. Eventually I'll loop back to Monterey, and by the time I do you'll be long gone."

It shouldn't bother me that he's trying to leave us. But it does. "And then what?" I demand. "We caught up with you at Del Monte so they wouldn't have a shot at you. But if you go back, they're going to have a pretty easy time snagging you."

He remains calm, empty almost when he replies, "I'm capable of taking care of myself, Wendy. I don't even know why you came to the mall. You should have just left. They might have taken me, sure. But if Robert is behind this, he knows the state of things between us. Soon we'll have no ties whatsoever. I'm no longer a good bargaining chip. And if you're gone and he can't hold anyone over your head, I'm as useless to him as the next person on the street."

And with those words, Gabriel and I are even more over. I thought I had decided the finality of our relationship already, but it keeps getting spelled out in new ways. Now he doesn't want me either. I guess he finally made that promise because he doesn't *want* to touch me anymore.

I feel around for my heart, looking for my own reaction to this new knowledge. I expect it to hurt, and maybe it does smart a little. Maybe it will hurt more later when I'm alone and haven't just come off an adrenaline high. For right now I'm mostly relieved. I've been worried I'd have to reject Gabriel outright and in person. I worried he'd waste his energy trying to get me back instead of moving on and trying to find happiness elsewhere. But it looks like we can part on… well maybe not *good* terms, but at least mutual ones. It's bittersweet.

I think this is what they call closure.

As we drive on in silence, I can't help drawing my attention to Gabriel, testing I guess, to see how this new state of things between us translates in his emotions. But all I feel from him is harrowed emptiness. It sits like a rock in my mind. I wonder how emptiness can feel so heavy.

45

When we reach Salinas we drive around for twenty minutes looking for a pay phone so I can call a cab. I can't remember the last time I used one, and apparently they have been removed since then because everyone has cell phones now. Gabriel has a phone with him, but I don't want to take the chance that it's been tapped or can be tracked.

We decide to try a gas station; I can ask to use their phone. Kaylen, Ezra, and I need a relatively untraceable ride to Watsonville, which is where I've decided we'll stay for the night. I also need to get my hands on some juice. I tested myself because of all the expended adrenaline of the last hour and I'm in the low sixties. Not in panic-range yet. But not good either. And after I just had that weird high at the fish and chips restaurant? What is wrong with me?

Ezra woke up only about ten minutes ago wanting to know what happened. Kaylen relayed the story without emphasis and it didn't take long for Ezra to realize that nobody was in the mood to talk.

Gabriel stops the car in front of a pump and I open my door and step out. "I'll be right back," I say to Ezra and Kaylen.

When I get into the gas station, a line of people are waiting for the cashier, and I down my juice as I wait nervously. If Robert's guys have been tracing Gabriel's car, I don't know how long it will take for them to catch up to us.

I look through the window as I wait, keeping an eye on the street. But my eyes rest on Gabriel's form instead. He has gotten out of his car and is leaning against it with his back toward me, filling his gas tank. Pretty soon he will drive away and I will never see him—maybe ever again. That will be for the best. He will be able to move on that much more quickly. I hope he's right though, and Robert won't see him as a target anymore. I'm not so sure, but I can't tell Gabriel what to do. I actually never have been able to.

My chest strangles in sorrow, the first inklings that I was right: I'm going to be hurting later. And if his emotions are any indication, Gabriel will be, too. My eyes water as I think that aside from Ezra and Kaylen's safety, my only wish is for Gabriel to be happy. I'm still amazed I can love him so much. Maybe I'm just in love with the *idea* of him. Maybe that's why things could never work out. He's amazing and genuinely good. He deserves happiness.

As for me, time will make it easier to bear. I should know. At sixteen, I suffered the worst kind of wound out there. It always seems unbearable at first. And then one day you wake up and realize the pain isn't as sharp. That day will come. It always does.

I finally reach the cashier. "Could I use your phone?" I ask him. "I don't have a cell phone and I need to call a—" I stop as I look into his face.

I stare at him for several moments to be sure he is who I think he is. Maybe recalling Elena has conjured a hallucination. Blond hair, a single light-brown mole on his chin. His hair is different, cropped much shorter than I remember. He's a little less youthful looking. But yes, it's him.

He looks up finally and his own eyes widen. I remember them well. His eyes always made him look relaxed even when he wasn't. "Wen?" he asks.

"Quinn," I say, almost whispering.

"Hey, how are you?" he asks cordially, although I can tell he's on defense.

"Fine," I reply, not sure what else I can say. I don't even know what I *want* to say, I am so in shock over seeing him.

"So… you're looking good," he replies nervously. Even without emodar I can tell my presence is making him really uncomfortable.

Quinn has questions, but he has no intention of asking them. He's not sure what's acceptable to talk about instead. There's no one behind me in line and it would be just… weird for me to take care of my business without saying anything else. I have always wanted the opportunity to read Quinn this thoroughly, to find the origin of whatever it was that made him fail me so miserably when I became pregnant with Elena. And now, as I listen to his emotions, he tenses in guilt. Shame.

I realize I don't hate him. I pity him.

"It's okay," I whisper without thinking much past the immediate stab of empathy I feel for him. "I forgive you."

He looks at me critically. I'm sure he doesn't suspect that I've read his mind, but he does know I've always been perceptive—we *were* together over six months. But he gets a little defensive anyway that I would presume he *wants* forgiveness—even though he obviously does.

I huff at his internal reaction and say, "I need to use your phone. I need a cab and I don't have a cell phone."

"Uh, sure," he replies. He turns to the side counter. "It's right here."

I come around. "Do you have a phone book?"

He reaches under the counter and hands it to me while I attempt to ignore his flustered confusion. I look up a number and dial while he helps another customer.

I'm told by the cab company that they can have someone to pick me up in half an hour. That's a long time, but hopefully Gabriel will be able to head Robert's guys off when he leaves—if they are, in fact, tracking us. I hang up, and as I do, a girl comes around the corner from the back room wearing the same color polo as Quinn—I guess she works here, too.

"Hey, Quinn," she says.

"You're late," he replies.

"Yeah, yeah. What, you have a hot date or something to get to?" she says, punching his arm.

"Whatever," he says, rolling his eyes. "You know I need to study."

"Yeah, I know. Monday right?" she says as she rings up someone's soda. "I can't believe you have the whole weekend off and you're going to spend the entire time studying."

"Story of my life. I'll see you on Tuesday," he says. Then he turns to me. "Can I talk to you for a minute?"

I shrug. "Sure. Cab won't be here for a half hour."

He motions for me to follow him into the back. It's stacked with boxes of soft drinks and snacks. A table with a few chairs are off to one side, and a refrigerator is stuffed in a corner. It looks like the place doubles as a stock room and break room.

He takes a jacket off of a hook and then turns to me. He tries to figure out what to do with his hands, eventually settling for the back pockets of his jeans. "I'm sorry, Wen. I've wanted to talk to you ever since… well ever since I moved."

I just look at him. This is… surreal. And I can't decide if there's anything I want to say to him.

"It got really crazy really quickly," he continues. "My mom wanted to get me out of there. She said you had a hard decision ahead of you and I was only going to make it harder if I stuck around."

"Harder?" I say just above a whisper. "But you left it all on me…"

"I was trying to give you the freedom to choose exactly what *you* wanted," he replies, confused. "It's your body. It's your life. You're a brilliant artist and you had so much possibility in front of you. I didn't want to do or say anything to take that away from you."

I stare at him again, somewhat in disbelief over how completely screwed up his perception of things is.

He sighs. "I know you think I did it to be selfish. But we were kids. I had to let you go so you could start over. And it all turned out for the best, didn't it? I heard you put the child up for adoption. He or she has a family… Was it a boy or girl?"

"Girl," I whisper, my mind reeling.

He nods. "*She* has a family. I'm glad you were able to do what you wanted."

My mouth hangs slightly open. Forget that he doesn't actually know about Elena's death. That has nothing to do with his inability to accept any responsibility. He doesn't get it. He genuinely thinks he did the right thing. That reminds me of someone else...

But they aren't the same. No way. Gabriel and Quinn are *not* the same. Gabriel did what he did out of love. Quinn did what he did out of fear. Instead of standing by me, he left. *He left.* All I wanted was one person to tell me I could do it, I could take care of her. But I had no one. Not even my mom wanted me to keep her.

"She wasn't just mine," I say, my voice starting to quaver. "She was *yours,* too, Quinn. Just because she was in *my* body doesn't mean that the decision was all mine."

"Wen," he says, irritated, "how would my being there have made the decision *any* easier?"

"The only thing you did by leaving was make the *wrong* decision easier," I say, my eyes watering. "If you'd stayed I might have had the courage to keep her. She wouldn't have ruined my life. She would have saved it. But I was alone. No one was on my side. No one. Don't you get that I needed you to be there, telling me we could do it, that we could get through it together no matter how hard?" Tears fall silently but in earnest. I sniffle a few times and wipe my eyes.

"I was your teenaged boyfriend, Wen," Quinn says in disbelief. "What were you expecting? Me to propose to you and start a family at sixteen years old?"

My eyes widen in surprise as his words wash me with clarity. That *is* ridiculous, isn't it? Commitment at sixteen. I remember expecting it at the time. I remember thinking I had it from him. But I had nothing. Quinn opted out of hard as soon as it reared its ugly head. And who would blame him really? Anyone would accept that we were too young. But excuses weren't who I wanted to be then *or* now. And I know what commitment is now. I've felt it's iron will. "You're right," I say quietly. "I always expected too much from you."

And from Gabriel I never expected enough.

I wanted Quinn to do exactly what I've been telling Gabriel to *stop* doing. Touching me aside, I've convinced myself that Gabriel is no good for me. That he pushes too much. That he keeps me constantly in doubt. I was even afraid of being afraid. Life feels out of control with Gabriel around.

But out of control isn't necessarily a bad thing. It can't be, because that's what I felt when I got Ezra, too. The difference is that I had little choice but to do what needed to be done where Ezra was concerned. I had to face the uncertainty of each month, wondering how we would survive on my meager income, worrying over Ezra feeling secure and loved. It was nearly a year of *constant* uncertainty.

Look what happened to me though… I *became* something I was finally proud of.

Tears spring to my eyes. Happy tears that always come when I think of what I gained from my relationship with Ezra. I fought for that relationship every day.

Why didn't I fight for Gabriel?

He's exactly what I need. I know it. I know it more now than ever before. He expects things from me. Hard things. Things I've never dreamed I'm capable of. But Gabriel believes me capable. I want someone that believes in me like that. I should have stuck it out. I should have seen my marriage to Gabriel as binding as my relationship to my brother.

I exhale heavily and wipe my eyes as Quinn waits awkwardly for me to break the silence. He said something to me while I was thinking about Gabriel, but I didn't process what it was.

It's too late for me and Gabriel though. He has made it clear both in his emotions and in his words that he just wants this over. If there was some chance Gabriel *did* want me, he would not have already given up. He would have made his intentions clear as soon as we saw him by the fountain. But he's made his decision about us. And when Gabriel decides something, he doesn't back down. He commits himself to a course of action no matter what stands in his way.

I won't stand in his way. Besides, if there was any chance he would want to try things between us again, it would probably come with the same stipulations as before: touching me. And I can't do that. It's the one thing that I haven't changed on. It's not Gabriel but my death-touch that continues to ruin my life just as I always knew it would.

I wrap my arms around myself, staring down at my scuffed tennis shoes thinking about Quinn again and comparing him to the enigmatic force that is Gabriel. It's not a fair comparison, but I can't help lamenting what my death-touch has cost me.

I look up at Quinn finally. "It's okay. You were just afraid. We are what we are and I don't want to be angry at you anymore. I'm too tired." And I'm more like Quinn than I'd like to admit. I'm afraid, too. I don't want Quinn because he proved he was willing to leave me out of fear. And I left Gabriel because I was afraid. No wonder Gabriel no longer wants me. I left him. Just like Quinn left me.

"Did you really care what I wanted at the time?" Quinn asks, looking for some way to end this amicably.

I look into his face. "Yes. It would have been nice to at least know you were as afraid as I was."

"I would have wanted the same thing you ended up doing," he says. "I would have wanted her to have a good family. I'm glad it worked out that way."

I struggle with whether to tell Quinn the real story. He was never around to tell at the time. And if I break it to him now, he will probably suffer the same guilt I do.

But I find that I want him to. Maybe it's because I've lost so much or maybe it's because the idea that Quinn imagines our daughter is playing and giggling with her adoptive parents rankles me.

I don't owe Quinn the illusion that everything worked out for the best. The burden of Elena was the catalyst for every bad decision I have made since. If there is a chance that knowing he shares the burden would make it lighter for me, I'll do it.

"She died, Quinn," I say, looking past his face. "Two months after she was placed."

He looks at me critically. I can tell he doesn't believe me. He thinks I'm trying to make him feel guilty. And maybe I am but it's still true.

"Whatever, Quinn," I say angrily, crossing my arms. "Don't believe me. That makes it all better, doesn't it? Put it *all* on me again. I've already suffered enough because of you. And I've had to do it all on my own. You go live your easy life thinking that your mistakes were all made right. This time *I'll* even do the running." I spin on my heel and head for the door.

"Wait," he says, catching up to me. He puts his hand on my arm, which is covered, thank goodness. "Gosh, Wen, how do you do that? I swear you can read my mind sometimes. I believe you, okay? I just… well I just don't *want* it to be true. That's all. I might have run away but that doesn't mean I didn't suffer."

"Oh really?" I spit. "You look like you're doing just fine to me."

"Yeah, it *looks* that way," he says, getting his own defenses up. "In the two years after I left, I got into a really bad crowd. Started doing drugs. I dropped out of school. That test on Monday? It's for my *GED*. I'm working at a *gas station,* Wen. Not Wall Street."

That's true. And if I'm honest with myself, I'll realize that Quinn sticking around and telling me he wanted our baby put up for adoption, too would have only made *that* decision easier. And that's the one thing I wish I *hadn't* done. The mistakes that followed were all mine.

"I look back on the possibility that I might have had to be a *father* through all that…" Quinn says, letting go of my arm and looking up and away from me. "Well I thank God the kid didn't have to suffer through me. I'm really sorry that the baby died, Wen. I really am. I'm so sorry you had to do that by yourself. I wish there was some way to make it up to you."

He sighs, wrenched with even more guilt. "So where are you taking a cab to? I can give you a ride if you want."

I realize my mouth is open and I close it. He *is* being honest. Quinn has always been a nice guy. Probably most of what happened between us that went wrong was because we were too young to know any better. "Watsonville," I reply quietly.

"Really?" he asks. I sense the budding of hopeful anticipation from him. "That's where I live."

“I’ll take a ride if you’re offering it. My brother and my... friend need a ride, too,” I reply, almost having referred to Kaylen as my sister. As far as Quinn is concerned, I only have a brother.

“Sure,” Quinn says, relieved and tentatively curious at the same time. He’s wondering if the flame still exists between us. It doesn’t, and it won’t again. I forgive him for what he did, but Quinn is too much like me to be someone who would do anything but drag me down.

And I already have a death-touch to do that.

46

Quinn and I walk out of the gas station to find that Gabriel has parked off to the side. Kaylen and Ezra are outside the car, and I see Kaylen leaning down to the driver's side window.

"What is he doing here?" Ezra demands, recognizing Quinn immediately.

"He's giving us a ride," I reply. "It will be cheaper than a cab, Ezra."

Kaylen looks up and glances between Ezra and me and Quinn with confusion.

"Like hell he is," Ezra says, crossing his arms.

"Calm down, Ezra," I say sternly. "We need a ride. He can give us one. I'm not going to waste what little money I have if I don't need to."

Ezra's snaps his mouth shut and grinds his teeth. I can tell he's trying to figure out a new way to protest.

At that moment Kaylen backs up a few steps and the car door opens. Gabriel emerges and looks at Quinn and me impassively over the top of his car. If the situation weren't so charged already it would be funny to see the difference between Quinn's gangly youth and Gabriel's refined maturity. It's like night and day.

"What is going on?" Gabriel asks calmly.

Please, Ezra. Keep your mouth shut for once. The last thing I need is for Gabriel to know who Quinn is. That's sure to make this whole last parting even more awkward.

"Quinn's an old friend. He's giving us a ride," I say simply. "So you don't have to wait around. Be safe when you go back, okay?"

Gabriel's eyes move from me to Quinn and then to Ezra's glare.

"You're alright?" Gabriel asks me. The concern in his voice jostles my barely-bandaged heart.

"Yes, I'm fine," I say, coming forward to check that I've gotten everything out of the back of Gabriel's car. "Quinn lives in Watsonville. It'll work out perfectly."

"This is bull," Ezra says, kicking Gabriel's tire. "You have got to be kidding me."

I give Ezra a warning look before leaning into the backseat, but he's not looking at me. Gabriel catches my expression though and says, "Old friend from where?"

I don't know why Gabriel would choose to be so curious all of a sudden. Surely he wants off this merry-go-round already. I know I do.

"From high school," I say, coming up with my test kit and tucking it back in my purse. "He moved up here a few years ago. It's pretty convenient, actually."

Behind me, I pick up Quinn's discomfort. He shifts his weight. Gabriel's probing glances are not lost on him. He is definitely wondering who Gabriel is.

"Yeah, *convenient*," Ezra snorts. "Did running away from your responsibilities work out as *conveniently* as you'd hoped, *Quinn*? If you think a *ride* will make up for the shit-storm you left behind, then you're still the sorry jackass you were four years ago."

"Ezra!" I yell, slamming the back door. "Watch your mouth! He's giving us a ride. Get over it!" I catch Gabriel's impassive expression out of the corner of my eye. He *has* to have figured it out. But his face reveals nothing.

Ezra looks from me to Gabriel and then back to me. "Fine," he snarls, grabbing my backpack from where it rests on the trunk of Gabriel's car. "Where to?"

My shoulders slump with relief.

Quinn recoils internally from Ezra's vitriol. He's always been good at staying calm. And he prefers running to fighting… "I'm parked right over there," he says, motioning to a small red truck only a few yards away from Gabriel's car.

Ezra stomps over and throws himself in the bed of the truck. Kaylen gives me a confused look but follows Ezra.

"I'll be there in a sec," I say to Quinn. I'd like to just leave, but I have to at least say goodbye to Gabriel, don't I?

Quinn walks past me and I step around the car to where Gabriel is, avoiding his eyes, holding my jaw rigidly so my feelings don't start pouring out of my eyes again. It's easier than I thought because Gabriel is back to the stone-cold detachment I felt earlier. Ice cold. It's actually intimidating in its intensity.

"I'm really sorry I drug you into this," I say to Gabriel. "Please… be safe."

"Is that him?" Gabriel blurts, his voice hardened. "The father of your child?" As he says it, his thoughts rebel openly against what I now realize is forceful self-restraint. It's like he took all his emotions and tried to put them under a massive boulder. And now even the boulder isn't doing a good job holding them down. He closes his eyes and reels in animosity and jealousy that's so strong I think it surprises even him.

I don't have it in me to lie to Gabriel. "Yes," I reply, still avoiding his face.

"You can't go with him, Wendy," he insists.

"It doesn't concern you," I say somewhat defensively. "It's not like I'm riding off into the sunset with Quinn. He's giving me a ride, not a promise of fidelity." *Why am I defending my permanently nonexistent love-life?*

"What are you going to do once you reach Watsonville?" Gabriel accuses, ignoring my statement. "What if he offers to let you stay with him? That's cheaper, isn't it? What then? You're going to move in with your ex-boyfriend who left you when you needed him most?"

I look at his face now, irritated by his level of outrage. "Oh sure," I say flippantly. "I'm going to move in with Quinn, the commitment flake. We're going to have wild sex, fall madly in love, and live happily ever after." I scoff. "Even if it were possible, do you seriously think that little of me?"

"I think… I think you're capable of overlooking what he did, yes. And I don't want to see you hurt by him again. As for… the other things, you're just patronizing me because you can *feel* from him exactly what I can see with my own eyes. He's hoping to rekindle something. Tell me I'm wrong." He stares at me with demanding eyes.

"Who cares?" I say, throwing my hands up. "I need a ride. He can give me one. He feels bad. I can give him a small way to alleviate his guilt. His feelings aside, what is so wrong with that?"

"Because of what he did to you!" Gabriel sputters. "It's reprehensible! And you're forgiving him! Giving him another chance!"

"Another chance? At what?"

"Winning you over," Gabriel says almost through gritted teeth. Another surge of jealousy burns through him and he leans against the car, one elbow resting on the roof, his hand over the back of his neck.

"Gabriel, you know that's stupid. For so many reasons." I tug my bag higher on my shoulder, awkwardly shoving my other hand in the pocket of my jeans and shift my feet, wishing more than anything that I could just walk away. “Why are you getting so upset?” I ask, hoping he’ll get whatever it is that’s really bugging him off his chest so we can move on.

He doesn’t answer, boiling over something he won’t share. Dammit, I can’t leave him this way! Why does the man have to hash out every last detail? Why can’t he just say, “Sorry it didn’t work out. Goodbye?” Maybe he just needs to yell at me. I can handle that I think. If it will make him feel better, I’ll stand here and take it.

“Gabriel. This isn’t how I wanted this to go. I’m sorry I drug you back into my life but here we are. So please just tell me whatever it is you don’t feel at liberty to say so you can get some closure and I don’t have to feel badly about how we said goodbye.”

He looks at me with the deepest pain in his eyes for several long seconds as he decides whether to speak. But even without speaking I think I begin to understand. The first hints of hope begin to trickle into me. I think Gabriel may not be done with me as I’d thought. I think… I think he might want me back.

“I’m upset because you are willing to give him a chance to make amends,” he almost whispers. “I’m jealous… well for a lot of reasons, but mostly because I wish it was me.”

I take my hand out of my pocket, gripping the strap of my bag in both hands now. “You want to make amends?” I work hard to temper my elation.

His brows knit in confusion. “Of course I do.” Then his eyes fall and his shoulders slump in disappointment—with himself. “I’m sorry,” he says in a pained voice. “I wasn’t going to do this. I wanted to at least give you an easy parting. But apparently I’m not even capable of giving you that.” His eyes meet mine for the briefest moment. “You’re right. I suck at making you happy.”

He turns away, angry at himself. He grabs the handle of his door, yanking it open.

I reach out and grab his arm before he can get in. “Wait, where are you going?”

He holds rigidly still under my grasp, not turning around. “I’m freeing you to find someone that can do a better job at making you happy. I should have done it long ago, but I can’t seem to help myself. I’m sorry for that… I’m sorry for everything.”

He pulls himself out from under my hand and maneuvers himself into the waiting seat of his car.

I reach for the door but I'm too late; he slams it shut. His window is still open though. "Gabriel!" I say, stepping forward and putting my hand on the door. But he already has the car on and he's rolling the window up. "GABRIEL STOP!" I shout, slamming my hand on the top edge of the glass while it rolls slowly upward.

He obeys. But he doesn't look at me still.

"What are you doing?" I plead. "Won't you talk to me?"

This scene feels familiar...

"I can't," he begs, staring straight ahead. "I wish I could say goodbye the way you want. But I need to leave now while I still can. Don't tell me where you're going or how to get in contact with you. I'm not... capable of being there for you the way you need."

I exhale, crouching down and setting my bag on the ground next to me as I cross my arms over the rim of the door so he can't take off. I petition the attention of his eyes with my own.

"Please just let me go," he breathes, his emotions begging me, but his heart accelerating at my nearness.

"I will," I say. "But first you have to tell me everything you're thinking."

"Why?" he whispers.

"Because... because I think you don't want to leave me. Is that true?"

He leans forward and puts his arms on his steering wheel, his head resting on them. "Why would you ask me that? Of *course* I don't want to leave you. How can you not know that?"

My heart stirs. "I'm not a mind reader, Gabriel."

He finally turns to look at me.

I smile softly at him and lift my shoulders. "There are unspoken words in that head of yours and I won't live with myself until they're out in the open. I've made all these assumptions about what you've been thinking but I'm starting to wonder if I'm totally wrong. But even so, life is happier when the truth is uncovered. Even if it's a hard truth. You taught me that."

He sits back in his seat but keeps his hands on the wheel, thinking for several beats. Finally he shifts in his seat and looks at me. "I'm thinking I have no idea what I'm going to do without you," he says, his voice cracking. "I'm thinking about what it will feel like going back to my empty apartment once more, this time with the sure knowledge that you'll never walk through the door again. I'm thinking I deserve it though. I keep looking back and wondering how I was so blind to what I was doing. I keep replaying it over and over again, trying to pinpoint the moment I decided to go so wrong—because I did go wrong, horribly wrong. But I can't find it and I'm terrified by the prospect that I'm just not capable of loving someone without trying to control them." His eyes bore into mine. "I'm helpless against myself," he says desperately. "And I've made you pay the price."

I hold my breath for several beats, trying to endure his pain and guilt ripping apart my insides. "You still… want to make me that promise?"

He tilts his head at me. "I already have," he breathes. "Over and over I've made that promise to you my head, knowing it was too late. Too late…"

I exhale long and heavily, closing my eyes, trying to wrap my head around this new Gabriel—one I might be able to have. Is this really happening? Are we really getting back together? I want it. I want it so badly.

I reach out and put my hand on his arm. "It's not too late."

His eyes widen in shock and confusion. He looks at my hand and then back up to my face, processing the words. "It's not?"

I shake my head.

"But… But you filed for divorce. You even filed a restraining order. What other conclusion is there to draw but that you want nothing to do with me? Is that not the case?"

"I did all that to protect you from yourself. You came to my house the day after you sent me that note about your theory about light bulbs, after seeing Kaylen touch me. You were there to corner me while I was alone. I had to take drastic measures. What did you expect me to do?"

Gabriel's mouth opens in surprise but no words come out for a moment. He puts his free hand on the back of his neck before saying, "But you told Letty you cared nothing for the promise that would have ended the stalemate between us."

My eyes fall to the ground. I guess Letty really *did* tell him what I said word-for-word. I had forgotten I even said that. "That's what I thought at the time," I whisper. I look up. "I was angry." I squeeze his arm. "But I changed my mind."

"When? How?" he demands, desperate. "After what I did to you? Tried to control you? Threatened you with killing myself? What on earth would prompt you to not just forgive me but also allow me back into your life?"

I rest my chin on my arms, gravel crunching under my feet as I shift to a more comfortable position. "Honestly, until fifteen minutes ago I thought I was done with you. I was so hurt, Gabriel…" I look up to see his red eyes tighten with regret. "And I began to look at our life together through the lens of that pain. It made me see all the things I love about you as *bad* things. The longer we were apart, the easier it was to come up with reasons why you were no good for me."

He closes his eyes. "I wasn't. I'm not."

"You *are*," I urge gently. "And it took seeing Quinn and remembering what he did to me and why for me to realize it."

His brow furrows with a bit of distaste as well as confusion. "Wendy, you don't have to settle for someone like me. Or Quinn. I appreciate being placed above him as far as your esteem—though I don't deserve it—but I want you to have better."

"Well I think you *are* better. I think you made a mistake but I forgive you. I understand why you did it."

"*Understand?* You *understand* my need to control you and dictate your happiness? Wendy, believe me, nothing would make me happier than to take you in my arms right now and never have to let go, but I know what I am. If I could tell you that I won't ever do that to you again, I would. But I can't because I don't know how I ever thought manipulating you with emotional trauma was a good idea. I'm afraid of hurting you like that again. I don't know how to stop from pushing people past the brink. I'm a *burden.* A burden you shouldn't have to bear."

"Stop it," I say, annoyed. "Why do you have to be so dramatic? Nobody is perfect, but I swear I have never known someone that can punish themselves to the point of ridiculousness. Now get out of the car." I stand up and jerk the handle to get the door open.

He doesn't move but looks at me with bewilderment.

"Out!" I shout. "Now. We need to get out of here already. And I'm taking you with me!"

He puts one leg out and then the other. When he moves too slowly I grab his arm and pull. Once he's outside the car, I lean in and grab his things, going through the glove box and grabbing anything that looks important and throwing it in my bag.

Once I have everything, I roll up his windows and lock his car. Then I drag him by the arm over to Quinn's truck.

"Ezra, you and Kaylen are in the cab. I need to talk to Gabriel privately," I order them. "And Ezra, you will shut your mouth and not say one word to Quinn the entire ride. Got it?" I look at him severely.

Ezra, obviously knowing that Gabriel's coming with us is significant, offers me a huge grin, though his emotions betray intense relief. "You got it!" He hops out of the bed, taking Kaylen by the hand and helping her jump down.

"Get in," I say to Gabriel, throwing my shoulder bag into the bed and climbing over the tailgate.

He obeys, at least conceding that this conversation needs to happen en route. We've been here too long.

Once everyone's in, we start moving, thankfully not too fast because it's not that warm out. Gabriel is sitting rigidly, nervously, completely unsure—both unusual emotions for him.

I pull up the hood of my jacket, not because I'm cold, but because I want to get close to him. We're moving and I want to protect him from my skin in case we get jostled. I squeeze next to him, my shoulder under the crook of his, my face resting against his shoulder. When he doesn't relax, I say, "Put your arms around me and stop thinking so much."

He doesn't move, hung in guilt and indecision.

"Dammit, Gabriel. I don't even get a chance to be angry at you over all the crap you put me through because you're already beating yourself up enough for the both of us. It's kind of unfair, you know?"

He remains quiet, *still* fighting against wanting what I know he wants.

"Gabriel. Hug me. Now," I say. "Or I'm going to tell your mother to smack you. I hear she won't let you in her house so I'm pretty sure she'd be on my side on this one."

He laughs, a quick, disbelieving sound and says, wrapping me in his arms finally, "I believe we've lived this moment before—you demanding I put my arms around you."

"Yeah," I say, sighing into the give of his arm now. "We seem to repeat things a lot."

The sound of rubber on asphalt consumes the next minute or so. But mentally it is not quiet. Gabriel seems to be working through whether it's okay to want me, whether he should give in to what I seem to want even though he doesn't think it's a good idea. "Wendy, you still want to be with me?"

"Yes," I reply.

"And you believe that I can make you happy?"

"You already have."

He snorts. "I'm not convinced I can. I'm a whole lot of trouble for too little return." His words infuse his emotions with even more uncertainty as he reconsiders his decision to come with me.

That ticks me off, but also strangely satisfies me. Gabriel, the man of action. Never the passive one, he'd leave me simply because he thinks he isn't good enough. Never mind what *I* tell him I want. Well he's not winning this round. I shift from under his arm and straddle his legs just over his knees, holding him down to keep him from running away. Even though being in a moving vehicle ought to prevent that, I wouldn't put it past Gabriel to jump to an escape if his mind convinced him to do that *for my sake*. He clearly has no regard for his own safety. I put my hands on his shoulders to further pin him against the truck—heaven knows what the people in the cab are thinking, probably that I'm seducing him. "I know exactly what you think. I don't care. We're married and I'm done treating what I have with you like a trial-run and I'm done cowering to your demands. I don't care what you do or say. I'm going to fight for this—even if it means fighting *you*."

His brow lifts in surprise, both at my words and my position over him. A new realization clicks in him, and for a moment he slumps in irritation. "There I go again, trying to tell you what you should want," he says to himself, gritting his teeth a moment. He looks at me finally. "El Ceilo, Wendy. I'm sorry. I'm terrible at this."

"At what?" I say, relaxing my hands from his shoulders to take his hands instead.

"After that first fight we had, I stopped listening to you. I don't know why—which is what scares me. But after that, I never let you tell me what would make you happy and then followed through on giving you what you asked. For someone who claims to value testing and evidence, I failed at even slightly entertaining possibilities outside of my own limited understanding. I treated you like your feelings didn't matter. I'm terrible at listening to *you* first and *me* second."

"You're listening to me right now."

“Only because you sat on me and told me you weren’t going to bend.”

“If holding you down and ordering you around is all it takes to get you in check, I’ll do it.” I grin at him and bob my eyebrows suggestively. “You gotta admit, this is kind of fun.”

Something overcomes him then, a sliver of titillation at my suggestiveness, but mostly relief. It entices him to reach for me and pull me in fiercely. It’s kind of awkward to lean over this way, straddling his knees, but I don’t care. I tuck my face into his shoulder and exhale as the boulder that’s been sitting in Gabriel’s mind lifts entirely away, releasing a wave of warmth and relief. It’s powerful enough to give me goosebumps. He squeezes me tightly as if he can’t get me close enough. Tears come to my eyes, not tears of pain but tears of happiness, *his* happiness.

And just like that, the piece of me that’s been out of place for so long, clicks back where it belongs. The peaceful rightness I feel when he’s near bleeds through me like a drug.

“I didn’t come to Robert’s house to touch you that day, Love,” he says, vulnerability finding its way into his voice—the kind of easy, raw openness that only Gabriel seems to possess. “I came there to beg you to take me back.”

“Admittedly, I wasn’t ready to *take* you back at the time,” I reply, taking deep breaths of him through his jacket. I find his hands, gripping them in mine bringing them into the tight space between our bodies.

“Wendy, I’ve not done a thing right since I married you. I can’t fathom why you put up with me, why you seem to love me like no one else has. Given that, you’d think I would have done everything I could to keep you—your spirit, your incorrigible morality, your self-sacrificial nature. You outshine me in every way. And I stupidly wanted to purge it from you.”

“Shhh,” I say. “Haven’t you punished yourself enough?”

“No,” he says, pushing me away gently to see my face. “I need to say this. I need you to know everything so you can decide if you truly want me still.”

I roll my eyes. “More self-flagellation? Fine. Get it over with so we can move on.”

“I’m a dictator, Wendy,” he says solemnly. My stomach roils with his disgust in himself. “I used your fear against you to try to make you do what I wanted. I thought it would be simple: leave you and let heartbreak spell out the error of your ways. I planned to *break your heart* to motivate you to do what I wanted."

My heart catches at the darkness of his admission. I suppose I knew that already, only I hadn't worded it in my head quite so… disturbingly.

He looks over my shoulder at the retreating ribbon of road. "I would break you in order to build you back into what I thought you should be," he whispers.

"Gabriel…" I say, putting a hand on his chest.

"No," he says, taking my hand in both of his and moving it back to my lap. "Let me finish."

I don't like this. Why did I tell him he could unload? The man never does anything halfway; why would I think an admission of guilt would be any different, any less difficult for me to hear?

"I didn't recognize that I was trying to rid you of the things I fell in love with. I had this beautiful thing in my life—you—and I wanted to eradicate it because I thought I could *make a better you.* How did I not see that when I devised the scheme?" He looks at me with anguished eyes.

The question is not rhetorical. He's genuinely asking. I take a deep breath, casting my eyes downward and trying to find an answer. I let my memory wander back to all the words we shared before our split. Our separation began on our wedding night. One fight. One stalemate issue: what was acceptably safe intimacy?

"You didn't see it because I was already pushing you away before you ever set that ultimatum," I say. "It made you desperate. When we're desperate we act without thinking things through."

"Don't you dare take any of the blame for this!" he cries indignantly.

"I will!" I insist. "There is no such thing as all my fault or all your fault! Not in a relationship!"

He puts his hands on my shoulders and shakes his head slowly. "It took me seeing you almost trampled to death by a horse to even *begin* to entertain that I might be wrong! Because then I imagined you dying while we were still estranged. It took the threat of your *death* to finally turn me around, Wendy. Would anything else have worked? Would I have had to see your emotional or mental destruction before I would relent? I don't know."

"You're not a bad person, Gabriel," I insist. "You're not."

"Bad enough," he says, looking down, disgusted.

"Shut up!" I cry. "Just shut up! Gosh, you're irritating. Yes, you screwed up. I never said you didn't. But we share responsibility for each other. If you do something wrong, I also have an obligation to look for how I could have helped you be better. And I did *nothing* to prevent what you ended up doing. You could even say I encouraged it. Subconsciously. Because I never could make myself believe that you could ever really want someone you couldn't touch. So I pushed you away without acknowledging it. We both did wrong. Both of us. And there's no point in arguing over who was more wrong."

Taken aback, his hands fall softly down my arms. "How do you do that? Be so wise?"

My posture eases. "Hindsight. It's 20/20."

"So they say. But that sounds more like 20/10. And you are far too young to have such keen hindsight."

I grin. "Well I *do* have exceptional vision. A lot better than 20/10 I imagine. Maybe it carries over into other things." Then my expression softens. "But it's more likely that it's because of my brother. Taking care of him was how I learned how to love people. And looking back on my relationship with him was how I realized what I gain from having a relationship with *you.*"

With my hands in Gabriel's, he pulls me back into an embrace. "Oh Wendy. I don't know how you managed it, but I feel a thousand pounds lighter."

"That's what happens when you talk. It sucks at first. But then it ends with smiles all around. You taught me that, too." I shift to sit next to him.

His eyes roam over my face and he becomes distracted by a fit of longing. "El cielo me ayude, I want to touch your face so badly. But I didn't bring any gloves. It never entered my imaginings that I'd be here again."

I sigh. "Well I'd like to be doing a lot more than having you touch my face. But deprivation seems to be name of the game for us, doesn't it?"

"Deprivation," he scoffs. "I know deprivation and it's not this. The last couple months, *that* that was deprivation. Like walking around with my soul dislodged and leaking."

His eyes find mine again, and I hold back none of the love and esteem I have for him as we release all of the strain of our separation, his affection for me building and wrapping my thoughts in a tender grasp full of the rhythmic movement I remember. It feels like coming home. Our minds meld finally and the connection we have always had is forged again, this time more strongly than before. It's palpable. I marvel that I can feel how Gabriel has become an even deeper part of me.

"I promise you, Wendy. I will not ever touch your skin," Gabriel says. "I promise you that as well as any other promise you'll have me make. I will be more careful around you. I never want you to be afraid where I'm concerned. You write the rules out and I'll sign them. I just want you in my life. That's all."

"Just promise me you'll never give up on me. Not ever." I say. "I love you and I need you. And no matter what happens I *will not* give up on you. No matter how crazy you make me."

"I promise," he says fervently. "May I be stripped of everyone and everything I hold dear if I should ever break it."

47

I sit really close to Quinn in his truck; smirking at Gabriel's utter silence toward Quinn since we moved into the cab. He hates that we're knocking elbows, but I wasn't about to let *him* sit next to Quinn. When we got to Watsonville I asked Quinn if he'd mind taking us on to Santa Cruz; I worried that our pursuers would find Gabriel's car and learn that we'd ridden with Quinn and figure out where we'd gone. He agreed and I told Gabriel we needed to ride up front. I don't really want to catch up with Quinn any more than I have already, but it just seemed rude to sit in the back like Quinn was my chauffeur.

"Your brother tells me you've been living in Monterey," Quinn says to break the silence. He's been wondering about my hand in Gabriel's for a while, but he won't ask.

"Yep," I reply. "With my uncle."

Quinn nods, searching for more small talk.

"So what are you going to do after you get your GED?" I ask to help him out. "Still planning on med school?"

"Yeah, I want to," Quinn says. "I need to do really well on my GED test so I can get into a pre-med program. So right now, that's my focus."

I can tell he has a lot of his own questions, questions he's unsure about asking. I can guess what they are and I toy with the idea of answering them. I may likely never see Quinn again after this.

We talk about his plans, which schools he wants to apply to, and what his parents and brothers are up to. I learn that he's still living with his mom—his parents are divorced, which is news to me—and that he's been working two jobs while studying toward his GED.

Finally, with the standard questions out of the way, Quinn's thoughts move back to what he was wondering about before. It's something that makes him a little sad and kind of nostalgic. Something that he's afraid of asking because he doesn't want to upset me—not to mention because Gabriel is right next to me.

"They named her Elena," I say deciding to give Quinn some closure. I wonder what it was like for him all this time having to wonder about a child whose gender he didn't even know. Even if Quinn had *wanted* to contact me after it, he would have had a hard time. We moved to Pomona from San Bernardino right after I gave birth. Even *my* mom wanted to get me away from the situation. Of course, moving wasn't uncommon for us.

That startles him. "How do you *do* that? Seriously, Wen, do you read *everyone's* mind the way you do mine?"

"You better believe it," Gabriel chuckles, his first words to Quinn.

I smile. "She was perfect. She hardly had any hair, and I remember thinking her eyes were going to end up being like yours. I only had her a couple of hours but she was really laid back like you. Kind of like she was good with whatever was going to happen."

My mouth turns down because I can't think about what actually *did* happen without being sad. In fact, I don't think I can even talk about it. But Quinn is going to wonder about it. I wish I hadn't told him she died.

"I'm sorry, Quinn. It would be easier to imagine that she was happy with some other family. There's really no need for both of us to be heartsick."

"Wen," Quinn says. "I don't even know what to say to you. I know you said my being there would have made things easier on you, but I don't think so. I probably would have been a bigger burden. Right before you got pregnant my parents were talking about divorce. That's why I started leaning on you and—" He stops and I can tell he doesn't want to continue with Gabriel in the car—someone I am obviously romantically tied to.

But I know exactly what he's talking about. At the time I saw it as Quinn *committing* himself to me, but looking back, it was more like I was an anti-depressant. I liked it too, feeling like he was finally letting his guard down with me. That's when we started sleeping together, and our relationship got really intense. He never told me about his parent's problems though, so obviously it wasn't commitment at all.

"It's okay," I say. "Really, Quinn. I don't hold any of it against you. I wanted to because I wanted someone to blame. But you were right. I was going to give her up whether or not you were around…"

I suck in a breath. I hate admitting that.

After another silent pondering minute or so he glances over at me. "Thanks for forgiving me, Wen. Of course it shouldn't surprise me. You've always been big that way." He pauses and thinks carefully about something that's bothering him. "It's none of my business... But I can't...Well I could be totally wrong but it sounds like... you blame yourself for her death."

I don't want to get into this with him so I remain silent.

"That's messed up," he says, accurately translating my answer anyway. "It's not your fault. Stop it." He puffs in annoyance. Next to me, Gabriel's indignation is in line with Quinn's and he grips my hand harder.

"You don't get to tell me what is and is not my fault," I say. "You weren't there so how would you know?"

Quinn groans. "Wen—"

"I'm not talking about this with you," I all but snap.

More silence.

Gabriel shifts his feet. "If Wendy's opposed to talking, I'd be willing to be a listening ear, Quinn."

Quinn glances over at Gabriel apprehensively and then at me. I give him a warning glare. "I don't think that's such a good idea," he says finally.

"Then *I'll* ask the questions and *you* answer them," Gabriel suggests. When Quinn gives him an incredulous look, Gabriel adds, "Heavens chap, the woman loved you, gave you her body, bore your child, tried to give that child a good life and has suffered for years since from guilt of her death. Then, as if bearing the consequences all on her own weren't enough to give you, she also *forgave* you for your egregious error in judgment. Don't you think you owe it to her to give her any closure and peace you might be capable of offering? What is it you're afraid of? That she'll hate you? You know that's not going to happen. You've already given her your worst. Yet she forgave you anyway. Muster your manhood and say your piece. We'll role play. You be you and I'll be Wendy. Pretend she's not even here."

I can't help the small laugh that escapes my throat. Trust Gabriel to say it like it is without concerning himself with people's sensitivities. This ought to be entertaining in the very least.

Quinn, taken aback by Gabriel's forwardness and somewhat intimidated by it, seems to take my chuckle as permission so he says, "I'd rather she blamed me. That would be easier to stomach than her blaming herself."

"Well it's too late for that, Quinn," Gabriel says, raising his voice in a slight falsetto to mimic me. "You don't get to decide blame when you weren't around for any of it!"

I snort and bite my bottom lip to keep from cracking up.

Quinn smiles, keeping his eyes on the road. "You're right. I wasn't. But you weren't around when she died either. How does that make you the one at fault?"

"*Because,* Quinn," Gabriel mimics, "if I would have kept her, she wouldn't have gotten sick! She'd still be alive!"

"What did she die from?"

"RSV," Gabriel says in an indignant shrill. "It's a common virus among infants. More than half of them contract it at some point before their first birthday. They don't usually die from it. But Elena did! And I just know if I'd had her with me, she wouldn't have!"

"You don't know that. Why did you put her up for adoption anyway?" Quinn asks. "It was because you wanted better for her, right? No matter what happened, how is that wrong?"

I glare at him and bite my tongue. Gabriel though, smacks his hand on the dash, startling both Quinn and me. "That is *not* why I did it!" he snaps, still in falsetto—It's really hard to be upset about the content of the conversation when Gabriel is making such a spectacle of himself. "I did it so I could go to art school!"

Quinn's brows pull together. He looks at me in confusion, then Gabriel. "Wait, what? When I left, you didn't even *want* to go to art school."

"I did too," I blurt angrily. "You don't know anything."

Quinn keeps looking between me and the road. Finally he says, "I *know* because you told me. Don't you remember? You said you wanted to graduate with me. And then you wanted to go to college like the normal kids and be an exchange student in Italy where you'd sample the food all day and sell art on the street."

I furrow my brow as I search my memory for what he's talking about. I'd say he's making things up, but I can tell from his emotions that he's completely serious. I do remember fighting with my mom about it. I was tired of art classes… I'd been doing them constantly for years... And my acceptance to art school with a full ride got my pride at an all-time high. I was *too good* for the confines of instruction. I wanted to be a *free spirit*. I believed I could make a name for myself away from home. Away from my mom who was always in my business and hovering.

He's right.

At first I didn't want to go. In fact, it wasn't until *after* I was pregnant that I decided to…

"I decided to go because I didn't want to be frivolous," I say in slight disbelief over the facts I have so long forgotten. "I wanted to make something legitimate out of myself because I—" The words catch in my throat and I look down at the floorboard. "I wanted to go to art school so I could be something better. I wanted to be a mother some day that *deserved* a child," I nearly whisper. "Like my mom."

Quinn doesn't know what to say. I don't think he really knew where he was going with his questioning. I don't know either.

Gabriel puts his arms around me and pulls me into an embrace. We ride in silence for several minutes as I dust off the memories I've buried. A few tears spring to my eyes but I feel a tremendous sense of relief in knowing that at least I had the good sense to give Elena up for better reasons. I've been carrying around a lie for so long that I think I've even manufactured memories to support it. It's an odd transformative moment, and it's hard to believe I've been compressing myself to fit a lie so effectively.

We reach downtown Santa Cruz and Quinn pulls up to a curb.

"You probably don't care, but *I* forgive you as well, Quinn," Gabriel says genuinely. "Thank you for reminding Wendy of the vital things she forgot." He reaches out a hand.

Quinn, surprisingly, seems to appreciate the gesture as he shakes Gabriel's hand. "Sure thing," he says, looking at Gabriel and regarding him differently, considering him now as something other than a rival—maybe someone to respect. Gabriel opens the door and steps out, waiting for me. Quinn looks at me as I scoot over the bench seat. Before I get out he says, "I'm sorry, Wen. I should have been there for you and I wasn't. But I'm glad you found someone that *will* be. He seems… good for you. But I have to ask, he's not married is he?"

For a moment I'm confused but then I remember that Gabriel is still wearing his wedding band; I'm not. Quinn must have noticed.

"He is," I say, smiling. "To me."

Surprised, he looks at my hand again, thinking he must have missed my ring.

"Long story," I say. "Take care, Quinn. Thanks for the ride." Then I get out and shut the door.

Kaylen and Ezra are waiting on the sidewalk, and I tell them to pick a restaurant. It's dinnertime and we need to regroup and come up with a plan. And I need a walk around downtown to… adjust to the whirlwind of change I've gone through in the past two hours.

While they argue over food ahead of us, Gabriel holds my hand up and kisses my palm. "I cannot believe I deprived myself of you for so long. That Quinn… Well I'm disgruntled to admit that he's not as terrible as I imagined him."

"Yeah. He's not as terrible as I *remembered* him," I say. "I wish I hadn't told him about Elena dying. I did it out of spite. He could have spent the rest of his life imagining I did the right thing and that leaving me helped me do it."

Gabriel stops and turns to look at me. "Wendy, you *did* do the right thing. The right thing isn't always based on the outcome—that is too unpredictable. The right thing is based on the intent with which we do things. And don't tell me you did it with ill intentions. You just proved that you've been lying to yourself about it all these years." Gabriel sighs. "I'm going to have to send Quinn a gift. He has proved invaluable to our relationship and to your internal peace. I'm jealous. Again. I've tried to figure out for months how to change your mind about Elena. It seems I didn't have all the facts."

"That all sounds really nice," I say as we start walking again. "But if I hadn't given her up, she wouldn't have died. If I hadn't given her up, I wouldn't have turned into a wreck. I wouldn't have wasted so much of my time and broke my mom's heart before she died."

"You don't know *what* would have happened if you'd kept her," Gabriel says. "She might have fallen ill anyway. And then what? You would have blamed yourself for not giving her up. There are a million possibilities. Sometimes circumstances are out of our control. The only thing you truly *can* know is why you did it in the first place. You did what you did out of love. You sacrificed your own immediate happiness for your child. What resulted doesn't change the beauty or meaning of that kind of love."

I'd like to believe that what he said is true. It sounds like a really lovely story…

For years I have wanted to go back and undo what I did. But Gabriel is right; there is no guarantee of what would have happened.

It was a hard thing. An impossible situation. And one way or another I would have been sad. At sixteen, taking care of a baby and giving up my dreams would have been hard. Not being able to give Elena everything I wanted to would have been hard. Depressing. It was a mistake that would include suffering no matter what I chose to do about it.

The only thing I have and can know for sure is what I *intended.* And I intended for my daughter to have a happy life.

I look up at the sky. It's grey and cloudy here just like in Monterey. The rainy season will be upon us soon. It reminds me of a day in July, years ago. It hardly ever rains in the summer in Los Angeles, but it did that day and had been for the few days previous. It was the day I gave birth to Elena.

I held her only once in the hospital. Right before I handed her over to her new parents. Tears ran down my face so I could hardly see her. I reminded myself over and over that I was giving her the best of what I had to offer. I took the opportunity to touch her parents so I could reassure myself that they would love her as much as I did.

They were awash in nothing but the most profound gratitude and wonder and relief as they looked back at me and then down at her. Without that touch, I don't think I could have done it. I could tell they were going to love her. They had waited a long time, never being able to have children of their own, so they were not going to take my daughter for granted.

Why have I not remembered that day until now? Why did I choose to push away everything that would have proven my intentions to myself?

Grief I guess. Anger, like always. The need to place blame for something that was so random and meaningless. Only I couldn't find anyone else to blame but myself so I built it up and justified it. I looked for evidence to support my belief until it became truth. Until it made it impossible for me to see things differently.

Thank goodness for Quinn. How ironic that he could bring me closure this way when I have resented him for so long.

Gabriel is right. I should be able to live in peace knowing that I did nothing out of selfishness when it came to Elena. And that matters.

I look around me at the quiet bustle of downtown Santa Cruz. My chest feels more open. I feel physically lighter. And perhaps it's just this new outlook on my past that has me noticing and appreciating the things around me, but I could swear things look more crisp and detailed. Even the cloudy haze over the buildings is stunning; I can make out the droplets of vapor in it. They're like graceful miniscule marbles in the way they float through space, finding every particle of light, using it to give their transparency a shape and form by way of reflection. Absolutely exquisite.

I guess it's true that happiness allows us to see more of the beauty around us. Or maybe it just makes us *want* us to see more of what's been there all along.

48

Rain taps sporadically against the wide window and balcony patio of my hotel room. A storm is threatening. It's far past sunrise, but the clouds still make it look like it's early morning. We ended up in a ritzy hotel on the San Francisco waterfront. In Santa Cruz we felt on edge because it was still close to Monterey, so we took a cab the rest of the way up here.

I was ready to settle for any place with a bed by the time we arrived, as late as it was and as crazy as our day had been, but Gabriel insisted. He said he had saved up money for our honeymoon that he never got to use, and he wanted this to mark a new beginning for us. Crazed energy healers were not going to stop him.

We seem prone to do-overs. Moments keep repeating, and despite all that's happened, I still have the nagging feeling that I'm stuck in a cycle I can't break out of.

Gabriel is sharing a room with Ezra and Kaylen and I have this room all to myself. I have to admit, when he arranged it that way, I was a little disappointed. It's a huge room and he could have safely slept in the other bed. I'm far less paranoid about my death-touch than I was before. I have better habits. But Gabriel was serious when he said he was going to back off. He always does what he says, and I didn't want to rock the boat. Kaylen and Ezra ought to have supervision anyway considering their budding romance.

I sigh. I miss him. I feel a little down for some reason and I can't figure out why.

Maybe it's the imminent rain.

I stand up, pulling a robe over my shoulders. I walk over to the glass doors, staring through them and into the greyness that has settled over the ocean. The sky and water have become one. I can't even see the horizon.

A knock sounds at the door then and my spirits lift.

I put my gloves on and go to open it, smiling. It's Gabriel dressed in jeans and a light sweater. He has two Styrofoam cups in-hand and he grins widely at me. "It occurred to me that I have no idea if you drink coffee. So I brought a package of instant coffee and a tea bag so you could choose."

"Thanks," I say, plucking the teabag package from between his fingers. "And I hate coffee but love coffee-flavored things."

"That robe looks smashing on you," he says, setting my cup of hot water on the end table.

I look down at myself and back up. "Really?" I say, putting the teabag in the water and swirling it around by the string. "It's a robe, Gabriel. Not a cocktail dress."

He shrugs, sitting on one of the armchairs near the patio glass. "I can't get enough of seeing you. My heart races away from me just to have you in the same room. Do you hear it?"

I listen and, truly, his heart *is* racing. "I guess I need to ask the hotel staff if I can get this robe in more colors then," I joke, moving to sit across from him in the other chair by the patio doors, tucking my legs under me.

He sighs in contentment. "We haven't talked in *ages.* Tell me what's bothering you."

"Something's bothering me?"

"Last night at dinner, when Kaylen and Ezra were telling me what you found at Robert's, you didn't say one word about it. " He takes a sip of his coffee. "No thoughts on how we should proceed from here?"

"I was pretty tired," I say. "I haven't slept much the last few days and I'm still in shock over things. Besides, *you* didn't have much to say about it either." Now that I remember it, that kind of bugged me. Ezra even asked him what he thought the difference might be between visuo-touch and hypno-touch, and Gabriel said, "I have no idea. And I don't much care about life forces and energy touch methods anymore. People are too inquisitive for their own good to safely explore something like that without causing damage. Suffice it to say, we need to keep these people away from Wendy to prevent further exploitation of people's souls."

Gabriel has been watching my face and he sighs after a few moments, crossing an ankle over a knee. I pick up a twinge of sorrow.

Before he can speak I say, "I told you I forgave you. Please don't beat yourself up anymore. I was mostly talking about Robert and his Minutemen. And seeing Quinn yesterday. The last five months.... I'm exhausted by it all."

"As would anyone be," he says. "I didn't have much to say about Robert because it's clear that he needs to be avoided. I think we all agree on that."

"Yeah, you said that yesterday," I reply, that same unsettled feeling prodding me.

"As for what to *do* about it in the long run," he continues, "I'd rather hear *your* thoughts."

"What to do about it? *My* plans were to get lost somewhere. Escape from the people hunting me down to torture me for information on the colorworld."

He raises his eyebrows, a little surprised. "Oh." He considers something and then looks at me. "So where would you like to go?"

"Wait, wait, wait," I say. "What was that?"

"What was what?"

"That… mental hiccup."

"Just me reorienting myself with you, Love. I've spent far too much time focused on how *I* can accomplish things. I am adjusting to focus my energies on how *you* want to accomplish them."

I look at him, lips parted in confusion for a few moments. Unsure of how to respond to that, I say, "Okay." But I don't know that I like this more… reserved Gabriel. Maybe I need to give him something to get his motor going. With his promise firmly in place, I don't have any qualms about sharing everything with him.

"I think I need a couple days before I can solidify plans," I say. "But right now I have some other things that might interest you."

"Do tell," he says, smiling.

I unload. All the things I discovered about the colorworld: the plane window, touching Kaylen, life force brightness, the colors that shift even more when you move around a room. As I talk, I feel lighter and lighter until I am gloriously exposed. The space between us, which hasn't changed all this time, *seems* smaller. More intimate. The dim light makes it even more so.

By the time I'm done, I sit back and sigh, the heaviness I felt earlier lifting. I think this is why. Truth is its own form of love making and I need it in order to connect to Gabriel, especially considering our other limitations.

I look at Gabriel expectantly, but he's not as excited as I anticipated. Instead he's beating himself up again. "I am so sorry, Love," he says. "That you never felt at liberty to tell me any of this only reminds me of the brute I've been to you. It's very hard to stomach."

"How long are you going to grovel?" I groan, impatient. "And anyway, aren't you going to tell me it's fascinating or intriguing or anything? Don't you have some new insight? I mean, we have more evidence now, don't we? That your light bulb theory is right? If I am an open circuit and souls power abilities, it totally explains why Kaylen gets recharged when I touch her."

"Yes, it is interesting. And from an academic standpoint I will file it away for perusal. But at present I am more interested in what *you* think of it. What *you* want to do with it. And I want you safe from Louise and Carl and Robert."

I balk at Gabriel's words. His emotions confirm that he is truly not expending any brain power on the new information I've given him. I've told him life forces vary in brightness from far away, that I power people like light bulbs, and he doesn't even stop to think about it a *little*?

"Since when have you not been able to think about two things at once?" I ask. "We're right here enjoying each other's company and it's an interesting topic. Plus, I'm dying to feel your brain move into action and you just sit there like I've made a nice comment about the weather? Who are you and what have you done with Gabriel?"

He looks at me, but all I can focus on is his definite restraint. "Your evidence does seem to support the theory, Love, but what does it matter? Overanalyzing what I think has literally pushed you away."

"So you're not going to think at all?" I ask incredulously, searching his emotions for the unadulterated movement that I'm used to. But it's not there.

"I have no interest in exploring things that might drive my maniacal mind to places my heart doesn't want to go. I let a *theory* about whether my soul was good enough for yours drive you away from me? Even if I were right about it, what would it matter? I am obviously *not* worthy of your soul. You would most assuredly kill me. To have tormented you the way I did… Wendy, I'm just grateful to be sitting near you. No more gilding the lily for me. I will be content with what I have. I don't want to live without you. I won't."

My fists clench involuntarily and I reach out to pick up my cup again to relax them. Those words... They always mean he is taking severe measures. My head is dizzy. *No more gilding the lily?* That fills me with so much sadness… like we've lost some essential piece of our relationship that made it what it was. And his thoughts… they have always been so free and open as they move from one thing to the next without regard for conclusions. He is stifling his open mental highways, shoring up the way so that nothing can get by.

"Gabriel?" I say, unsure of what I want to communicate.

"Yes, Love?" he says, watching my face.

I take several long, pondering sips, not tasting the tea, rocked by the idea that is beginning to take shape in my head.

I stand up, putting my cup down and crossing my arms. I step over to the window and bring my face inches from the glass door where tiny specks of water splatter the surface on the outside.

Gabriel's groveling has pushed past unacceptable boundaries. The man can *never* do anything without taking extremes. Not *worthy*? That's ridiculous!

My weakness is not his fault. His strength is what I need yet he thinks it's a flaw. I *love* Gabriel. I love everything about him. I don't *want* him to give up. I don't want him to dispose of any part of himself.

Gabriel appears next to me. I feel his eyes on my face. But he doesn't ask why I look so distraught.

Why doesn't he ask?! He should be demanding that I tell him what I'm thinking. Instead he waits patiently. Even his inquisitiveness is stifled.

The wedge that was driven between us was mine as much as it was his. *I* am the one that is too afraid. My stubbornness has made Gabriel feel like less of a human being, has made him lose his incorrigible tenacity that I love so much. And I've accepted that ridiculous promise of his, forced him to give up entertaining his own thoughts.

What have I done to him?

The better question, actually, is what am I going to *do* now? But I scramble my thoughts to push against the answer I feel coming. I don't have the courage to face it.

I try not to cry, and all of a sudden the room feels frighteningly still. I slide the glass open. A few rain drops wet my face as the wind blows teasingly through my hair. It feels so much better than the inside of the room so I step out completely, coming to stand with my hands on the balcony railing.

So many moments I have loved having with Gabriel. But each of them were stained in fear… It has ruled me and stifled what joy I might have had all this time. What's worse, it has metastasized. It has infected Gabriel. Made him half of the man I love by forcing him into a reality I refuse to be swayed from. How can I live with a man who stifles himself for me?

Is this what we give up to be together? Relationships can't work without sacrificing some part of ourselves, can they? Gabriel doesn't know how to be who he is *and* submit to my conditions.

What about me? Trying to live a contradiction. I already admitted that I can't ever pull the trigger. Gabriel *knew* that, which is why he threatened to touch me in the first place, so why should I care what Gabriel thinks about evidence? I can't expect him to both push me and hold himself back at the same time. That's impossible.

There has to be some happy median… some way to do this that won't mean destroying us.

I really am crying now, softly. Gabriel is next to me and we're both getting slowly dampened, but I barely notice.

"What's wrong?" he asks tentatively. But even worse than those hesitant words is his burning current of dread. He expects me to reject him.

The reality of the moment creates a paradox that has only one resolution. Before, I felt like I had no choice but to *leave* Gabriel. Now I have no choice but to *touch* him. How else will I prove to him the worth of his own soul?

I cower. The revolver is in my hands. I *beg* the universe to just show me where the bullet is.

Just show me!

"Wendy," Gabriel quavers. "What can I do?"

More inhibited words. It makes me sick inside. Tears fall in earnest, mixing with the few droplets of rain on my cheeks. For several long moments I grip the railing, fighting the weight of doubt. The war rages until I look up into the grey sky. The sight of it makes me bitter. More clouds. More fog. More obscurity. It's all around me. And in this moment, when a little sunshine and clear skies might give me courage, I get the gloominess of cloud-cover.

The weather was just like this the day I gave up Elena. I felt the same way about it then as I do now. In fact, until that day, I had loved rain. If it rained, I would run outside just to feel it pelting my face. But I gave up rain the same day I gave up Elena.

All of a sudden, a flash of light splits the ashen horizon. And several seconds later, the rumble of thunder.

I gasp in alarm.

Lightning?

Gabriel turns his head toward the ocean, surprised by it as well.

I don't think thunder and lightning are regular visitors to the San Francisco area. I only remember it a few times as a child in LA—that was the only thing that could get me *out* of the rain. I had to sleep with my mom because I feared it was the Apocalypse.

Another flash. Another crack. The sky lights up over and over with veins of light. It's beautiful and terrifyingly powerful.

I don't realize I have backed away from the balcony until I feel Gabriel take my hand. "Are you okay?" he asks.

"Um… just scared me is all," I reply.

"Yes, it's unusual, isn't it?" Gabriel says, turning his attention back to the sky.

He's right. It's impressive. Violent. And now that it has started, the flashes don't let up. Lightning strikes every ten seconds or so followed by thunder. Over and over. A grand light show put on by nature. Compelling.

"Should we be worried standing out here this high up?" I ask.

He shakes his head. "It's far away, several miles at least."

I move back to the railing, Gabriel's hand still in mine. We watch and all the while trepidation over my behavior eats at Gabriel.

"What's wrong, Wendy?" he asks resignedly. "You look… indecisive about something."

I nod.

"You can tell me anything," he says, but his voice falters; he's so sure I'm going to say something he doesn't want to hear.

I look at him for a few moments to see if his face will give me courage. But all I see is the light of life. I can't bear to think of it leaving.

Lightning flashes again and Elena is in my head once more. And memories of that day—the granite sky that deepened the stillness. I felt sure if I willed it hard enough, time would stop moving and I could stay next to the nursery window, staring at her forever. Yet anxiety over what was to come wouldn't allow me to fully enjoy the moment.

It was like death. I hadn't lost my mom yet, but looking back, giving up Elena was exactly like that. The day my mom died, I counted out her breaths, feeling both a mixture of sorrow and anticipation. I wanted her to stay so I wouldn't be alone. I wanted her to go so she wouldn't suffer anymore. In the end, I just wanted the moment to be over. But it passed with unbelievable slowness.

A flare of brilliance lights up the horizon again. I know I'm stalling the decision, but I can't find bravery anywhere. The sky fills me with nothing but foreboding. I'm stuck to this spot.

"Wendy, please. What is it?" Gabriel pleads. "What did I do wrong?"

"Nothing, Gabriel," I sigh. "You have never done *anything* wrong."

"Then why do you look so pale and afraid?"

I turn to him. "Because I *am* afraid."

"Of what?" he asks softly, bringing my gloved palm to his mouth, holding it to his face as the wind whips my hair about.

I shiver with cold.

"We should go inside," he says.

I shake my head. "Not until I decide something." And truly, I mean it. Every big decision has moments where time stands still, giving you the opportunity to choose. If I allow time to move forward again, things will happen how they may. I can't be passive. I have to choose or I'll live in indecisive hell again.

"Decide *what*?" Gabriel begs when I don't elaborate.

I ignore him. Instead I close my eyes and lean on the railing again as wind blows my hair into disarray and the sprinkling of rain slowly dampens it.

There's not enough evidence to be sure. I just need to gather a little more. There's no need to be hasty about it. I'll get a little more proof and then I'll touch him.

But I have a *mound* of evidence... What more do I need? When is it going to be enough?

That's the point.

There will never be enough evidence to erase all fear. At some point I have to trust what I know. I have to make the leap. If I don't, fear will *always* keep me from happiness.

I shake my head in wonder. Robert was right. I don't trust the guy about anything else but he was right about that. I have perpetuated my misery. I have chosen to control in hell rather than imagine heaven—what it might require from me to find. And if I continue to choose hell I am going to drag Gabriel down into the depths of it with me.

"Wendy," Gabriel pleads. "Why aren't you talking to me? You're scaring me."

I look up again as another thunderclap sounds. It's so hard to think with the calamity of the elements in my ears. The colorworld is always a good place to gain courage…

"Give me your arm," I say. "I want to see what this looks like in the colorworld."

Gabriel moves closer, utterly confused. I know I'm stalling my decision further. And the chill outside is starting to penetrate my robe, but thunderstorms aren't something I get to see every day, and certainly not in the colorworld.

I close my eyes, anticipation elevating my mind to the right place. The sensations of the colorworld flow over and through me with gentleness.

When I open my eyes, the sky, as usual, is the first thing I notice. It looks *exactly* how it always does: a panorama of fluctuating color.

But where are the clouds?

My eyes dart this way and that. I see none. If it weren't for the sounds, I would think this was a regular day with the sun shining.

"There are no clouds in the colorworld," I say in astonishment.

Gabriel's anxiety leaps into curiosity, but just as quickly he tempers it. "So you're saying clouds are invisible?"

As soon as he asks, I hear a clap of thunder. But I didn't see any flash precede it.

"No lightning…" I marvel. "No rain. Clear skies."

If it weren't for the rain hitting my face, I would swear it *must* be a cloudless day.

"Water is invisible?" Gabriel asks.

Both awed and disturbed by the lack of thunderstorm in the colorworld, I let go of Gabriel's arm.

I blink into the darkness, shivering again as a gust of wind sneaks beneath the hem of my robe.

"I think so," I say, remembering the tank of fish; invisible is probably exactly right. "I can see right through it. It doesn't have a color. I only see the things that float *in* it."

"Interesting," Gabriel says. And then he turns to face me. "Wendy, what are you deciding? You are behaving so strangely and I'm sure you can tell it's frightening me."

"I know," I sigh. "I'm stalling. I'm just hoping that if I stand here long enough things will get clearer—" I stop, my eyes wide.

Clearer. The colorworld in perfect clarity… While everything on this side is hidden in fog.

I move into action. For this brief moment I've found courage. I force myself not to overanalyze it. I start taking my gloves off, reminding myself that Gabriel *needs* this. *I* need it. I believe in the colorworld. I believe in what I see and experience there. It's just as real as this world, if not more so.

"I'm going to touch you now," I say quietly, using the words to strengthen my resolve.

"Is that a metaphor for something?" Gabriel asks. But he looks down at my bare hands with uneasiness.

His look of worry gives me further determination. A few moments tick by and Gabriel decides I'm being completely serious. As soon as I feel that, I dart to the door, putting myself in front of it to bar the way. I pull it closed behind me.

He looks around frantically, positioning himself behind the two patio chairs in the corner between the railing and the wall. He is genuinely afraid now. The more afraid he is, the more sure I become.

"W—Wait, Wendy," he stammers, feeling for the railing, translating the change in my countenance. "*This* is what you were deciding? Don't do this. I don't want it. I want *you*, Wendy. I want to be with you. No contact."

I hope he keeps talking. Everything he's said is proof positive that he truly thinks himself inferior. I have the power to make things right. It just takes one bullet in an otherwise empty chamber. Uncertainty will always be there. And I think I trust the colorworld more than this world. It has never lied to me. The colorworld doesn't give me clouds.

I step forward, pick up one of the chairs carefully. I place it in front of the door. I pick up the other chair and put it next to the first as Gabriel grips the railing.

I take another step toward him. His fear and confusion have grown so much that it's becoming difficult to hang on to my conviction. I opt for moving toward him because I trust that I still have it. What I feel is not mine. Another step.

"Wendy, stop!" he says, putting a hand out. "Please! Why are you doing this?"

"Because I can't live with you like this," I say gently.

"Like what? What am I doing wrong?" His hand falls slowly to his side and my eyes follow it, imagining with a twinge of excitement that in moments that hand could be touching me. I become distracted by it, wondering at the feel, the temperature, the way it will move against me.

"Nothing," I whisper. "I told you you've done *nothing* wrong. You've only tried to be what I asked you to be." Tears spring to my eyes, not of fear, but of the sight of his hand, of his *skin,* anticipating the unspoken way it could change *everything* between us. I love him so inexplicably in this moment that it's hard to breathe. The need to touch him—to show him his worth to me—suffocates me.

Realization washes over me with the force of an undertow. Why do we not see the unparalleled ability of our skin? The things we choose to touch or not touch. The *people* we touch. We should be more aware of what we think we're saying with it, because if the eyes are the window to the soul, skin is the doorway. We can touch someone's soul through our skin more easily than with any other method. And when we do, our souls communicate trust in an unspoken language, remembering and retaining what our minds do not. Skin-on-skin. So simple. So powerful and lasting. Our souls thirst for contact; I've seen that with my own eyes in the colorworld.

It all clicks into place then: Gabriel's theory, what it feels like when I touch people, and what skin can do. Being denied physical connection has led me to ponder it more deeply than I realized was possible. My soul can touch the soul of another when my skin meets theirs, probably in a more profound way than usual. Somehow I know this. It makes sense, and a feeling of calm moves through me as I accept it, as if the idea has seamlessly overlaid everything I know about life. Like a new layer of understanding, bringing with it poignant peace.

"If what I am is not what you want, tell me how to change. I'll do it," Gabriel pleads as I take another step toward him.

"Do you promise?" I ask. Gabriel has no intention of letting me touch him. And I really don't want to chase him.

"Of course," he says fervently.

I smile, wrap my robe tighter around me.

"I want you to let me touch you," I say. "It's the only way to get my husband back."

His jaw drops. "That's not fair."

"You promised," I insist, coming to stand only a foot from him. He flinches, but doesn't jump away.

"I thought you'd be honorable in your request," he says weakly.

"This is the most honorable request I've ever made of you," I say. "This is me loving who you are, without inhibition. I want you to see what I see, even at the risk of death."

"I *will* die though," he says softly, looking into my eyes. "I will do what you ask, but no one knows what I am capable of better than me. You overlook my crimes because for some unknown reason, you love me. But even though you overlook them doesn't erase the blackness of my actions. It doesn't erase the blackness that is obviously a part of my soul."

His words coupled with his conviction stab my heart, but at the same time the depth of his belief in what he's said about himself is maddening. How can he possibly think that? It's ridiculous! I close my robe tighter again in a vain effort to keep out the wind. I prefer the warmth of dryness for this moment, but I think the numbness of my physical body has given me clarity. I don't want to lose that.

I reach out.

Gabriel lowers his eyes in defeat, in the throes of distress. "When this is over, please remember *I* drove you to this. Don't blame yourself. Please promise me that?" As he speaks, the wind stills, settling the cold grey over us.

With my hand only a few inches from his face, I fumble my confidence, withdraw my hand. To imagine what this will be like for me if Gabriel dies suffocates me with fear.

And then the rain comes. Suddenly and insistently. It quickly gathers and pours down our faces, and it feels as if my very soul weeps with it.

But in the colorworld it is clear.

"No," I say angrily, eyes flashing. A fire blazes to life within me. A fire of confidence. I don't think I have ever felt so fearless—and so suddenly. "I will *not* promise you that. Because you will *not* die." His eyes are still downcast. "*Look* at me," I demand.

He looks up.

"You are the *best* man I have ever known. Your soul is *not* black. It's the most beautiful thing I have ever experienced. *I* know your soul. Better than you do. I *see* it. *Hear* it. *Smell* it."

I hold his frightened eyes with my own.

"I'm going to touch you now," I whisper gently. I reach out once more, my hands wet. He searches my face, bogged down with the struggle of wanting to accept what I've said but not truly believing it. I hate this look on his face, hate how I have made him feel. It's so wrong. I will take this risk it if it means Gabriel getting himself back. I broke him, I can tell. And now I'm going to fix him—or kill him maybe, but I can't imagine that happening now. I'm going to touch his soul and he will live because I've touched it before, in so many ways, but namely that night in our apartment. Never mind that we didn't use our skin. His soul *can* survive mine.

I lean toward him and our breaths mingle in the soggy air. He looks at me lovingly, saying goodbye again. "If you need to touch me, then my life is yours, Wendy," he says. "I love you. No matter what happens. Please don't forget that."

"And that's exactly why you will live," I say softly.

And then I press my bare hands to his cheeks.

49

I count the beats of Gabriel's heart.

Lub-dub, lub-dub, lub-dub.

I search his eyes for a change.

Animated. Expectant.

His emotions. Are they here?

Bated in anticipation. But full and present. And getting fuller.

Has time stopped?

My eyes dart to where my hands rest on his face, checking that I really am touching him. I almost expect that I forgot to remove my gloves.

My skin. On his skin. It's real.

I don't know what to do next. So long I have spent stifling my need to touch him, I did not consider what I would do once I did.

Something warm touches my fingers. It's Gabriel's hand. He brings his other one up to match it on the other side. He holds my skin to his face, his eyes fall shut. His disbelief rages against a warmth of happiness. Happiness wins. He inhales and exhales slowly, testingly.

I'm touching Gabriel.

Time inches forward.

Explosions of heart-throbbing amazement.

Just the sensation of his warmth—and the current like I experienced with Ezra—passing from his skin to mine and back… I feel nothing else.

"Wendy…" Gabriel breathes, not yet opening his eyes. He drags my hand across his cheek slowly. It glides like vibrant silk, that simple movement alone enough to elicit a sigh from my throat. My hand comes to rest on his mouth.

His lips are touching my palm, soft and giving. I don't think I have ever felt anything so perfect. It sends tingles of sensation all through my body. But I don't want to move. Where my skin touches Gabriel's mouth, heat starts to build and percolate like a net of warmth that encapsulates me even though I'm drenched in rainwater.

And then he kisses me there on my palm. That simple shifting of his lips against my skin… It's like tenderness embodied. Like love shaped by the molecules of space that moves between his lips and my hand. This language of love… the motion of this single aspect of his body… It communicates clearly, down deep to my very core, the depth of my soul. There is no mistaking the gentle affection that his skin speaks to me.

Tears spring to my eyes. Of joy. A depth of exquisite contentment that permeates my bones.

Gabriel, eyes still closed, kisses the tip of each of my fingers. Reverently.

Each one experiences the attention of his mouth as if singularly priceless.

I'm mesmerized. I'm on an upward quest and I come to life with each finger he explores. With each kiss, his affection probes further and further still, finding more permanence in my heart. It reminds me of when I experienced his soul for the first time in the colorworld. All along the way his lips record the journey, testing carefully the shape of each fingertip.

Mapping it.

Memorizing it.

One finger after another until I am shaking, overcome with emotion.

When he is done, he opens his eyes. Looks into mine. "May I kiss you, Wendy?" he asks.

Overwhelmed by the measure of his care, I don't answer for a moment until his expectancy breaks through my daze. "I think you just did," I say, my voice cracking.

He smiles. "No. I meant, may I kiss your lips?"

My heart flutters and I'm sure that I flush, not from embarrassment, but it's the way he asks… It makes me weak in the knees. My lips ache in anticipation.

"Yes," I whisper as I step forward, my arms resting against his chest now, my hands shaped to the curve of his neck, his hands shaped to mine.

He moves to touch my face, starting at my temple. His finger moves down, next to my ear, and then sweeps the length of my jaw. My eyes close. Both warmth and chills move over my skin in a symphony of sensation as he touches me. Rain droplets bathe my face, but I barely notice.

Gabriel accentuates every moment in the journey across my face. Every sensation he stops to appreciate until he knows it completely before moving to the next one.

He leans down slowly.

His mouth is on my forehead, tasting the rainwater there. Lingering.

With his mouth that much closer to mine, I can hardly stand it anymore. My body, which has been fighting for my attention all this time, demands to be party to Gabriel's skin as well.

"Please, Gabriel," I beg. "Kiss me already. I'm going to pass out if you keep this up."

That rouses him into slight amusement. "I'm not skipping to the end," he says softly as his hands, which have been caressing the skin of my face, stop at my jawline. "Besides, I feel a bit like a naughty teenager, trying to get a kiss on the first date."

"But it's not the first—" I stop because his lips have moved to my cheek. My mouth has gone dry and I breathe heavily. As he tests my skin, memorizing the feel, desire builds within him—within both of us. The closer he gets to my lips, the more thirsty I become. What was once delicate sweetness now becomes fodder for a building fire. It may rage out of control at any moment.

He fights it, although I don't know why. We are both breathing heavily now as his cheek rests against mine. My insides are in such a twist of anticipation that I can't think straight. Gabriel remains as he is, sitting in the coals, waiting for them to get too hot to stand.

His cheek moves gently across mine until his breath moves gently over my ear. He brings his hand up, moves my hair behind my shoulder and exposes my neck. My heart thumps erratically, and my neck begs for contact. I lean my head to the side, inviting it.

When the warmth of his mouth finally touches my skin, just behind my ear, my body folds. But he catches me, holding me to himself as I cling to his arms.

He kisses me there again. My hands climb upward to his neck. I pull myself closer.

That small movement throws gasoline on the blaze. Before I can react, Gabriel's mouth is on mine.

His lips are warm. Wet. And they fit mine perfectly. He kisses each of my lips, top then bottom, struggling to hold himself together with patience.

I have no such patience. I tug on him to bring him closer. I press my lips more firmly to his. I kiss him hungrily, wanting him to release himself to me.

He groans as I do so, giving up. His wanting engulfs mine quickly, and he squeezes me to himself firmly. He explores my mouth vigorously, but it's never enough. We both want more. But instead his lips retreat from mine for a few unbearable moments.

I search for them, meeting them once more with relief. Over and over he pulls away, and each time I find him. The power of his movement exalts the connection I find whenever my lips make contact with his. His mouth may be unfamiliar, but his soul and heart and mind are not. And his lips compliment the rest of him perfectly in the coordination of motion. Because of that, I already know *how* to kiss him. We release ourselves to abandon and it's easy for me to follow where he leads.

My hands on his neck have become slippery in the rain. But it adds a new perspective: our skin can glide against each other with little friction. Gabriel pauses then to taste the rainwater on my lips, and I dissolve into dizzying hunger. I find the bottom edge of his soaked shirt and my fingers explore, pushing upward to his chest. I moan softly. The rest of me is now aching to be in contact with him. I want to drink in more of the sensation of his body against mine, but our clothes are in the way.

Gabriel is no less wanting, yet still he holds back.

"Touch me," I plead, needing his hands somewhere other than my face.

"Are you sure?" he asks, his forehead to mine, our breaths inhaling the muggy air.

"Of course I'm sure," I gasp. "What kind of question is that?"

He brushes my wet hair away from my face, kisses the rainwater from the tip of my nose, tenderness returning to his movements. "We shall never have this moment again," he says.

I raise my eyebrows. "There will always be new moments," I say, thrilled by the possibilities.

He sighs, my cheek cradled in his hand, his thumb tracing the curve of my lips. "Never like this one. Never like the one after it. Every millisecond. I want every one of them to last forever."

"No moment lasts forever," I say, running my hand under his shirt and around to his back. I pull him to me to convey my urgency. "And I want this one right now."

He holds himself in check. I grab one of his hands, bring it down under the neck of my robe until it rests just under my collarbone. "Touch me."

He closes his eyes and groans, fighting for restraint as fire blazes where his hand rests on my skin. I take his other hand now. He doesn't resist. I bring it to my waist, under my robe, beneath the camisole I'm wearing.

He loses all semblance of control then, devouring my lips, and tugging at my body, grasping me to him fiercely.

But still he does not move me from where we stand in the rain. "Gabriel. Inside. Now," I demand, gasping.

He laughs between kisses that he plants on my neck and my mouth as his hands explore my body. I'm so starved for his touch that it's hard to breathe. "I'm not done with this moment," he says. "It's unbearably erotic."

Now he's just teasing me. Kissing behind my ear. Caressing me without *really* touching me in the places I want. His torture is deliberate. He's enjoying it even! It brings a smile to my face.

"You're back," I say, standing on tip-toe to press my face into his neck. He is back to the strong charismatic force I love, mastering me with his incredible self-control. He's back to the man who takes every situation and ekes out every spare molecule of experience he can get. He is the man who never looks for the end-point. He always lives *right now*.

"Forever," he sighs, hunger rippling through him again. He shudders.

"Yes. And I'm ready to *start* forever. Get me inside, you stubborn man. Your ambition to prove yourself is going to end with us being on the ground right here and I will *not* be pleased with that."

Without a word he scoops me up into his arms in one swift motion. He kicks the chairs aside and pulls the door open.

A bolt of lightning shatters the horizon behind him. It's followed by the loudest crack yet. It doesn't startle me though. I'm lost within my own body.

Except for one thought: I will never give up the rain again.

50

The thunderstorm has not let up. Or maybe multiple storm clouds have been passing over this area. It's bizarre, actually. But not so bizarre that it trumps this day and the fact that I have never in my life done something so reckless. One minute I'm thinking, *Well of* course *he lived. How could you have ever expected anything different?* The next minute I'm wondering what came over me and if it's possible to ever duplicate that kind of daring.

"Why did you *really* do it, Wendy?" Gabriel says, stroking circles on my back as I lie against him, marveling still at the surrealism of this moment. His skin is a new discovery, a side of him I thought I understood was missing, but never grasped how incredible it could actually be.

I spread my fingers apart, laying my hand against his bare chest and then lifting it up, testing the strange sensation of magnetism. I discovered that, with Gabriel, the faint current I felt with Kaylen and Ezra is much stronger. It feels like it binds me to him. I already asked Gabriel about it, but he doesn't feel anything like that.

"Wendy, why?" he asks again.

I prop my chin on his chest. "We've been over this. I'm not sure what else I can say. I broke you of all the things I loved the most. You said no more gilding the lily. And I couldn't stand for it."

"But that's not what I—" Gabriel complains. "I had no idea you would see me that way when I told you I was going to content myself to not gild the lily. I thought… I thought it would reiterate my commitment to you."

"Yeah, your commitment to destroy yourself for my sake. I didn't sign up for that."

"Why wouldn't you just tell me to stop doing whatever it was that was bothering you?"

I shake my head and roll my eyes. "Because what I wanted from you was contradictory. To push me yet not push me. To believe in yourself yet *not* believe in yourself. To question everything yet not question everything."

"Okay, fine," he grumbles. "But that could have been worked out without risking my life."

I lay my cheek on his chest, closing my eyes to soak his warmth directly into me. I can't get enough. I don't know if I ever will.

"I'm done trying to explain this to you," I say when his thoughts prove that he's waiting on an answer.

He sighs. "Your logic doesn't make sense to me. I understand the issue you had. I just don't understand the leap in deciding to touch me so suddenly."

"Isn't me touching you *exactly* what you set out to do by leaving me?" I ask. "So your plan worked. Why are you so surprised by it?"

"Because it was wrong!"

"Sometimes we need wrong things to move us."

He snorts.

"I needed you to do exactly what you did."

Gabriel relents, distracting his irritation by looking at my hands. He holds one up and then the other, looking at my fingers, testing his hand in mine like he just can't believe it.

His wonder stops with my left hand though. Sadness fills his heart. I turn my head to look at him and that's when I realize he's looking at my ring finger—my *empty* ring finger.

"In approximately thirty days, we will officially be separated," he says, choking on his words. His eyes water. "They served the papers two days ago. And in about five months after that, you will no longer be my wife."

"Well *that's* not going to happen," I say. "A trip to the courthouse will fix it."

That doesn't deter him as he looks at my hand, his brow knit in sadness. Then he brings it to his cheek, desperate and pleading. "I am so *so* sorry. Yo no merezco tu perdón."

"It's done, Gabriel," I say. "Let it go. I forgive you. I forgave you. I cannot possibly ever look back on it with disappointment."

He looks at me. "How can you so easily forget months of emotional abuse? I disregarded you in every way imaginable. I shouldn't be *rewarded* this way. It's not right."

I make a fist with his hand and hold it in my grip. "How can it be ultimately wrong if this is the result? Your mind…" I shake my head in wonder. "Your mind always gets you to the right conclusions. Look, I told you before, I understand why you did it. You didn't want to make me a promise that would jeopardize my future happiness. Meanwhile I dwelled on uncertainty. It was an equal blunder but you were right the whole time."

Gabriel puts his other hand over mine and says intently, "It only resulted this way because you allowed it. Not because of anything I did right. My actions arose from a need to control. Your actions were out of love. That is not equal."

I groan and roll off his chest to lay on my side, my head propped up on my elbow. "I don't care. I am done with this conversation. There is no point to hammering out blame."

"No, come back," Gabriel pleads in a voice that makes him seem younger than he is. He grabs my wrists and pulls me back up to his chest. "I can't take your skin being away from mine. Even if your refusal to answer has me floundering in guilt and uncertainty inside, and I have no idea why you love me, I'll drop this topic. I'll do whatever you ask, you know. I'm under your spell and obliviously, happily so."

I brush his hair off of his eyebrows and sigh. "Would it help if I told you why I love you?"

"I certainly wouldn't be opposed to that."

"I love you because you drive me crazy."

His face screws up. "That doesn't sound pleasant at all."

"I've never had anyone make me so passionately love them and hate them all at once for the exact same things. You bring me to life. You make me sad, mad, desperate, furious, elated, amazed, baffled, confused, joyful, and everything in between. Our relationship is volatile. It's alive. I've never felt that before—like what I have with someone is a living thing, something to be nurtured and sustained. I'm still trying to figure out all the ways to take care of it and it keeps me on my toes, makes me feel like I'm part of something bigger than just me. The fragility makes it that much more beautiful. And it makes me that much happier."

He considers that. "You *like* when I make you feel those things?"

"Maybe not at the time for some of them. But… after the fact, sure. Every time I get through your latest meddling in my head, jerking around my emotions, I feel as if I've conquered something. As if I've grown. I love that you can give me that feeling." I look at him. "Weird huh?"

He spends a few moments deciding how he feels about that. "You love me because you like *enduring* me…" He looks down at my face. "Is it bad that I like that?"

I grin. "About as bad as me liking you putting me through hell. We are two messed up people."

"Messed up?" he says, excitement over some realization building in his head. "If this is messed up, I'm curious what is considered 'well adjusted' in a relationship. It sounds boring. Heavens, Wendy, we're perfect for each other. Because I like the same thing—persevering. I just realized it after you said that. I think that's why I never let things go."

"I don't doubt it," I say. "If I like enduring *you,* you like enduring every*one* and every*thing*. I think you *like* life telling you no just so you can find a way around it."

He chuckles and gathers me in again, content finally.

"I have a surprise for you," I say

"It cannot possibly rival anything you've given me thus far."

I lean over to grab my backpack from the floor. I reach into the very bottom and pull out a small plastic bag, holding it up for Gabriel.

His eyes sparkle with delight. "You took them with you?" he says, grabbing the bag from my hand and opening it. He upends it and the two silver rings fall into his hand.

"Yes. I almost didn't though…" I furrow my brow as I remember. "I had to decide what to do with them before I left so—" I stop and look up at Gabriel. "Did you know I was going to fly to Virginia yesterday?"

"Virginia?" Gabriel asks. "Why?"

I tell him about the plans I had made with Robert and what happened after we went to the airport. "Seriously, Gabriel, my intention to get away from you was thwarted so many times it's like someone *wanted* you and me together. And get this: I went to clean out my desk drawer after making plans with Robert and I had the rings with me because I was intent on doing something with them once and for all. Throw them in the ocean maybe. Give them away. I didn't know. I was about to leave my office, still not knowing what to do, and I stood there looking at them in my hand a minute. The cleaning lady, Antoinette, came by about then. She asked me if I needed anything thrown out. She was talking about my desk, but I took it as a sign, you know, that I needed to get rid of them and not think about it so much.

"I knew I was going to need as much cash as I could get so I asked her if there was a pawn shop in the area. She peeked at my hand and commented on how unusual the stone was. 'Are you sure you don't want to hang on to them? Something that unique is hard to come by.'"

My chest feels hollow as I remember it. "I was confused all over again and decided I didn't have the energy to make a decision right then and I'd take them with me."

Gabriel has been listening to everything I've said with silent, wide-eyed wonder. "Santa madre de María," he exclaims. "Wendy… Do you also realize that if we hadn't run into Quinn, we wouldn't be here either?"

I raise my eyebrows and smile. "Why, because you turned into a raging jealous boyfriend as soon as you figured out who he was?"

"You act as if I should be ashamed of it," he says, affronted. "But yes. Because I was *trying* to let you go. I had already done so much to hurt you I told myself I owed it to you to not lay down and beg. I didn't want you bearing any guilt or sadness over me if I could help it. You deserve better. So your plans to get away and my plans to let you go would have happened. If Quinn hadn't shown up, I know I would have kept my feelings in check. I would have driven away and been relieved to accomplish it. But I saw him…" Gabriel takes a deep, agonized breath. "And I couldn't control my feelings for you from pouring forth. I was powerless. At that moment I was sure Quinn's taking you away was punishment for all that I'd done to you."

"Thank goodness for Ezra's big mouth," I say, shuddering as I imagine what would have happened if I'd not felt the stirring of feelings for me in him. "I really thought you didn't want me anymore. That's why I didn't push it until I felt your reaction."

He continues to turn the rings over in his hand, rife with guilt.

"Don't do that," I say. "There are a lot of what ifs. But a possibility isn't reality. This is reality and we eventually did the right thing. So put them on me already. If you don't I'm pretty sure the universe is going to get mad. Each time we resist it, crap hits the fan and we collide into each other with more force than the last time… You know, that reminds me of a song." I think for a minute, testing my memory of the melody. And then I sing to Gabriel,

"*Even the best fall down sometimes*
Even the stars refuse to shine
Out of the back you fall in time

I somehow find
You and I collide."

"Howie Day, right? That song is nearly ten years old," he says. "I can't believe you know it. But it does fit, doesn't it?" Then he sighs and runs a finger along my jaw. "Your voice is lovely. I can't believe I've never heard you sing. And you sang *to* me." He melts as he gazes at me. Gabriel is the sappiest person I know, but I love it because it's his honesty not having enough outlets. It just pours out of him.

I hold up my left hand expectantly.

He smiles and takes it gently, running his own fingers the length of mine. He looks at me. "Do you still want to be Mrs. Dumas?"

"Yes!" I say impatiently. "Gabriel, you're making me nervous. I already feel the forces of the universe ready to spring if you don't put the damn things on me already. We might be struck down if you don't do it—pretty sure that's why there was some freak lightning storm earlier."

He chuckles and rolls his eyes. Then he slips them on my finger, one by one. "Trust you to ruin a perfectly good romantic moment. And with such uncouth language, no less."

"That's how I roll," I say, admiring the shifting colors of my engagement ring and remembering when he gave it to me months ago. "And like I said: universe, wrath. All that. In fact, I think I heard the elements sigh with relief when you put these on me just now."

"I guess you would know," he says, smiling. "Super-hearing and all."

"Don't you forget it," I say, jabbing his chest with a finger. "I can see the invisible forces at work."

"No doubt," he says, pulling me into an embrace.

I close my eyes to the rise and fall of his chest. I listen to his pulse and time my breathing to its rhythm. As I pay attention to only his body, I can even hear *rush, rush* of his blood in time with his heartbeat.

Wow, that is some serious hearing ability.

After a long time of melding my skin with his and listening to his vital sounds, I realize they have slowed, as have his mental processes. I lift my head up and see that he is asleep, one arm fast around my waist and the other hand buried in my hair.

It's early afternoon; I have no idea why he would be tired enough to sleep in the middle of the day. I chuckle though and disentangle myself carefully from his arms to go to the bathroom. As I start to sit up, I marvel at the sensation his skin elicits from mine. It feels like Velcro wherever our skin separates. As I stand up and move away from him, the peculiar pull is still there, but it's more like a tingling, a hum in the space that divides us. Even standing on the floor, several feet away, I feel a draw toward him like the very cells of my being are willing me toward him. I take measured steps back, the sensation weakening the further away I go until it's gone at about the same distance as my emodar—*his* range, not my usual five feet. How odd that the two phenomena should coincide this way. I wonder what Gabriel will say?

In the bathroom, washing my hands, I catch sight of my rings again. I kind of want to send Antoinette, the cleaning lady, a present or something for preventing me from selling them. She's not someone I know well, only in passing her occasionally and saying hello, but her words meant something. She couldn't have known the story behind my rings, but she said the right thing at the right time.

Bracing my hands on the counter, I'm struck with the utter irony of my standing here right now. Gabriel should not be in the other room. I should not have just shared the depth of intimacy with him. Yesterday, about this time, I was sitting at the airport waiting for my flight to leave. Determined to get away from him. I never would have imagined *this* would be my tomorrow. The events that transpired truly feel like the collision I told Gabriel about. Sure, lots of little things happened to bring me here, but it was directional. Like someone picked me up and placed me in a completely different setting from the one I was in.

I remember thinking everything was conspiring against my happiness. Like my birthday: Maris' phone call, the courthouse, Robert's lecture. So many things I saw as working against me, but they weren't. They were signs of something else entirely and I nearly missed them completely. I focused on every detail along the timeline of my past and saw nothing but hopeless sorrow.

That's how we naturally look at life—in the details as they happen, through a telescope or a magnifying glass, analyzing them to death. But now I can actually see through the opposite end of the telescope, zooming out, seeing the whole picture. Everything *did* conspire, but it conspired for my benefit, not my undoing.

Ezra and my near accident when he touched me. All the evidence of Gabriel's theory in the colorworld like the souls I saw in wonder from the plane window. Kaylen touching me…

The accident on the horse. I gasp as I remember it. It was so random but resulted in Gabriel's change of attitude. It was… necessary to the moment I enjoy right now.

What if Gabriel had decided to make me that promise early on? I shudder to think of it. I came to not only recognize but *value* his tenacity and commitment to a cause during our separation. And by virtue of understanding and loving that part of him, I found enough value to justify the risk and take a leap of faith finally so I could *keep* that part of him.

My mind explodes in awe at the comprehensibility I feel I've grasped. So many events… all working to help me get here…

My cloud sculpture... I reel in amazement once more as I remember that day I saw it at his parent's house. How on earth did I forget that all these months?

If only I'd *looked* at things *differently.*

But I was laser-focused on that one thing I could see through the telescope, thinking *that* view was the *only* view. Not recognizing that there are numberless other views. Numberless pieces in an overall picture.

Tears fall from my eyes as I am overcome with joy and gratitude for every single moment of the last three months. My life is not a curse after all. It's a miracle. Some kind of masterfully woven miracle that I can see clearly now that I've turned the telescope around.

Epilogue

"I hate contemporary art," Ezra says from where he sits on one of the benches in the gallery, a sullen look on his face. Gabriel stands in front of Ezra with his chin in his hand, tilting his head this way and that as he looks at the photograph on the wall.

"Five," I say loudly to Ezra, leaning against a wall and crossing my arms. I'm having a hard time not laughing at Gabriel's clear frustration.

Ezra rolls his eyes. I've been keeping track of how many times he's insulted the art since we arrived at the San Francisco Museum of Modern Art.

"I hate contemporary art," Ezra says again, sticking his tongue out at me.

"Six," I reply, smirking at him.

Kaylen walks over from where she's been looking at one of the other pieces and stands next to Gabriel. This particular exhibition features photographs of the inside of homes. Each photo is overlaid with thin tissue paper. Different shapes are cut out of the partially see-through paper, highlighting various points of the room in the photo.

Gabriel sighs in irritation. I bite my lip to suppress my giggle. This entire outing has been nothing but entertaining. I've spent the entire time amused by his effort to understand what he's looking at and hearing Ezra come up with new ways to insult modern art. I've also been testing my eyesight because I think it improved again. Like right now I'm looking at the photographs—the parts not covered by tissue anyway—and am disturbed that I can actually see pixels—tiny smudges of color that make up the overall image. I wonder if I can see anything more in the colorworld?

"My dad told me once that the problem people have with contemporary art is that they try to get it," Kaylen says.

"Oh gee. That helps so much," Ezra grumbles.

"I'm not sure," Kaylen says, turning around to look at him, "but I think that means you're supposed to look at it without guessing at the artist's intent. Instead, you focus on your own perspective. Do you like it? Why? People have different tastes. So if something speaks to you, that tells you something about yourself."

I regard her with surprise. That's pretty intuitive. I don't know why that should surprise me. Kaylen has always had an innate maturity about her.

Gabriel turns around. "Well I don't like any of it. What does that say about me?"

"It means you have taste," Ezra says. "And since this was your idea and you finally see the error of your ways, can we leave now? I think we should spend our spare time doing other things. Like figuring out what we're going to do about Robert. Isn't your dad a lawyer, Gabe? Can't he like… put some legal pressure on Robert or something?"

"Seven," I say.

Gabriel looks at me. "What do you think?"

"About what?" I ask, my arms still crossed. "Your dad helping us?"

"No," he replies. "The art. Isn't this your area?" I can tell he's not only frustrated with the art but also with my close-lipped attitude since we came into the museum.

"Not really," I reply.

He scrutinizes my face, wishing he could read my mind. "No advice on how to appreciate this kind of… visual stimulation?"

I look past Gabriel to the photo beyond, telling myself that it's stupid to be so defensive. Ezra's eyes are on me. He knows I quit art years ago. He tried to tell Gabriel that nobody wanted to go to an art museum, but Gabriel wasn't having it. I think Ezra agreed to come along just for me—maybe to protect me from Gabriel interrogating me about it. I think Ezra's worried that Gabriel and I are going to start fighting again and split up—which is silly. I'm in this for the long haul.

Gabriel takes a few steps closer to stand in front of me. He runs his hands gently down my arms and pulls them apart so they rest at my sides instead. "You look like the curator's bouncer standing like that."

I raise an eyebrow. I guess I *have* spent this entire tour in defensive positions. Of course Gabriel would notice something like that.

To prove that I'm not uptight—even though I am—I say, "Look. The thing you need to get about this kind of art is that it's always about breaking out of the mold. Choreographers are always looking for new ways to move the body. Writers are always looking for new ways to put words on paper. Musicians are always looking for new sound. It's about giving you something you haven't seen before. A modern artist is driven by the need to create something novel because art is a visual representation of some aspect of the artist's soul. Art is proof that the human soul is unique, so the possibilities for visual representation is, in theory, infinite."

I'm a little surprised that all that came out of me so easily—maybe Gabriel's psychological manipulation of uncrossing my arms did it. It's been a *long* time since I've even *thought* about art, let alone tried to articulate artistic theory. But I go with it. "It's an obsession, really, to search out the parts of yourself that are unique, separate from others. The artist doesn't create for the patron, yet every artist wants to show what they've done. That applies to anything though. You're supposed to appreciate the imagination and admire the uniqueness of the human soul."

Gabriel thinks intently, his eyebrows knit together.

"Of course," I add, "Even my opinion of the purpose of contemporary art is subjective. That's the beauty of it. It is whatever you need it to be, whatever you want it to be. The more you wonder, the more it moves you. And that's the point of sharing art in the first place."

"Well I need it to be not in front of me," Ezra says.

"Eight," I say. "You're on a roll, Ezra."

"But how do you appreciate something that looks like it obviously didn't require much effort?" Gabriel asks, hands on his hips now as he scans the room.

"I take it you're talking about minimalist art," I reply. "If you're looking at it in hopes of marveling over the artist's skill, you're looking at it for the wrong reason. You're overcomplicating something that isn't trying to be more. It's minimalist because it strips down your reaction. It's non-complex. That makes it beautiful. I challenge you to have a really stressful day and not feel better after you walk through a minimalist exhibition without expectations. It's a way to simplify human experience."

Gabriel nods slowly, thoughtfully, and then turns back to the photograph he was looking at before. He takes cleansing breaths and tries again to appreciate the piece.

"I'm pretty sure that means I have a right to hate it if I want," Ezra says. "And I've hated every bit of this field trip. So I'll ask again: do you guys have plans about Robert?"

"Nine," I say. "And no. We have no plans yet."

"It's been three days since we split from Monterey and you haven't even *thought* about it?" Ezra whines.

Kaylen sits next to Ezra. "We're going to have to do something drastic: take a stand. Maybe we should go to the police."

"And say what?" asks Ezra. "'Excuse me, there are a bunch of crazed energy healers after us because they think my sister is the key to unlocking human potential, and she kills people sometimes when she touches them. Could we file a restraining order, please?'"

Kaylen giggles, nudging Ezra's foot with her own. "It'd be pretty awesome to see how they'd respond, wouldn't it?"

"It'd be nice to know what Robert and Louise seem to know about me that I don't know," I say. "I get that they want to give people superpowers, but the way they've gone about it isn't straightforward enough for me to believe that it's as simple as that."

"I guess I can't look at something without analyzing it," Gabriel says, turning around, having concluded his mental experiment with contemporary art. "I'm always looking for connections to things I already know about so I can put it in context. I'm not sure how to not do that."

Ezra hops up. "Well let's move on to the next gauntlet of eyesores. This exhibit is starting to make my nose run. To think they cut up perfectly good tissues... Some people in the world don't even *have* tissues. And we're over here hanging them on a wall. It's a shameful waste."

Kaylen laughs again and Ezra holds out his hand to her. She takes it and he pulls her to her feet.

"Yeah," I say, smiling at the two of them, "that was definitely number ten."

Gabriel entwines his fingers with mine—which are gloved since we're in public—and when I try to head around the corner, he doesn't move and doesn't let me move away either. He puts his hand on my neck just below my ear, his thumb on my cheek. Then he leans down slowly, puts his lips to my forehead. After two beats he puts his arms around me, squeezes me carefully to himself as if embracing something fragile and priceless, his cheek now against my head, his fingers caressing my scalp.

I melt into him, relaxed for probably the first time since we started the tour. It's difficult not to be when he touches me with such profound reverence. I decide to remove one of my gloves so I can hold his hand—even that minimal contact always gives me a thrill. This place is pretty much empty since it's mid-morning on a weekday.

"I can't tell if this is better or worse than eye-groping," Ezra says. "You're not even making out but it still feels like you are."

I catch Ezra out of the corner of my eye, wrinkling his nose.

Kaylen smiles as she watches us. "Shut up, Ezra," she says. "Do you have to complain about everything? If you don't like it, look away."

"I have a better idea," Ezra says with a mischievous look. "How about we make out, too?"

She smacks his arm. "No way."

The next exhibit is a set of glass sculptures.

"Sweet!" Ezra exclaims, running up to one of the displays. "A Klein bottle?"

I glance over at what he's talking about. It looks like blown glass, horn-shaped. On closer inspection, I think the small end of the horn is inserted into the side of the horn itself where it expands to become the main opening. A kind of illusion maybe?

Ezra catches sight of another display. "A Möbius strip..." he breathes. It looks like a strip of glass wound into some kind of figure-eight... but not exactly. It's confusing to trace its surface with my eyes.

After a few moments of drooling over that one, Ezra moves to the next one. "A Roman Surface... That is so swag."

"So pretty," Kaylen says.

"Now *this* took skill," Ezra says. He looks up, noticing another display down the way. "Holy father of Wonder Woman. An icositetrachoron!" He darts over to it.

It looks like some kind of complex geometric shape, a lattice of interconnecting bars inside of it. Very intricate. Crystalline almost.

"I don't even know how to say what you just said," Kaylen marvels.

"The edges aren't perfectly proportioned," Ezra says. "But whoever made this knows their geometry."

Gabriel's interest has perked up as well and he says, "You can really tell whether they're proportioned correctly?"

"Oh yeah," Ezra says.

"How?" Kaylen says in disbelief.

"I don't know. It just looks off," Ezra says, walking over to yet another strange geometric object. "A tesseract."

"Tesseract?" Kaylen says. "Looks like a cube within a cube to me."

"It's a representation of a cube in the fourth dimension," Ezra explains.

"It's beautiful," Gabriel says, walking up next to Ezra to get a closer look.

I laugh. "Count on the analytical-minded scientists to get excited about geometric shapes—something that has obviously been done before."

Gabriel straightens and looks at me enthusiastically. "That's a fascinating philosophical idea."

"What is?" I ask.

"Which is more beautiful? That which appears random and meaningless or that which is ordered and reproduced? Which ought to be valued more?"

"Different strokes for different folks," I say, not getting why Gabriel feels like a light bulb just went off in his head.

Gabriel sits down on a bench and crosses his arms, his brow furrowed as he thinks. Finally he says, "I'll have to spend more time on that later, because the tesseract has given me an idea."

"Which is what?" I ask.

"A fourth dimension."

"Elaborate?" I say.

"First, a question: do you think it likely you could see the colorworld before you had hypno-touch at Pneumatikon?"

I consider it, remembering how Gabriel thinks the reason I can see the colorworld is because I have exceptional senses—something I already had somewhat before I ever went to Pneumatikon. "If my senses are what allow me to see it, then yeah, I guess so."

"Which begs the question: why did Carl and Louise have hypno-touch done to you at Pnuematikon at all?"

Kaylen gasps. "They *wanted* to give her a death touch?" she breathes.

"Exactly," Gabriel says.

"Or they just wanted to improve her sight," Ezra says. "Didn't Carl say Wen's sight in the colorworld was better than his?"

"Yes," Gabriel says. "There must be another dimension to the colorworld that we're not aware of. And it either has something to do with Wendy's lethal skin, or it has something to do with being able to perceive something in particular in the colorworld. I'm inclined to say both. We need to find out what that is. That will put us ahead of Carl and Louise."

"What kind of dimension?" I ask, looking at the tesseract and trying to visualize a fourth dimension in the colorworld... I don't know what that even means.

"Not an *actual* fourth dimension in space. But there is some other ability you possess that you aren't aware of. Just think about how people can speak to you telepathically. You weren't aware of that ability until we discovered it by accident. There is more to your lethal skin. That current you feel is a clue."

"They're always messing with fourth dimensions in comic books," Ezra says. "It always ends up screwing with reality."

"Great," I grumble. "I need more of *that* in my life."

"That's why I like comic books," Ezra says. "It may not be perfect science, but they breathe life into theoretical ideas. Like a tesseract. One title uses it as the cosmic cube."

"Cosmic cube?" Kaylen says, amusement curling her lips. "You are such a nerd, Ezra."

"Hey, the cosmic cube is no joke," Ezra says defensively. "It has the power to make any desire a reality."

"That's nonsense," Gabriel says. "You can't make any desire a reality without disrupting the order of things. It's non-sustainable."

Ezra gives him a withering look. "That's the point, Gabe. It's considered a dangerous weapon."

Gabriel snorts. "Doesn't sound like a very engaging plot. You can't wish things into existence. It destroys the integrity of reality."

"I'm pretty sure that's what God does," Ezra says defensively. "And almost everyone believes in that."

"That is a ridiculous notion," Gabriel snorts. "If there actually is a god, he or she fully comprehends the laws that govern reality. He or she does not operate outside of reality. That's implausible and, frankly, bad theology. But then again, theology in itself is generally senseless."

"Whatever, Gabe," Ezra says.

"You're saying that... God would have to follow *rules*?" Kaylen says, furrowing her brow.

"Of course," Gabriel replies, extending his legs. "How else would it be possible to comprehend a god?"

"Uh, I thought God was supposed to be incomprehensible or something," I say.

"More bad theology," Gabriel says, getting riled. "More likely, we should say, 'it's unlikely God can be comprehended by any one person in their limited life span.' Don't those religious types always like to say that we're supposed to know God? Explain to me how you are supposed to know someone you can't comprehend—that exists and operates in a reality outside your own? That's impossible. Religion is ridiculous."

"So you don't believe in God?" I ask, confused.

"I'm open to the idea. But I'm not sold one way or another."

Ezra laughs drily. "*Open* to the idea? You're waiting on empirical evidence? Get in line. They've been working on that for millennia."

Kaylen looks distraught. "How can you not believe in God, Gabe?"

I look at Gabriel, too. I don't know if that bothers me, but I *am* asking myself how I never knew this. Gabriel's mother is definitely religious. How did he end up so *not* religious?

"Why does it matter?" he asks. "I believe in the laws of nature. The cycle of the seasons. The breadth of the universe. The beauty of the intricacy of our world. Love. Compassion. Human capability. I believe in everything that people claim God made. I believe in the struggle of opposing forces. If I have faith in the consistency of the universe, then if God does exist, and as scriptural accounts claim God is in everything, then I believe in him by default, don't I?"

"No wonder you're such an arrogant bastard," Ezra muses. "But I have to admit that does make sense."

"But…" Kaylen says, still bothered. "What's the harm in accepting God as real if it won't alter anything else you believe in?"

"You're saying that because my idea of God is compatible with how I view the world, then I should acknowledge his existence?"

Kaylen shrugs.

"That's a worthy question," Gabriel pensively. "I would counter with, what is so terrible about indifference? It's not as if I am rebelling against God's supposed work of creation. I don't look at a tree and call it a stone just because I have the power to say so or believe so. Let's say I declare God exists. What more does that require of me? A duty to behave morally and to love others? Do I not already strive for that? If there is something beyond simply trying to be a better person that I am supposed to *do* to uphold a belief in God, what is it? Religion?" Gabriel laughs incredulously. "Which one then? Which set of arbitrary rules shall I choose? And what will I gain from it other than a means to exclude people? No thank you. If that is God's idea of veneration, I'll have none of it. And that's why I don't acknowledge God: not because I dislike or discount the possibility, but because it's far more pleasant to be condemned to hell than to argue with a religious person about who or what God is and what he or she wants from us. Religion convolutes the simplicity of the truth that is present in every molecule of nature. You don't need a belief in God to see it or appreciate it."

Kaylen, Ezra, and I watch Gabriel with wide-eyed amazement. I think I've had my mind blown by yet another Gabriel-ism. My mind feels twisted into an unfamiliar position. But that's not the half of it. It's the way he delivers it… The man is sitting on a bench, his legs extended casually, but yet his presence commands my attention like a magnet. And even though what he has said is deeper than anything I have ever considered—and certainly heretical by most standards—it makes utter sense on a level that goes beyond the words he has said. For several moments I wonder how he did that. How did he move me so easily and send chills down my spine?

Gabriel leans forward and props his chin on his hand, his elbow on his leg. "If God really decreed absolute belief in him or her was necessary for some kind of eternal salvation, I'd think God would have done a better job making his or her existence unmistakable and irrefutable."

Ezra is the first to find words. "Her?"

"Why not her?" Gabriel says in a lighter tone, and with it, the intensity of a moment ago melts into casual consideration. "We just demonstrated, didn't we, that the male members of our group have a lack of appreciation for creativity and unconventionalism? You and I value reproduction more. Seems like if there really is a creative force at work in the universe, a woman would have to at least be involved. And I'm not about to cater to the religious preference of a patriarchal deity. For all I know, God is more than one being. But it doesn't much matter to me, so long as he or she or it follows the rules and keeps from destroying reality."

I stare at Gabriel. I honestly had no idea he held such strong opinions about God. He believes whatever aligns with his logic. A god that abides by rules? How did he think of that? And what was with that weird, 'I say it and thus it is true!' ambiance surrounding him earlier? If that's how he teaches his students, it's no wonder he was voted favorite teacher.

I wish my head worked the way his does. Maybe it has to do with courage—the courage to believe contrary to everyone else and then say it without a lick of doubt. I wonder if Gabriel even possesses inhibition.

"Geez, Gabriel," I say. "I've never even thought about half of the stuff you do."

"And that's what makes you so amazing, Love," he says as he gives me an adoring look. "To live morally and purposefully without a basis for doing so. What I wouldn't give to experience being you for a day."

"Well I wish I saw the world like you do," I say. "It sounds incredible."

"We're well-matched then, aren't we? Looks like we each have something to teach each other."

"Ugh," Ezra breaks in. "Please don't start adoring each other again. In fact, all this God-talk is making me hungry. Can we go now?"

Gabriel stands up. "What an enlightening trip this has been. I may have to make more regular visits to art museums."

No kidding. I feel like I just went to a philosophy class. "Let me check my blood sugar before we go eat," I say, pulling out my test kit and sitting down.

Ezra drags Kaylen back to the tesseract and starts trying to explain the fourth dimension to her while Gabriel hangs over my shoulder, watching me.

296 is the reading. *What!?* I haven't eaten anything since before the last time I tested.

"Good heavens, Wendy," Gabriel says. "Didn't you take a couple units before we came here? That was only an hour and a half ago."

Ignoring him, I test again but get a similar reading. What is going on with my blood sugar these days? Even with my Louise and Robert problem, I don't think I've ever been more content.

Now that I can touch my three favorite people without worry, my stress level has gone down significantly.

I give myself an injection, and when I put everything back in my bag and take Gabriel's hand, I see him watching me with stern concern. "We need to get you to a doctor in the near future and see what's going on with you."

I shrug. "We will. It's been fluctuating a lot the last couple months but it's still not anything like the horror stories I hear about other people with juvenile onset. Don't worry. I probably just need to get back to some kind of regular life. I guess I'm more stressed than I feel."

That seems to appease him as he leads me out, Kaylen and Ezra behind us. As we near the exit we find a large installment piece: water bottles glued cap-end down to a platform raised over a huge rectangular vat of water.

Ezra stops and gives it a look of disgust. "What in the Joker's insane head is that?"

I burst out laughing and everyone joins in. Once I find my voice again, I read the placard. "It's a concept piece about the conservation of water, Ezra."

"It's an atrocity against recycling, that's what it is," he replies.

Gabriel chuckles again and shakes his head. "I'm trying to be open-minded here, but I'm afraid I jump too quickly to the same conclusions as Ezra. Nevertheless, I find myself grateful that someone out there is trying such interesting new things. Things that don't make sense keep me on my toes."

I lean against his shoulder and sigh. I can't believe I almost let Gabriel go. He's the yin to my yang, and without him I don't think I'd have learned half of the things I've learned about myself in the past five months. And chances are, without him I'll never figure out this fourth colorworld dimension he talked about.

It reminds me of the last time I was in the colorworld. It was during that bizarre thunderstorm. In that instance, the colorworld did make things clear. But not in the way I expected.

It's hard to believe that water, something we have so much of on earth, that's literally in everything, would be invisible in the colorworld—the place where the souls of things are revealed.

Seeing the vat of water before me makes me curious to confirm if what I saw the other day still stands. I saw the fish tank at the aquarium once of course, but I was too mesmerized by the fish to notice whether I was seeing any semblance of water in the tank itself. I've seen the ocean, but it's full of sediment. And far away it mostly reflects the sky. It's not clear like this water.

"Hold on," I say before Gabriel can pull us to the door. "I want to look at all that water in the colorworld."

Gabriel's instant curiosity waits. Instead of hovering my free hand over his arm, I hold his hand. I wonder if touching someone's skin will get me there even faster?

I close my eyes. I've had so much experience in the colorworld that my efforts get me there in no time. I open my eyes to the swirl of color, resting my attention on the plexi-glass basin of water.

It looks completely empty… Despite expecting it, it's still strange. Water really is invisible in the colorworld. What does that mean?

Gabriel is gripping my hand kind of hard and it distracts me.

"Wendy?" he whispers intently, intimidated. But that quickly explodes into wonder so awesome that my heart hammers with the feel of it.

"What is it?" I reply breathlessly.

"I think I just found that fourth dimension we were talking about."

"Where? What?" I ask, looking around although I'm not sure what for. I *do* know that Gabriel has come up with something. And it's big.

But his answer is totally unexpected.

"I can see the colorworld," he replies.

Look for book 3 of the Colorworld series:
Lumaworld

Visit the official site at:
www.colorworldbooks.com

Made in the USA
Charleston, SC
13 May 2014